Abo

When Virginia Heat... to fall asleep, so she n... the time while she wa... older, the stories beca... taking weeks to get to the happy ending. Then one day, she decided to embrace the insomnia and start writing them down. Over twenty books and three Romantic Novel of the Year Award nominations later, it still takes her forever to fall asleep.

Regency Secrets

Regency Secrets:

The Wild
Warriners

VIRGINIA HEATH

MILLS & BOON

First Published in Great Britain 2023
By Mills & Boon, an imprint of HarperCollins*Publishers*
1 London Bridge Street, London, SE1 9GF

www.harpercollins.co.uk

HarperCollins*Publishers*
Macken House, 39/40 Mayor Street Upper,
Dublin 1, D01 C9W8, Ireland

This book is produced from independently certified FSC™ paper
to ensure responsible forest management.

For more information visit: www.harpercollins.co.uk/green

Printed and Bound in Spain using 100% Renewable electricity at
CPI Black Print, Barcelona

A WARRINER TO
PROTECT HER

For Tracy Croft.

Mentor, friend and feisty heroine.

Chapter One

1st December 1813. One month, three days and approximately eighteen hours remaining...

The thin cord dug into her wrists painfully. Letty ignored it to focus on the practicalities. She barely opened one eye and peeked through her lashes. The Earl of Bainbridge's crinkly, grey head was lolling sideways, swaying slightly with the motion of the carriage—eyes closed, mouth slack—and she experienced a moment of relief to know he had finally nodded off. She risked opening her eyes properly for the first time in the better part of an hour, raising her head carefully from the seat to look out of the small strip of window still visible between the dark curtains which hid her from the world.

It was black as pitch outside.

A good sign.

It meant they were deep in the countryside, miles from any life, and the fact she could not even see the stars suggested this part of the Great North Road was edged with sheltering trees. Bainbridge's tatty coach was also flying along at speed, another indicator that they were a long way from the next inn or village. So far, each time the driver had approached one, the wheels had slowed and he had rapped loudly on the roof. Then the Earl had violently restrained her, his gnarled hand clamping tightly over Letty's already gagged mouth, the point of his boot knife pressed ominously against her throat as they had either passed through or the horses were quickly changed.

As he dozed, that very knife was still resting on his knee, his fingers loosely clasping it. Just in case. There seemed little point in trying to wrestle it from him when her main priority was escape. The last time she had showed any signs of struggle, Bainbridge had swept the back of his hand maliciously across her cheek with such force, his signet ring had sliced through the soft skin on her lip, leaving it now swollen and painful around the gag. For protection, she had pretended the blow had rendered her unconscious and had not moved a muscle since. If it had achieved nothing else, it had given Letty time to think.

As stealthily as she could, she rose to sit up and silently edged her bottom incrementally towards the door. If she could reach the handle, she could throw herself on to the road. After that, if she survived, she really had no idea what she was going to do. It was not really much of a plan, but as she had no desire to go to Gretna Green and she would much rather be dead than married to Bainbridge, it was better than nothing.

The Earl began to snore. But it was erratic on account of his upright position, the sort of snoring which woke a person up. There was no time to lose. Letty stretched out her bound hands and lunged at the handle desperately and, by some miraculous twist of fate, she managed to do this as the carriage veered slightly towards that side. She crashed into the door, wrestled with the handle and it flew open, taking her with it and tossing her sideways.

Instinct made her curl into a ball before she hit the ground, to protect her head and her limbs. Still the impact was sheer agony, pushing all of the air out of her lungs and blinding her with pain. Sharp stones embedded themselves in her skin as she rolled; muddy water shot up her nose and seeped through her closed eyelids, stinging them mercilessly. Almost as a blur in the distance, Letty heard a shout go up from the carriage, now further ahead, then the squeal from wheels when the brake was suddenly applied.

She rose to her knees, forced her bruised and battered body to move, practically dragging herself into the dark and silent trees. Then she ran. There was no thought as to direction. Just as long as it was away from the road, it didn't matter where she was going. She ignored the way the tangled branches seemed to reach out and grab at her clothing, nor did it matter that the deeper she plunged into these woods, the darker and more terrifying they appeared. Nothing could be as terrifying as being caught again by that dreadful man.

In the distance, she could still hear their angry voices, yet with every yard, those voices became fainter and fainter, spurring her to put even more distance between them as she ploughed recklessly forward. Until her lungs burned and her muscles screamed and she could run no further.

What Jack *should* have done was go straight home. But hindsight, in his experience, was overrated. It only served to bring about regrets, and frankly, Jack Warriner had quite enough of those already. So what if he was now drenched to the skin and frozen to the bone? The inn had been warm, the ale good and the company, for once, friendly. He had meant to stay for just the one drink. Just to clear the dust of the road from his throat and to enjoy a few minutes of respite from all of the responsibilities which stifled him before he wound his way down the last three miles to home. But one drink had soon turned into three. And three became six. Then the innkeeper had brought out the whisky and someone else had produced a fiddle, and before he realised it, he had been singing loudly with the rest of the patrons, stamping his feet, clapping his hands and behaving like a young man without the entire oppressive weight of the world on his shoulders.

Now he was paying for his rare moment of weakness. The rain was impressive, even by December's standards, and would have been coming down in heavy, vertical lines had it not been for the wind. But to compound Jack's current misery, as he fought the inevitable aftereffects of far too much alcohol in too short a period of time, the relentless north-easterly was forcing the fat rain drops almost horizontal. Right into his face.

Thank goodness there was only a half a mile or so left. Soon he would be home. Safe in the house which ate money for breakfast, luncheon and dinner. His grand stately pile, the opulent legacy of his lofty title, a leaking, creaking, millstone around his neck. The place where all hopes and dreams were mercilessly crushed under the hobnail boot of responsibility, while Jack sunk deeper and deeper into debt with every passing year. Just thinking about it made him lethargic.

And slightly nauseous.

Or perhaps that was merely the whisky and the ale. Jack wiped his dripping face with the back of his sleeve and almost lost his seat when his horse suddenly reared noisily. He struggled with the reins to bring the beast under control and that was when he saw her. Almost like a ghost, the woman appeared out of the trees. Her skin eerily pale in the flimsy moonlight, hair and thin dress plastered to her body, eyes as wide as saucers as she stared back at him. Then she fled, wet skirts and a pronounced limp hampering her progress.

It took several seconds for his alcohol-impaired mind to register what else he had seen. A vicious gag. Bound hands. Sheer terror.

She was stumbling ahead of him along the narrow, rutted lane which led to his house as if her very life depended on it. Judging by the state of her, it probably was. Jack's wits finally overpowered his inebriation and he swiftly directed his horse after her.

'Miss! Wait! I mean you no harm.' The wind carried away his words.

As he came alongside her, Jack bent low in the saddle and grabbed her arm. She spun around and tried to extricate herself from his grip, fighting like a cornered fox to escape him.

'I mean you no harm!'

He could tell by the way she struggled that she was exhausted. Shouting at her was not going to calm her.

'Let me help you.' He said this quietly and he saw her blink as she heard him. To prove it, he released the grip he had on her upper arm and held up his gloved hands as if in surrender. Automatically, she went to bolt and he forced himself not to try to stop her. It was the right thing to do. She hesitated. Turned back. Her wide eyes locked on to his and she simply gazed at him, as if she were searching the depths of them to the man he was inside, to see if he could be trusted. Then, almost as if all her strength and determination was gone, she began to slip to the ground.

Jack managed to grab her arm again before she crumpled into a heap and used all of his formidable strength to pull her now deadweight body on to his saddle. He cradled her in his lap; her damp flesh was like ice and it made him wonder how long she had been out here, exposed to the winter elements. She felt so very delicate in his arms. Precious.

He tried to work the gag free. It refused to move. Rainwater had sealed the knot tight and whoever had tied it had done it so harshly, he could not move it. This close, he could just about make out the bruising on her face. Her lip was badly cut and swollen, suggesting she had been beaten as well as bound. And the very fact he had discovered her stumbling blindly along a deserted lane, past midnight and wearing what appeared to be only a bedraggled, sleeveless silk gown meant she had probably managed to escape. Only then did it suddenly dawn on him that her captors might be searching for her. Whoever had bound and beaten this delicate woman was not going to be the sort of person to listen to reason. If she had escaped, it went without saying they would stop at nothing to get her back. Whoever she was, she needed his help.

Without thinking, Jack kicked the horse into a gallop, holding the reins tightly with one hand while the other held his unconscious passenger close to his body to keep her safe. He ignored the sting of the wind and rain on his face. Nothing else mattered but getting her home and to safety. Markham Manor might well be in dire need of a new roof, but at least his troublesome ancestors had had the good sense to surround it with a twenty-foot wall and an archaic pair of similarly proportioned gates which weighed a ton. He had a feeling tonight, for the first time in over two hundred years, the Warriners might actually need them.

Chapter Two

One month, three days and approximately
sixteen hours remaining...

Jack carried her limp body into the hallway and shouted for his brothers at the top of his voice. Used to jumping to attention at his tone, they arrived one by one on the landing. First came Joe, the second youngest and only four years his junior, and by far the one he was keenest to see first. He took one look at the woman and the physician in him burst to the fore.

'I'll get my things.' And he was gone again.

Then came Jacob, the youngest, who crossed his brother on the landing, dark hair on end and rubbing the sleep from his eyes. Close behind him limped Jamie, the closest in age to Jack. Both men instantly sprang into action the moment they spotted the burden in Jack's arms.

'What the hell?'

Jacob just stood and gaped as he reached the bottom step, trailing after Jack as he hauled the woman into the high-ceilinged great hall which now served as the drawing room. He had already lowered the woman on to a sofa by the time Jamie managed to get there. Like the brilliant soldier he had been before his injuries, it did not take his brother long to assess the situation.

'Where did you find her?'

'She just appeared in the middle of the road. She was conscious then.' That she had failed to regain consciousness in the last twenty minutes was a worry. In the dim lamplight, her skin now had a grey pallor beneath the caked mud which did not bode well.

'Any signs of whoever did this to her?' Jamie asked.

Jack shook his head. 'But the storm is still raging outside. Even if there had been an army right behind me, I doubt I would have heard them. Make the place secure!'

Jamie responded immediately to Jack's command, turning to Jacob. 'Get my sword and pistols from my bedchamber, and grab something for yourself. We're going to close the gates.'

The two brothers were gone by the time Joe returned with his medical kit. Despite the fact there had been no money to send him to university again this year, Joe had still relentlessly studied medicine in the vain hope he would one day qualify as a doctor. He had done since he was a young boy. What he did not know about the workings of the human body was not worth knowing. He watched Jack carefully cut through the gag and the cord at her wrists, then remove them, before kneeling to examine her.

'She's like ice, Jack! We need to warm her up.' Joe fished in his bag for some scissors and began to cut the woman's clothing open from the hem up.

'What do you think you are doing?' Jack exclaimed,

because somehow stripping the poor girl seemed a bit extreme.

'I have to get her out of these wet things, Jack, and dry her off or it will be impossible to warm her. Hypothermia can kill. Fetch some blankets.'

For once, Jack did exactly as he was asked. His younger brother might well bow down to him on all other matters, but in this situation, he trusted Joe more than anyone else to help the stranger. Secondly, Jack had precious little medical knowledge, had no idea exactly what hypo-whatever-it-was meant and it felt morally wrong to stand by gawping while she was relieved of her clothing. Wasting no time, Joe was in the midst of his examination when Jack came back, his patient's torso thoughtfully now covered in a coat.

'I do not think she has suffered any broken bones, though until she is awake, it is difficult to know for sure. There are cuts and bruises all over her—see?'

Jack passed the pile of blankets towards his brother and glanced down at the poor girl's visible bare arms and calves. His brother was not wrong. Filthy wounds and grazes marred the pale skin. 'Look at the bruising here.' Joe pointed to the left arm. 'If I had to take a guess, I would say she had a bad fall from something and landed on her side. Judging from the size and colour of the bruise, it's a miracle her arm or collarbone did not shatter from the impact. Some of these punctures are quite deep. The cut on her lip is nasty too. And her wrists have been rubbed raw by the cord around them— those wounds are angry and prone to become infected. She had to have been tied up for hours. I need to clean them all thoroughly.'

Relegated to the role of nursemaid, Jack busied himself by boiling kettle after kettle of water and traipsing the heavy buckets backwards and forward from the kitchen to the hall, leaving his brother to do what was necessary and feeling impotent in the process. As each layer of grime and embedded grit was removed, Joe commented on how miraculous it was that the woman was not more injured, yet she did not regain consciousness nor did she lose her deathly colour. Despite the now roaring fire in the enormous stone fireplace and the heap of blankets that swaddled her, her core temperature did not increase. Her swollen lips were blue tinged, her hands and feet like icicles.

'She must have been out in the cold for hours, Jack. I am worried she actually *has* hypothermia. She's barely breathing now and her pulse is definitely slowing.'

'What can I do?' Because there had to be something. The idea of her dying in their house tonight was horrifying. Not after he had done his best to save her, seen the stark terror in her eyes.

'You gather her up, Jack—share your body heat with her while I finish with all of the other injuries.'

'Share my body heat?' It sounded far-fetched, but Joe had proved to be right before. 'How exactly do I do that?'

'Hold her in your lap like a child.' Joe lifted her carefully at the base of the shoulders, exposing her bare back. They swaddled the blankets around her like a baby's shawl and Jack sat so the pair of them could manoeuvre her into his lap.

It was all well and good Joe telling him to hold her like a child—but it was blatantly obvious she was no child. There was too much of her, so his brother tucked her legs up beneath the covers to warm her extremities, while Jack smoothed his palms briskly along the sides of her arms in an attempt to create some heat from the friction. Her back and bottom were so cold he could feel the chill through the layers of woollen blanket and his clothing, and if she had not been breathing he would have thought he was holding a long-dead corpse. He gathered her close protectively and wrapped his arms about her, hoping she would absorb whatever warmth she needed from his body, crooning to her as his brother towel-dried her sodden, matted long hair before wrapping a blanket around her head too.

'If she was awake, I could make her drink something. Warm milk or tea might help to speed up the process.' Joe ran his hands through his thick dark hair in agitation. 'I suppose I could try and spoon some into her?'

All Jack could do was shrug. He had no clue as to what should be done and from his position beneath the girl, he was hardly in a state to assist his brother further. Being powerless was not something he excelled at. He hated feeling so useless when he was usually the one in control. All he could do was continue to hold her cradled in his arms, searching her wan face for signs of life. As he waited for Joe to return from the kitchen, his other two brothers returned. Both looked as if they had just walked through a hurricane.

'Only an idiot would be out in that!' said Jamie, shaking off the rain. 'But the gates are bolted and we saw nothing in the lane. If somebody turns up, we'll all deny any knowledge of your mystery damsel until we know what the hell this is all about. How is she?' He limped painfully towards the sofa and stared down at the still bundle in Jack's arms.

'Joe's patched her up as best as he can for the time being. Now we're trying to get her warm.'

Jamie did not instil a great deal of confidence with his next words. 'I've seen many a man killed from exposure to the elements. It's when they stop shivering you have to really worry. Is she shivering?'

She was not. Jack did not want to think about what that meant. 'She won't die!' Not if he had anything to do with it. 'Joe is fetching some warm milk.' As if milk was some magic medicine nobody had known about which would miraculously cure a poor girl who was almost frozen to death. Jack stared down at her. She was so still, and so frighteningly pale, she could almost have been carved out of alabaster. He remembered the fear he had seen in her wide eyes when she collided with him and hoped those awful few minutes would not be the last she was doomed to remember. 'I don't even know her name.'

Jacob, so far silent, went to the pile of wet clothes discarded on the floor and began to rifle through them.

'She was not in the army, fool,' Jamie said dismissively, 'I doubt she will have her rank, surname and number written on her petticoats.'

'You'd be amazed what ladies keep in their petticoats.' Jacob did not look up from his task. 'Although to know that, you would have to know how to charm the ladies, Jamie, which you don't.' He sat back on his heels and triumphantly waved a small square of intricately embroidered linen. 'I, on the other hand, am very charming. Her name is Letty.' He balled up the damp cloth and threw it at Jamie's head. 'It says so on her handkerchief.'

Jack stroked his index finger gently over her cheek and willed her to wake up. 'Letty. Letty, sweetheart, can you hear me?'

* * *

Letty. Letty, sweetheart, can you hear me?

She did not recognise the voice, but it had a calming lilt to it even though it came from a strange man. It was not Bainbridge and it was not her uncle. That was all that mattered. Letty struggled to open her eyes, but they would not budge. She was so very tired. So tired she did not have the strength to be frightened. Something was pulling her upwards to a place she wanted to go, yet something, *someone*, held her firm, preventing her from floating away. She was cocooned rather than imprisoned. Safe.

She felt something warm trickle down her throat. She couldn't taste it. Strong arms around her. More of the warm liquid. *Letty. Try to swallow, sweetheart.* Sweetheart? That was nice. Nobody had ever called her sweetheart before. *We need to warm you up.* Now that she considered it, she was cold. Every part of her ached. Not surprising considering what had happened to her. Bainbridge. The carriage. The woods.

Panic came afresh. What if they had found her? She forced her eyes open. Intense blue eyes met hers. *You're safe, Letty.* They were beautiful eyes. Troubled eyes. Reassuring eyes. *I am going to look after you, sweetheart. I promise.* The deep lilting voice crooned against her ear. She sighed. It was all she had the strength to do and her eyes fluttered closed again. The painful gag was gone. And he was holding her.

There were worse ways to go.

Chapter Three

One month and one day remaining...

Letty experienced the sensation of falling and it woke her with a start. It took her a few moments to focus in the daylight, but when she did two pairs of identical blue eyes were staring down at her. Frightened, she had intended to scream; the strangled mewling noise she managed was really quite pathetic.

'Shh…' said one of the pairs of eyes kindly. 'Everything is all right. You are safe here.'

She could make out the blurry edges of the speaker's face. Dark hair. Smiling. Next to him stood another man who looked strikingly similar. They were definitely related. The same dark hair, the same deep blue eyes, but he was frowning. She knew those eyes.

'My brother rescued you from the road,' the smiling man said, stroking one of her hands, 'You have had a bit of a fever and you are badly bruised, but miraculously you have made a very fast and splendid recovery. What you need to do now is rest. Give your body time to heal. In a few days, you will be as fit as a fiddle.'

Letty tried to speak, to ask where she was. However, her mouth felt so woolly, her tongue would not move. Her eyes flicked to the frowning man and he continued to frown, until the smiling man next to him gave him a sharp nudge in the ribs and he forced himself to smile. It did not touch his eyes. Letty could not quite make out whether the emotion swirling in those fathomless blue depths was concern or annoyance.

'Why were you tied up and wandering in the woods?' The smile slipped off his face as he stared down at her.

Again her stupid tongue would not move and she made some garbled sound.

'Leave her be, Jack. You can interrogate the poor girl once she is better.'

Interrogate? Were these men her enemies, too? She did not recognise either of them as her uncle's or the Earl of Bainbridge's men—yet that didn't mean they were not in their employ.

'Here, Letty, take this medicine. It will help you to sleep.'

She was powerless to stop the spoon being pressed against her lips and recognised the bitter taste of the liquid. Laudanum. The exact same drug her uncle had forced down her throat before he had handed her over to Bainbridge. Letty struggled as best she could. To her surprise, it was the frowning man who came to her aid. The one with the familiar deep blue eyes.

'Stop it, Joe. If she doesn't want it, you shouldn't force it on her,' he commanded.

The young man instantly withdrew, concern etched on his handsome face. 'I don't want her to be in pain, Jack. She needs to sleep.'

Apparently, enough drops of the liquid had already

entered her system because her eyes were suddenly very heavy. She felt another hand touch her face softly. She knew immediately whose hand it was and also knew she liked this man's touch.

'That's a good girl. Close your eyes, sweetheart. Everything will be all right...'

It was still dark when she woke properly, but not so dark she could not see. Opening both eyelids, however, proved to be problematic. The left one would not open at all. The room was strange. The bed was warm and comfortable, and every bone in her body hurt like the devil.

The only illumination in the room came from a solitary candle on the nightstand and the moonlight streaming through the uncovered window panes. Letty tested her arms and found that she could, in fact, now move them. The tight cord her uncle had bound her with was gone then. Those bonds had left their mark on her wrists though; they were both sore and painful. She reached her other hand over to touch the opposite arm and felt her left wrist bound with bandages. More bandage bound her upper arm. She attempted to sit up, but gave up when her head began to spin and pound once again.

Bringing her hand to her face, Letty felt her swollen lip. It was sore still, although the cut caused by Bainbridge's signet rig was healed over. She must have been here asleep for hours for that to happen. Or days? Further probing led to the discovery of a huge lump on her temple. It was hot and tender, the bruising spread over the front of her forehead and just above her left eye. The lid felt swollen and explained why it was so difficult to open. She probably looked a fright. Her hair felt gritty and matted with a substance she did not recognise, but suspected was mud. She was also beyond thirsty.

For a few minutes she simply lay there, wondering what to do and trying to take in the unfamiliar surroundings. The bedchamber was large and simply decorated. There was a plain, mahogany dressing table against one wall and a matching, and equally enormous, wardrobe on the opposite one. The small nightstand next to her and the bedstead were the only other pieces of furniture. The heavy curtains at the leaded windows hung open, giving her a good view of the night sky beyond. The steady patter of raindrops on the glass suggested that the dreadful weather had not improved at all. The window was closed, but not barred or locked. That was a good sign surely—unless she was so high up escaping from the window was an impossibility. There were lots of castles in Scotland, after all, and the walls and ceiling did have an air of the ancient about them, although the ceilings were too low to belong to a fortress.

Letty scanned the rest of the room for clues. There was one large rug on the wooden floor. It looked to be good quality despite its obviously advanced age. The lack of artwork on the walls or little knick-knacks strewn about gave the room a distinctly impersonal feel. She had no idea whether she was in an inn or a private house and, as she was completely alone in the room, there was nobody to ask. There was also nobody to help her. However, the bedchamber door was open, which made her feel better. If she was a prisoner, then her captors would hardly leave her unattended with the door open—not after what had happened in the carriage. Perhaps she was safe at last?

Slowly, Letty shuffled her body to a more upright position, pausing to let each new wave of dizziness pass. Her shoulder throbbed, the wrist on her left hand was still immensely painful and her left ankle was also a bit tender, but other than that she had escaped the carriage remarkably in one piece. Stretching out her good arm, she could just about touch the rim of the cup on the nightstand. She used the soles of her feet to push forward a little more until she could grab the top of the cup with her finger and thumb. Judging by its weight, she thought the vessel must be filled with liquid. However, the flimsy grip she had on it was not strong enough. The cup slid out of her fingers and crashed to the wooden floor below, taking the precious fluid with it.

The noise created a flurry of activity, accompanied by manly-sounding grunts, on the floor on the other side of the bed. A bewildered dark head appeared first, blinking eyes heavy with sleep, taking in the surroundings as he dragged one hand over his face and through his unruly hair. 'You're awake!' he slurred, peering at her through semi-closed eyes.

'Sorry,' she croaked, 'I dropped the water.' Letty did not recognise him as one of her abductors, but there was something oddly familiar about him. Bizarrely, she had the distinct impression she could trust him and that she was safe with this complete stranger. Then she remembered him as the man who had prevented his accomplice from forcing more laudanum on her. If either of them had meant her harm, she was certain he would have held her down so the drug could be properly administered.

'It's all right.' Stiffly, he raised himself to his feet and stretched his back and neck before shuffling around the bed to the nightstand. He was tall, and from what she could make out, broad to go with it. Older than her, but not by more than a few years. She felt a pang of guilt for inconveniencing him, whoever he was. It could not be very comfortable, or warm, sleeping on the floor. With his back to her he poured a fresh cup of water, then sat on the mattress next to her and guided it carefully into her good hand, wrapping his warm palm around her chilled fingers until he was sure that she could manage it alone. Letty greedily drank every drop so he refilled the cup without her having to ask. 'It's the laudanum,' he explained gruffly. 'My brother says it makes you thirsty.'

How his brother knew this, she had no idea, but he was right. Letty could not remember ever needing to drink quite as much as she did at this moment. She sipped the second cup more slowly, feeling self-conscious as he watched her. Even befuddled and crumpled from sleeping on the floor the man in front of her was very pleasant to look at. He was nothing like the men she had known in the *ton*. His hands were obviously used to hard work and had felt calloused when they'd rested briefly over hers.

'My name is Jack Warriner, in case you were wondering.'

Jack Warriner was also a man who spent a great deal of his life outside. Even in the poor light of the bedchamber she could see evidence of a tan—tiny white crinkles fanned out from the corners of his eyes suggesting that he often squinted in the sun. Yet his accent was not coarse and his diction unmistakably pointed to that of a gentleman. The untucked, and undone, linen shirt he still wore emphasised his wide shoulders and strong arms. The thick column of his throat would look strangled in the high collars favoured by the men in society. And what gentleman of means would sleep on the floor next to an injured stranger? Such an onerous task would be delegated to a servant while the master slept. Unless he was her guard and was merely lulling her into a false sense of security? He was the sort of large, imposing man who would be suited to the job.

Letty watched him carefully as she finished the last drops of her water before passing the cup back to him. 'More?' he asked, lifting the stoneware jug for emphasis and she shook her head gingerly. 'You gave us quite a scare, Letty, I don't mind telling you.' How did he know her name? 'I found you in the road. You passed out, no doubt from all of the trauma and the cold, and you've been out like a light since. My brother Joe is training to be a physician. He patched you up, so you probably have him to thank for saving your life.' His tone, his delivery was matter of fact. 'Do you remember how you came to be bound and gagged and wandering alone in the forest?'

Before she answered his questions, she had a few of her own before she trusted him with the truth. Her uncle was no fool. He would offer an impressive reward to anyone who found her. His own future depended on her marrying the odious Bainbridge. And if the Earl was looking for her and retrieved her...well, she already knew how cruel he could be. She pretended to think and then shook her head. The motion caused a fresh wave of dizziness which he spotted.

'Lie still. Try not to move your head too much.'

'Thank you, sir. You are being very kind.' Letty attempted a smile in the hope he would not realise she was already suspicious.

'Call me Jack,' he said with a wave of his hand, 'ev-

erybody else does.' The corners of his own lips curved
upwards slightly, giving some respite from the perpet-
ual frown he had worn since he had awoken, but it was
still not a smile. He stared at her awkwardly for a few
seconds before speaking again. 'Would you like some
more medicine?'

She shook her head. The black void that came with
the laudanum would rob her of any control. Besides, if
she needed to escape quickly from here then she needed
to be lucid. She also needed to plan an escape route.

'Can you tell me where I am… Jack?'

He sat back down on the mattress again, disregarding
any of the rules of propriety, and sighed, as if answering questions was a great chore to him. 'You are in my
home. Markham Manor. In deepest, darkest, dankest
Nottinghamshire. Retford is the nearest village, almost
three miles away, but if it's a proper town you need,
then Lincoln is probably the closest.' That put her in the
north of England. Just. A long way from Gretna Green
at least. 'I found you near the woods a good mile away.
Soaking wet and frozen stiff. I reckon you had been out
in the storm for a couple of hours before I came along.
I have no idea where you sprang from either and since
nobody has come to claim you, I think we can assume
whoever tied you up was not able to follow your tracks.
My brother Jamie has battened down the hatches in
your honour, in case they come visiting, and is taking
turns with my youngest brother Jacob to keep watch,
so you are safe.'

For some inexplicable reason, Letty believed him.
She had actually done it! She had escaped Bainbridge
and now she was hidden in a house. Her relief must
have been obvious because he shot her a dubious look

which suggested he did not believe her pathetic claim to have no memory of the event.

'What day is it?' The passing of time was her only hope now, yet she had no idea how long she had been here.

'It is past midnight so it must be Friday.'

Letty risked another tenuous shake of the head. She could not work out how much longer she needed just from that information. 'The date?'

Intelligent eyes sought hers and she had the uncomfortable feeling that he could see into her very mind and knew she was lying. 'As I said, it's past midnight, so I suppose that would make it the fourth.'

'I see.'

'Yet you have not enquired as to the month, so I must assume you remember some things. Are you sure you have no memory of what happened?'

Letty looked down towards her hands. This man had been nothing but kind to her so lying to him made her uncomfortable—but there was no guarantee he wouldn't be tempted by a ransom, so with no other choice she did it anyway.

'I do not recall the accident at all.' She would never, ever forget it. Her heart began to knock against her ribs at the falsehood and her palms felt sweaty. What she was claiming did not sound plausible to her own ears.

'Do you remember any details about your family, Letty, so that I might be able to inform them of your predicament?'

Letty would rather die than admit the truth. If her uncle knew where she was then her life might as well be over. Correction—it likely would be over and pretty sharpish, too, if he and the Earl of Bainbridge's hideous plan came to fruition in the next few weeks. No matter what, she needed to stay hidden until then. She stared down at her hands again and shook her head. 'I am afraid I do not... My head feels so dizzy.'

Whilst this was true, she only mentioned it to stop him probing further. Lying was not something that had ever come naturally to her. Her mother and father had always caught her out when she had tried to do it, joking that her guilt was plainly written all over her face. Just in case he could read it in her eyes, Letty hastily closed them with a sigh, but not before she saw scepticism in his own intelligent blue gaze. 'Perhaps I will feel better with a little more sleep,' she mumbled, trying her level best to sound exhausted rather than terrified of imminent exposure, and felt him rise from the mattress next to her.

'Perhaps I should fetch my brother so he can check on you. You have been very ill.'

'There is no need to wake him at such a late hour. I have already inconvenienced you and your family enough. I shall sleep for another few hours, I think.'

She heard, rather than saw, him hesitate for a few moments as he decided whether or not to grant her request. 'I will be right here next to you should you need anything,' he said gruffly, perhaps a touch begrudgingly. Then she heard the rustle of blankets and the sound of him easing his big body back down on to the hard, uncomfortable floor.

Letty was peculiarly grateful that he did not intend to leave her alone in her current state. She felt too vulnerable and his solid presence was strangely reassuring. 'I am so sorry for being so burdensome,' she added lamely, hoping to convey to him her appreciation for all that he was doing for her despite the fact she was lying through her teeth. He grunted in response, but offered no soothing words to contradict her nor did he make any attempt to prolong any conversation between them. She heard him punch the pillow into shape and hoist the covers over himself as he settled into a suitably comfortable position to sleep in.

Whilst Jack Warriner lacked the gentlemanly politeness she was accustomed to, Letty could not help but admire his honesty. He did not want her here, she was a huge burden, but he would not turn her away just yet either. She would be safe here, temporarily. It was a small weight off her mind. A day or two of respite in this remote oasis was a blessing to be sure, although she would have preferred not to have been flung from a speeding carriage in order to have achieved it.

On the other hand, neither her uncle nor the odious Earl was likely to take her escape lying down. Now she was out of their clutches, if she managed to make it intact for her twenty-first birthday, both men were now in very precarious positions indeed. She was not entirely sure what the penalty for abduction, forced marriage and then bridal murder was—but she would be extremely surprised if either of them was allowed to live if they were ever sentenced for the crimes. They would move heaven and earth to find her, and to silence her, and they would endeavour to do so well before the fourth of January.

Letty could not afford to rest on her laurels while she recovered. She needed a plan. A proper plan this time, which would keep her safely out of harm's way until it was too late and she would have full control over her inheritance. She also needed to think of something to tell her clever, reluctant host. Bumbling excuses were not going to work indefinitely on him. But could she really risk telling him the truth? Until she knew more about the situation and the man himself, it would surely be prudent to keep quiet. In the last few days, Letty's blind trust in mankind had been smashed to smithereens with a pickaxe. Trusting anyone after what she had been through was not going to be particularly easy.

To her side, she heard the steady deep breathing of a man already lost in slumber. Letty had never shared a bedroom with a man before. A few short weeks ago such a scandalous act would have brought ruin to her name. Then she had cared a great deal about her reputation—as if it was all that mattered. Of course, she had not realised her life and liberty were in danger and she had believed she would be free to select the husband of her own choosing from the ranks of willing gentleman who swarmed around her at every social function. Her enormous fortune gave her the pick of the bunch, so there had been no need to be hasty. Years ago, when she was young and foolish, she had even written a list of attributes the lucky candidate must possess. He had to be handsome, witty, titled, an excellent horseman, a connoisseur of the theatre, a patron of the arts, the absolute envy of all her friends and, of course, and most importantly, he *had* to be *hopelessly* in love with her.

Whilst she had managed to find suitable gentlemen with nearly all of those qualities, the last one was always the sticking point. After several Seasons her youthful hopes had become quite jaded. So far, she had not found one man who she was wholly convinced loved her, Letty the woman, rather than Violet the Tea Heiress. Her huge fortune, instead of giving her a reassuring sense of comfort, had become a massive weight on her shoulders. Did anyone of her acquaintance actually like her for herself? Or was it merely the piles of pound notes and all the luxury that came with her legendary generosity that drew people to her? She could never tell.

There was one promising candidate who was already close to proposing marriage—the Duke of Wentworth. However, Letty could not quite fathom him out either. Until she did, there was no way she was going to commit to something as permanent as marriage. She was still young; what was the rush? Besides, for a while now she had been distracted with other thoughts. Ideas of actually doing something with her fortune, something that mattered, something which gave her shallow, empty life some purpose. Perhaps create a home for foundlings? Other orphans who were all alone in the world, just as she was, but who did not have the benefit of a fortune to keep them safe, fed and warm. Unfortunately, while she had been lamenting the huge burden of her fortune and what to do with it, and putting off journeying on the path to find her one true love, she had neglected to consider her uncle's personal ambitions for *her* money or the fact that she was bound by law to do his bidding until she reached the age of majority.

Which was only one month away now, give or take a few hours.

Chapter Four

Exactly one month left...

Jack eagerly swapped his nursemaid duties with Joe well before dawn. The hard floor had not been conducive to sleeping on for any longer, not that he ever had time to sleep in, but still, even by his standards the hour was early. The mystery woman had been in his care for a few days now. However, last night had been the first time she had been in any state to speak for herself and her cagey responses to the questions he had asked her did not quite ring true. In fairness, the poor girl had been bound and gagged and horrifically abused beforehand, so it was hardly surprising she was reluctant to trust him, but as she was now his responsibility, he reasoned he did have the right to know what sort of trouble he had brought to his own door.

And she was going to be trouble.

He knew that with the same certainty he knew the sun would rise every morning. Trouble had been Jack's constant companion for a decade; he knew the scent of it too well to ignore.

He wasn't surprised when he found Jamie already up and dressed in the kitchen. Since his brother's return from the Peninsula, he apparently did not sleep. And he smiled even less than Jack did. Both states worried him, yet he had no idea how to fix them. Jamie had always been a closed book. Any loose pages he once had were now glued together firmly and no amount of cajoling would pry them free again.

'I thought I would head to the village and see what I can find out about our guest.' After cradling the woman in his arms for hours and sleeping alongside her for two nights, much as he did not want to, he already felt responsible for the chit. And strangely protective. Clearly he was going soft in his old age.

Jamie handed him a steaming mug of tea and an assessing stare. 'Good idea. I've been thinking much the same myself. It is fairly safe to assume the girl is in danger, but if you go there asking questions, you could stir up a hornets' nest.'

'I am not a fool.'

'I never said you were; however, you are not known for your subtlety. I'll come with you and show you how it's done.'

Without thinking, Jack allowed his gaze to wander to his brother's wounded leg and regretted it instantly when he saw his face cloud with fury. 'I am not a blasted cripple, Jack! I can still ride a horse.'

He was in no mood to try to reason with him today. Jack had barely slept properly in three nights so his temper was closer to the surface than usual and he would likely say something which couldn't be undone. Since Jamie had come home, he was still so angry at the world and convinced he was good for nothing. Any attempts at brotherly concern about him over-extending himself and putting back his recovery would only aggravate him further.

'I shall saddle the horses then.'

It was market day in Retford and by the time they arrived the square was already bustling with activity. At his brother's suggestion, they went directly to the inn in search of breakfast and information. It made sense. If strangers were in the area, they would be staying at the inn. Jack would not have thought of that first, so perhaps having Jamie in tow would prove to be beneficial.

'Just eat your food and listen. The trick to good recognisance is to appear disinterested. If we hear anything vaguely interesting, leave it to me to do the probing.'

Jack grunted in response, a little put out by his brother's lack of faith in his abilities. Jamie selected a table in the centre of the dining room and they ordered food, then his brother disappeared to do some quiet digging and left him to his own devices. For want of something useful to do, he scanned the patrons to see if he could see anything suspicious and conceded that perhaps his brother was right. He knew nothing about gathering information subtly. In fact, his relationship with subtlety of any sort could best be described as tenuous. Jack was a doer and acknowledged his usually straightforward methods of getting to the truth might not be what was needed today. Because it was market day, almost every face was new to him—and therefore, by default, instantly suspicious to his untrained eyes. His first instinct was to go and thoroughly question them all, which was exactly what his military-trained brother had feared he would do. 'You cannot help yourself, Big Brother,' he had said as they had ridden over, 'you are too used to being in charge.' Acknowledging his own character flaws always made Jack wince; having them pointed out correctly by a sibling was galling.

At the bar, Jamie had sidled up to the innkeeper. Being a recently returned war hero from the infamous family who lived near the forest made him of significant interest to the innkeeper. The locals did love to gossip and the Warriners had given them plenty to feast on over the years. Jack watched the man ask his brother question after question with barely contained curiosity and, as usual, Jamie dealt with them with his customary surliness, staring into his drink and never meeting his interrogator's eyes. To all intents and purposes he appeared exactly like a man who wanted nothing more than to be left alone rather than one on a quest for information. Jack had to admire that talent, even if he was still slightly sulking and did so begrudgingly.

A few minutes later, Jamie limped back to the table and spoke in a voice so low, Jack had to strain his ears to hear it.

'There are a group of men from London staying here. A pushy lot, by all accounts, who the innkeeper would be glad to see the back of. They have been here since the morning after you found your damsel in distress. Came in soaked to the skin, despite the two fancy carriages they arrived with. The carriages and half the men left the next day, leaving three of them behind. The rooms were all booked under the name Smith. The innkeeper says they've been asking questions about a girl. An heiress, by all accounts.' Jack raised his eyebrows at this news. 'They are claiming she has been kidnapped and they are searching for her. They haven't surfaced yet this morning, but he expects them presently on account of it being market day and filled with new people to talk to. So far, each morning they have done the same thing. They ask questions, eat and disappear for the day. He has no idea where they go to—but they come back very frustrated. As if they are in a great hurry to get the job done.'

Jamie shot him a warning glance as their breakfasts were brought over. How he noticed the impending arrival of the food was also impressive, Jack mused, seeing as Jamie was not facing the kitchen and would have needed eyes in the back of his head to have seen anyone behind him. The innkeeper's wife plonked them down unceremoniously in front of them, her hostility towards not one, but two Warriners so early in the morning written all over her face.

'Have you paid for these?'

Their father's legacy still blighted them. The bastard had been dead seven years and still the locals believed a Warriner equalled nothing but bad debt and aggravation. Jamie shot the woman an evil look and was about to put her in her place when Jack intervened. 'I paid up front, Nelly. As I always do.' He was trying to build the broken bridges, had been trying for years to mend them, and as much as the slights still wounded he understood them. For centuries the Warriner family had always been a bad lot and it would take a darn sight longer than seven years for the brothers to repair the damage their ancestors had wrought. It was only in the last eighteen months that Jack had been able to lure a few rag-tag tenants back to his land and even they were not originally from around these parts. Nelly sniffed and stalked off.

'Perhaps they are Letty's family searching for her? Maybe she *was* kidnapped.' Conjuring the image of her terrified and running away from him made Jack feel a strange combination of protectiveness and fury all over again.

Jamie shrugged. 'Or that is exactly what they want us to think. They could hardly tell people they are the kidnappers and they would like their hostage back now, can they?' That argument made a lot of sense too. 'Besides, if they are above board, why the name Smith? It's too convenient, Jack. My gut tells me it's not right.'

As Jamie's guts had saved his soldiering bacon on more than one occasion, Jack decided to go along with them. They ate in virtual silence in order to overhear the tangled conversations around them. In the main, they were all tradesmen here to make some coin. One or two piqued their interest, but nobody mentioned a bound and gagged girl in the woods.

Their food was long finished and they were about to leave when three burly men walked in and scanned the room like hawks seeking prey. Jamie picked up his empty mug and pretended to drink. 'Here we go. This is them, I reckon.'

The three men instantly split up and began approaching the other patrons jovially, moving from group to group after friendly handshakes were exchanged and ever closer to their table.

'Remember. Act bored. And keep your mouth shut.'

Jack gave his brother a sarcastic look. 'I appreciate your confidence in me, Jamie.'

'Hello, gentlemen—might I trouble you for a few moments?' The man who pulled up a chair next to them was all politeness. Jamie flicked him a detached look and shrugged. Jack copied.

'Do you live locally?'

'What's it to you?' Jamie replied suspiciously.

'Merely a friendly enquiry, sir.' The man's diction was crisp, but his appearance belied it. Underneath the fine clothes and the oily smile, he was not from the gentry, Jack was certain of that. He might lack Jamie's skills as a spy but he knew a wrong 'un when he saw one. This man had fists like hams, for a start, and a nose which had been often broken. The bridge had collapsed beneath his forehead before jutting out at an odd angle, making him appear more like a bare-knuckle fighter from a travelling carnival than a discerning gentleman of taste passing along the Great North Road. A fine, white jagged scar bisected one cheek. Its presence spoke volumes. This man was a close acquaintance of violence.

'My friends and I are looking for someone. A young lady.' The man gave them a knowing smile. 'There's a reward.'

Jamie stared down into his empty mug as though he was only interested in how soon he could fill it up again. 'A reward, you say?' It was quite a masterly performance. Casual disinterest which gave the interloper just enough hope the lure of money *might* tempt him.

'Indeed. A handsome one. A hundred pounds to anyone who aids in her safe return.'

Jamie let out a slow, impressed whistle. 'A hundred pounds—that's a lot of money. Why so much?' He glanced casually at Jack, his lips curved in a disbelieving half-smile before he turned back to their visitor. 'Is she wanted by the Crown?'

'No. Nothing like that... She has gone missing.'

'We are on the road to Gretna Green. Hundreds of young girls go *missing* along this road every single year. If yours doesn't want to be found...' Jamie shrugged again, allowing the implication to ferment.

'Unfortunately, we believe the young lady in question was kidnapped rather than eloped. Her family are extremely keen to have her back. They fear for her safety.'

'If she's been kidnapped, why not wait for the ransom demand and simply pay it?' Jamie was back to being bored again. His amused eyes met Jack's. 'We are not the sort of men to take on a gang of kidnappers. Not even for a hundred pounds. We value our own lives too much.'

The man smiled and nodded. 'I understand, gentlemen—but the lady in question is rather...resourceful. *If*...she managed to escape their clutches, it might explain why no ransom demands have been made yet.' It all sounded so reasonable—yet alarm bells were ringing in Jack's mind. 'All I would ask is that you keep a watchful eye out for her. She is gently bred, unfamiliar with the area and there are so many places she could get lost here. If you did come across any information as to her whereabouts, her family would be very grateful... And it might prove to be very lucrative for you gentlemen also. Everyone wins, as it were.'

Jack had had enough of playing the mute sidekick. 'If we did see her, what does she look like?' He ignored his brother's warning glare.

'Very pretty. Blonde hair. Green eyes. Only twenty. She's quite a striking little thing. A bit prone to fancy though, as so many young women are, and after such an ordeal there's no telling what sort of state her poor mind will be in…' The man shook his head as if he were genuinely concerned and it raised the hackles on Jack's neck further. 'Her family are hoping to get her back quietly. You understand. The poor girl would be ruined if the world knew what had happened to her. If you see or hear anything, you can find me here at the inn.'

'And your name is?'

'Smith. Mr John Smith.'

'And the girl's? Is she a *Smith* too?'

'No, sir. I merely work for the family. Her name is Violet.'

'No surname?'

The man smiled again, but it lacked any sincerity. 'That's right, sir. The family would prefer not to create a scandal…the young lady would be quite ruined if news of her abduction leaked. Therefore, I am certain you can see now why the family are keen to get her safely returned into their loving arms as swiftly as possible.'

Jamie pierced the stranger with his steely glare. 'If the reward is one hundred pounds, then I am assuming the family is important. That is a large amount of money for a lady of little consequence. Therefore, it stands to reason they can spare more than a paltry hundred pounds for her safe return, don't you think?'

The other man stood, his face a frozen mask. 'May I enquire as to your names, sirs?' There was suspicion in his cold eyes now as they flicked between them.

Jack stared back, all smug arrogance. 'Warriner. I am Jack and this is my younger brother Jamie.'

For a second he saw Jamie silently querying the logic behind giving this fellow their real names, then realising it was sensible. If they aroused this man's suspicions he would likely check on their story and a great many of their neighbours would happily sell the 'Wild' Warriners down the river.

'Well, Mr Warriner, I am sure the *family* would be open to negotiations. Should you have anything of... interest to them.'

Jack laughed and slapped his brother heartily on the back. 'I think me and you should go heiress hunting, Jamie. What do you say? What could we do with at least a hundred pounds, aye?' Never a truer word was spoken although it was a drop in the ocean compared to what he actually needed to stop the rot in their ailing fortunes.

Jack smiled enthusiastically back at the still-loitering man, ignoring the bad taste in his mouth which came from coveting the reward and for hoping the scarred, creepy fellow was, indeed, telling the truth, despite his gut feeling that he wasn't. The Warriners could do with one hundred pounds. It might be enough to send Joe to medical school for a while and ease his guilt at failing to get his brother there sooner.

Then again, wanting that money already felt disloyal to Letty, although he had no idea where his overriding loyalty to her had come from. Unless it was just the crushing burden of yet more responsibility he did not need. Jack apparently had a soft spot for damsels in distress. 'Where did you last see her, Mr Smith?'

The man's expression instantly changed to one of friendliness again, believing he had won them over. 'We suspect she might have been taken along this section of the Great North Road.'

'You *suspect*?' Jack shook his head at his brother and laughed derisively. 'So we would not be chasing a fact—merely a suspicion? Only about ten villages and a hundred square miles of Sherwood Forest to search then!' He stared back at the man with pity. 'I think my brother and I can find better things to do with our time than searching for a needle in a haystack—but I wish you well with your search. If, by some miracle, we do hear something, rest assured, Mr Smith, you will be the first to know.' For good measure, he toasted him with his own empty mug.

Chapter Five

Still just one month to go...

Her attentive physician tied the last of her clean bandages, then sat back on the mattress to smile at her. 'It is indeed a miracle you are this hale and hearty. I was convinced you would die when Jack brought you home, yet now there are just a few sprains and cuts left to heal. You obviously have a strong constitution indeed. A day or two of rest and I dare say you will be as good as new.'

Letty certainly felt better. And cleaner. The youngest Warriner, Jacob, had brought her a bucket of hot water, some soap and towels at her request, so she had managed to rinse the mud and grit from her hair. She was sat up in bed, her belly pleasantly filled with food and dressed in a freshly laundered gentleman's shirt. She bestowed her healer with one of Violet's best smiles—the one which had been fêted in society as the most stunning of the Season—and hoped her swollen lip would not spoil its impact. 'Thank you, Doctor. I am grateful for all you have done.'

'I am no doctor yet,' he said a little wistfully, 'but perhaps one day.'

This surprised her. 'I was certain you were a proper physician. Your medical knowledge is excellent. Without your help, I do not doubt I would have died. Why do you not get a proper licence to practise medicine?'

He stood and busied himself with tidying away the soiled bandages. 'I study and read extensively, and I am sure that one day I will qualify. However, it is not just my efforts that saved your life. The majority of your thanks should be directed at my brother Jack. He was the one who brought you home and he has scarcely left your side since your arrival. He was the one who spent the nights tending to your fever and making sure you were kept warm.'

Letty recalled the eldest Warriner had slept on the floor beside her last night. Clearly, he had spent a few nights on that hard floor on her behalf—odd when he had appeared so suspicious and put upon, although, for reasons she could not fathom, his diligence did not surprise her. 'Then I shall extend my gratitude to him also, *Dr* Joe, as soon as I see him next.'

He had not been there when she had awoken this morning, which at the time Letty had been relieved about. Jack Warriner saw too much. Whether or not he really was a good man, as both of his younger brothers had suggested, she would have to see. However, neither Jacob nor Joe Warriner had been guarded in their answers this morning when she had bombarded them with a stream of questions. Thanks to them, Letty now knew for certain she was not a prisoner in this house. Jack Warriner had found her on the road and brought her home, and by doing so, had saved her life.

Home was a four-hundred-year-old manor house surrounded by thirty acres of park and farmland. Mostly farmland. The Warriners grew wheat and raised sheep, and hardly moved in the sort of circles Bainbridge and her duplicitous uncle did. Apparently, only the second eldest, Jamie, had been to London and then only once on a fleeting visit, so they would have no idea who she was either.

They all worked on the land, with the exception of Jamie who had only recently arrived back from the war, and was still recovering from the damage Napoleon's army had done to his body. The three younger brothers also had enormous respect for Jack. It shone out of their eyes whenever he was mentioned in a conversation and they clearly deferred to his leadership on all matters of importance.

The Warriners were fiercely loyal and hugely protective of one another, the sort of tight family bond Letty had never experienced, yet always yearned for. They loved one another. It was plainly obvious and she could not help envying them for that. It must be nice to know there was always somebody there for you, ready to support you or simply to commiserate with when times were tough. To always have someone to turn to. Letty had not had such support since the untimely death of her parents at seventeen. She had ostensibly been all alone in the world—yet nobody had really pitied her because she was the Tea Heiress after all, as if her money could somehow fix her broken heart, or banish her loneliness and make everything bright in the world again.

If something happened to one of the brothers, the others would move heaven and earth to rectify things or would support each other in their grief. She had been missing from Mayfair for days—and sincerely doubted anybody had missed her at all. Not really. Her swathes of friends might comment on her absence at a ball or afternoon tea, but Letty was not convinced any of them genuinely cared enough to investigate the true cause of her absence. She did not possess one true friend, the sort a girl could confide in or depend upon. Nobody had ever assumed she might want one and she had no idea how to go about getting one. And that was a humbling thought, as well as a depressing one. She had more money than she could ever spend in one lifetime, yet she envied the Warriners.

She got the impression life was tough for the family—although such disloyalty had not been vocalised explicitly—and she suspected the main obstacle between Joe qualifying as a doctor, and not, was decidedly financial. That might work in her favour. In her experience, those in need of money were easily bribed and her father had often commented on the benefits of 'greasing a few palms'. In a few weeks, she could easily fill the palms of all four Warriners with gold and still not make a dent in her reserves.

And then again it might not. If they desperately needed money quickly, they could well sell her back to Bainbridge if the opportunity presented itself. At least Bainbridge could pay them instantly—Letty would have to wait weeks to get her hands on her own money. The appointment was already made with the solicitor on the day of her birthday to sign the papers which would give her her longed-for independence. It was also the day she would consign a generous portion of it to the charitable trust she intended to set up in her name and begin carving out a new life filled with noble purpose rather than pampered inertia. Once that was done, she intended to begin searching for premises right away and nobody would be able to stop her.

Her uncle had always been most dismissive of her desire to put her money to work and had refused to allow her to spend it on anything apart from gowns and fripperies she did not need and had long ago ceased to want. But on that glorious day, in one month's time, she could do with it whatever she pleased. The Warriners might not want to wait.

The fact that she had not been attended to by the family servants niggled. It was almost as if the brothers were intent on keeping her presence here a great secret. Why would they do that unless it was for sinister purposes? Was it for her protection or was it for theirs? The most pressing problem was that Letty really did not know if this family was to be trusted.

Until she did, it was probably sensible to have an escape route. As soon as Joe left her on a quest to fetch her some tea, Letty eased her legs over the side of the bed. After carefully testing her weight on her bad ankle, she hobbled across the room to the faceted, leadlight window and peered out.

Markham Manor was indeed in deepest, darkest, dankest Nottinghamshire. One side of the estate was fringed with dense woodland. The outer edge of the estate ran directly alongside the River Idle, so unless they came by boat or battled their way through the trees, the only way Bainbridge could enter the grounds was to the east, and via the narrow, rutted dirt lane her rescuer had found her on. A lane whose only destination was here.

In the distance, Letty could just about make out the high wall which she now knew enclosed the Warriners' land. She also knew the huge gates were now locked because Jacob had moaned about the effort it had taken to do so and the splinters he had received in the process. A little further along, and purposely hidden behind tangled vines, was a smaller gate, a secret escape route which sounded positively medieval and very romantic. The Warriners of old must have needed such a device, as well as a great deal of fortified protection, if they had built such defences, yet those same defences now gave Letty a great deal of peace of mind. She had been here three days and nobody had come a calling. The more time passed, she hoped, the less likely it was they would do so.

Directly below her window was a cobbled courtyard which housed a large iron pump handle and a small mountain of buckets balanced haphazardly on top of each other. Other than that, the courtyard was bare. Her bedchamber must face over the kitchens then, in the rear of the house and well away from prying eyes in the lane. The drop from her window to the courtyard was significant enough to cause injury, she estimated, yet not quite high enough to result in death. There was trellis alongside her window, covered in the gnarled old branches of a wisteria left quite barren by the winter. If she had to, she could lower herself from it carefully and make a dash for the woods.

Satisfied the outside was safe, Letty turned and began to hobble towards her bedchamber door to investigate the layout of the house when the door opened and Jack Warriner strode in.

Then stopped dead.

She was wearing his shirt. That should not have come as a surprise because his brother had dressed her in his shirt when they had transferred her unconscious body to Jack's bedchamber because the only other one in any habitable state had mould creeping over the damp, cracked walls. Except the sight of her standing there in it was simply staggering. She had legs. Lovely, shapely female legs which were bare to mid-thigh where the tail of the shirt hung. And the most wonderful golden hair Jack had ever seen. A tumble of corkscrew ringlets fell past her shoulders, the short curls around her face framing it like a halo. His words dried in his throat and his eyebrows shot up as he stared at the beautiful creature right in front of him.

Emerald-green eyes stared back at him in surprise before she crouched and her arms covered her thighs. 'Would you mind turning around, please!' she squeaked and his wits returned.

'Yes, of course! Sorry!' Jack spun on his heels and faced the door, grateful for the opportunity to catch his breath and simply breathe.

There was a woman in his bedchamber.

Because after seeing her legs there was no way he could continue to think of her as a patient. There had not been an actual woman in Markham Manor since his mother had died a decade ago and he could barely remember the last time he had seen a woman's bare legs. May? Last spring, in Lincoln? Although at the time he had not really taken much notice of the tavern maid's legs because he had had to travel home before dark and he was more concerned with other parts of the woman. Perhaps he should have, because surely one pair of legs was much like the next? What was it about these particular legs he suddenly found so alluring?

He heard her scramble back towards the bed and the

rustle of the covers as she made herself decent. 'You can turn around now Mr… Jack.'

Somehow, seeing her sitting up in his bed, all tousled and proper, made it worse and he felt the falls of his breeches tighten uncomfortably. She looked as tempting as a baker's window and, by God, he was desperate to taste her. But he had no time to spare to consider such unexpected yearnings, definitely not for a woman in his care and definitely not when he sensed impending danger.

'We need to talk… Violet.'

Her lovely eyes widened further in alarm at the use of her proper name and Jack finally knew for certain she had been economical with the truth. However, it was difficult to be annoyed at her for the omission. In her shoes, he'd have probably done much the same.

'There are men in the village looking for you.' A look of terror washed across her delicate features which he experienced an enormous desire to soothe. 'We did not alert them to your presence here. I thought it prudent to talk to you first before I entrusted them with any information.'

She visibly sagged with relief, the motion causing the open neck of the capacious linen shirt to fall to one side, exposing the smooth, pale skin of her delicate, feminine shoulder. Jack's groin tightened again and to cover it, he sat down heavily on the mattress in front of her. 'I think it is time you told me the truth. Don't you?'

Her golden head bobbed in assent, causing the blonde curls nearest her face to bounce. He suppressed the urge to reach up and touch one. Run his fingers along the length of it to see if it actually did feel like spun silk. She worried her bottom lip nervously with her teeth, drawing his hungry eyes there too. Her mouth was pink and plump and ripe for kissing. For some inexplicable reason, Jack was sorely tempted to kiss her. Not that he would, of course. The poor girl was frightened enough already, the last thing she needed was his case of rampant, wholly inappropriate lust.

'How many men?'

'Three. The others and their coaches have gone elsewhere to search for you, although I doubt they are too far away either. There are not many villages in this part of the county. They claimed to be working for your family.'

Her expression hardened. 'In a manner of speaking, they are.'

'They also claimed you were abducted, although I gather you would rather not be returned to them?'

He watched a flurry of emotions play on her face. Fear, confusion, mistrust, then finally acceptance. She stared back at him levelly. 'Those men—was one of them an older man? Grey hair tied back in an old-fashioned *queue*?'

Jack shook his head. 'No. The man I spoke to called himself Mr Smith. He had a scar across his cheek here.' He swiped his finger in a jagged line down his own cheek to the jaw in demonstration.

'Layton. His name is Layton. He works for the Earl of Bainbridge.' She sat back on the pillows, tucking her knees to her chest and hugging them. It was an unconscious gesture which suggested she needed to protect herself from whatever it was these men had come to achieve. It sparked something visceral inside him. Something primal and male and territorial. It made him want to slay dragons for her—a ridiculous notion which suddenly came out of nowhere and blindsided him. She could be lying through her pretty teeth, yet that made no difference to his urgent need to be her knight in shining armour. What was wrong with him? It wasn't like him to be so fanciful. Jack did not usually have those sorts of feelings for women. He liked them well enough…but always in a pragmatic and sensible way. He had never been a *romantic* man—although a part of him was certainly feeling that way if he was thinking of himself as her knight and conjuring imaginary dragons in his obviously addled mind.

It was probably because of the golden hair, he reasoned, he had always had a penchant for blondes. The legs were a bonus, of course, and then there was the fact that she was lying in his bed. Staring a little warily at him with her beautiful green eyes. She regarded him thoughtfully for several moments, then sighed.

'Letty *is* my name. It is the name I prefer to be called, at any rate, because my mother used to call me it as a child. However, my full name is Violet Dunston.' She paused briefly as if he should recognise the name, and when he didn't she seemed a little surprised, but continued. 'My parents died in a carriage accident a few years ago and since then I have been under the guardianship of my father's brother. Whilst I have never been particularly close to my uncle, I had no reason to suspect he wished me ill. He moved into my family house to fulfil his guardianship duties, although apart from that we really had little to do with one another.'

'A few weeks ago, he introduced me to the Earl of Bainbridge, a man old enough to be my grandfather who apparently had expressed a desire to marry me. Unsurprisingly, I was not thrilled with the proposal and turned him down. He is a completely odious man, who has already outlived two wives and has the reputation for being a dreadful gambler. I was surprised he would even condone such a proposal. However, since then, my uncle has been relentless in his insistence that I marry the vile man—because they were friends, or so I was led to believe. We argued about it a great deal and eventually my uncle ceased pressing the suit. I assumed I had convinced him that Bainbridge was the very last man on earth who I would consider marrying. Unfortunately, I could not have been more wrong.'

Just thinking about her uncle's treachery made her angry. All this time she had been duped into believing he had only wanted the very best for her...but he had designs on her fortune just like every other man who came knocking on her door. 'On the night in question, I had only just dressed for a ball and was waiting for the carriage to be brought around when my uncle asked to speak with me. He offered me a glass of wine, which stupidly I drank. It was laced with laudanum. I was barely conscious by the time Bainbridge arrived, but I overheard the gist of their conversation nevertheless. Bainbridge had agreed to give him half of my fortune in return for my hand in marriage—payable as soon as Bainbridge could obtain legal access to my money. It is held in a trust, you see, until I reach the age of majority. They tied me up and I was taken to a carriage bound for Gretna Green.

'By the time I came to, we were speeding along the road. I told Bainbridge that no court in the land would condone a forced marriage. I threatened to have the pair of them arrested and tried for their crime and that I would move heaven and earth to have the sham of a marriage annulled if he succeeded.' Her voice wavered then, because Letty still could not quite believe it herself. 'He laughed, claiming he had no great desire to be shackled to me for any longer than was necessary to get his hands lawfully on my magnificent stack of money and said…' her voice faltered '…he said that if I failed to comply and made his life difficult, then I would force his hand. He said I would find it difficult to get a marriage annulled from the grave.'

Jack Warriner's dark eyebrows came together fiercely as he absorbed her words. Other than that, she really had no idea what he was thinking. His very handsome face was quite inscrutable.

'So you were kidnapped, then?'

Letty nodded. 'Yes—but effectively by a member of my own family. If they find me, Bainbridge will drag me to Gretna Green. As soon as we are married, English law grants him my entire fortune.'

'And then your uncle would receive his half?'

'My father left him nothing in his will, aside from naming him as my guardian and giving him some control as trustee of the estate. As soon as I turn twenty-one, control of my entire inheritance reverts to me. The blood money earned by selling his niece to Bainbridge was obviously more palatable to him than living out the rest of his days with nothing.'

He stood and pinned her with his stormy blue gaze, giving nothing about his ultimate intentions away.

'I need to talk to my brothers.'

Then he stormed to the door.

Chapter Six

~~~~~~~~~~~~~~

Thirty days and twelve hours left...

'Violet Dunston?' Jacob exclaimed and then appeared frustrated when all of his three brothers stared back perplexed. 'Seriously? Do you three never read the newspapers?'

'I don't have time to read the newspapers.' By the time Jack finished his never-ending round of daily chores, he could barely stand, let alone read.

'Scarcely a week goes by without a mention of society's darling Miss Dunston. She is the *Tea Heiress*.'

Jack was losing patience. 'Spare us the dramatics, Jacob. Surely it is quite apparent none of us knows what you are blathering on about. Kindly put us out of our misery, Little Brother.'

Jacob leaned forward on the scarred kitchen table as if imparting some great wisdom. 'The Dunston family were *serious* tea importers and by serious I mean they made oodles of money from it. Or they did, before old man Dunston sold the business for a king's ransom. I believe he died a few years ago. Violet Dunston is an only child; heiress to it all. Lock, stock and barrel. She is a renowned beauty and now that I've seen her I have to concur.' Watching the twin smiles of male satisfaction appear on Jacob and Joe's faces caused Jack to experience an unfamiliar pang of jealousy, but he held his tongue. His siblings all had eyes, after all, except the thought of his brothers sharing the magnificent spectacle of Letty's legs particularly bothered him. He needed to find her more suitable clothing as soon as possible. Something shapeless, large and concealing. Something that would put a stop to his brothers' wayward gazes. Begrudgingly, he turned his attention back to his youngest brother.

'The gossip columns are filled with speculation about whom she will choose to marry. It is all anyone can talk about. The gentlemen of London are falling all over themselves to court her.'

Jamie, always the least impressed by anything, was scathing. 'Hardly a surprise when the girl is obscenely rich. I should imagine, just like her uncle and the Earl of Bainbridge, they would be delighted to get their hands on all of that lovely money. She could have a face like a horse's behind and they would probably still want to marry her.'

'True,' agreed Jacob, 'but it is not only fortune hunters who are courting her. There are a few wealthy peers too. I read something about the illustrious Duke of Wentworth throwing his hat into the ring, and he is as rich as Croesus and has his pick of the ladies. She's famously charming—in fact, Miss Dunston is viewed as a diamond of the first water. An *incomparable*.'

An incomparable! If ever Jack needed proof that his misplaced lust was barking up the wrong tree, there it was. Letty had queues of eager, *solvent* suitors and would never look twice at a humble Warriner for anything more than necessary protection. She was so far out of his league he would need a stepladder to reach her. Perhaps twenty stepladders. Not that he had hoped for more, of course. Lust was a natural, human response to such a beautiful woman. Even bruised and dishevelled, Letty *was* a beautiful woman, so his instantaneous and physical reaction was also, therefore, quite understandable. Besides, Jack was too pragmatic, too wise to be disappointed in the ways of the world and too burdened already to even consider something beyond the carnal. These overwhelming feelings of protectiveness towards her obviously stemmed from the unyielding and irritating sense of responsibility he had been cursed with since birth. She was a damsel in distress. Ever since his mother, he had a soft spot for them. He had found Letty stumbling in on the road to his house, therefore, until he could take her safely home to Mayfair, it stood to reason she was also his responsibility, just as his mother had been. Another one. To add to the thousands he already had and didn't need.

Lucky him.

'We will need to get her back to her people in London as quickly as possible if her life is in danger. There must be another relative there who can keep her out of harm's way while this uncle and Bainbridge are brought to justice.' And out of his sight.

'It's too soon to make her travel yet.' Joe immediately leapt to her defence. 'Yesterday she was still burning with fever. She needs a few days to properly recuperate.'

'Nobody is planning on moving her yet. With that Layton and his cronies still at large in the village, a trip now might arouse suspicions. I will not put either her life or any of yours in danger by acting rashly. Once the dust has settled and I deem it to be safe, I will return her.' Although how Jack was going to pay for an unforeseen trip to London without their finances suffering too much, he had yet to work out. All of the spare money left over from last year's harvest had already disappeared in new lead for the decrepit roof on the east wing. Every other penny had been accounted for. He supposed they could overnight in one inn on the way there and on the way back he could find a quiet barn somewhere...

'You will not be making the trip alone. It's too dangerous. I will be coming with you,' Jamie announced. Nobody dared point out that Jamie was lame and in no state to endure such a long and demanding ride south. However, he had apparently already considered it himself. 'I might be useless on my feet, but I can still sit on a horse and shoot straight, should the need arise.' And nobody commented on the peculiar arsenal their brother now housed in his bedchamber either. Not after Jacob had found out the hard way that the former soldier slept with a knife under his pillow. 'Do any of you know how to cover your tracks or live off the land?' He scanned their faces and shrugged smugly. 'I thought not.'

As always, Jamie made a valid point. Despite his physical limitations, he would be useful to have around. Especially if the Earl of Bainbridge's men decided to follow them. 'All right then. It's settled.' He pointed at Joe and Jacob. 'You two can stay here and convince those scoundrels all the Warriners are where they should be, in case they come calling. Layton has nothing to link us to the girl as yet—I would prefer to keep it that way. Jamie and I will escort her back to London.'

'You most certainly will not!'

Letty had become increasingly anxious waiting for Jack Warriner to return to her room and appraise her of her fate, so she had wrapped herself in a blanket, hobbled down the creaky wooden staircase and followed the sound of male voices. Now, it seemed, she had timed her arrival to perfection. 'I cannot go to London until the fourth of January!'

Jack stood and glared at her. 'Your family will know how best to keep you safe.'

'To the best of my knowledge, my entire family only consists of one treacherous uncle. To return me to him is tantamount to signing my death warrant! I am too well known and there are too many people who would sell me down the river for a reward.'

'Surely there must be someone else you can go to?' He was looking at her as if she was clearly stupid and his patronising tone rankled.

'I believe, sir, I would remember if I possessed any other living relations. Do you think I have mislaid them somewhere?' Her head had started to spin, but she ignored it. 'For the time being, I would prefer to hide, just for a few days while I decide what to do next. Perhaps I could remain hidden here?' Without thinking she cast her eyes around the shabby room and smiled kindly. 'I can pay you, if it's money you require.'

The three younger Warriners all exchanged a telling look. Joe winced. Jamie shook his head and Jacob simply closed his eyes.

'I don't need your damn money, woman!' Jack stalked towards her in outrage. 'We are not paupers,

Miss Dunston, and I resent the implication. Whilst you are here, you will remain as our guest and that is that. Taking you safely home as soon as possible is the *right* thing to do. I find it hard to believe there is nobody in London who is worried as to your whereabouts and would be a more suitable guardian for you than myself. There must be somebody—a cousin, a close friend, perhaps?'

She had to make him understand. 'The Earl of Bainbridge and my uncle will find a way to silence me if they have any inkling I am alive. I know of their nefarious plan, remember? They will be in fear for their own lives now. Don't you see? Desperate men like that will resort to desperate measures. Travelling anywhere, even in the dead of night, will put my life in danger.' The toll of the last few days had made her body weak. Her knees threatened to buckle so Letty locked them to stand proudly in front of this domineering man who thought he knew best. 'You have witnessed already the lengths they are prepared to go to. Not only will my life be in danger, yours will be too.'

'Then that settles it. You will remain here for the entire month,' Jack decreed.

An entire month! Here? 'Once I am fully recovered I will seek sanctuary with the local authorities of my own accord. I will not be held responsible for putting you and your brothers at risk.'

'I do not hold the authorities in Nottingham in particularly high esteem. Once they know you have been here, with the Warriner family, I doubt they will act with the necessary diligence your circumstances demand. I believe I am quite capable of protecting you and my brothers against any threat for a month, Miss Dunston.' Letty went to interrupt and he stayed her with his hand. 'It is settled. My decision has been made. Until I can return you to London and alert the proper authorities there as to what danger you are in, you are now my responsibility and will abide by my rules.'

'But you are four men, Mr Warriner! Four men and I am a woman alone.' Letty had intended to sound reasonable, but the words came out in a screech. She had only thought to stay here for a few days, not several weeks. If she were ever to be discovered here her good reputation would be in tatters.

'Yet you are safer here than you would be out there!'

A very valid point. She remembered the huge gates and walls. The isolation. Nobody knew she was there. The idea had merit, but she had to be in control. 'Only on the condition that I recompense you for your services.' Surely her money would give her the upper hand against this domineering man she hardly knew?

Jack's thunderous expression said it all. 'Out of the question.'

Letty shook her head stubbornly, a movement which brought about a wave of dizziness so intense she had to grab the doorframe for support. 'I will not be in your debt, sir. You have already done so much and I can well afford it.'

The three seated Warriners all stared at their feet in silence. Clearly she had said the wrong thing again, because Jack was looming over her now.

'I do not require money for doing a good deed, madam. As the master of this house, it is my responsibility to keep you safe, and after what you have told me, I honestly believe the best way to do that is to hide you here. You will not return back to London until I deem it safe to do so. It is decided.'

It took a great deal of pride not to burst into frustrated tears at his dictatorial tone. 'Decided? Am I to have no say in my own future?' Such a concept was beyond ridiculous. Letty always got what she wanted. He stared back, his steely blue glare unmoved. 'I am not a child or a chattel, Mr Warriner. I am perfectly capable of looking after myself. *You* have no authority over me!'

As parting shots went, she was quite proud of it. His intense blue eyes narrowed as he digested her words and Letty decided now would be the opportune moment to make a well-timed exit. The walls of the room had begun to sway and tilt quite ferociously as she turned smartly to storm back upstairs. Letty took two steps forward, then the floor began to list too. Her grand gesture of defiant independence collapsed the moment her knees did and she found herself crumpling woozily to the floor. Most irritatingly, it was Jack's strong, capable arms that caught her. He lifted her into them as if she weighed practically nothing, with a distinctly paternalistic, put-upon expression on his face.

'Joe?'

'She's still weak from her ordeal—she shouldn't be out of bed. No wonder she swooned.'

Jack did not even bother responding to his brother, he merely turned with Letty still in his arms and began to walk briskly towards the staircase. It was disconcerting being held so close by him—yet bizarrely not in a bad way. She felt safe, protected and stupidly impressed by his strength and undeniably manly physique. And he smelled positively sinful. Some sort of spicy, fresh, male smell which Letty wanted to inhale deeply while she burrowed her face into his neck. His overbearing, single-minded, irritating neck. 'You can put me down. I can manage.' There would be absolutely no burrowing. Not while he was being so…domineering and non-compliant.

His irritatingly beautiful, blue eyes flicked to hers for a second. 'We can't have you *swooning* now, Letty. Can we?' The very idea of it seemed to amuse him, which of course, seriously rankled.

'I am not a woman known for swooning, Mr Warriner. Anybody who knows me will tell you that.' Not that there was anyone left alive who truly knew her. Her parents had. Everybody else saw what they wanted to see and Letty found it easier to hide behind that convenient façade than allow anyone to see she was lonely and unhappy. 'Had I not been forced to wander in a freezing forest for hours in the rain, after being bound, gagged and abducted, it would not have happened today.'

He stared ahead, apparently bored. The dark stubble on his chin tempted her fingers to touch it, so she clasped them ineffectually across her middle as he started up the stairs.

'Are you too proud to let me pay for your services?'

Silence.

Clearly it was time to become the confident Violet Dunston. Whenever she met a brick wall, and Jack Warriner was definitely a big, thick, brick wall, Violet's charm had never failed to quietly knock it down. Men, especially, were particularly responsive in her experience. She could not spend a month being dictated to by this stubborn man. She would run mad.

Letty unclasped her hands and rested one palm gently over his heart, moistened her lips to give them some gloss and peeked up at him through her lashes in the manner which she knew all men found utterly delightful. 'Perhaps I could fund your brother's medical studies, Jack?' For good measure she blinked a little erratically so he could see just how long and lovely those lashes were and how very upset she was by his insistence on being in charge. 'Surely you would allow me the pleasure of doing that one, small thing out of gratitude.' Something which would keep this infuriatingly dictatorial male in check.

He glanced down at her face and she was certain she felt his heartbeat speed up beneath her fingers, but when his jaw hardened and those dark eyebrows came together in a forbidding line, she realised she might have seriously misjudged the situation.

'You might have my brothers falling all over themselves to do your bidding, Letty, and I am sure you are quite used to getting your own way in practically everything with your *fêted* beauty and *piles* of money, but your pouting and flirting will not sway me. You can stay here for as long as I am prepared to be your keeper—and once I decide it is safe to take you back to London, then you will go. In the interim, you will do as you are told, Miss Dunston, because I am master of this house and you would do well to remember it. No amount of pretty eyelash fluttering is going to change my mind.'

Chapter Seven

Twenty-eight days remaining, give or take a few hours...

Letty stared at the trunk full of outdated ladies' dresses with a sinking heart. The heavy brocades and stiff skirts would take hours and hours to turn into anything vaguely presentable, even with her talent with a needle. She had dispatched Jacob up to the attic to find her something to wear, other than Jack's shirts, and this was the best he could come up with. With amazing forethought for a man unused to having women in his house, the youngest Warriner had also brought his mother's old sewing basket down too. Now that she was more herself again, altering these clothes would give her something to do while Joe had confined her to yet another day of bed rest, which frankly she did not need.

'Thank you, Jacob. I am sure I can make use of these. I have not been allocated a maid yet. Now that I am feeling better, could one be arranged?'

'A maid? Of your own?'

'Yes—somebody who is handy with a needle and

good with arranging hair. And could you ask your cook to vary the menu a little bit? Whilst the roast meat is always very nice, I find the lack of sauces and the boiled vegetables a little bland.'

Jacob's face began to split into a wide grin. 'I have no authority regarding the distribution of *staff*, Letty, or the menu choices. You should probably ask Jack. He organises all of those things.' His eyes were twinkling mischievously. 'However, perhaps he might be more open to such requests if they came from you. You are our *guest*, after all.' He looked like he was about to burst out laughing. 'Aside from that, is there anything else you require?'

'Some tea would be nice, Jacob. In about half an hour? And I don't suppose you could bring some cake with it?'

He playfully tugged his forelock. 'I shall see what I can do, Letty.'

Left alone, the silence of her lonely room began to feel oppressive. Letty was already way beyond bored with staying in bed, certain that it was Jack who was insisting she rest rather than have her under his feet. For the sake of peace, she would comply today, but wild elephants would not keep her in this bedchamber tomorrow.

Her only company came in the shape of either Joe or Jacob Warriner and usually only briefly when they could be spared from other chores. They brought her tea or books or whatever else she requested—but those visits were still few and far between. Thus far, she had not had any dealings with the gruff Jamie and she had only seen fleeting glimpses of the domineering master of the house since he had unceremoniously deposited her back on his bed two days ago, after her failed attempt at getting him to bend to her will.

The fact he had seen straight through the reasons for her flirting was embarrassing. Usually men scurried around Letty to please her, even without her resorting to using her feminine wiles. When she did bestow one coy look or a faint flutter of her eyelashes, even the most hard-nosed gentleman was won over and keen to earn her good favour. She was the *Tea Heiress*, after all. Judgemental Jack had managed to make her feel like a fool, and what was worse was the fact that she had been the one trying to make him feel off-kilter. Instead, it had been her pulse which had ratcheted up several notches; her kilter that was off.

Being held in that man's arms had been overwhelming enough. She had felt protected, delicate and, despite his grim demeanour, quite special. Galling when she was so determined to be independent. It almost felt like she'd taken a step back towards the old Letty, the one who wanted to marry a man to feel worthwhile. But touching Jack's hard, warm chest had been, frankly, beyond heady. Letty had never experienced a reaction to a man quite like that one. She had wanted to curl her arms around his neck instantly and experience how splendid she imagined it would be to be draped fully against him, properly wrapped in those magnificent, ungentlemanly muscled arms. Shamelessly staring up into his fathomless, beautiful blue eyes…

Oh, stop it, Letty! She had a tendency to be prone to flights of fancy and silly daydreams—but to be having such thoughts about a man who saw her as a great inconvenience and was completely immune to her womanly charms was ridiculous. Jack Warriner was not the sort of gentleman she usually favoured. Yes, he was handsome and, yes, he was deliciously burly and easy on the eye—but he was also a stubborn, dominant and unbendable male! Just like her uncle. A man who refused to listen to her—and, although she sincerely doubted Jack shared any of her insidious uncle's other, reprehensible character traits, Letty was all done with domineering males. Her fanciful mind had no place constantly wandering back to *him*. She knew exactly the sort of man she wanted and that man was nothing like Jack Warriner.

He was someone more like the Duke of Wentworth, for example. A polite, solicitous and gentlemanly man. Letty doubted he was that interested in her fortune, because he had a vast one of his own, although one could never tell. She supposed the title could be considered a bonus, except she had little interest in such things any more. The trouble with Wentworth was that he was a collector of all things beautiful and he always had to have the best of everything. The opulent new house he was having built in Mayfair was a great source of society speculation and he had reportedly sent out emissaries to the furthest reaches of the globe to bring back rare treasures to fill it with. Despite his charming manner and seemingly besotted demeanour, Letty had a horrible suspicion his interest in her stemmed from the ridiculous label she had been given of an *incomparable*. The *diamond* of the Season. And being desired simply as another adornment to a man's house, rather than for the woman she truly was, was somehow worse than being merely a source of income. At least money had a use. Ornaments got dusty when their appeal faded and the owner forgot about them. Until Wentworth proved otherwise, Letty was not particularly tempted to become his duchess either. Whoever her future husband turned out to be, he had to be hopelessly in love with *her*.

Not a handsome, domineering farmer to whom she was an unwelcome burden. She wanted a man who would put her on a pedestal, didn't she, not one who put her in her place… Although, in typically contrary fashion, she immediately decided it was quite refreshing that he had not fawned all over her. She quite respected his strength of character even though she disliked his heavy-handed approach. That intrigued her. He was the first man she had encountered who appeared totally oblivious to the fact she was an heiress—in fact, any mention of her money seemed to get his dander up. And he was very, very handsome. Those eyes of his were positively swoon-worthy and his muscles were so…so…

Clearly, she had to get out of this dull room or she was in danger of running completely mad if she was actually debating the merits of Jack Warriner as a potential suitor! He had three equally handsome brothers, two of whom were closer to her own age and both thoroughly charming. If she was going to have peculiar fancies for a Warriner brother, she would do better to direct them towards the capable, kind physician Joe, or the roguish, flirtatious Jacob. Any Warriner, in fact, who was not Jack.

With a sigh, she padded across the bedchamber to the large wardrobe and rooted through it for something which would render her decent enough to eventually leave this room. All she could find were more shirts, plain waistcoats and breeches. After comparing a few pairs for size, she pulled on a soft pair of buckskin breeches which were far too big around the waist but fit her well enough everywhere else. A quick rifle in the sewing basket produced a reel of scarlet ribbon. She cut off two lengths. One was tied tightly around her waist to hold up the sagging breeches, the second she used to tie back her unruly hair. With no hairpins apparently anywhere in Markham Manor, and no maid as yet, it was the best she could do with such limited resources. Her request, made via Joe yesterday, for some feminine items to be purchased on her behalf in the village came back, also via Joe, with a terse '*Are you mad, woman?*' from He Who Must Be Obeyed.

Now she considered it fully, she was prepared to concede that the oldest, most irritating Warriner had made a valid point. The purchasing of anything feminine for a house filled with men was a tad suspicious and, if she wanted to remain out of Bainbridge's gnarly clutches, she should probably make do with her ribbon. Although making do was not something she was used to. If she was being completely honest, it was not something she had ever experienced—which made her feel like some spoiled, selfish brat and the sort of woman she loved to loathe.

But she wasn't incapable of making do, was she? And she certainly wasn't useless. Hadn't she already proved herself to be resourceful by escaping her captors? If she could do that, then she could fashion herself a perfectly serviceable wardrobe without inconveniencing her vexing host further or tipping off Bainbridge's lackeys as to her whereabouts. Besides, she could hardly roam around the house in men's breeches, even if they were surprisingly comfortable. Imbued with a self-righteous sense of purpose, she had soon ripped open the sleeves of one of the dated gowns and had spread the fabric pieces on the floor to cut.

Jack tossed his wet greatcoat in the hallway and took the stairs two at a time. His trip to the village this morning had bothered him. The reward money was no longer a generous one hundred pounds. It had been raised to a princely five hundred and the whole village was buzzing with the excitement. Folks in this particular corner of Nottinghamshire rarely, if ever, saw such a vast sum of money in one go and the anticipation of securing those riches had inspired several packs of locals to form teams scouring the forest and neighbouring areas. It was only a matter of time before some of them made their way up the lane towards his house—and if they found the gates bolted to them, they would become suspicious. Hardly anybody trusted a Warriner at the best of times. A wary, non-compliant Warriner would likely result in a siege when five hundred pounds was at stake.

Much as he railed against the prospect of keeping her here for the entire month, moving her now was completely out of the question. And much as he wanted to avoid the prospect of spending any more time in that minx's company, he needed to tell her of the heightened danger. While he was about it, he was also going to set some well-needed boundaries. Letty Dunston was running his two younger brothers ragged with her demands.

No, that was not strictly true. Neither was run ragged—it was more that they were eagerly hopping up and down to do her bidding, which was taking them away from their usual chores and forcing Jack to pick up the slack. Only yesterday, when Jacob was supposed to be chopping wood for the fires, he had learned his brother had, instead, taken himself off to the village because Princess Violet had asked for some biscuits.

Biscuits indeed! Biscuits were not going to keep the house warm or the sheep fed. And the woman apparently needed a near-constant supply of tea brought to her bedchamber, yet barely drank more than a single cup at a time. Last night, when Joe had helpfully wrapped the pot in some towels to keep the heat in it longer, she had complained that her tea was now too stewed to enjoy properly and sent his foolish brother to bring her a fresh pot. Had Jack not been avoiding the temptress, he would have stormed up there and given her a piece of his mind right away. Tea was an expensive commodity. So were biscuits, when the only place you could get them from was the local bakery because not one of the Warriners knew how to bake the damn things.

But he was avoiding the temptress—and temptress was the only word for her. Every time he laid eyes on her he was tempted. His mouth dried, his blood heated and his eager groin hardened. When he had carried her up the stairs he had been only too aware of the way her trim waist had curved out to a fine pair of rounded hips. He had also remembered, with far more clarity than he was comfortable with, the soft press of her unrestrained bosom resting against his body as he held her. Carrying Letty to his bedchamber held a great deal of appeal—although his rampant mind and body would have preferred the circumstances to be very, very different.

However, the woman was quite certain of her appeal towards the male sex, and was not averse to using it to her own advantage. The brazen way she had walked her fingers up his chest when he had carried her back upstairs had been one of the most calculated displays of feminine manipulation he had ever seen. The fact she had tried to use her wiles on him in an attempt to control him, and the fact that his body had betrayed him and reacted instantly to her touch, was beyond the pale. Worse still, now random images of her kept creeping into his dreams and disturbing his sleep. And his work had suffered too. Jack had thought about nothing but blasted Letty all morning and only a small fraction of those thoughts had been concerns for her safety. That hair. Those seductive green eyes and, God help him, those legs! Even avoiding her, she was driving him to distraction.

He eyed the open bedchamber door cautiously. There was no avoiding her now. They needed to talk about her precarious safety and he needed to stop having errant thoughts about her and remember she was another unwelcome responsibility he did not need. She was a spoiled heiress and an armful of trouble. Mentally fortified, Jack strode purposefully in and stopped dead in his tracks.

The damn woman was going to kill him!

First there had been delicate bared shoulders, then the loose hair and long legs and now her fantastic bottom was displayed to him in all of its round, feminine glory as she was, for some inexplicable reason, bent on her knees on the floor rather than recuperating in his bed. At this rate, his imagination would be able to piece her intriguing parts together bit by bit—and it only made him wonder more about the parts he had not seen. And if he wasn't mistaken, her tempting bottom was currently encased in *his* breeches. How exactly was he ever supposed to wear them again knowing they had touched that magnificent backside?

'Ahem.'

Her golden head whipped around at his cough and she smiled at him around a mouth full of pins. A slight blush touched the apples of her cheeks in a most becoming fashion and he wondered, rather uncharitably, if it was genuine or another beguiling feminine tool she could summon at her will.

'I need to talk to you.' Jack stood stiffly at the doorway, unsure of whether or not he should enter. It was his room, after all, but while she had laid siege to it, it felt wrong to just barge in. There was already the air of the feminine about it. She had made the bed differently. The pillows were plumped and stood on their sides; the bedcovers draped in an aesthetically pleasing fashion.

He watched her carefully pop the pins back into his mother's old pincushion and then sit up on her heels. 'Talk away. I am all ears.' She wasn't. She was all hair and legs and curvy bits, but that was not what he needed to discuss. The bed suddenly loomed larger in the room.

'I am afraid your Mr Layton has upped the reward for your safe return.' Jack saw a flash of panic cross her face and realised with dismay that she had immediately assumed he had surrendered her for the larger amount of money. As if he were a low, immoral creature who would do such a thing! 'I do not need Mr Layton's five hundred pounds, Letty.' The numerous, urgent things he could do with five hundred pounds did not bear thinking about. 'I prefer to earn my money through honest labours. Thank you for your lowly opinion of me, though.' He ignored the fact that his father would have pocketed the money without a moment's hesitation. As would all of his other dead ancestors. A Warriner with morals was a new, and decidedly outrageous, anomaly which the world was clearly still not ready for, despite almost a decade of him trying to change the past, yet still he was mortally insulted.

'I did not think you would hand me over to him, if that is what you are insinuating, I was just thinking how much more attractive a prospect finding me has suddenly become to all and sundry. I think it is *you* who has a lowly opinion of *me*, Jack, if you believe I would think such a thing about you after all you have done for me, although I am not sure quite what I have done to deserve it.'

He could see now that he had really upset her. Her green eyes became greener when she was troubled, her golden eyebrows were drawn together and she frowned. Now it was Jack's turn to feel bad for his uncharitable assumptions. Letty had no idea of their wild Warriner reputation and he could hardly admit to a rampant case of lust as the cause of his disgruntlement. 'I'm sorry, Letty. The implication was uncalled for. We Warriners are considered the scourge of the earth, thanks entirely to my forebears. Unfortunately mud sticks and we are doomed to be tarnished by it for ever. It makes me defensive—although in this case unfairly.'

She dazzled him with a smile then. A proper smile that made her fine eyes sparkle and transformed her face from a thing of beauty into some sort of transcendental manifestation of total perfection which rendered him momentarily stunned. 'Then I shall forgive you, Jack. Perhaps we should start this conversation again?'

Or perhaps he should just give in to temptation and run over there and kiss her. When he found his voice it came out a little strained. 'In view of the increased in-centive, I believe it would be prudent to expect visitors to come here searching for you. I have told my brothers to re-open the gates, Letty, but do not panic, during the night they will be secured again. Those ridiculous for-tifications will only serve to arouse suspicion during daylight hours if they are closed. If anybody arrives, I shall have to appear willing to co-operate. I will invite them in and listen to whatever they have to say—and, however long that takes, you will have to remain hid-den up here.' The lovely smile had slipped.

'I have to stay in this room.' Whilst she was grateful for his protection, Letty would go quite mad confined in this one place for hours on end with nobody to talk to.

'No, of course not. Only if and when we have visi-tors. The four of us will take it in turns to work near the top of the lane. That road is the only way in and out of Markham Manor. If we spot anyone, the man on watch can alert the rest of us to an impending visit and you can slip up here.' He stared at her seriously. 'Just in case anyone should force their way up these stairs, I need to show you something.'

He motioned for her to follow him and, intrigued, she did. He led her down the landing a little way to a painting on the wall. The portrait was undoubtedly a Warriner. Almost jet-black hair, handsome features and striking blue eyes stared back at her. 'This is Sir Hugo Warriner. A troublesome fellow by all accounts—but then most of my ancestors were. He had the enormous wall built around the house when he decided to help Mary Queen of Scots plot against Queen Elizabeth. Fortunately, his involvement in high treason was never discovered, or else I would not be here. Old Hugo was a cautious fellow—he also installed this.'

Letty watched fascinated as he opened a secret door in the oak panelling and then peered inside. 'A priest hole?'

'More of a Hugo hole really.' Jack grinned rakishly like his troublesome ancestor, showing a row of perfectly white straight teeth, and somehow being roguish suited him. For a moment she caught a glimpse of the young man who lurked beneath the serious exterior, the one he hid from her and perhaps the rest of the world, too.

Of course, it helped that when Jack Warriner smiled he became even more handsome, if such a thing was indeed possible, and the way his deep blue eyes sparkled make her feel all fizzy inside, like champagne. 'I doubt he would have been charitable enough to consider hiding a worthy fugitive. I believe this little room has hidden a great many Warriners in its time. My ancestors have always had a canny knack of being on the wrong side of everything. They fought with King Charles during the Civil War, supported the Jacobite uprising—there is even a suggestion that one of them was a member of the gang who tried to blow up Parliament with Guy Fawkes—but again, he was never caught. In fact, history is peppered with infamous, and decidedly slippery, Warriners. I am yet to find any evidence of a good one…but I live in hope.'

Letty laughed then, as she was sure she was meant to. 'Well, you and your brothers are good men, so I can only assume the family has changed its errant ways. Your father would be proud to know that he did such a good job with you all.'

His face clouded briefly. 'I doubt it...however, I digress. Should you feel threatened in any way, Letty, or hear someone coming whom you do not recognise, I want you to come here. It locks from the inside. Do not open it unless either myself or one of my brothers comes to tell you the coast is clear.' He promptly closed the panelling again and stood stiffly beside her as he stared at Sir Hugo's picture rather than at her. 'I will keep you safe, Letty.'

'Thank you, Jack.' After everything he had already done for her, plain old words were a poor expression of her gratitude. All at once, she felt emotional at his continued kindness. It was on the tip of her tongue to say *I am in your debt and will repay you as soon as I am able*, but stopped herself. The last time she had offered him a reward he had reacted badly and, as they had declared a truce, of sorts, bringing up the subject of money would probably bring stern Jack back. Letty rather liked the slightly shy Jack. Without thinking, she laid her hand on his forearm and watched his blue eyes fall on the place where it rested. 'I shall sleep easier now.'

Their oddly intimate moment came to an abrupt end when he simply nodded and stalked off in the direction of the stairs.

Chapter Eight

Twenty-five days remaining...

When Letty woke she decided she was all done being treated like an invalid. Today, she would breakfast with the family, whether they liked it or not, and explore the house. Aside from her one trip downstairs when her head was still spinning and her eyes practically crossed, she had no idea what the rest of Markham Manor was like. As nobody had yet come to attend to her because it was still dark outside, she washed in the ice-cold water on the nightstand, before pulling on the breeches and a fresh shirt and tying back her unruly hair in the scarlet ribbon. Barefoot, because she had no idea what had become of her evening slippers, she padded out of the bedchamber and headed down the creaking, wooden staircase.

The sun had not risen properly, yet the servants had lit no candles to illuminate the dim hallway. However, it was plain to see that the standard of cleanliness was not quite what it should be. It wasn't filthy, nor was it overly messy, but there was an air of neglect which

Letty supposed came with a house full of men who did not have the exacting household standards a woman did. The mistress of a house would ensure the corners and nooks would be properly dusted and the house properly maintained.

As she wandered slowly along the hallway, her critical gaze saw plenty of evidence of the servants' slackness. The wooden panelling looked to be in dire need of a good coat of fresh beeswax to bring out its lustre, the rugs needed beating, the floors polishing properly and the beautiful leadlight windows would positively gleam with a treatment of vinegar. So far this morning, she had not encountered one of the lazy staff, which was a shocking disgrace. At her house in Mayfair, she ran a tight ship. Her servants were busy from six o'clock, ensuring everything was properly done so the correct standards were maintained. The servants here were practically fleecing the Warriners!

If she could do nothing else in the short term to repay the brothers for their benevolence, she could take the servants in hand and make this house shine. It might make them like her. And when her fortune was hers to control she would buy new furniture to replace the old and purchase each of the brothers a special gift...

She paused and sighed. There it was again, her pathetic need to get people to see her worth. Her true worth rather than the value of her fortune, yet she was using her fortune to try to buy their favour. She really needed to stop doing that. If she truly wanted to be liked for herself, then perhaps it was time she stopped feeling the urge to buy their affections. For the next few weeks, Letty was basically a pauper who was doomed to accept the Warriners' charity. What better opportunity to find out if she possessed the characteristics of a woman who was liked purely for herself?

Joe and Jacob already liked her, or at least she thought they did. She had no idea what Jamie thought of her and was not entirely sure she particularly cared—but she wanted Jack to like her. She really wanted Jack to like her...at least then she would not feel quite so awkward about liking him as much as she did, even though she got precious little back except for commands or put-upon stares. Although, as he had been her own personal knight in shining armour, she supposed it was only natural that she would like him far more than his equally handsome brothers. Most of the time, she got the distinct impression she irritated him. If she could do something useful to repay him for saving her, Letty would definitely feel better about the whole thing. Especially as he vehemently refused to take her money.

Markham Manor was actually quite a charming old building which certainly did not deserve to look quite so dingy and neglected. The ceilings downstairs were high and vaulted, while the aged oak panelling gave the whole manor an air of gravitas Letty found pleasing. With a good clean, about a hundred candles, some fresh flowers and a few homely, feminine touches, it would be a delight.

Letty pushed open one of the many closed doors off the long passageway and was surprised to find the room beyond draped in dust covers. Behind the next two doors it was exactly the same, which was odd. Why would so much of the house be closed up when the four brothers were in residence? The fourth door led to a formal dining room dominated by a long banqueting table, but no sign of breakfast. The dull layer of dust on the mahogany suggested this room has not seen a family meal in some considerable time. Yet another mark against the staff. Meals should always be served in the proper setting. It was uncivilised to do otherwise. In her mind's eye she had already pictured a large formal dining room in her foundling home; cheerful, happy conversation over a plate of good food. If such things were good enough for foundlings, Jack and his brothers should insist on such things as their due. Shaking her head, she closed the door and continued onwards. Finally, she found herself at a pair of large, arched doors which opened on to the impressive great hall she had glimpsed on her one trip downstairs. A roaring fire burned in the biggest stone fireplace Letty had ever seen, casting the room in a warm, cosy glow. She could have easily stood in the grate with all four Warriner brothers and there still would be space for another person.

This room looked to be in full use despite the fact it was currently vacant and the welcome heat drew her in. Evidence of the four men who lived here was everywhere and made it easy to determine exactly who sat where. Next to the big, comfortable chair closest to her was a neat pile of books topped with a folded pair of wire-rimmed spectacles. A weighty tome lay face down on the chair: *On the Fabric of the Human Body* by Andreas Vesalius. That meant this was Joe's seat. Across from that she recognised several London newspapers strewn about the floor in front of a brocade sofa. As she already knew Jacob had a penchant for society gossip, he had to sit there.

Closer to the fire sat another chair twinned with an enormous footstool. On the side table were some medicinal bottles, clearly pain relief for the dour Jamie, although the easel and paints nearby surprised her. She wandered over and was taken aback at his current work in progress. For a withdrawn man with a military past, she did not expect to see a beautiful watercolour picture of a garden filled with fat, blooming roses. Obviously, Jamie hid a poetic heart to choose such a romantic tableau. Intriguing.

Finally, opposite Jamie's chair was the sturdiest but shabbiest-looking chair of the lot. Jack's seat. The ancient upholstery bore the indents where his big body rested to such an extent she could instantly picture him there, sat leaning slightly to one side if the over-worn left arm was any indicator, although Letty doubted he spent much time relaxing. Piled next to the chair were ledgers, books on animal husbandry, arable crops and a dull-looking pamphlet entitled *The Manner and Proper Drainage of Clay Soils*. The sight of so much work occupying what should have been his leisure time troubled her. The proverb 'all work and no play makes Jack a dull boy' immediately sprang to mind. It probably explained a great deal about his character and the burdens he carried. Despite his patriarchal bearing, Letty estimated Jack to be well shy of thirty. This manor, an estate and the responsibility of his brothers was a considerable load for such a young man to take on his shoulders. Yet he carried it effortlessly, just as he had carried her effortlessly up the stairs in his strong, comforting arms.

She allowed her fingers to trail lightly over the back of his chair and spotted another book tucked down between the arm and the seat. Curious, she plucked it from its hiding place. She instantly recognised it. *The Soldier's Daughter* was one of her favourite plays, although it had not been on the London stage for a few years now, but she had fond memories of seeing it as it was the first production she had been taken to see by her parents upon her come-out. It had been responsible for her life-long passion for the theatre. Jack had good taste in plays, as well as a sense of humour about his ancestors. Two things she liked about him. Three, if you included his arms.

Letty's stomach rumble reminded her she had come down here in search of breakfast first, so she carefully slipped the slim book back into its hiding place, feeling a new affinity with Jack Warriner. They had something in common, albeit a very small thing in the grand scheme of things. Why such a thing mattered, she could not say, aside from the possibility that the pair of them could converse on topics which did not always have to be about her current predicament. It would be nice to get to know him better—the real man she had glimpsed a few days ago rather than the overbearing master of the house—the man who grinned rakishly and yet took his responsibilities seriously. Letty was rather drawn to that version of Jack.

Back in the hallway she heard the distinctive sound of hearty male laughter and followed it to the kitchen. All four of them were there, sitting around a big oak table, sharing the noisy, boisterous sort of family camaraderie Letty had never known, even when her quiet parents had been alive. While the brothers were blissfully unaware of her presence, she simply stood and listened, enjoying the way they parried insults and quips to and fro. It did not take long to get the gist of the conversation—Jacob had made yet another conquest. A farmer's daughter. The brothers were joking about the possibility of her father coming after him with his pitchfork if word ever got out. The youngest Warriner apparently took all of the ribbing in his stride and looked inordinately proud of his achievements with the farmer's wayward daughter.

It was Jack who spied her first and instantly brought his brothers to heel. 'There is a lady present!'

Four sets of deep blue eyes swivelled to her spot by the doorway and both Jack and Joe stood politely.

'I am not sure you should be out of bed, Letty,' said Joe with his usual air of concern, 'Do you feel dizzy or light-headed?'

'I am feeling perfectly well, Dr Joe, although I am positively *dying* of boredom stuck in that room.' Letty boldly walked towards the table in case anyone wanted to argue and pulled out the only spare chair. Instantly, Jack sprang to attention and solicitously pushed it back in when she sat. He had gentlemanly manners, too. Another thing to like. 'I thought I might have breakfast with you all. That is if you do not mind my company?' She smiled at the men hopefully. One of her real smiles rather than one of Violet's. A test for herself.

'It will be delightful to see a pretty face at the table rather than this ugly lot.' Jacob grinned back at her. 'Would you like some tea, Letty?' She nodded happily to be included and was surprised when it was Jacob who poured, in the absence of a servant, while Joe wandered to the hearth and retrieved a covered plate and placed it in front of her. He whipped off the silver cloche and her face fell at the sight of yet more bacon and shrivelled-looking fried eggs.

'Is everything all right?' He stared back at her, concerned.

'Would you ask your cook if I might have something different this morning? Only I have had bacon every day so far and I am not overly fond of it. Some sausages, perhaps, or some scrambled eggs?'

There was a moment of strained silence at her request, then Jamie scowled and pierced Jack with his stare. 'I am not cooking her anything different.'

Jacob grinned at his brother. 'That's because you can't cook anything different, Jamie. I, on the other hand, have a particular way with eggs.' He went to stand, but Jack stayed him with his hand.

'We eat what we are served in this house, Letty, and we are grateful for it.'

The four men focused intently on their plates as if the discussion was now over. Letty considered letting sleeping dogs lie, then decided she could not. These four men obviously worked tremendously hard, so it was a travesty that their lazy staff should hold so much power. The youngest Warriners clearly found it easier to step into the breach rather than bring the help to heel. As she had suspected, this was an area in which she could make a contribution.

'Please do not be embarrassed. I would hardly expect four men to know the best way to deal with unruly servants. Fortunately, it is an area in which I have a great deal of expertise.' Letty had been running her Mayfair house since the age of seventeen as her uncle was not used to dealing with such a large household, or, indeed, even interested in learning. If anybody could get the best out of the Markham Manor servants, it was her. 'Why don't I oversee the indoor staff while I am here? It would be no trouble. If nothing else, I can improve the quality of our meals.'

For effect she picked up the abandoned silver cloche and popped it back over her plate. 'It is a sorry state of affairs when the servants are too lax to serve breakfast. We are *grateful* for what we get indeed! Where is the choice? Why, there is not even any jam on the table! How can one be expected to have a civilised breakfast without preserves? I fear that your good natures are being taken gross advantage of by all of your servants. I intend to speak to your cook personally and explain the proper way for a good kitchen to be run.' For emphasis, Letty stood and picked up the offending plate. 'Where might I find your belligerent chef?' Because things were going to improve at Markham Manor starting right now. It would be her gift to this generous family. One which would cost her nothing but her own efforts. 'And whilst I am about it, I should like to speak to your housekeeper as well. It is criminal the way the housework has been neglected. The maids need to be told to dust all of the nooks and crannies and their work needs to be thoroughly checked to see it is up to standard.'

Letty would start with the kitchen and then move on to the rest of the staff. By tonight, this house would run like clockwork. She smiled reassuringly at the stunned-looking gentlemen in front of her, except their reactions to her sudden decisiveness made her nervous. Joe and Jacob exchanged a telling look before staring mournfully at their empty plates, while Jack's jaw hardened. Jamie Warriner rose slowly to his feet and folded his arms angrily across his chest.

'I am the belligerent cook. And the current lazy housekeeper.'

Letty had not been expecting that. 'Surely not?' Her eyes scanned the other faces around the table for confirmation. Only Jack met her gaze, although she could not accurately discern what stormy emotion was currently swirling in those cobalt eyes. Annoyance? Shame? Pride? Perhaps all three? She stared at him beseechingly. 'Are you having difficulties hiring servants?'

That was clearly another wrong thing to say, judging by the snigger which emitted from the vicinity of Jacob and cut through the brittle silence like a knife. Letty turned to him in question and even he began to look guilty. The wretch had encouraged her to talk to Jack about the staff when she had enquired about a personal maid and now she had a sneaking suspicion he had led her on a merry dance for his own amusement. He had set her up for a fall and she had indeed fallen for it like a silly, spoiled fool. Whilst she enjoyed a good joke as much as the next person and had always had an enormous appetite for mischief, Letty had the distinct feeling she had just horrifically insulted Jack Warriner. Inexcusably insulted him, if what she was coming to suspect was the case, and that was too awful a prospect to have to contemplate after all he had already done for her.

Jacob's guilty smile slipped off his face under her scrutiny and he coloured up in embarrassment. 'It's not so much we have difficulty hiring servants, Letty, it's more we have difficulty paying for them....oomph!' He sagged when Joe's elbow collided sharply with his ribs and knocked the air out of him.

Realisation began to dawn. Her outburst had not only been crass; it had been cruel. Unforgivably cruel. 'There are no servants at Markham Manor, are there?'

Jack stood, clearly furious, and his voice was more clipped and frigid than she had ever heard it.

'I am sure back in London you have an army of obedient servants to cater for your every whim, *Princess* Violet. Here, we have to work for our supper. Seeing as you are now up and about, and we are apparently stuck with you, it's time you stopped leeching off our hospitality and earned your keep. Fortunately, you have helpfully pointed out how criminally the housework has been neglected. It is difficult to find the time or energy to dust every *nook* and *cranny* when you have to work in the fields from sun up to sun down. Therefore, those *neglected* nooks and crannies are now yours, Miss Dunston. I look forward to checking your work later. I would hate for the standards to not be properly maintained.'

The walls of the kitchen shook with the force he put into slamming the door on his way out.

Chapter Nine

Twenty-four days and fourteen hours...

Complete humiliation had never brought out the best in him, but for some reason, complete humiliation in front of Violet Dunston was worse than any Jack had ever experienced before. And he had a wealth of embarrassing experience to draw upon. When she had declared her intention to take his cook and housekeeper to task for their ineptitude, he had wanted to curl up into a ball and die from the shame. It was one thing to know your home was turning into a crumbling hovel before your very eyes, but it was a very different kettle of fish to have it pointed out by the most beautiful woman you had ever seen. A very different, totally unappetising kettle of fish indeed when he had spent the night lusting after her. Again. Clearly he was a glutton for punishment.

Doubtless her good opinion of him was now in question, especially at his surly reaction, and that bothered him a great deal too. For once, he wanted to be judged on his deeds rather than his family's past, and as Letty's views had not been tainted by the locals he had been hopeful she would regard them as decent, civilised people. However, his pride would never allow Jack to show her how much her thoughtless words had hurt him, so he had barked at her in retaliation instead, because attack had always been his default form of defence.

Even now, after a full day of hard work in the constant pouring rain, he was still smarting. He knew she had meant well and suspected Jacob had a hand in her belief that they had staff, but neither of those things were any consolation. The lofty lord of the manor *should* be able to afford servants. That was the way of things. He could hardly blame her for her blatant disbelief at his failure to provide something so fundamental when he owned a house with fifteen bedchambers, even if only four of the damn things were safe to sleep in. How was Letty to know the last of their servants had left a year before his father had drunk himself to death? Understandably, they were unforgiving of the Earl of Markham's habit of prioritising his brandy ration over their wages. The fact the man had put his brandy above everything else, the welfare and futures of his four motherless sons included, was even more unfortunate. If he had not felt an overwhelming responsibility towards his younger siblings, Jack would have cheerfully joined the fleeing servants and never looked back. Except, after their mother had chosen death rather than seeing them all grow up, Jack could not be cruel enough to desert them, too.

When the selfish old bastard had finally turned up his toes when Jack was just twenty, there had been nothing left for the boys except weed-choked fields, huge debts lodged with every merchant from here to Nottingham and the reputation of being the lowest of the low and little better than vermin. It was widely held that the family would cheat you in business, despoil your women and sell their own grandmother on a whim for their own benefit. Those that remembered his father in London, where he had been all of those things and had then scandalously compromised an heiress into marriage to round it off, probably thought much the same still, too. Nobody trusted a Warriner.

They had even less respect for the Earl of Markham, a title his father had bandied about to justify his selfish vileness to such an extent it was now infamous, so Jack had never bothered using the tarnished title he had inherited with the crushing debt and crumbling house, in the hope the unpalatable legacy would blur with the sands of time. Seven arduous years on, they were still tarred with the same old brush and Jack sincerely doubted anyone would work for him even assuming he could, somehow, miraculously pay their wages. Those old wounds ran too deep, no matter how hard he tried to improve the family's reputation.

Of course, it did not help that all four of them were the spitting image of their feckless father. Everyone assumed the similarities went much further than skin deep and that it was only a matter of time before history repeated itself. The villagers were so wary of the Warriners that no shopkeeper would even allow them to open an account. Everything had to be paid for in cash there and then. No leeway, no benefit of the doubt, no better than any common vagabond who happened to be travelling through Nottinghamshire. Servants? That would be a funny joke if it wasn't entirely on him.

With a grunt he hauled down a fresh bale of hay and

heaved it on to his shoulders to carry to the few cows in the other barn. Not that it wouldn't be nice to have the extra hands. Especially as the health of the farm slowly recovered and required more and more of his time. Two years ago, his working day was ten hours long. Now it was nearer fourteen and that was pretty much non-stop, even in winter and with his brothers pulling as much weight as he did on a daily basis.

The cows, horses and chickens needed feeding twice a day in this weather. The sheep on the grazing land fed themselves, but thanks to the heavy clay soil, needed constant supervision. The stupid animals were forever getting stuck in the mud, or stranded in the flooded areas nearest the river, and the least said about the constant risk of foxes the better. But the lamb he raised was good quality and he received a reasonable return for it now that he was building up a good relationship with a butcher in Lincoln. He was paid a little lower than market price for it, in view of the risk involved in doing business with a Warriner, but it was a start. It was a shame nobody would do any business with him closer to home. The long treks to the cathedral town and back wiped out a whole day he could ill afford to lose—but beggars could not be choosers. At least somebody bought his produce. Even the wool made some money, although not nearly as much as he needed or as much as it should.

Despite all of the work and the paltry financial rewards, Jack was secretly proud of his achievements. In seven years he had turned the majority of this estate from barren wasteland into farmland and with no outside help at all. He had single-handedly rebuilt two of the dilapidated tenant cottages, cleared the tangled brambles from the plots around them and rented them out. Granted, for a pittance and the few pounds' return a year was not much of an income, but it was considerably more income than this land had raised in his lifetime, not to mention the joy that came from gradually clawing his way out of his father's debt. If only the price of corn would improve, then he might be able to turn an actual profit. In another few years, if the roof of the house held up and he could find the time to fix up the remaining tenant cottages, and after he had paid for Joe to finally go to medical school and then perhaps send Jacob to university, he might be able to employ one or two people to help ease his burdens. It all seemed very far away and he dared not hope.

And now he had a blasted tea heiress criticising him. Perhaps he should have taken her up on her offer to pay him to hide her, except being paid to do a good turn for another did not sit well with him. It was something his father would have done unthinkingly—which, categorically, also made it the wrong thing for Jack to do as a matter of principal. Whilst there was no doubt he could use the woman's money, his pride would never allow him to accept her charity—because that was what it would be. Charity. If he had a decent home, rather than a ramshackle manor, and if he'd had proper servants as earls were expected to have, she never would have offered such a preposterous thing after her horrific ordeal. But the bewitching Letty Dunston saw things exactly how they were and had offered him money because she meant well. In the same, humiliating way she had meant well when she had commented on the disappointing food and the dire state of his dusty nooks and crannies.

Jack had never asked for hand-outs and he never would. He toiled and suffered and paid his own debts and stood proudly in front of those who judged him. If it killed him, which he suspected it all probably would in the end, he would turn this family's fortunes around—and perhaps their reputations, too—and the tart opinions of well-meaning heiresses would not change that. He doubted she'd done a day's work in all of her charmed life, so what right did she have to judge him anyway?

And why should he care one way or another what the girl thought of him? He hardly knew her despite his odd feelings for her and, at best, their acquaintance was only temporary. As soon as it was safe for her leave, she would merrily skip back to her perfect life and become the darling of society again. He sincerely doubted she would ever give him a passing thought he was so far beneath her.

Perhaps it had escaped her notice, but *he* was the one doing *her* a huge favour. If his humble home was not good enough for the princess to live in, then she could go elsewhere as he had originally wanted, to people who were more her sort or who would happily take her money to keep her safe. But as soon as he thought it he discarded it. He knew that he didn't trust anyone else except himself and his brothers to keep her safe, so she *would* remain in his house until the blasted fourth of January, when he could finally stop thinking about the minx every minute of the blasted day and feeling so ashamed of who he was in her presence.

Letty was exhausted. Up until this moment, it had been a word she had blithely thrown about when she had been shopping for hours in Bond Street or had danced every dance at a ball. Now she fully understood what being truly exhausted meant, she promised herself she would never say it in vain again. She also had new respect for her maids, although there were at least ten of them in her Mayfair house working downstairs alone and she was only one. Nevertheless, Letty experienced an enormous sense of accomplishment when she cast her eyes critically around the great hall. The vaulted room looked positively homely thanks to her labours and she was looking forward to showing it off.

Unfortunately, there was nobody to show it off to. She had spent almost the entire day completely on her own after insulting the master of the house so spectacularly at his breakfast table. Afterwards, Joe had dismissed Jack's order that she pull her weight as merely his temper talking and had insisted she continue to rest in her bedchamber. Jacob had apologised profusely for his mischief and told her to do the same.

'Jack has a temper,' he'd said with a shrug. 'But it disappears quickly.'

Then the two youngest Warriners had donned heavy coats and plunged out the back door into the elements to begin their own work, leaving her alone with Jamie. The most taciturn Warriner did not offer her platitudes or reassurances. Instead, he wandered to a cupboard, pulled out buckets, mops and brooms, then silently put on his own coat and disappeared after the others. But she had seen the fierce loyalty towards his brother and the latent hostility in his eyes.

She supposed they all thought she was not up to the task and that she would admit defeat before she had even started because she was a silly, spoiled heiress who was completely out of touch with the harsh realities of life. And perhaps she had been a few weeks ago. Not one of the brothers thought her capable of anything resembling work and, despite her own significant reservations, her pride refused to allow her to live up to their low expectations and surrender. There was more to her than everybody realised. She had determination and drive. She was capable of more than lighting up a ballroom or shopping for ribbons. She always excelled in everything she put her mind to. Letty had escaped kidnap and survived a night in a frozen forest. If she could manage that, she could certainly clean this house.

And she had cleaned. Slowly at first, but once she got the hang of it there had been no stopping her. Years of supervising her own servants had taught her that polishing and dusting required vigour and it took her a while to learn the proper application of polish or how to avoid unsightly smears. Using all of her pent-up rage at her traitorous uncle and Bainbridge she had scrubbed and swept and buffed until her arms screamed and her back ached. Now, not a speck of dust dared linger in any of the corners. The old Persian rug had been beaten to within an inch of its life, largely because she had pictured the Earl of Bainbridge's wrinkled face in the centre of it and had found thwacking it therapeutic. The windows glistened and the chandelier shimmered in the soft candlelight. It had made her smile to see the transformation and went a little way toward easing the guilt she felt at her horrendous faux pas.

Once the room was clean, Letty had then set about rearranging it to make it look pleasing. After hunting under the dust covers in the adjacent rooms, she had found more furniture which suited the main room. Now, the worn chairs favoured by the brothers were covered in soft throws and cushions she had salvaged and she had added another chair for herself, as well as a low footstool and some well-positioned extra candlesticks. If she said so herself, it was a vast improvement on what it had been before. The only thing missing was a cheerful bunch of flowers—and she sincerely doubted she could summon one of those at will. A house which could not afford servants would hardly have its own hot-house. But perhaps some branches of holly and some cheerful winter berries would not go amiss?

A quick dash upstairs to rummage in the trunk of old clothes and she procured a pair of lady's walking boots. They were a bit big—Mrs Warriner was clearly built in a sturdier fashion than Letty—but she padded them out with an extra pair of thick woollen stockings, then headed to the back door through the kitchen, clasping a pair of lethal-looking shears she had found.

Leaves and flowers were homely and Markham Manor could do with a lift. Letty pulled on a heavy greatcoat which was hanging on a peg by the door and clomped out. The crisp fresh air was a welcome change from being stuck inside. Even the rain was refreshing. For several seconds she simply stood and enjoyed it all before she went hunting for foliage to complete her masterpiece.

Finding holly in the early evening darkness proved to be more of a challenge than she had first anticipated, meaning she had to trudge further from the house than she'd intended. Eventually, she found some and began snipping away with the shears until movement in the distance caught her eye.

Initially, Letty was scared and darted behind the

bush in case it was somebody sinister looking for her, but the more she watched the lone figure, the more convinced she was that it was Jack. There was something about the way he held himself, the long, sure strides, the broad shoulders, the strange attraction which pulled her to only him rather than any of his three brothers.

Letty owed him an apology and the chance to do it in private, rather than in front of an audience of his brothers, was too appealing an opportunity to miss.

Jack kicked open the barn door and set about breaking up the bale of hay and distributing it amongst the horses. He never heard her behind him until it was too late.

'Hello, Jack.'

At the soft sound of her voice he instantly stiffened, but did not turn around. Looking at Letty made him want her and he was still embarrassed at her obvious reaction to his failings. 'You shouldn't be outside.'

'It's getting dark and nobody can see me. I wanted to apologise for what I said earlier.'

'There is no need.' He didn't need her well-meaning pity either. He would rather pretend it hadn't happened. 'It was a misunderstanding.' Jack busied himself by refilling the water troughs from the big barrel in the corner and hoped she would go away and stop dredging the sorry episode up. Unfortunately, he heard her move to stand next to him.

'It *was* a misunderstanding—but that does not excuse my thoughtlessness. Without meaning to, I insulted you. I feel dreadful, if it's any consolation.' It wasn't. 'You must think me very spoiled.' He did. 'After everything you have done for me, I am heartily ashamed of myself.'

Jack really did not want to look at her, but his eyes strayed towards her anyway. She certainly looked like the dictionary definition of remorse. Her face was downcast, her delicate shoulders slumped and her lovely eyes were troubled. Even as he fought it, she plucked at his heartstrings. 'It really doesn't matter, Letty. I am over it.' And now he was lying to make her feel better.

'Still, I should like to make it up to you.'

His teeth ground together unconsciously in protest. 'For the last time, I do not want your money, Letty...'

'I know that. I also would not insult you by offering it again. But I can help in other ways. I have already started on the nooks and crannies.' The corners of her plump mouth curved up into a nervous smile. 'Although I have only done one room so far.'

Jack experienced a rush of guilt. 'I never really intended for you to do the cleaning.' She shouldn't have to debase herself like that, especially after everything she had gone through. It was not as if she was responsible for the mess. He was.

'I quite enjoyed it, actually. I had a sense of purpose which has been missing this last week. You have no idea how mind-numbingly boring staying in bed is.'

Her open smile made him feel a little better. She was trying to smooth things over, therefore, he should meet her halfway. 'I should like to try it one day. A whole day of doing absolutely nothing appeals to me.' Why was he ruining a perfectly nice moment by complaining about his lot?

'Spoken like a man who would rather do everything himself instead of delegating. I get the impression you do far more than your fair share, Jack.' She gazed around the barn and noticed the hay bale he had brought. 'Why don't I help you now? You will be finished more quickly if both of us do it.'

Her assessment of his character followed by her offer to assist surprised him. Instantly he refused it. 'There is no need. I can manage.' Letty simply grinned and ignored him. She had discarded her lamp and branches and was pulling huge clumps of hay from the bale before he had finished his sentence, positively throwing herself into the task. Clearly she did not realise how dirty one could get in the company of horses. 'Try to avoid the end without a head on. Horses can be...unpredictable at times.'

Her laughter was not the tinkling sort he imagined normally issued from gently bred ladies. It was a throaty giggle accompanied by the occasional snort. It sounded positively naughty. God help him.

'What a gentlemanly way of putting it, Jack. But I am used to the *unpredictability* of animals. My horse has no manners at all. He is ruthlessly *unpredictable* at every available opportunity.' Methodically she distributed the hay as if she fed animals all of the time.

'You ride?'

'Like a hellion, I am told. I particularly like fast and fearsome horses like this fine chap.' She reached up to stroke the muzzle of Jamie's temperamental black stallion.

'Satan doesn't like to be stroked,' Jack said quickly.

Letty smiled and ignored the warning, and for once the troublesome horse appeared to welcome the attention, pushing his big head against her open palm like the biggest of flirts. 'You poor thing,' she crooned, 'What did you do to deserve such a horrible name? You're a sweetie, Satan, aren't you?'

In Jack's experience, the horse most definitely was nothing of the sort. 'Usually, the only human he allows near him is Jamie and even then he barely tolerates him. Jamie brought him home from the Peninsula with him. When I say brought him home, it would probably be more accurate to say that he stole him. The horse gave him so much trouble, he called it Satan, but despite all that Jamie still kept him.'

'I can't say I blame him. You are such a handsome boy, Satan, aren't you?' To Jack's amazement she then kissed the tip of the animal's nose before stepping away. It was a sorry state of affairs when a man found himself jealous of a horse. 'I bet he is very fast.'

'He is. Dangerously so. Jacob tried to ride him when Jamie first came home and Satan threw him in a ditch. We didn't see the horse for hours afterwards, not that Jamie was concerned. He simply shrugged and said Satan would come back when he was good and ready. And he did as well. Wandered back into the barn eventually as if nothing was amiss.'

'Do you think Jamie would let me ride him?'

'I don't think it's down to Jamie. Satan can be particular. He's a one-rider-only sort of chap. I doubt he would make exceptions, even for a hellion.'

'My mother used to tell me off for riding with reckless abandon and then she would tell my father off worse for encouraging me.' Her lovely face clouded at the memory.

'You were close to your parents then?' Now there was something he had no concept of. He had never understood his, let alone been close to them. Neither his mother nor his father had wanted much to do with their offspring.

'Indeed I was. It was always just the three of us. Until it wasn't. I miss them dreadfully.'

She had brought them up, so Jack decided she probably didn't mind talking about them. 'You said they died in an accident—how old were you when it happened?' He returned the water bucket to its proper place at the same moment she brushed the last of the hay from her hands.

'Seventeen,' she said without hesitation, 'Far too early to be without any parents—especially a mother. But I suppose you would understand how devastating that is. Jacob told me you were all still children when your mother passed away.'

'He was seven, I was fourteen.' Except he hadn't really had the opportunity to be devastated. His three younger brothers had needed a buffer between them and their father's belt strap, just as his mother had needed one from his father's drunken fists. Not that she had ever been grateful for his interference or tended to his bruises afterwards.

'You were even younger than I, then. How did she die?'

Years of being the wife of a Warriner, estranged from her family and all good society, the harsh realities of her isolation and the constant poverty had driven her to do the unthinkable. 'Suicide. She drowned herself in the river.' It had been swollen and raging after a week of storms, just as it was now, so she had jumped in on purpose without a backward glance because she mourned the life she had lost and could never regain.

Jack still hadn't fully forgiven her for leaving them, when they had loved her even though she could barely look upon them without seeing the face of her hated husband. The man who had compromised her into marriage to get her dowry and then had them chased out of London because of his mounting debts. Lord only knew what had happened to the dowry, but Jack doubted it went on anything sensible. Letty's face was filled with pity. 'And before you ask, my father followed her into the ground seven years later. He was fond of the bottle.' Why was he telling her that? Although it was hardly a secret. Being drunk was one of the few things his father had done well, to the detriment of everything else, and for some inextricable reason Jack had wanted to tell her because she appeared to care.

Letty stared at him for a long time, her golden head tilted to one side as she considered what he had unintentionally confessed. Where he thought he might see horror, or judgement, he saw only sympathy. 'Oh, Jack,' she said at last, with a sigh, 'now I understand why your brothers all look up to you so. You have had to be both a mother and a father to them all these years. And run this estate. What a lot to take on.' She smoothed her hand down his arm almost affectionately. He felt the touch everywhere. 'You should be proud. You have done an excellent job of it. Your three brothers are all good men.'

If he had been expecting a compliment, or an affectionate touch, he might have had a glib answer ready for her. Instead, he experienced a rush of gratitude so acute it caused a lump in his throat. Nobody had sympathy for a Warriner, not usually, which made Letty's reaction all the more special. He dipped his head to avoid her gaze and tried to change the subject.

'Why have you been picking holly? Surely it is a bit early to be making garlands for Christmas?'

She shook her head, the motion causing one damp

corkscrew curl to bounce enticingly over one eye as she grinned. 'I thought I would make a pretty arrangement for the drawing room. A homely touch to cheer you all—perhaps it might even raise a smile from Jamie.'

The curl bounced again, tempting him. Unconsciously, Jack reached out and tucked it behind her ear, his fingers grazing the silky, soft skin of her cheek in the process and she smiled up at him. More words tumbled out unchecked.

'Sometimes it is difficult to know exactly what Jamie is thinking. Since his return home, his withdrawal worries me. I wish I knew what to do to fix it.' And there he went again, telling her things which he did not share with his family. Confiding in her. Letty Dunston was doing strange things to his heart.

'Perhaps you cannot simply fix it. I suspect Jamie needs time to come to terms with his experience of war himself before he can explain it to you. Give him time to heal mentally as well as physically. All grief heals eventually.'

'Maybe. It is hard to simply stand by and watch.'

'Why? Because you are used to being the one in control of everything?'

'I suppose.'

His fingers were still playing with the soft curls by her ear, lingering too long on her skin until he realised he was beaming back at her like a besotted idiot, something he was quite sure she was used to, but not something he ever did. Jack dropped his hand as though he'd been burnt and quickly turned back to finish his work. He really had no right to touch her like that, no matter how easy he found it to confess things to her, and quickly quashed the overwhelming urge to touch her again. The girl was trouble he did not need. Another unwelcome, unwanted responsibility. One who was only biding her time here until she could return to her splendid life and her fancy Duke, and one who certainly would not be impressed by his overwhelming attraction to her.

She stood waiting silently as he blew out the lamps in the barn, a task he instantly regretted the moment he turned around. The soft glow from the lantern in her hand cast her in an ethereal light which made her look just like an angel. Once again, she took his breath away and he could think of nothing to say to relieve the wave of desire which suddenly swamped him. Her beauty and his spellbound reaction to it almost made him physically flinch.

'Dinner will be ready soon,' he said abruptly. Standing alone with her, here in the dark, was foolhardy. If he was not careful, she would know he was attracted to her and he would spill out all of his troubles, and that would never do. Then she really would pity him, poor, unworthy pauper that he was, and he would look completely pathetic. It was far better she thought he saw her as a great inconvenience rather than the greatest of temptations. 'We should go.'

With brisker efficiency than he felt, Jack led the way out of the barn and secured the heavy door. They walked a few yards in painfully awkward silence while he racked his brains for something—anything—sensible to say which did not make him appear to be the lustful, uncivilised nobody he had a frequent tendency to feel around her.

'It's been raining for days.' Good grief! Was that really the best that he could do? Only the dullest of fellows talked about the weather. 'I am worried the river will flood.' And now he was burdening her with more of his problems, as if she would care about something so...mundane and beneath her.

'I suppose a flood would damage your crops, wouldn't it?' She was trying to make the best of his feeble attempts at scintillating conversation and he cringed inwardly at his lack of charm. Even Jacob had better luck with females than he did. This was a woman who was the darling of society. An incomparable. And he was a crass oaf who couldn't even afford one servant and became overwhelmed after receiving one, tiny compliment. But the die was cast, he had started the boring conversation, and he had to answer her polite question even if neither of them really cared about the answer.

'It is the wrong time of year for crops. However, if the river does burst its banks it can be dangerous for my animals.'

As if to prove a point, one of those animals cried out in panic. Letty's eyes widened. 'What was that?'

'A sheep.' And if Jack wasn't mistaken, it was a sheep in distress. Just what he needed in the pouring rain, despite the fact it got him out of being the dullest conversationalist Letty had ever had the misfortune to talk to and gave him an excuse to escape from her tempting presence. 'I will meet you back at the house, I need to go and see what is wrong.'

'Something, I suspect, you might find much easier with the lantern, don't you think?' She grinned and wiggled the lamp for emphasis and sealed his fate. 'I shall come with you.'

Chapter Ten

⟨~⟩

Twenty-four days and thirteen hours to go, give or take a few minutes...

Letty had never heard the sound of a panicked sheep before, but it was quite unsettling and almost child-like. The nearer they got to the pitiful sound, the more her too-big boots stuck in the sodden ground beneath her feet. More worrying, in view of Jack's sad tale about his mother's untimely death, was the unmistakable noise of the angry river as they trudged ever closer to it.

Jack had relieved her of her lantern and held it aloft following the noise deftly. He let out a frustrated groan when he spotted it. 'There it is.'

In the darkness, Letty could just about make out the shape of a sheep. Its head and flank were thrashing from side to side as it stood rooted to the spot. Jack simply stared at it in disgust. 'Their hooves become embedded in the mud. I live in hope the silly animals will eventually learn from their mistakes and avoid the river bank. But they are sheep and sheep are reliably stupid at all times.'

He put the lamp down on the ground and shrugged out of his heavy coat, passing it to Letty to hold, and then began to unbutton his waistcoat quickly. She watched transfixed as the second layer of clothing came off, unsure as to why he was stripping off, but when he gripped the hem of his shirt and began to pull that over his head too she began to panic.

'W-what are you doing?'

'Clearly you have never wrestled with a wet sheep, Letty, else you wouldn't ask.' The shirt joined the pile of clothes in her arms and he stood in front of her naked from the waist up and clearly irritated. 'They can be ridiculously absorbent.'

The glow from the lantern made his skin appear almost bronze and cast interesting shadows around the large muscles on his arms and shoulders. A dusting of dark hair fanned over his chest and narrowed before disappearing under the waistband of his breeches. Jack appeared blissfully ignorant of how vastly improper their current situation was and Letty was loath to appraise him of the fact in case he reassessed the situation and put his clothes back on. Did that make her a hussy?

Probably. But she didn't care right now.

'I will be soaked to the skin instantly the moment I touch it. At least this way, I will have something reasonably dry to put on afterwards.' He stood on one leg to tug off a boot. It was swiftly followed by the other one. She held her breath and scandalously hoped he would shimmy out of his tight breeches as well. Without the covering of his coat, the soft fabric clearly encased an impressive pair of thighs and a pleasingly firm, rounded bottom she had not noticed before. Had she ever noticed a gentleman's bottom before? If she had, it was no wonder she did not remember it. For several seconds she scanned her memories for the Duke of Wentworth's bottom and came up blank. Whatever his posterior resembled, all previous bottoms of her acquaintance paled into insignificance in comparison to her present company. To Letty's complete disappointment, the breeches remained resolutely on.

'This shouldn't take long.' With that, he strode purposely towards the sheep.

Further conversation proved impossible because Letty's body was behaving in the most peculiar way. For a start, she could not tear her eyes away from his powerful back as he grappled with the animal. How could she when those muscles moved intriguingly under his smooth skin? It took a tremendous amount of fortitude to force them elsewhere and even then they kept drifting back guiltily until she realised he could not see her eager staring with his back to her. After that, she allowed herself to ogle him shamelessly. His back, his broad shoulders, the muscles in his arms and his delightfully firm bottom were all studied far more than was really necessary because, it went without saying, they would be seared on her memory for ever. But as she did so, to her consternation her knees were definitely becoming increasingly wobbly and her heart was beating so loudly it drowned out the bleating of the panicked sheep. And she was hot. Very, very hot. All over.

Whilst such an unexpected display of his own nudity did not apparently bother Jack, Letty was definitely overwhelmed with the impact of his raw manliness. Her arms had involuntarily tightened about the warm pile of his clothing she held. Better that than to give in to the desire to march over there and touch him herself. But his garments were an unsatisfactory substitute.

How would he feel? She definitely should not allow her errant thoughts to wander there! Unfortunately, those thoughts were not done wandering and refused to listen to her.

Would his skin be soft like hers? She already knew his body would feel deliciously firm beneath her palms. Her fingers itched to be able to explore all of those indents and bulges properly. Just to be certain.

Letty had never experienced desire like this before. She had flirted with battalions of men, usually just for fun or because that was what everyone expected Violet to do, yet once or twice she had been curious about what it would be like to kiss a man. She had recently given a great deal of serious thought to kissing the Duke of Wentworth—just in case she did end up marrying the man. However, whilst she definitely wanted to kiss Jack, she also wanted to touch, lick and nibble him, too.

All over.

A new and blush-worthy development she had not considered before—even with her dashing Duke. She sincerely doubted she would ever be able to talk to Jack again without thinking about him *without* his clothes on. It was a good job it was dark. From the intense heat radiating from her skin, Letty knew she was flushed. Flushed rather than blushing all over, which was scandalous in itself. She should be horrified to witness such an improper display of naked male. Not be revelling in it. Fantasising about it. Wishing it would never end.

It did not take Jack long to dislodge the sheep's hooves from the mud and, rather ungratefully, the animal struggled in his arms as he carried it to the safety of firmer ground. 'You have done that before.' Letty's voice was undeniably hoarse as she attempted to sound nonchalant. For good measure she sucked in a few calming breaths in an attempt to bring her fluttering pulse under control. It didn't work.

'Too many times.'

He grabbed the shirt from her arms and to her total fascination, began to use it as a towel. First he rubbed it briskly over his head, unaware that in doing so the muscles in his arms bunched in a most appealing way and he gave her a glimpse of the two dark patches of hair beneath them which held her transfixed. Then he used the balled linen to roughly dry his exposed skin. It was on the tip of Letty's tongue to offer to do it for him and that shocked her so much she forced herself to stare at her feet rather than gaze longingly at his splendid body.

Too soon, he relieved her of his heavy coat and slipped it on, stuffed the sodden shirt into one of the pockets, then bent to pick up the lantern, leaving Letty still holding his waistcoat and her holly, painfully aware of the fact she could still see tantalising glimpses of his bare torso as they walked back towards the house and feeling very, very aroused by the sight.

When they entered the kitchen, Jamie Warriner took in the scene with his usual blank look, but his eyes lingered on Letty's flushed cheeks and wide eyes and she was certain she saw a flash of amusement in his inscrutable gaze.

'Dinner is in half an hour.' Then, as an afterthought, he smiled at her.

Oh, good heavens! He knew what she was thinking about his elder brother. A blush joined the flush and heated her face further. Letty probably resembled a beetroot. She tried to brazen it out. 'Excellent. That gives me time to freshen up then.' And to have a lie down, ostensibly, she reasoned, to think about how she was currently feeling. However, her legs were now so unsteady, Letty knew if she didn't lie down soon, she would probably fall down. Or swoon. Swooning was more likely. 'If you will excuse me, gentlemen.'

She was still clutching her bunch of holly as she scurried upstairs and didn't care. Jack had unsettled her. He kept doing that, she realised. His smile, his manner—rakish one minute, domineering the next—his kindness, fierce loyalty and, not least, his pride. He was absolutely right to be proud, she supposed. He had been so young when he had taken on the burden of responsibility for his brothers and the estate, something she found both admirable and touching. Then, of course, there were his gorgeous deep blue eyes and now his truly magnificent body was thrown into the heady mix. Letty gratefully sank down on the mattress and flopped back against the pillows to allow her mind to properly consider it now she was alone. One did not need a vast amount of experience with the male form to know when one had seen a singularly perfect specimen...

Jack stood next to Jamie and surveyed his drawing room. Letty had not exaggerated when she had claimed to have cleaned all of the nooks and crannies. He could not remember the last time anywhere in this dilapidated old house had ever felt so inviting or smelled so overwhelmingly of polish.

'She did this all by herself?'

'It was impressive to watch. The woman is a demon

when she gets going. I genuinely feared for the windows when she started cleaning them.'

'And you didn't help her move the furniture?' Jack was still baffled as to how she had managed to drag in the heavy oak side table from the other room all alone. On the surface, Letty appeared to be such a delicate little thing.

'By the time I came home she had already moved it all. Neither Joe nor Jacob helped her either.'

Jack scratched his head and smiled. 'She's done a splendid job.' Who would have thought a spoiled heiress was capable of actual graft?

'Indeed she has. Your Letty is a feisty one.'

Jack was reluctant to take the bait, but knew from bitter experience it was better to tackle it head on rather than leave such an outrage unchecked. 'She's not *my* Letty, Jamie, so have your fun elsewhere.'

Jamie shrugged and feigned disinterest. 'Is she not? Perhaps I misread the obvious signals she was sending out.'

He couldn't ignore that. 'Signals?'

'You fluster her.'

'I do?'

'I'll say. Just now she was all pink and nervy. What did you do her?'

'Nothing. She apologised for this morning, we chatted and then I had to pull a sheep out of the mud.'

Jamie allowed his eyes to travel slowly down Jack's body and then pulled apart the front of his greatcoat. 'Like that? Where has your shirt gone?'

'You wouldn't wear your shirt if you were handling a wet sheep either.'

'That explains it, then. You gave her a show of your

raw manliness—women like a bit of the untamed savage in their men. Displays of half-naked brute strength have a tendency to make females swoon. I don't suppose your Letty is any different.'

'Stop calling her *my* Letty. You know full well there is nothing untoward going on.' Much as he would like there to be. Jamie merely shrugged again, but it was a gesture loaded with meaning.

'I rather think she is *your* Letty, Big Brother. There are four devilishly handsome Warriners in this house, yet she has taken a fancy only to you. There is no accounting for taste.' Jamie turned and limped back to the kitchen, forcing Jack to follow him like a lapdog, desperately hopeful to hear more of his brother's tantalising theories, but Jamie did not elaborate. Instead, he poked the point of a knife into his boiling potatoes and pretended Jack did not exist. Asking anything now was tantamount to a confession of guilt and he did not need his astute brother knowing he was burning with lust and fraught with longing for the woman, so Jack poured himself some milk. He tried to choke it down nonchalantly when all he really wanted to do was shake his irritating brother by the shoulders and demand he explain himself. Immediately.

After an eternity, Jamie spoke again with far more measured casualness than even his acting skills extended to. 'I suppose it doesn't hurt that she is an uncommonly pretty little thing.'

Jack experienced a surge of possessive jealousy at his brother's comment. 'Is she? I can't say I've given it much thought.'

'Liar!' Jamie threw his head back and laughed then, something he rarely did. Jack had never craved the satisfaction of punching his brother in the face more. 'Every time you look at her your tongue is hanging out and you practically drool.'

The best form of defence, even when your brother had your exact measure, was attack. 'I wonder if Napoleon's troops didn't injure your thick skull as well as your leg, Jamie. Clearly you have begun hallucinating.'

Jack stalked from the room to the boisterous sound of his brother's laughter, feeling a strange mix of emotions which unnerved him. Was Jamie right? Was it within the realms of possibility that a fêted society beauty might have taken a fancy to him? While the prospect warmed him, he would have to be an idiot to give the theory any credence. If she was flustered, it was probably due to his uncouth disrobing in the presence of a lady. At the time, he hadn't given it much thought. He always stripped to the waist when he rescued wet sheep. They all did. Now that he considered it, he supposed proper gentlemen would never do such a thing. His instruction in correct etiquette had been woefully neglected by both of his parents, so was it any wonder the poor girl had been shocked by his crass behaviour?

Letty's flush would have been pure embarrassment, not admiration for the *untamed savage* as his brother had suggested. Instead of being impressed at his display of brute strength, all Jack would have managed was to cement her opinion of him as a brute. The very last thing he should be doing was holding out a preposterous hope of anything else with her.

In Jack's experience, hope in any form was normally the kiss of death. Every single time he had experienced that fickle emotion, fate had had very different ideas. As if Violet Dunston, incomparable diamond from sophisticated London, would seriously lower herself to be with somebody like him. Even if he weren't a Warriner, he boasted little to tempt her. No money, poor manners, a crumbing house and the son of a man who had ruined another heiress once upon a time. Yes, indeed—plenty to turn her head there!

And besides, he had enough burdens in his life already, without yearning for the additional complication of a woman in it. Even if by some miracle she did find something attractive in his *brutish savageness*, wives and Warriners did not mix. The Warriner men were doomed to make women unhappy, and although he was not a violent man, like his father, or a drunk, again like his father, he was loaded with far too many responsibilities to take on another one and he could not bear the idea of reading the inevitable disappointment in any woman's face when she realised she had made a huge mistake in shackling herself to him.

Added to that, it certainly did not help matters that Jack's estate was in the direst of straits, he was tarred with the worst reputation possible, barely had twenty measly guineas to his name and was definitely not the sort of man an *incomparable* would ever consider as a potential mate in any lifetime, let alone this one. Not when she had wealthy dukes falling all over themselves to court her, who definitely did not need her money at all and could give her exactly the sort of life she had been born to live and doubtless yearned to get back to.

Chapter Eleven

Twenty-two days left...

'What are you doing?'

The barked question nearly caused Letty to lose her tenuous balance on the tiny occasional table she was teetering on. 'I would have thought it obvious, Jack. I am cleaning the chandelier.' The large, only remaining dusty thing in the vaulted hallway had been taunting her.

'You are going to break your neck, woman!' He strode towards her, looking simultaneously annoyed, windswept and enormous in his undone greatcoat. Unfortunately, this time there was both a shirt and waistcoat firmly in place beneath it. His big hands steadied the table and he stared up at her with barely disguised irritation. 'Get down this instant!'

Every time Letty heard his dictatorial tone it grated and childishly she became more set on doing whatever it was he disapproved of, even though she knew he was right. Her position had been dangerously precarious and she should be grateful he had come to her aid. She should be, but she wasn't. 'No! Just look at all the dust and the cobwebs.' With a flash of ill-advised defiance, she wielded her feather duster on the dingy glass droplets again and the table wobbled ominously beneath her feet despite his hold on it.

Letty's arms waved as she tried to balance herself, only to find this completely unnecessary when his hands gripped her thighs in a most improper manner. 'Oh, for goodness sake, you stubborn wench!' Seconds later her feet left the table top as he hoisted her into the air until her shoulders came level with all of the cobwebs.

Suddenly, cleaning the silly thing as quickly as possible became her main priority, because his head was inches from her navel and those distractingly strong arms were wrapped very tightly just below her bottom. Never had a feather duster moved so fast, yet as rapid as her movements were, they did nothing to take her mind off their intimate position.

Letty could feel his breath on her skin. Warm, slightly laboured, it floated through the soft linen of the shirt she was wearing. *His* shirt. The heat of his hands seared through the buckskin of her breeches, *his* breeches, until she was aware of the exact shape of his palms and the weight of each of his fingers pressed against her legs. And there was nothing else between the fabric and her skin. She had no underwear. The corset and chemise she had been wearing on the night of her abduction had been ruined along with her evening dress and slippers. Letty had never wished for a corset more than she did right at this moment, because it would have acted like armour. A boned and impenetrable layer of protection between this vexing man and her decidedly vexed body.

Almost desperately, she scrabbled for the last of the cobwebs. 'All done!' This was sung with far too much relief and in a voice a great deal more high-pitched than normal. 'You can put me down now!'

Misguidedly, she had assumed he would plop her back on the table and then help her down. He did no such thing; instead he carefully lowered her to the ground by sliding her down his body. Whilst this probably made sense in view of the feeble nature of the table she had chosen to use, the logistics of the task proved to be more disconcerting than merely being held aloft. It involved Jack's arms shifting position as he shuffled her downwards. They grazed over her bottom before circling her waist, his face now level with her breasts. That warm breath did peculiar things to those as it permeated the flimsy linen.

A moment later and her breasts were pushed flush against his chest, and Letty hoped he was not as aware of her suddenly pert nipples as she was, although she suspected they would be awkwardly apparent through the fine linen of his shirt now that only two layers of thin material separated them.

Her eyes locked with his as they came level. Up close, there were darker flecks of sapphire in the intense blue and his pupils were larger than she was used to seeing them. Unnerving. Her pulse leapt further when they briefly flicked to her lips. He blinked and for a moment Letty thought he might kiss her, so intense had the atmosphere between them suddenly become—but if he was as attracted to her as she was to him, he hid it well. Effortlessly, he lowered her until her feet came into contact with the floor; her neck tilted back to look up at him, reminding her of the huge difference in their heights. The peculiar exchange had probably taken no more than a few seconds in total, yet her fevered imagination had slowed it all down in order to savour the whole experience.

It was Jack who stepped back and broke the sensual spell she was under. 'Do not attempt to clean another chandelier without one of my brothers there to help you!' The gruff tone was a dash of cold water which brought Letty up short. 'And please try to keep yourself out of trouble for the rest of the day.'

He turned and strode towards the kitchen, that greatcoat billowing behind him as he disappeared around the corner. Letty heard the door slam as he left the building and realised her foolish idea that he might kiss her had been exactly that. Foolish. The man thought her the greatest of all inconveniences and clearly still did not like her despite her pathetic efforts to try to make him do so.

More than a little unsteady and now quite miserable, she considered admitting defeat. Jack Warriner would never warm to her and perhaps without the protective aura of her fortune to seduce people with, she wasn't particularly likeable. A sobering thought.

A defeatist's thought.

Letty had thwarted kidnappers, for pity's sake. If she could manage that then she could make Jack like her. Perhaps she simply needed to go about it in a different way...

As she had never cooked anything before in her life, the recipe before her might as well have been written in a foreign language, but now that the lower floor of Markham Manor was shining like a new pin, Letty was

determined to serve a proper meal in the newly spar-
kling dining room. One with a sauce. And a dessert.

Letty had never as much as peeled a carrot before, so
to make a meal entirely from scratch would gave her an
inordinate sense of achievement. Her uncle had often
accused her of being spoiled and having no understanding of the real world. She needed, her uncle explained
in that patronising way that he had, a sensible man's
guidance because she was incapable of being independent. Well, thanks to his treachery, she had learned a
completely new set of skills recently which she had
hitherto not needed. Escaping a moving carriage, for
instance. Or dusting. Or doing laundry. Yet she had not
only tackled each task with vigour, she had emerged tri-
umphant, as she always did, and excelled at every one,
with the exception of yesterday's unfortunate chandelier
incident. Now she would teach herself to cook as well.
What was that if it was not independence?

It had also been nice to be able to do something for
this family who had taken her in. She had already developed a great affection for the three younger Warriners,
even the taciturn Jamie, and there was no denying the
physical attraction she had to their brooding big brother.
Since their memorable meeting in the barn, closely followed by the peculiar incident in the hallway, he had
been doing his level best to avoid her. That was plainly
obvious to anyone with eyes and she clearly still irritated him, as even in the evenings when she sat in the
drawing room with the whole family he remained aloof.
She chatted and laughed with Joe and Jacob, occasionally Jamie added some pithy comment which made them
all smile, while Jack occupied himself with his ledgers

and barely grunted if she tried to include him in the conversation.

And there she had thought they were beginning to get along the other night. Only to spoil it by climbing on that silly table and making herself look inordinately silly in his eyes once again. With Jack Warriner, every time she took a step forward, she seemingly took two steps backwards. She had never been more confused by a gentleman in her life. Men usually courted her good favour. Jack now totally ignored her.

If she said so herself, making dinner was a stroke of genius. For days now, Jack's unfriendly behaviour towards her had put Letty on edge. She was not used to being either invisible or disliked. People always adored her—well, on the surface they did anyway. Did they only see Violet, rather than Letty? The very fact that she continually thought of herself as two people, and only Letty was real, did little to ease her unease. Violet was rich, charming and enigmatic. The catch of the Season.

But Jack did not want her money, or appreciate Violet's charms, nor did he appear to like Letty very much. The real her. Once again Letty felt like an inconvenient burden to him and she was now so desperate for his approval she was prepared to try anything to get it. Something, she was prepared to concede, which was completely pathetic and said a great deal about her need to belong and, more to the point, her underlying lack of confidence.

Doing something productive for the family helped to alleviate some of the guilt she felt at straining their already limited resources and, if Jack would not accept her money, he was jolly well going to accept the fruit of her labours…and perhaps, if the way to a man's heart was truly through his stomach, he might stop treating her like a plague victim come to contaminate them and smile at her again. One of those unguarded, roguish smiles which made his eyes twinkle mischievously. The one which made her heart melt. She frowned. No wonder she needed to keep herself occupied. Every time Letty stopped moving, she found herself thinking dreamily of him. Usually without his shirt on.

When she had informed Jamie several hours ago of her intention to make dinner, his only reaction was to quirk one eyebrow, then disappear into the courtyard. When he returned a few minutes later, he handed her two dead chickens which were still warm, their broken necks swinging menacingly as she held them tenuously by their feet. 'There are vegetables in the pantry,' he had said and then had promptly disappeared outside again.

It was just as well. Cooking was proving to be much more troublesome than polishing and dusting, and the ancient cookbook she had found in the long-forgotten library was not a great deal of help. *The Art of Cookery Made Plain and Simple* was a misnomer. The recipe for 'Fowl à la Braise' was neither plain nor simple and took it for granted that the reader knew the fundamentals of the culinary arts before commencing. What, for example, did '*reduce*' mean? And how could one '*add enough flour to make a thick sauce*' if one had never made a sauce of any sort before? How much, exactly, was enough? In desperation she had added spoonful after spoonful to the pan, only to watch it congeal into lumps before her very eyes. Far from being in a sea of thick, delicious sauce, her fowl *à la Braise* was now floating in a stagnant pond in the middle of a heatwave.

And with less than half an hour before dinner was due to be served, she was beginning to lose all hope of the final dish being edible.

Jack worked himself into a state of exhaustion. He had not needed to spend an hour in the barn chopping wood, the wood pile already being quite healthy, but he could not face going back to the house until it was absolutely necessary. Not while she was there, tempting him with her glorious riot of corkscrew curls and still wearing his breeches. Looking and not touching was killing him. Looking, while not appearing to look, was driving him insane. He had never been so frustrated in his life. Unfortunately, as it was almost dinner time it was absolutely necessary to go back inside so he could not put it off any longer.

With a sigh he piled up the last of the wood and shrugged on his coat. The last three days had been tortuous. He was wary of even glancing at Letty in case Jamie had been right and he did openly gape at her with his tongue out, drooling, and after he had shamelessly enjoyed the feel of her in his arms yesterday and had very nearly kissed her because he was so consumed with lust, the only course of action available to him now was to have as little to do with the temptress as possible.

In the mornings, Letty's company had been more bearable because he had a distinct purpose—eat breakfast and then leave as quickly as possible. But in the evenings…well, frankly they made him cringe. If sitting silently through dinner trying not to explode while conversation wafted around him wasn't painful enough, at the end of the evening he would then have to watch her perfect bottom sway up the stairs, in *his* breeches, on her way to bed. *His* bed. Both things drove him mad with unfulfilled desire. It was all he could do to mutter goodnight.

Things would be a lot easier if she was an ordinary-looking girl, but of course he was never that lucky. Instead she had those lovely, big green eyes and those plump, pink lips which appeared to have no difficulty talking. There was an animation about the way that she spoke which made even the most mundane topics sound interesting. But that was entirely the problem. Her life had been far from mundane. She knew everyone in London, had been invited to every ball, had danced with dukes and solvent earls, and even the Prince Regent himself.

Twice.

How exactly did a humble, financially embarrassed farmer from dankest Nottinghamshire even begin to compete with all of that? She positively reeked of effervescence. Jack probably stank of the sheep he wrestled like a savage. Half the time he felt unworthy, the other half merely miserable. Letty was perfect. There was no other word for her. And perfect, when you were a penniless Warriner with an incurable case of lust and no prospects, was intimidating. Jack used to be master of the house, but now he was reduced to being a slave to his urges, and a mute slave to boot.

Despite his inability to reciprocate conversationally like a civilised gentleman, or indulge his rampant desire, having Letty in the house made everything about the place seem a little brighter. Not to mention cleaner and more…homely. It was almost as if she belonged at Markham Manor—which was, of course, ridiculous. An *incomparable* did not belong here. With him.

He took a calming breath and then opened the door.

'Letty has been cooking!' announced Jacob with a grin.

Letty was stood at the table looking lovely, a leather-bound tome entitled *The Art of Cookery Made Plain and Simple* at her elbow and a huge smudge of flour on her cheek. It was quite an arresting sight. She looked like a beautiful depiction of the perfect farmer's wife. Jack managed a smile despite the sudden tightness in his chest. Farmer's wife? Where the hell had that come from?

'So I see.'

Joe was stirring a big pot on the range and appeared to be on the cusp of hysterical laughter. 'She has made Fowl à la Braise and potatoes—which is apparently a fancy name for a chicken stew from what I can make out. For pudding we have baked apples with cream.'

'It sounds delicious,' he said carefully, although it did not actually smell particularly delicious. It smelled burnt—and ever so slightly fetid.

'Why don't you sit down, Jack?'

With a sinking feeling Jack realised he was trapped. He had to make conversation now after she had plainly gone to so much trouble. It was expected. 'Have you had a good day?' It was a reasonable start.

She smiled at him and gestured to the mess around them with a spoon. 'I have been learning to cook. I did not realise that it was so complicated—but it has proved to be very entertaining. I had originally intended to make an apple pie for pudding, but I am afraid that the pastry proved to be a little too challenging.'

'I see.' Dull. Dull. Dull. Jack racked his brain for another topic. 'The rain has stopped.' Good grief, could he be any more boring?

'It has?' This news appeared to cheer her. 'That will make your work easier.'

'I hope so, though it could take a day or two for the water to subside. Once it does, I should be spared from rescuing sheep for a few days. Three of them got stuck in the mud today. Sheep are such stupid creatures.' Much better. He had actually managed to string several sentences together quite effectively.

'They taste good, though, so that is some consolation.'

She gave him such a lovely smile and he found himself grinning back at her like an idiot before he checked himself. 'Indeed it is.' Jack took a grateful gulp of his tea.

'I think that the potatoes are done, Letty,' Jacob called from across the room. 'You had better get those plates ready, Jamie.' When Jack stood up, intending to help her, Letty turned to him and stayed him with her hand. It touched the back of his briefly and sent tingles up his arm.

'Sit down. The three of us can manage well enough. You work too hard, Jack.'

Letty insisted they all eat in the formal dining room so the brothers carried the steaming pots to the table, but when the lids were removed she stared at her creation with a sinking heart. They all did. It might well smell like food, but it looked terrible. The sauce around the chicken was thin, lumpy and grey in colour. The two chickens looked anaemic. The least said about the accompanying vegetables the better. Mush was a more fitting word for them now. Bland, pale, unappetising mush.

Jack politely served himself a chunk of the chicken.

As he lifted the sorry-looking portion on to his plate Letty could see the tell-tale signs of feathers still on the greasy, gelatinous skin and winced. The spoonful of mush Joe served him landed on his plate with an ominous-sounding splosh.

'This looks lovely,' he said with the falsest smile she had ever seen and then he proceeded to help his brothers load their own plates with a completely straight face. Letty wanted to curl up and hide as she watched them all pick at the food dubiously. Poor Jack had no option but to fill a fork with the slop and choke it down.

'Mmm…' For good measure he nodded sagely, rolling his eyes at his siblings as if his mouth was filled with the nectar of the Gods and she realised he was actually being kind. To her. Letty wanted to die. But they all made a polite and valiant attempt at eating the meal despite the fact it was beyond awful. Jamie curled his lip in disgust and shovelled the food in fast, a technique he had probably learned in the army when the rations were terrible. Jacob and Joe appeared so disappointed upon swallowing their first mouthful, but they looked to their elder brother, who kept making encouraging sounds as he attacked his plate with gusto, and they did the same. At one point his eyes rested on hers. For once, it was not irritation she read in them, nor was it disappointment at the shameful ruination of good food at her clumsy hand. To her complete surprise he seemed to find the whole thing very funny.

'I am so sorry about dinner,' she blurted out and then instantly blushed from the roots of her hair down to the tips of her toes, 'It is a travesty.'

Those intense blue eyes lifted slowly from his plate

and regarded her with obvious amusement. 'A travesty is a bit harsh.'

'How would you describe it, then?' Letty's cheeks were burning hot, but she forced herself to meet his gaze. 'I have even ruined the saucepans.'

For a moment he shrugged, then a devastating boyish grin transformed his face. 'There are some redeeming aspects. You make excellent tea—so the beginning part of the meal was very good.'

To her horror, both Joe and Jacob burst out laughing. Even Jamie smiled. 'In the army I had to eat some pretty inedible things, Letty. But this? This is by far the worst meal ever to pass my lips.'

Letty buried her face in her hands and groaned. 'It all appeared to be so straightforward in the book.'

Jack's eyes were still laughing, but he spoke kindly. 'Perhaps you should have started with something simple first. I confess I have never heard of fowl *à la Braise* before today, but I think you should master something basic like roasting a chicken before you move on to something as advanced as trying to cook it *à la Braise*.'

'Would you consider boiled potatoes and carrots advanced? I ruined those, too.'

'You are being too hard on yourself.' The three other Warriners nodded enthusiastically, in a valiant attempt at making her feel better which failed completely. Feeling inordinately stupid and angry at herself, Letty stood and began to snatch up the still-full plates, stacking them in a pile in front of her.

'The baked apples might taste better!' Although she did not hold out much hope. The acrid smell of burning fruit was unmistakable.

To compound her misery, Jack started laughing. 'I

thought the stewed chicken feathers were a particularly *nice* touch. I have never seen that before. Was it in the recipe or a little twist of your own?'

'I enjoyed those, too,' said Joe, fishing one from his mouth and waving it for emphasis. 'They gave the meal a little extra something…'

'Texture.' Jacob was holding his ribs, he was sniggering so much. 'If you ask me, there are not enough feathers in food. They are wasted in pillows.'

Letty pouted in consternation. 'I have never plucked a chicken before,' she admitted with the beginnings of a smile because it was funny. 'It was horrible. They were still warm. I gave up plucking when I thought one of the birds was still twitching. I foolishly thought the remaining feathers would burn off as they cooked. But at least I got one thing right. My fowl *à la Braise* was accurately named. It was truly foul.' The infectious sound of Jack's laughter was interrupted by the sound of a fist pummelling on the front door.

Chapter Twelve

Twenty days left and all is not well…

The five of them stared at each other, although Letty appeared truly terrified. She needn't have worried. Jack would slay dragons before he ever let anyone get near her.

'Go upstairs. Stay out of sight. We'll deal with this.' She didn't have to be asked twice and sprinted from the dining room with her lovely eyes wide.

The fist pummelled the door again and the four of them walked warily towards it. 'I'm coming!' Jack shouted with feigned irritation, conscious that his heart was threatening to beat its way out of his chest. This was his fault. No doubt the change in the weather had influenced this visit. For once, Jack was not pleased the incessant rain had stopped now that they had a fair-weather search party at the door. He chastised himself for not realising this was bound to happen. Thanks to his own stupidity, he had inadvertently put Letty in danger. But he could flagellate himself later, when the threat was gone.

He turned to his brothers and whispered instructions. 'Whoever it is, we know nothing. We have seen nothing.' They nodded and headed into the great hall, led by Jamie. When Jack saw they were all sat in their usual places, pretending to be reading something, he slid open the latch and the heavy front door swung open. There were three men standing on the dark threshold, all with lanterns in their hands. Jack recognised only one of the men.

Layton. When this was all over, he promised himself he would enjoy making the weasel pay for his part in harming Letty. But not tonight. In the nick of time he remembered that calling him by his real name would tip the man off.

'Mr Smith? What brings you here at such a late hour?'

The scarred man leaned sideways to look suspiciously past him down the hallway before returning his gaze to Jack. 'Sorry for the unexpected disturbance, Mr Warriner, only we are still looking for the missing girl. After talking to some of the locals and after having been informed your estate was quite extensive, not to mention so remote, it occurred to me that Violet might have taken refuge here somewhere.'

The man's pale eyes searched Jack's expression for any sign of emotion which might give something away. He forced himself to appear amused. 'With your reward now at a princely five hundred pounds, you can be assured if either myself or my brothers had seen her, we would have delivered her safely back to you immediately.'

Layton smiled, although his eyes remained cold and inscrutable. 'I am sure you would, Mr Warriner. I am

certain five hundred pounds would be extremely useful to a man in your position...' He would pay for that
comment, too. 'However, the young lady in question
is a resourceful thing. In her panic, she may well have
ensconced herself in one of your outbuildings without
your knowledge—'

Jack cut him off curtly. 'In her panic, Mr Smith? I
thought the girl had been kidnapped.'

Layton never missed a beat. 'We now believe she
may well have escaped her abductors, Mr Warriner.
We have still received no ransom note and a few of the
locals have mentioned seeing a young girl of her description on the night in question. They say she was all
alone and obviously terrified.'

Jack had never seen a person lie so effortlessly. Nobody else had seen Letty, on the night of her escape or
since. The only people who knew for certain she had
been alone on the road hereabouts at that particular time
were her abductors and him. The only truth in Layton's
claim was the fact Letty had been terrified. That, Jack
had seen first-hand. Now he knew exactly who her abductors were, the need to cause Layton harm was visceral. But Letty's continued safety depended on his
performance right this minute.

'Perhaps you had better come in, Mr Smith. Seeing
as the rain has stopped, we can all search the outbuildings together.' For effect he called to his brothers. 'Joe,
Jacob—fetch some lanterns. We need to go outside.'
Jamie would guard Letty in his absence.

The three interlopers stood in the hallway and Jack
did not leave their side until Joe and Jacob came to
relieve him. Both had donned coats and serious ex-
pressions. Jamie limped behind them, his limp more

pronounced for dramatic effect. As he had hoped, his brother knew exactly what do without Jack needing to explain. For good measure, Jamie behaved exactly like a Warriner was expected to behave.

'If she's in our barn, then she's ours until you pay us for her,' he said with an unpleasant leer.

Layton eyed him with hostility. 'Perhaps...'

'There's no perhaps about it. If she's there, none of us will let her leave without our pockets being filled with that five hundred pounds.'

Jack stepped in. 'Now, now, Jamie... We can discuss terms *if* we find her. I won't let them sell us short either. Follow me, gentlemen. If there is a reward due, we'd best get to it.'

They had trudged through the house noisily, their heavy boots echoing on the old wooden floor below, yet even when all she could hear was silence, Letty refused to move from her position on the landing. Hearing Layton's voice just a few scant feet away had rendered her almost frozen with fear.

'Go into your bedchamber, Letty. And for God's sake don't light a candle. Sit on the bed and don't move. We don't want that man hearing a sound from upstairs. He's a canny one. And no matter how much you are tempted to look, stay away from the blasted window as well. One of us will tell you when the coast is clear.' Jamie's hushed voice floated softly up the stairs and gave her some comfort. For a brief moment, when she had heard him talk so convincingly about wanting the reward money, she had wondered if he might betray her. Now she felt ashamed at the thought.

'Thank you, Jamie,' she whispered and did exactly as he said.

The minutes ticked by slowly. Occasionally, she saw the light of one of the lanterns reflected on the walls of her bedchamber or heard muffled male voices. One thing was for certain, the search was a thorough one. Letty did not know whether that was at Jack's insistence or Layton's, but she told herself it was a good thing. If their search proved fruitless, then they would surely be less inclined to come back.

After what felt like hours, she finally heard the men stomp back into the house, where their conversation continued until she was so jumpy and panicked she could barely hear the words over the noise of her pulse beating in her ears. Snippets of conversations wafted through.

'We will keep an eye out...'

Jack's voice. *'She might well be dead...'*

Jamie. *'Nobody could survive the elements for this long without shelter...'*

'Could she have found someone on the road travelling back towards London?' That came from Dr Joe.

They were putting doubts in Layton's mind. Even when she heard the front door creak open and heard it close firmly behind them again, she could still not bring herself to move from her position perched on the edge of the mattress. Jamie said one of them would come when it was safe, and right now, being safe was her only priority.

More silence stretched out ahead of her. When Letty thought she would die from the not knowing, she finally heard footsteps on the staircase and instinctively held her breath as they moved swiftly towards her door even though she knew, in her heart, they were friendly feet.

'It's me, Letty.' She slumped at the reassuring sound of Jack's voice and felt tears wet her cheeks as the door cracked open. 'They've left. Jacob and Joe have gone to secure the gates.' Fear had closed her throat, making a verbal response impossible, so she nodded slowly and tried to stand, only to find her knees would not support her either. 'Hey—don't cry.' He crossed the room in three long strides and sat down beside her on the mattress. 'I think we did a pretty good job of convincing them you weren't here. They should leave us alone now.'

Hearing Layton's voice again had reminded Letty of how precarious her situation still was. 'Th-thank you.' Her voice caught on the final syllable and to her complete horror she was unable to stem the flow of tears which were now pouring down her cheeks. When Jack wrapped one strong arm tightly around her shoulders and pulled her closer, she burrowed against his chest and wept, conscious of the fact she was behaving like a silly dolt, yet desperate for the comfort and protection he offered.

His other arm came around her and he rested his chin on the top of her head, rocking her slightly as he soothed her with gentle words. 'It's all right, sweetheart. You're safe now. I promise.'

Letty did feel safe with him, but still she could not stop crying. After the worst of the racking sobs had subsided, Letty tried to speak.

'I w-was having such a l-lovely evening—for a while I had f-forgotten about it all.' She had as well. Despite the disastrous dinner, the easy banter and the sense of camaraderie this evening had been something special.

Letty could not remember ever feeling quite as comfortable anywhere, not even her private rooms in her house in Mayfair. For a while there she had been part of the family. Except they weren't her family. She was the interloper and they had generously taken her in out of the goodness of their hearts. Her only family member had sold her to a complete villain without so much as a by-your-leave, for his own financial gain. Letty was nothing but a healthy purse to him. And Bainbridge. The thought of him sent ice through her veins. They were hot on her heels and baying for blood.

Letty's blood.

She knew too much.

Jack must have seen the panic on her face. He cupped her cheek with his palm, swiping away the fresh tears she had not realised were still falling with his thumb. 'We knew they would come here at some point. Layton's visit was inevitable. If anything, I am angrier at myself. I should have known they would turn up as soon as the weather eased. When it stopped raining earlier, I should have insisted the gates be closed before we had dinner. But they came, and they are none the wiser. I doubt we will see them any time soon. You don't need to dwell on it for every second of every day, Letty.'

'But the threat is still very real, isn't it? They haven't given up. Even after a fortnight, they are still here. L-looking for me.' Fresh tears threatened, but she ruthlessly fought against them. Self-pity was not going to keep her alive. Crumbling in Jack's capable arms would only ever bring her temporary relief as well. In a few weeks, she would have to return to London and use the power of the law to bring her uncle and Bainbridge to justice. Then she would be alone again in her big house in Mayfair, where there were no noisy males to laugh with and nobody who cared one whit about the real her. Funny, a fortnight ago, she had never wanted to leave London. Now, she could scarcely imagine wanting to go back.

Letty moved to sit upright, but Jack's arms tightened around her protectively and held her so close, she could feel the steady beat of his heart against her own ribcage so she allowed herself this brief moment of comfort. Her own heart swelled and tried to match its rhythm, as if they were meant to beat together in harmony. She felt his warm breath in her hair. 'They still have no idea what happened to you or where you are. I will keep you safe, sweetheart, in whatever way is necessary, for as long as it takes.'

Letty melted against him, needing the contact. However, it was not only the comfort of his arms she craved. Being held by Jack Warriner was a heady experience. He was so big and solid. Commanding. When he said he would keep her safe, she believed him. Time and time again he had proved himself to be trustworthy. Loyal. Kind in his own brooding way. And she liked it when he called her sweetheart. Perhaps far more than she should. Letty tilted her head back to gaze up at him. 'I can't stay here for ever, Jack. Can I?' *Please tell me I never have to leave,* she thought, hoping he would hear her. Because suddenly, staying here with Jack felt like exactly the right thing to do. She belonged here.

Didn't she?

She certainly felt more herself here than she did in any of the London ballrooms. There, she had to be Violet Dunston, wealthy society beauty, but somehow separate from the proceedings. Human contact was transient, meaningless. The world only saw the confident heiress, not the lonely, uncertain girl beneath. The one who had no one who really loved her, yet everyone believed they knew her because they had read so much about her. Letty had read those same accounts, bemused. She did not recognise the frivolous, but much-emulated creature they wrote about, the girl whose concept of fashion was exquisite. Who danced like an angel floating on air. Whose laugh was like the gentle tinkling of a stream. However, the more nonsense she read about her mythical self, the more Letty pathetically tried to live up to the ideals. More and more new dresses, elaborate hairstyles, honing her skills at flirtation or eyelash fluttering and practising her laughter in the mirror so that the sound of it in public did not disappoint. At best, she had become a spectator to her own life, more concerned about what others thought than being true to herself.

And all for what? A bunch of acquaintances who never thought to look past the façade? All of them far more impressed with her money than with the girl. It was laughable, how empty her privileged existence actually was. Internally, she craved a life enriched with love and genuine purpose, not money, yet she played to the gallery regardless. The Duke of Wentworth was actively courting her, yet he had no idea he was courting Violet Dunston the *Tea Heiress*, and not her, Letty, at all. She had not even sought his opinions on her grand plans to create a foundling home. Why not? Did she really care if he disapproved? Or was she as indifferent to the perfect Duke as she was to her empty shell of a perfect life? Things she would happily walk away from as soon as she took control of her fortune and began her life properly.

Here she was Letty. Nobody cared if her hair wasn't correctly dressed or if she snorted when she laughed or failed disastrously at cooking. Being part of this family was wonderful. Bizarrely, being the butt of their jokes was also wonderful and already she dreaded leaving them. Her life in Mayfair would feel sterile in comparison. But she dreaded leaving Jack the most.

There was something about him which drew her and tugged at her heart more than any man ever had before. When she was with Jack, she could scarcely remember what the Duke of Wentworth looked like. That was hardly a surprise when Jack Warriner was quite the most spectacular specimen of a man she had ever encountered—but it was more than just his good looks that enticed her. Everything about him appealed to the woman within and his sense of duty went above and beyond. Even now, despite all of his many heavy responsibilities, he was trying to take away her pain and fear by absorbing it himself. Making her problems his and asking nothing in return.

How utterly romantic was that?

Without thinking, Letty snuggled her cheek against his chest contentedly and sighed. Except, the sigh sounded more like a groan of pleasure than an expression of relief. Probably because being held by him *was* pleasurable. In his arms, she felt dainty and womanly— while he was just so manly and strong. Letty allowed her hand to snake up to rest on his chest, splaying her fingers so that her palm could touch more of his body in one go and revelling in the solid feel of him. Wanting even more.

They stayed like that for almost a minute, just holding each other, until something shifted in the atmosphere between them. His eyes were still locked with hers, but his breathing was shallower. Next to her his heartbeat was quicker and she suspected hers was, too. She watched his Adam's apple bob as he swallowed warily and realised it was she who made him wary. Not Layton or Bainbridge. Her.

He was not immune to this intense attraction either, yet he held himself rigid, maintaining the small distance between them because, despite his rough edges, he was a proper gentleman who would never take advantage of her. Yet Letty desperately wanted him to. Her arms brazenly wound her way around his neck and she watched his eyes darken. He stared down at her for several long seconds without releasing his tight hold on her, his mouth hovering only a few inches away from hers, giving her hope that he also felt the intense pull of desire she did, that she had not imagined the tension between them when he had lowered her from the chandelier, but then his blue eyes became stormy. His features troubled. Another minute and their perfect moment of connection would be gone. She was damned if she would let that happen again. Letty closed the distance between them and pressed her lips softly to his.

He'd almost kissed her. It took every ounce of willpower Jack possessed not to claim her mouth with his and demand she never leave him when he had thought he'd heard her ask to stay. Letty belonged here. In his house. In his bedchamber. In his arms...but common sense intervened. The girl was overwrought and understandably scared for her life. Taking advantage of her while she was this upset would make him the lowest of the low. No better than the vile Warriners of old and his father in particular. A man who had compromised a vulnerable heiress to get his hands on her fortune. Jack sincerely doubted anyone would believe he was not a chip off the old block if he actively pursued his attraction to Letty. She did not belong here—her real life was in London and it was the sort of life so far removed from his own that to fool himself she would seriously consider staying in this house, with him, was beyond even the realms of fantasy.

Jack had been about to put some distance between them, for his own heart's safety, because he feared the yearning he experienced was threatening to burst forth, leaving him exposed and vulnerable, and doomed to be in receipt of her pity. Then miraculously, it had been Letty who had kissed him and, like a starving man at a banquet, all his body could do was satisfy the physical need which had consumed him from the first moment he had seen those bare legs displayed beneath the hem of his shirt.

One gentle brushing of lips was never going to be enough to sustain him for a lifetime, so Jack kissed her again with more urgency than he had intended, pouring all of the unexpected tenderness he felt for her into it until the emotion threatened to choke him. It made his mouth more passionate than it should have been, a kiss that should have terrified an innocent like Letty. Yet she met his lips with the same enthusiasm, winding her arms tightly around his neck as he hauled her into his lap roughly and dragged her womanly body flush against his. Because he had to, Jack buried his fingers in her hair, sliding off the ribbon which bound it back until the riotous curls sprang free.

When he felt the seam of her mouth relax, the kiss became more carnal. He explored her mouth thoroughly with his tongue and teeth and then trailed heated kisses along her throat, surprised by her needy passion and revelling in the way she arched against him in mindless desire. Through the soft, worn linen of the matching shirts they both wore, he recognised the pebbled hardness of her nipples against his body and found his hands stroking up the side of her ribcage in search of better contact. Letty did not appear to mind his presumptuousness. If anything, she welcomed it. As his hand cupped one soft swell reverently, she pressed it urgently against his palm and purred with satisfaction. Her own hands tugged his shirt from the waistband of his breeches, then burrowed underneath the fabric to stroke the skin on his back.

Blinded by another surge of desire, he eased her back on to the mattress and allowed his mouth to trail moist, searing kisses across her collarbone, then down on to the upper swells of those lush breasts. Her ribcage was rising and falling rapidly and she sighed his name with her eyelids closed, her head writhing against the sheets with each impertinent flick of his tongue. Jack's fingers pushed the fabric aside and touched her properly. Her puckered nipple hardened further when his thumb grazed it. Simultaneously, the motion caused his groin to tighten more and he kissed her deeply to hide his own needy moan. God, he wanted to be buried inside her. Deep inside her, branding her as his for ever.

'I've made some tea—shall I bring it up?' Joe's voice in the hallway below dragged him abruptly and painfully back to reality. Jack sat back, panting, only to see Letty sprawled wantonly across his bed, her hair fanned out around her head, one perfect, aroused breast bared to his hungry gaze and her desire-darkened green eyes as wide as saucers.

'No need!' he called, hoping the panic was not audible in his voice. The bedchamber door was wide open. Anybody could have seen what he had done, the full, shocking extent of how he had greedily and shamelessly taken advantage of a frightened woman in his care. He was no better than his hateful father after all. 'We are coming down now.'

As Letty had not already done so, Jack pulled the neckline of the shirt upwards to cover her modesty and tried to make sense of what had just happened. If Joe had not called out, he wouldn't have stopped. Now that he had, reason *had* to replace desire. What had just happened, should never have happened. He had put his own selfish needs above Letty's. Hadn't he?

Although she had instigated the kiss and she was smiling at him shyly. Perhaps she really did want him? If she wanted him, too, then maybe this kiss was the start of something. He glanced back at Letty, only to see her smile had gone and she was hastily tying her hair back with the ribbon. She did not meet his gaze. Did that mean she regretted it? Or was it that she was only equally as horrified as he at the prospect that they might have been caught? Jack sincerely hoped it was the latter because the glimmer of hope that she might, miraculously want him—*him!*—as much as he wanted her was overwhelming and too ridiculous to give credence to.

Except such unruly thoughts were as impractical as her reciprocating his feelings in the long term was improbable. Aside from the fact that only the biggest of cads would try to take advantage of a woman who was as distraught as Letty currently was, Jack had nothing to offer her. Nothing positive at least.

He could offer her a life of misery and of being shunned by society as his father had his mother, he supposed, or he could doom her to an eternity with a man who was as suspicious of love as the world was of a Warriner. Hadn't he seen first-hand how such a marriage could destroy a woman? Jack would not follow in his father's footsteps and simply take what he wanted, and to hell with the consequences. Letty deserved more than that. She was bright and resourceful, tenacious and charming, and so beautiful it made the air catch in his lungs every time he saw her.

Yes, she might well have been staring at him as if he were her knight in shining armour a few moments ago, clinging to him and tempting him to kiss her because she was desperate, so very frightened and he was the only one here. But he also had to remember she had just been crying like a baby in his arms beforehand. He had felt her fear as he had held her and knew she had nobody else to turn to except him and, under difficult circumstances, people rarely thought straight. That fact he also knew well. After the death of her parents, hadn't his own mother mistakenly believed herself to be in love with his father the moment she had met him, when it had really only ever been lust tinged with loneliness? She had ended up ruined, then embittered and resentful for ever afterwards because she had confused one powerful emotion for another one. Such was the inevitable way of things.

Jack watched Letty lick her plump, kiss-swollen lips

and wondered, fleetingly if she had actually wanted him to kiss her or if, like his mother, she had simply needed someone to be there for her. She had unmistakeably enjoyed his kiss. He had seen and felt her earthy response to his touch. Perhaps the very fact their kiss had turned incendiary the moment it had started was a sign that she felt more for him than simple gratitude.

For a brief moment, Jack allowed hope to bloom again and then he banished the thought angrily. He was confusing Letty's obvious gratitude for an invitation, when the poor girl was terrified out of her wits. It was then that he knew if he stayed here with her for much longer, his resolve to do the right thing would disintegrate. It was sobering to realise there was more of his father in him than he had believed. The temptation to bolt the bedchamber door and kiss her again superseded all thoughts and took every ounce of determination to ignore. But he *had* to be the responsible one. Letty was so full of life and laughter. He would not be the one to kill those lovable traits with the cold, hard truth of an eternity stuck with him, here in this demoralising place.

Of course, she would initially make the best of it because that was the way she was made, but month after month, year after year, her effervescence would diminish and the light in her lovely green eyes would dim. Letty belonged in society where she could sparkle. He had to do the right thing and nip this in the bud now for her sake, before real, irreparable damage was done.

'Tonight has been a bit of an ordeal, hasn't it? Neither one of us is thinking straight.' Jack passed her his handkerchief and watched a myriad of emotions play across her expression. One looked like confusion, another disappointment, and he could have sworn he thought he saw desire, although he could well have been mapping his own desires on to her. Wishful thinking? He just didn't know any more. In the end, she stared right at him and frowned.

'Not thinking straight? I am not a silly girl, Jack, if that is what you are implying.'

'I know you are not a silly girl. You are a frightened girl, which under the odd circumstances of this evening is perfectly understandable. And fear can unsettle us.' Jack was definitely unsettled and currently terrified that the part of him which was like his father would win. She was still frowning.

'So you are saying what we just did happened only because you think I was unsettled?' Now he heard anger, too.

'What I mean is, in view of everything that has happened, it would be inadvisable to confuse one charged emotional state with another. Kissing me is not going to make the dangerous situation we find ourselves in any better, nor is it advisable. We both know it was nothing more than a silly mistake on your part.'

'A silly mistake.' Her tone could have curdled milk. 'On *my* part.'

He smiled as best as he could at her admission, even though he had secretly hoped she would disagree with his practical logic. At least now he had made her understand what had really made her kiss him, his conscience would be clear. Almost. 'I would prefer to pretend it never happened.' While he would cherish the memory of their kiss, the last thing he wanted was for Letty to feel awkward around him. He would feel awkward enough for both of them. And disappointed. And perhaps even a little heartbroken.

'I see.'

She wasn't looking at him again, therefore he had no idea whether she agreed with his assessment of their current situation of not. She rummaged on the bedside table for the elaborately embroidered handkerchief he had found her with that fateful night and watched her clean her face with it, then tried to smile back at him bravely. Clearly she was grateful he had extricated them out of a potentially awkward situation and was relieved to be able to pretend nothing was amiss, although the knowledge did not bring him any relief.

He had kissed her. Intimately. And not only in the physical sense. His strange, powerful feelings for her had been poured into the kiss as well. If she'd have had more experience of a man's kisses, she would now know he felt more for her than just passion. Jack had been so caught up in the moment, so caught up in the idea of him and her together, he had never wanted it to end. Even now, he felt uncharacteristically unsteady and shaken. Letty, on the other hand, was definitely *not* still reeling from the intensity of the unexpected emotional and physical bonding. She appeared to have recovered her equilibrium without much effort at all. Further confirmation he had done the right thing—if perhaps a little insulting.

'How terrible do I look?'

Not nearly terrible enough to stop his body's yearnings. 'Nobody would know you had been crying.' Jack held out his hand and tried to ignore how perfect hers felt clasped in his. She was a damsel in distress and a true knight in shining armour would put aside his own feelings for the sake of hers. Theirs could only ever be the sort of courtly love from a bygone era. Jack was her protector, nothing more. She was a princess. 'Please try not to worry about those men any more. One way or another I will get you home safely, Letty. You have my word.' He pulled her up to stand next to him and then forced himself to let go of her hand. 'Until then, you will remain here. With me.'

God help him.

Chapter Thirteen

Fifteen days and thirteen hours remaining...

With only four days to go till Christmas Eve, Letty was determined to get into the spirit of the Season despite everything that was presently wrong with her life. Even if one put aside the trials and tribulations of an uncle who had betrayed you and a gnarly old earl who intended to wed by you by force, then potentially kill you for your money, or the sad fact that not one of the London newspapers Jacob read so avidly had printed any story suggesting she was missing or so much as *missed*, there were more pressing matters which Letty found vexing. All of them involved the eldest Warriner and her stupid, pointless feelings for him.

Why Letty was so besotted with the surly brute, she could not say. He was nothing like the man she had promised herself she would fall in love with. Not that she was in love with Jack, of course. Only a fool would develop such a powerful emotion for a man who largely behaved as if she didn't exist. Ever since their kiss five days ago, he had either avoided being left alone with her, or treated her like somebody suffering from a delusional mental state. Yes, he was polite and more sociable than he had been. When he was accompanied by any one of his brothers, he laughed and chatted to her as if she were one of them. But if she tried to corner him on his own he bolted. On that fateful night, he had dismissed her one and only attempt at seduction as merely being a weakness of the mind brought about wholly because she had been distraught. As if she, Letty Dunston, thwarter of kidnappers and now master baker, was even capable of behaving like such a ninny.

To save face, she had turned into Violet once more and gone along with it, when in truth his speedy about-turn from ardent, passionate lover to patronising, over-bearing protector had hurt. Letty had kissed Jack because her body had told her to, because being held in his arms had made her forget about Layton, Bainbridge and the danger she was in. Because it simply felt *right*. And not, as he had oh-so-reasonably stated, because she had been in a *charged emotional state*, brought about by fear. She had been in a charged emotional state all right, only it had been brought about by being in such close, intoxicating proximity to *him*.

And to make matters worse, and perhaps even more galling than being chastised like a child for wanting something she couldn't have, was the sorry fact that she *still* wanted him. Body and soul. Every loyal, upstanding, brave solid inch of him. He had pushed her away and then, to her utter mortification, informed her he would rather pretend it hadn't happened. Letty was so angry at him, and so utterly demoralised and humili-ated by his rejection, that five days had done nothing to close the wound. Yet barely an hour of the day went by when she didn't remember how marvellous it had felt to have his mouth and hands on her. Or to have her hands on him. She had never behaved in such a scandalously wanton manner—but acknowledged honestly to herself that she happily would again.

With him.

Any time that he saw fit!

Angry and frustrated in equal measure, Letty stared down at the bread dough on the table in front of her. After her disastrous Fowl à la Braise, and after failing so spectacularly as a seductress, conquering *The Art of Cookery Made Plain and Simple* had become something of a mission. Everything in her life might well be miserable in the here and now, but she could at least learn to make bread. Punching the air out of the soft dough gave her some satisfaction and she continued to pummel it, imagining it was Jack Warriner's handsome, patronising, kissable face.

If he were a normal gentleman, he would be flattered by her interest. In Mayfair, suitors had been queuing up to catch her eye. Some handsome, almost all titled and eligible. It was rare a day went by without a bouquet arriving from one of her admirers, complimenting her on her beauty, charm and wit. Any one of them would have been thrilled if she had kissed them—not that she had ever wanted to kiss any of them. But when the patronising, supercilious, condescending Jack looked at her, all he saw was an emotionally feeble girl with an addled mind, so of course, the *responsible* thing to do was to pretend it hadn't happened or avoid her like the plague. Nobody had ever avoided her before—and certainly not someone she had a soft spot for. Yet despite his annoyingly patriarchal manner and apparent immunity to her charms, Letty still had a particularly soft spot for the vexing man. When she didn't feel the overwhelming urge to kiss him, she simply wanted to hold him and talk to him. Be there for him as he was for her. Ease his many burdens.

From the sounds beyond the back door, and the way her traitorous skin tingled, the vexing man himself was back from the village. Irritated at the realisation her body now apparently sensed his presence before her eyes did, Letty continued to ferociously knead her bread dough and did not do him the courtesy of looking up as he burst through the door.

'You're back then,' she said with her eyes fixed on her dough.

She heard him and Jamie take off their greatcoats and shake the rain out of their hair like a pair of wet dogs.

'They've gone—Layton and his men.' This came from Jamie, never one to mince his words or over-embellish a sentence with more words than were absolutely necessary. Letty did look up then.

'Gone where?'

Jack shrugged. 'Bound for London, we believe. Three weeks of fruitless searching, constant rain and the rapid approach of Christmas have forced them to give up. The innkeeper said they paid their bill in full and passed on a forwarding address in Mayfair in case anyone heard anything interesting.' He thrust a piece of paper at her and she stared down at the address dispassionately. She had been expecting to see her uncle's address—*her* address—and she was not disappointed. She hardly needed further proof of his treachery.

'Do you think they will come back?'

His blue eyes flicked briefly towards hers. Obviously, even looking at her for short periods of time was something he found distasteful. 'Hard to say. The reward is now a thousand pounds, so even with them gone, finding you is a massive temptation for the locals. Except now the reward is for any information that leads to your whereabouts or the discovery of a body... so perhaps they have given up hope that you're even still alive.'

'Well, my uncle will be in for a surprise when I turn up on my birthday then, won't he? You must be relieved, Jack. You only have to suffer through another two weeks of my burdensome company.' Letty was not sure what sort of reaction she had been expecting from that harshly delivered statement, but with hindsight, she supposed she should have anticipated stony indifference. Jack did stony indifference so well.

'I'm going to chop some wood.' He stalked to the door and retrieved his sodden coat from the peg. The door slammed behind him and Letty punched the dough again, feeling decidedly shaky and thoroughly upset. Jamie limped around the table to sit opposite her and stared.

'Have you two had an argument?'

'Of course not, to have an argument, one would actually have to converse in private. In case it has escaped your notice, your brother prefers to avoid me.'

'He has been absent quite a bit lately. And now that I think upon it, he's been rather quiet. For him. Clearly you bring out the worst in him.' His mouth quirked in an approximation of a smile.

'I am well aware he doesn't like me, Jamie.'

'Oh, I wouldn't say that...'

Letty snorted her disbelief. 'I would! Of course he doesn't like me. Aside from that one night...when Layton turned up here...we have scarcely exchanged any words which were not completely necessary or spoken across the dinner table.'

'The night Layton turned up, you say? Wasn't that the night the pair of you kissed?'

Letty's head shot up and she felt the beginnings of a blush stain her cheeks. 'He told you about that!'

Jamie tried to act innocent and then grinned. '*He* never said a word—*he* didn't have to. I have eyes. Even a short-sighted fool with no sense could have worked out what the pair of you had been up to that night. You both arrived downstairs looking rumpled, couldn't meet each other's eyes and had those swollen mouths that only come from some serious—'

'Stop!' Her cheeks were now positively steaming so she covered them with her hands. Not much got past Jack's intuitive brother. 'Does everybody know?'

He shrugged. 'Hard to say. We haven't spoken about it—but they have eyes, too.'

This was awful. 'Oh! I feel like such an idiot.'

'Don't. Jack is a big boy. If you didn't want to be kissed, you had a right to put a stop to it.'

'What?'

'Well, I assumed from his odd mood, longing glances and solitary tendencies you refused his advances.' His blue eyes, so like his older brother's, but not as addictive to her, narrowed as he scrutinised her. 'Am I wrong?'

Letty stared down at the floor, willing it to open up and swallow her whole. When it didn't, she covered her face with her hands again so that Jamie would not see her shame. 'I kissed him. *He* was the one who put a stop to it.' As she had always suspected, when you put aside her fortune, there was nothing particularly special about her.

This statement was met with silence. After several moments, Letty peeked out between her fingers to gauge his reaction. Instead of looking amused at her confession, Jamie appeared exasperated. 'My brother has a very distinct sense of right and wrong. And it usually works to the detriment of himself.'

'What is that supposed to mean?' she asked curiously.

'Jack will always blame himself or put himself last. He always *has* to be responsible.'

'You are talking in riddles, Jamie. Whatever it is you clearly feel the urge to say, I wish you would just say it and be done with it. I am already completely mortified. With any luck, any further shame will result in my immediate death from it.'

'For goodness sake, Letty! For a beautiful woman you can be daft sometimes. Did *he* put a stop to it immediately?' Of course he hadn't. If he had, then she would not have had to deal with the shame of knowing he'd seen her bare breast. Touched it. At the time, she had hoped he would very much want to kiss it, too. 'I shall judge from your colourful reaction, that things developed into a bit more than a chaste kiss.'

In the absence of anyone else to confide in, Jamie, it seemed, would have to do. 'Jack said I was in a *charged emotional state*, brought about by fear due to Layton.'

'And were you?'

'Not at that precise moment, no.'

Jamie stood awkwardly and began to limp out of the kitchen, their uncomfortable conversation now obviously at an end. What was it with the Warriner men that they were happy to leave so many important things unsaid? She pouted. 'So that is it, is it? I bare my soul and you walk away.'

'I assumed you were off to the barn.'

'And why would I go there?'

Jamie sighed and raised his eyes heavenwards. 'I'd have thought it was obvious.' She watched his retreating back as he disappeared down the hall, but still heard his parting words as they drifted back to her. 'My principled brother is clearly as daft as you are.'

The log split with a satisfying sound. Only two more weeks to go. Two weeks and she would be back where she belonged, being courted by her rich Duke and robed in her missing finery. Then Jack would be spared the torture of seeing her every day. Perhaps then he would finally locate the peace of mind which was currently evading him.

He would take her back to London, they would say a stilted, awkward goodbye, and then he would head back here where he belonged. And as long as he never read one of Jacob's blasted newspapers, he would never again be confronted with the temptation she presented. For the sake of certainty, Jack would even speak to Jacob and warn him never to tell him any news about her. All talk of Letty would be forbidden from that day forth, so Jack could properly banish her from his mind. The very last thing he ever wanted to hear was a story about Letty marrying her wealthy, powerful Duke. He didn't want to have to picture her in another man's arms, in the full throes of passion, making those arousing, sensual noises she made and pushing her perfect, bare breasts greedily into another man's filthy hands.

The axe came down on the next log with such force it embedded itself in the ground and, for a moment, he experienced a raw surge of hatred for the faceless Duke he had never met. A man who, in all probability, never had filthy hands. Whoever he was, however much money the man had, and however clean his hands were, he did not deserve Letty. But then again, neither did Jack. Therefore, all of this effort he was putting into yearning, and being consumed with irrational jealousy, would be better directed elsewhere—and perhaps, in view of the wall of chopped logs stacked neatly along one whole side of the barn, he would do better to vent his frustration elsewhere as well. At this rate, they wouldn't need wood for several months. Another week and there would be no more trees left on his land.

He heard the barn door creak open behind him and turned. Then wished he hadn't.

'Can we talk?'

Typically, like the uncivilised savage he was, he had discarded his coat and waistcoat again. He was sure the sight of him sweating from exertion in only his shirt was offensive. And he probably should have shaved this morning as well. Her Duke would have shaved. 'If you want.' Which Jack certainly didn't. He placed another round log upright on the floor and swung the axe again. If he kept busy, remained aloof, she would leave quicker.

'Why don't you like me?'

The next stroke was off, splintering through the bark and sending the log rolling towards her legs. If he went to retrieve it, he would have to offend her nostrils with the scent of honest labour. If he began chopping a new piece of wood, he would look like he was scared to go near her. Neither option appealed, so he leaned his forearms on the axe handle and tried to appear bored.

'Letty—I have work to do. I don't have the time to flatter your ego. When you go back to London, I'm sure there are plenty of gentlemen there who will fall over themselves to tell you how wonderful you are.'

'I don't care about their opinions. I want yours. And I don't want you to spare my feelings. What is it about me that you find so distasteful?'

'I think you are imagining things.'

'And I think you are patronising me and doing your level best to avoid answering my question. Why don't you like me, Jack? Do you find me irritating? Am I huge burden? Or do you think me silly and empty headed? Or perhaps you find me unappealing. And if that is the case, why did you kiss me back?'

Chapter Fourteen

Fifteen days and twelve hours to go...

Letty had gradually edged closer towards him and reached out to touch his arm. 'Does the sight of me disgust you?' Because she had to know. No matter how difficult it was to hear, she had to know why Jack had recoiled from her that night the very moment he had come to his senses.

'Of course not!' He looked and sounded outraged. 'I thought we agreed to pretend it never happened.'

'But it did happen and now you cannot even look at me without wincing.' He stubbornly stared back at her, but she saw the slight flinch anyway. 'There it is! You're doing it again. Just admit you can't stand me.'

'Oh, for goodness sake!' He raked one hand impatiently through his overlong dark hair and huffed out a sigh of complete exasperation. 'The thing is… I like you well enough. It's just after what we did, it makes things awkward.' He was resolutely staring at his folded hands on the axe handle. 'It shouldn't have happened, Letty. Everything about it was wrong.'

It. He couldn't even say the word kiss. That did not
instil her with confidence in her abilities as a temptress.
Automatically, her fingers went to her lips as she tried
to recall exactly where she had gone wrong. 'Did I do it
incorrectly? Was I too brazen?' Those intense blue eyes
almost popped out of their sockets as he glared at her,
then quickly looked away to hide his reaction, giving
her all the answer she needed. 'Oh, my goodness! I *was*
too brazen. I'm sorry, Jack—I don't have much experience of kissing and…well…kissing you was more than
a little bit overwhelming.' Letty had the urge to cover
her breasts with her hands because he'd seen them, or
at least one of them. Her hands flapped ineffectually
in the vicinity of them, causing his eyes to widen even
more, so, swamped with shame and self-loathing, she
covered her face with them instead. 'I behaved like a
hussy, didn't I?'

There was a long, loaded pause. The only sounds
filling the silence were the laboured sounds of Jack's
breathing as he tried to think of a polite way to tell her
she had disgusted him with her shamelessness. Letty
heard him move towards the hay bales and lower himself heavily on to one of them. It sounded as if he was
trying to calm his breathing by inhaling deeply.

'No, you didn't. Please don't think you did anything
wrong. I just… God, this is awkward.' Jack sounded as
miserable as she felt. She risked a glance at him and
saw his expression appear completely wretched as well,
sat there with his hands tucked underneath his thighs,
his posture rigid. 'You are under my care, Letty. I cannot protect you properly if my mind is elsewhere. Does
that make sense?'

'And kissing me sends your mind elsewhere?'

'Kissing you sends me out of my mind, woman! I'm only human.'

Although it was a pretty compliment, he did not appear to be particularly happy about it. Carefully, she moved towards the bale and sat down next to him. 'Kissing you sent me out of my mind, too, Jack. If we both feel the same way about it, surely that is a good thing?'

He shot her an odd look through half-hooded eyes and shook his head decisively. 'It's lust, Letty. Pure, raw, human lust. Nothing more. Don't try to rationalise it as anything else.'

'It could be...' He stayed her with his hand.

'No, Letty. It couldn't.' He shook his head again and sighed. When he next spoke, he did so kindly, as if to a child. Or a woman with an addled mind who struggled to see the nose on her own face. 'I won't lie to you and pretend it could lead anywhere, even though doing so would be in my best financial interest and would completely benefit me in the long run. Once the lust is spent, Letty, there would be nothing left between us and I respect you too much to ruin your life like that. If things had gone any further the other night, we would have had to marry, and once you realised the truth, you would quickly have come to regret it. We Warriners are not good with wives.'

Well, that killed her blossoming hope stone dead, swiftly and clinically.

An emphatic no.

No maybe. No perhaps. No hesitation. Just no. He desired her body, albeit temporarily, but not her. Whilst the rejection cut like a knife in her gut, at least he was honest. There were no games with Jack Warriner. 'I suppose I should thank you for your principles. Most men of my acquaintance would have happily ruined me in order to marry me.'

'I dare say they would happily marry you before ruining you, too. You are a beautiful woman.'

'I doubt they truly notice my face. My looks, nor my character, hardly matter when I come with such an enormous mountain of money.' Letty stood despondently and walked towards the door. At least being desired for only her body was marginally more palatable than just her purse. There was something about her that Jack found attractive, even if the idea of spending a lifetime with her was wholly unappealing. His passion and desire had been genuine. He simply knew he could never love her enough to spend a lifetime with her.

'You are being too hard on yourself. I am informed you are courted by all manner of worthy men. Even a wealthy duke. Once I return you safely home, you will see things with clarity again. You belong in Mayfair with a man like him, with your fancy clothes and an army of servants. I don't mean to hurt your feelings, Letty. I am simply being a pragmatist. You have a particular life to live and so do I. Your life is in London, at parties and soirées, surrounded by your admirers, and mine is here, and that is how it should be. You were not born to be a Nottinghamshire farmer's wife any more than I could pretend to enjoy the superficial conversation of the privileged.'

He smiled, as if it could soften the blow he had just dealt her. 'The trouble with our current situation is that everything is exaggerated. We have been thrust together, when under normal circumstances our paths would never have crossed. But they did, under an extreme set of conditions where our emotions are heightened and everything feels intense. But it's not real, Letty. We are like oil and water, you and I. No matter how hard we tried, we could never mix.'

More painful honesty that threw salt on her already gaping wound. She should have ignored Jamie and continued pummelling her bread dough. At least then she had been only angry and confused. Now she felt truly bereft, spoiled and insignificant. *Superficial.* The first time she had made tentative advances towards a man she actually trusted, a good man who would not take her money, and humbled herself by suggesting that there could be more between them because she had *wanted* there to be more between them, and her worst fears were confirmed. When the lure of her fortune was stripped away, Letty really had nothing except a pretty face going for her. It was a hard, cruel way to learn that lesson.

Letty lingered in the doorway, tempted to tell him that there was more to her. That she had plans to help people with her money. Make the lives of lonely orphans, like her, easier. Make a difference because she hated the parties, soirées and disingenuous admirers— but she knew he wouldn't listen. Like her uncle, he did not think her capable of such depth so she painted on one of Violet's sunniest, emotionally vapid smiles. The one which told the world she was perfectly comfortable with a situation and had already forgotten why she had been bothered by it in the first place. 'You are probably right. The circumstances we find ourselves in are somewhat unique. Thank goodness you are so sensible.' She only had to survive for two, interminable weeks in his company, then she could go home and lick her wounds in private. Immerse all of her frustration and passion in the poor foundlings and prove everyone wrong about her. Including him. It was cold comfort. For the first time since she had arrived at Markham Manor, Letty wanted to leave.

'I suppose we should begin to plan how I am to safely return to London now that the Earl of Bainbridge has seemingly given up his search here. I don't want to walk straight into a waiting trap—and I suspect that will be their next plan of action in this whole ghastly mess.'

Jack, understandably, appeared greatly relieved by her change of subject. 'Yes...definitely. Why don't we all discuss it over dinner tonight?' He retrieved the fallen log from the floor and placed it end up on the ground, effectively dismissing her from his presence with the gesture. He was already swinging his axe before she closed the door behind her.

The loud explosion made the windows rattle while the accompanying burst of lightning lit up the bedchamber with the mouldy walls. Jack forced his exhausted, sleep-numbed mind to focus as he sat bolt upright in the bed he'd slept in ever since Letty had recovered enough not to need him to sleep on her floor. The leadlight glass sounded as if it was being pelted with handful after handful of gravel. He came to rapidly, blinking hard to squeeze blurriness from his eyes, then padded to the window and yanked open the heavy curtains to squint outside and groaned.

The storm that raged was one of the most ferocious Jack had ever witnessed. He could just make out the shapes of trees in the darkness, their branches bent over from the power of the wind. Rain fell in sheets rather than drops, pouring down the window pane like a waterfall. Another clap of thunder rumbled ominously, closely followed by the blinding light of a mighty fork of lightning. It split the sky and briefly, terrifyingly, illuminated the swollen banks of the river. So swollen now, the trees on the top of the steeply inclined bank were standing in a foot or more of boiling, furious water.

Another handful of gravel hit the window and he realised it was hail. Only small hail, but enough to panic the sheep, who were probably already panicked quite enough by the wind, rain, thunder and lightning. If they ran for the cover of the trees near the river bank, the stupid animals would likely be swept away on the current. And there he had been, less than an hour or so ago, praying for something, anything, which would take his mind off Letty and allow him to finally get some undisturbed sleep. There was nothing like the threat of impending doom and the prospect of several hours outside battling against the elements to distract him from his unwanted, but incessant, thoughts about her.

Jack was in the process of buttoning the falls on his hastily dragged-on breeches when Jamie stepped through his door. 'Good. You're up.'

As his brother was already wearing his greatcoat, it was fair to assume that Jamie, as usual, had not bothered going to bed. 'Have you woken Joe and Jacob yet?' Jack tugged on one boot as he hopped on the spot before collapsing to sit back on the bed to pull on the other.

'They're dressing, too. I'll meet you downstairs.'

Less than a minute later, Jack strode on to the landing, only to be confronted by the sight of Letty looking deliciously sleep rumpled at her door. She had only opened the door enough to poke her head around, but Jack saw the tantalising glimpse of a female leg where it poked beneath the hem of yet another one of his shirts and the sight irritated him. The blasted woman was handy with a needle. She had started embroidering little patterns on everything from napkins to pillowcases. Weeks ago, she had begun making a dress—which was still not finished—so why could she not fashion herself a proper nightdress? One that came to the floor and covered all of her soft, silken skin. And while she was about it, she should probably plait the wild, golden riot of curls that hung past her shoulders and tempted him to touch. An ugly nightcap would not go amiss either.

'What's happening?' she asked.

'There's a storm. We need to round up the animals. Go back to bed Letty. You're in no danger.'

'I can help.'

Jack was in no mood to be tactful. 'No, you can't. Go back to bed.'

The storm would take his mind off her; he didn't need the additional burden of an heiress faffing about and getting in his way when he had a serious job to do. He saw her fine eyes narrow just before she slammed the door shut and he turned away, striding briskly to the stairs. It was just as well. If she had argued with him, he would have bitten back twice as hard. Lack of sleep always brought his temper close to the surface and, as Letty was responsible for the deficiency, he doubted any confrontation would end well tonight. Not after their splendid chat in the barn earlier, when she had thanked him for being so sensible, then blithely gone about her day as if the words he had wrenched out of his gut and choked hollowly out of his mouth had not sounded the death knell on all his secret hopes of a miracle.

She might have argued then, as she was prone to

when she heartily disagreed with something, and perhaps given some credence to the idea that their two worlds could merge if they both wanted them to. But of course she hadn't. Only a tiny part of him had expected her to—a part which he hadn't even realised existed until he had categorically listed for her all the reasons why there was nothing except lust between them. Even as he said the words he knew them to be false. What he felt for Letty was more than just desire. He genuinely admired her tenacity and her sunny disposition. Her indomitable spirit. The woman never let anything beat her, whether that be kidnappers or roasted chickens. And since the very first moment he had found her frozen and terrified in the road, a part of his jaded, wary, Warriner heart would always be hers. Yearned to be hers. Maybe those rash feelings were due to his customary and ever-present sense of responsibility—but if that was entirely the case, why, when he had held her chilled body in his arms that night, had her presence in them felt so very…right?

If only she had been a random, ordinary girl of no consequence instead of The Tea Heiress. Then maybe he would have stood a chance and taken a gamble. It didn't help knowing, thanks to hours of rifling through Jacob's collection of newspapers when nobody was looking, that when the newsmen wrote the words *Tea Heiress* they were always put in italics, as if she were so special, so above everyone else, that only a select few in society were on a par with her. Now he knew her, he realised they were right. Letty was an incomparable…and so very far out of his reach as to be laughable.

Unfortunately, that same tiny part of him which had held out for the miracle earlier was now disproportion-

ately grieving the inevitable loss of her in his life, even
though he never really stood a chance of her remaining
in it. He had also read about *her* life in those same newspapers and it was a life he could never hope to give her.
The finest clothes, balls, jewels and a prominent and re-
vered place in society. The moment Jack had reminded
her of her wealthy Duke, she'd nodded and smiled and
immediately switched her thoughts to getting home to
Mayfair. Which had been his intention. Because any
hope of a future between them was ridiculous. Wasn't
it? So he should be happy he had been the sensible one.

But he wasn't.

'We need all the ropes we can carry.' His three brothers were assembled in the kitchen, the lanterns already
lit. 'The river has burst its banks. If one of us has to
venture into it, then we'll be tethered to something first.
If we drive the sheep to the west pasture, they will be
safe. Jamie—check on the horses, then the cows. See
that none of them have injured themselves.'

His brother's face clouded with barely suppressed
fury. 'I am not a blasted invalid, Jack. I'll help you
three with the sheep first. The horses and damned cows
can wait!'

'I'll see to the horses and cows.' Jack spun around
to see Letty marching towards him in a greatcoat that
swamped her and wearing an expression of complete
and total defiance. Jamie nodded and handed her a
lantern, clearly delighted not to be relegated to lighter
duties because of his injuries.

'Go back to bed, Letty! It's dangerous out there.'
And Jack could already feel the beginnings of a knot
of worry at the thought of her out in that storm. The

last time she had been exposed to bad weather she had almost died. 'This is no place for a woman like you.'

She marched fearlessly in front of him and stuck out her chin, not the slightest bit intimidated by the angry way he loomed over her. 'I am not some silly, spoiled, empty-headed fool.' Her finger prodded him firmly in the chest. 'And whilst your brothers might well listen to your orders, you are not my master Jack Warriner. Or my husband. And you never will be. So don't expect me to obey you. I am helping. Deal with it.' She spun on her heel and stomped stubbornly towards the back door. Without a backward glance, she flung it open and flounced into the raging tempest.

Chapter Fifteen

~~~~~~~~~~~~~~~~~~~~

Fourteen days and approximately twenty-two hours of misery left...

The tiny hailstones burned her face as they blew about in the wind, but Letty ignored them. Jack's idea that she should stay in bed when there were potentially distressed animals on the estate was ludicrous. It was not as if she had actually been sleeping. Try as she might, sleep had proved to be elusive after he had knocked her down a peg or two earlier. More than a peg or two, if she were being honest with herself. In actual fact, Letty felt as if her legs had been brutally cut out from under her. Now the hurt she had felt at his words had curdled and marinated into anger. How dare he suggest she was not up to the task of being a Nottinghamshire farmer's wife! Since she had been ripped from Mayfair, she had attacked task after task and emerged victorious.

Jack's pithy assessment of her lifestyle grated. Superficial conversation for the privileged. Balls, soirées, jewels, fancy clothes. All external trimmings which had absolutely nothing to do with who she really was inside.

Just like everyone else of her acquaintance, the thick-skulled eldest Warriner could not see further than skin deep. Letty was more than all that and, if Jack couldn't see it, then, quite frankly he didn't deserve her either. And she was not some feeble, delicate ornament incapable of knowing her own mind!

She slammed into the cow barn first. Aside from the noisy mooing one would expect from cattle in the midst of a thunderstorm, everything appeared all right. To be sure, Letty held her lantern aloft and checked each beast as best she could for signs of injury or undue distress. Finding nothing, she distributed some fresh hay and water before securing the barn door carefully closed and battling her way across the yard to the other barn where the horses were kept.

The closer she got, the clearer Letty could hear the door to the barn swinging noisily against the hinges. The wind must have dislodged it and the bashing sound would only serve to spook the horses. She dashed inside and was not even slightly surprised to hear the sounds of agitated animals in the pitch-black enclosure. Again, as she had in the cow shed, she raised the lantern to check on each one and began soothing the mounts by stroking their muzzles and whispering words of reassurance. It took a few moments to realise the end stall, Satan's stall, was open.

Letty went to it, peered inside and, finding it empty, used the glow of the lantern to search the rest of the cavernous building for signs of Jamie's temperamental horse. But it was nowhere. Outside, in the storm, with thunder, hail and explosive lightning, she seriously feared for the animal's safety. This was really not the night for the horse to go wandering around loose.

Making sure the rest of the animals were secured, Letty grabbed a set of leather reins hanging on the far wall. If she could locate Satan, she would need to put him in a halter in order to bring him back safely. She bent to pick up the lantern again, then plunged into the dark field beyond the barn, hoping against hope it would be miraculously easy to find a jet-black horse in the oppressive darkness.

After twenty minutes of searching, she caught sight of the men in the field beyond. With their similar heights and appearances, it was difficult to discern who was who from a distance. However, the closer she got, it became obvious which one was Jack. It stood to reason that he would be the one who put himself in the most peril. Currently, he was thigh deep in the raging water, holding a wriggling sheep in his arms and wading back. Behind him, the river gushed violently, tossing the occasional broken tree branch effortlessly up into the air before sucking it mercilessly under the water. Surely, he didn't put the life of his sheep above the safety of his own?

Without thinking, she broke into a run to drag him away from the danger. When she got nearer, Letty noticed he had thick rope knotted around his waist and shoulders. The other end of the rope was tied to Jamie and wound around the trunk of a sturdy tree. Jamie spotted her first and waved. She could just about hear his voice over the gale as he pointed.

'Help Joe and Jacob move the sheep!'

For a second, she hesitated, as the need to reassure herself of Jack's safety warred with her desire to help, but when she saw him deposit the sheep carefully on solid ground and glare back at her menacingly, the decision was easy to make. She knew exactly what he would say. *Go inside, Letty.* As if she were wholly useless. This field, in the midst of this storm, was no place for a silly, decorative society princess. Letty turned to search for the two youngest Warriners and saw them just to the west. She headed directly towards them until something else, something big, frightened and horse-shaped appeared in her peripheral vision.

It took Jack far longer than necessary to reach his brother. The ground was like a bog, sucking on the soles of his boots and hampering every stride. When he reached him, Jack didn't mince his words.

'Go after Letty and send her indoors!' He had no idea what Jamie had thought he was doing to send her to help the others, but a raging storm was the very last place on earth he wanted her to be. Not after the last time.

'Don't be daft, Jack. Letty is perfectly capable of rounding up some sheep.'

Jack folded his arms belligerently in the stance he knew his younger brothers called his Do-As-I-Command posture. 'I don't *want* her rounding up sheep. I *want* her out of harm's way. She's not built for this sort of work. Any fool can see how delicate she is!'

'Letty? Delicate? That girl is as strong as an ox. She can move furniture on her own, remember? And clean several years' worth of grime in minutes.'

Jack winced. He hated the fact that Letty still cleaned for them. When he had initially told her to earn her keep, he had never actually intended for her to do anything, it was merely a tactic to put her in her place that one time. Very well, she had done a splendid job that first time and one which had made him feel bad for underestimating her, but he had certainly not wanted her to continue to do it. Yet every day, his house improved as a result of her labours and every day he felt guiltier and guiltier she had to demean herself like that. His mother had never lifted a finger. Would never have dreamed of lifting a finger. And now Letty was demeaning herself here, too, being pelted with rain and hail, getting soaked to her lovely skin and covered in muck. 'I want her inside!' he roared.

Jamie nudged him and pointed back towards the river bank. 'There's another one.'

The stupid sheep stared back at him in a blind panic, its hooves slipping as it struggled to maintain its footing on the steep bank already under several inches of water. With a groan, Jack ensured the rope about his middle was tight and trudged back towards the water.

Being a sheep, and therefore in possession of absolutely no sense, the animal fought against being rescued. Jack was breathless by the time he had wrestled it free and his leg muscles were screaming from the exertion. His passage back towards firmer land was painfully slow and, as he traipsed towards his brother, he automatically scanned the horizon to check on Letty. He soon spied Joe and close by him Jacob, but there was no sign of the petite, stubborn vixen who didn't do as she was told. Perhaps she had found the going hard and given up already? He certainly hoped she had.

Relieved, he turned back towards Jamie, only to see his brother's eyes widen ominously. Jack followed his gaze off into the distance and made out the small square of light from a lantern on the ground. Thunder began to rumble, then an enormous fork of lightning crackled overhead, illuminating the field and silhouetting Letty. She was walking, hands outstretched, towards a rearing, kicking Satan. Jack experienced a moment of sheer, gut-wrenching terror.

'Letty, stop!'

The gale took his warning and blew it back in his face and the pasture was plunged into darkness again. Both Jack and Jamie hastily tugged at the rope that bound them together, clawing at the sopping knots with chilled fingers until they gave.

'That horse will kill her if she goes near it.'

His brother's stark words echoed Jack's own fears. Letty might well have a soft spot for horses, but Satan had earned his evil name fair and square. Once he was untied, he stumbled towards her, calling for her to put a stop to her madness. Either she did not hear or she did not listen, leaving him powerless to do anything but watch the awful drama unfolding before his eyes.

She lunged and caught the horse around the neck, hugging him and, from his position too far away, it looked as if she was talking the beast. It fought against her hold at first, then miraculously stilled. He watched her retrieve a halter from her shoulder and slip it over the animal's enormous head, all the while soothing him with her palms and voice. Within moments, the horse was obediently following her as she tugged gently on the reins, but not back towards the barn, towards the low stone wall which separated this pasture from the next. It was only when she clambered to stand atop the wall that Jack realised what she intended to do and fresh panic surged through him, forcing his tired legs to pump the ground to reach her before she effectively committed suicide.

But without a saddle, and while another rumble of thunder sounded ominously overhead, she climbed on to Satan's back, her golden head bent low over his so that he could hear her. The huge horse reared then, causing Jack's heart to skip a beat, yet she held her seat magnificently, holding the reins with one hand while the other smoothed down the stallion's mane. Satan's jerky motions calmed slowly, and as if nothing at all was the matter, he finally came to stand obediently beneath her.

They stood like that for several moments while Jack stood frozen to the spot, too scared to move in case he spooked the horse and signed her death warrant. But to his horror, Letty gathered the reins tighter, and before Jack knew what was happening, she set off swiftly. Fearlessly. Heading towards the scattered sheep, leaving Jack powerless to stop her.

He stood breathless and gaped at the spectacle. Despite the howling wind and violent storm, Letty had full control of the enormous beast. As another tremendous crack of lightning set the sky ablaze, she galloped to the rear of the furthest sheep and began to herd them towards the open gate of the west pasture, using Satan like a mighty, disciplined sheepdog, which she rode instead of whistled at. By the time Jamie caught up with him, all the pair of them could do was stand and watch as she made short work of finishing what the men had started and failed to achieve.

'I see exactly what you mean,' Jamie drawled as the last sheep disappeared into the adjoining field, 'Your Letty is a delicate one.'

'For the last time, she's not *my* Letty,' he said through gritted teeth.

'Yes, she is. The girl is mad for you. It's beyond me why you are so hell-bent on resisting her.'

Jack felt his throat constrict at the memories. 'You know why, Jamie. This place is not suitable for a gently bred woman.'

Jamie turned slowly and stared. 'Because of what happened to our mother?'

Jack did not want his brother to see how much the painful recollections hurt and how much his feeble attempts at easing her burdens had failed, so he stared out towards the raging river rather than meet his eye. 'She came from London, too. You saw what living here did to her.'

'Our mother was delicate—that I do agree with. But in spirit, Jack, not body. Every memory I have of the woman is of her complaining about her lot in life, blaming our father, or us, for her situation rather than doing something about it all.'

'She was miserable because of our father's selfishness. I won't do that to Letty.'

'No, Jack. Our mother was just miserable! Did it ever occur to you that she had a hand in what happened to her, too? Our father had a terrible reputation long before he met her, yet she allowed him to seduce her. People don't change. Did she think he would? She was one of the most selfish people I have ever known. All she ever cared about was herself. How unhappy with her lot she was. How difficult her life was. She wasn't a mother, Jack. As a parent, she was no better than our useless father. Thank God we all had you, else I don't doubt we'd have turned out little better than feral.'

In the distance, they heard the whoops of joy as Joe finally closed the gate on the last of the sheep. Letty held Satan on the spot, effortlessly using only the lightest touch on the reins while Jacob appeared to be congratulating her. She threw her head back and laughed, enjoying her moment of triumph, then her gaze locked on to his across the field and neither the distance nor the darkness could not diminish the defiant pride which radiated off her as she sat astride Jamie's unmanageable horse.

He could just imagine her thoughts. *You underestimated me, farm boy, and I proved you wrong.* She kept proving him wrong. So much so, he was starting to doubt his own firmly held beliefs.

'Letty wasn't born for this sort of life.' Just because she could round up frightened, scattered sheep in the rain didn't mean that she should. In her world, such degradation would be unheard of.

'You're probably right, Big Brother.' Jamie spun on his heel and began to limp towards the celebration. 'The girl managed to thwart a gang of kidnappers and escape from a moving carriage unaided. She should have frozen to death or died of fever afterwards, but within a few days she was up and about. And, of course, she is so delicate that she doesn't balk at the challenge of single-handedly cleaning a mansion *and* she can tame a crazed, temperamental horse by riding it bareback in a thunderstorm. The more I think upon it, Jack, the more she resembles our mother in her weak character. Being leg-shackled to an imbecile like you might be the one thing that breaks her.'

Chapter Sixteen

Eleven interminable days to get through...

It had been an uncomfortable few days. In a reversal of roles, it was Letty who now avoided Jack. The bitter sting of his rejection still hurt and she was counting down the hours until she could leave so that she would be spared the trauma of seeing him again. Each time she looked at him, his well-meant words flooded back and alternately upset her or spiked her temper. To make matters worse, Letty was certain she kept catching him staring at her, a slightly perplexed expression on his handsome face, almost as if she were some peculiar specimen he was studying through a microscope and one which he could never hope to understand. It was most unnerving.

Even mealtimes were awkward. Not with everyone else, of course, just with Jack. Both of them actively joined in the boisterous conversations, but they were careful to avoid directly answering or directing comments at each other. At times, it became almost impossible to keep track of it all and Letty's near-constant state of self-consciousness, growing lack of confidence and her determination to hide it all behind the cheerful façade of Violet was becoming exhausting.

The only light at the end of the tunnel was that Letty would be leaving in a week. Four days before her twenty-first birthday Jack had decided they would journey to London. He planned to do the journey in segments, travelling overnight so as not to arouse suspicion and resting during the daylight hours well away from prying eyes. With a reward for one thousand pounds hanging over her head, reporting a sighting of Letty was potentially the most lucrative Christmas present anyone would ever receive. She made no arguments on his insistence they err on the side of caution. Once in London, she would be handed over to the authorities where she could finally bring her uncle and Bainbridge to justice.

Whether or not Jack would be staying to witness the ugly aftermath, she had no idea and her pride would not allow her to ask. She was putting all of that nonsense out of her head for the time being. It was what it was. All she could say with any certainty was that she would soon be all alone in the world again, devoid of any real human attachments and with only her money to keep her company. It was cold comfort for a woman whose dearest wish was to belong somewhere and be understood. No, that was a lie. She wanted to belong *here*. With Jack. Never mind—she had had real plans before she had met the man, plans that did not include a patronising male who thought he knew best, and she would start on them the second the ink was dry on the official papers giving her control over her own fortune.

Jack might not need her. but those foundlings did. She would belong with them and he would be forgotten.

Or so she hoped.

With a sigh, she reached for the greatcoat by the back door. Today was Christmas Eve, and Letty was damned if she would allow her melancholy to spoil her plans for the festivities. Right now, because she could finally risk going outside in daylight, she was going to fetch holly to decorate the great hall in readiness. Tomorrow afternoon, after the essential farm chores were done, they were going to celebrate properly. Jamie had killed a fat goose which was hanging ready to be roasted in the oven and Joe had gone to the village to buy some wine to accompany their feast. With Jacob, Letty had organised games for afterwards and she had made each of the brothers a small gift. It was nothing special, only handkerchiefs she had embroidered using their mother's old silk threads, but each one had the man's name and a pattern which suited his character. Jamie's had colourful paint palettes and brushes, Jacob's had books and newspapers and for Joe she had recreated the snake-and-staff motif used by healers since ancient times.

Jack's handkerchief was a cause for concern, but it was far too late to change it now. She had been umming and ahhing for days about whether or not it was appropriate, being uncharacteristically indecisive, to the extent that it was now far too late to change it even if she wanted to. Which she definitely did. Unsurprisingly, she had made his first and put far too much care into the design. If compared alongside his brothers', it would be plain to see it had been made by a woman completely besotted. But Letty had made it before she had humiliated herself before him in the barn and then could not bring herself to change it because to do so involved thinking about him, when she would prefer to avoid doing that at all costs. It was a decision which would probably come back to haunt her. Everyone knew what a lion symbolised.

The whole of England was peppered with them. The monarch's crest had three, for pity's sake, and every other door knocker in Mayfair had one. Lions stood for power, strength, courage and fortitude. Four attributes which Jack Warriner possessed in spades. However, for Letty it stood for Jack's other attributes, too. Loyalty. Self-sacrifice. Leadership. He was the unchallenged leader of this pride. The king of all beasts had seemed strangely fitting for a man who allowed himself no time for hobbies. Their protector. Her protector.

Her rejecter now as well, which was as devastating as it was humiliating.

Why hadn't she chosen something more innocuous and perhaps a little insulting, like a sheep? Jack owned sheep and they vexed him a great deal. He thought them stupid creatures. Last night, she had considered unpicking her work and replacing the majestic lion's head with a fat, woolly sheep just to spite him, except, she was concerned he might see this as a reminder of her shameless reaction to him when she had first witnessed him pulling one of the stupid creatures from the mud. He must have noticed she had become a flushed, stuttering fool at the sight of his bare chest. Jamie certainly had. However, the awful truth was that Letty would blush scarlet when she gave it to him, no matter which design she had chosen. At least she could fib her way out of the lion.

It could, she reasoned, also represent his superior,

dictatorial manner, aloofness and coldness. From what she had read, your average lion would not think twice about ruthlessly killing its prey and eating it, just as Jack had not so much as blinked when he had denounced her existence as superficial and privileged. If questioned, she had already prepared a little speech to make the others laugh and put their eldest brother in his place. Letty hoped she didn't have to use it because none of it was true. She adored the fact he was noble and steadfast. In a world where Letty found it difficult to truly trust anyone, she trusted Jack implicitly. Heart and soul. He always did what was right and proper. He was reliably, solidly responsible.

However, she hated that he insisted on maintaining those iron-clad morals all of the time. Just once, she wished he would forget about them, kiss her and lose his mind completely. The noble Jack was so frustrating, or perhaps it was simply because *she* was frustrated.

Using shears, she snipped boughs of holly from a bush which was a bit sparse. The leaves were curled and browning without a single berry in sight. Disappointed, she scanned the grounds for a better specimen. Off into the distance, close to the river's edge, she thought she spied something red and walked towards it. On closer inspection, it proved to be the perfect example of a Christmas decoration. Shiny, waxy green leaves resplendent with ripe, crimson berries. She was so excited with the find and engrossed in cutting armfuls of the stuff, she failed to notice the two children peeking at her from behind a matching holly bush on the opposite bank. Nor did Letty see them scurry off before she bent down to gingerly pick up her thorny decorations and drag them carefully back to the house.

* * *

Jack had got up especially early today in order to be finished, and bathed, in time for the planned dinner. He couldn't remember when he had looked forward to a Christmas Day as much as he did this one. Christmas had always been a day much like any other in Markham Manor. When his mother had been alive, he had vague recollections of fraught Christmas dinners in the formal dining room, which inevitably deteriorated into another violent argument between their parents. After his mother had died, his father preferred to spend the entirety of Christmas in a state of constant inebriation, but then again, as he was so regularly in that state, it had not exactly been a surprise. He couldn't remember presents or games, and the Warriner brothers had barely acknowledged the significance of the day in the years since. It was just another day of sweat and toil.

This time, there was an unmistakable atmosphere of excitement in the house which dragged him along with it, whether he wanted it to or not, and that came directly from Letty. The woman was determined to have a proper Christmas and had roped his brothers into her plans. Entertainments were planned, every nook, cranny and surface in the great hall was bursting with sprigs of holly and the festive aroma of cinnamon and baking had tickled his nostrils whenever he set foot in the kitchen. Joe and Jacob had been talking about it for days and even Jamie appeared a little cheered by the prospect.

All three of his brothers had quietly explained to him that there would be presents, all homemade and inexpensive, and that he should probably acquire something nice for Letty. After racking his brains for ideas and having no talent for making anything at all, he was quietly confident he had found her something nice although it was not homemade. It also, in all probability, would earn him a sound ribbing from his brothers. But she deserved it regardless. A small token of his gratitude for all of the work she had done in his home and for bringing the old place alive these last few weeks. He already knew Markham Manor would feel cold and empty when she left. He felt cold and empty himself knowing that day was rapidly drawing near.

Since their last conversation, she had resolutely, but politely, avoided him. Not that Jack could blame her. With the benefit of hindsight, he could see he had been dismissive and harsh, and a huge part of him bitterly regretted it. At the time, he had hoped to nip their inappropriate attraction for one another in the bud. He had been convinced Letty was unsuited to the life he could offer her. After witnessing her conquer Satan during the storm, he was prepared to concede he had unfairly underestimated her, which then led to him wondering if he had made a terrible mistake. Perhaps, at the time, he should have welcomed her tentative suggestion that there could be more between them? Jack still couldn't get over her admission that his kisses had driven her out of her mind. Only a fool would turn down such a wonderful woman, which meant, as he had long suspected, he was the biggest fool to ever walk the earth.

However, in view of her new reluctance to have anything to do with him, and her constant excited chatter about her impending return to Mayfair, it was probably for the best. Even if he had succumbed to temptation, she would have come to her senses eventually and regretted him—regretted them—and he was not certain he could bear that. It was better to extinguish all hope than to have to witness her inevitable disgust of him.

He hoped this little memento might make her eventually come to remember her time with him fondly, but he suspected once he was out of sight, and she was surrounded by her sort of people, Jack would be out of her mind. Ironic, really, when he was slowly going out of his. Good grief, she had made him utterly pathetic!

Jack dragged on a clean shirt and popped his gift safely in his pocket before heading downstairs. His brothers were already seated at the formal dining table, each with their hair combed and wearing their Sunday best. Dishes filled with potatoes and a steaming array of vegetables covered the linen-draped table. Where had she found a tablecloth? Jack never knew they possessed one. It all looked, and smelled, quite splendid. He scanned the room quickly for Letty, which typically, Jamie noticed straight away.

'Letty has gone to get the goose,' he explained, starting to rise. 'I should probably help her. That bird is heavy.'

Jack quickly stepped in. 'I will go.' It might be his only opportunity today to see her on her own and give her his inappropriate gift away from prying eyes. He walked briskly towards the kitchen and stopped dead.

Letty was wearing a dress.

Jack had never seen her in dress before, aside from the one ruined, soaked one she had arrived in which didn't count, and the unexpected sight of it was quite overwhelming. She turned towards him and he watched her green eyes widen with surprise.

'Oh! Hello, Jack.'

Her golden curls were arranged on top of her head,

exposing the swanlike curve of her neck. The bodice of her dress was cut in a scoop. The merest hint of cleavage rose above it; acres of creamy, alabaster skin were on display for his greedy gaze to feast upon. Even the sight of her bare arms, beneath the feminine capped sleeves, reminded him that he was a man and she was a woman. A very beautiful woman. A beautiful and very passionate woman. Instinctively, and completely beyond his control, his groin tightened and Jack was grateful that, for once, he had put on a coat.

'I've come to carry the goose.'

His voice came out gruff, angry. Hardly festive. And he had no idea what to do with his hands. Why now, after all of this time, had she decided to finally finish making the blasted dress? Letty in breeches was a temptation. Letty in a gown was pure torture.

'Here it is.' She smiled tightly and gestured to a huge platter on the table. 'If you carry that in, I shall bring the gravy.'

She picked up the gravy boat and briskly manoeuvred around him to lead the way, clearly keen not to be left alone with him. With a sinking feeling, Jack heaved the platter into his arms and trailed after her. The view was almost as breathtaking from the rear. The neckline of the gown dipped low, showing the delicate shape of her shoulder blades and the velvety skin on her back. The fabric draped along the contours of her body, highlighting the womanly flair of her hips and the juicy peach of her bottom as it swayed before him. Jack gripped the platter for grim death, fearing his stupid knees might buckle from sheer lust, sending her lovely Christmas dinner crashing to the ground.

They sat at the table. As far as Jack could see, the

impact of Letty in a gown had no effect on the others. Either they had already seen her and recovered from the shock or the only man she had the power to bewitch was him. To his consternation, his brothers insisted he carve the bird as the head of the household, effectively putting him on display when he was in no fit state to be so. Having a throbbing bulge in his breeches, obviously he made a hash of it. Stupid, *stupid*, uncultured, clumsy fool! It would have been more fitting if he had simply torn the goose limb from limb with his bare hands like the most uncivilised of savages.

Conversation flowed around him and Jack did his best to join in, only his eyes kept drifting towards Letty as he picked at his food and chewed without tasting it.

'What is the first thing you are going to do when you get back to town, Letty?' Jacob kept asking for titbits of society gossip because that world intrigued him. Each one served to remind Jack he was unworthy of her.

She shrugged her slim shoulders and beamed at his brother. 'I don't know. Something *frivolous*, I suppose, like shopping on Bond Street.' Jack could have sworn he saw her eyes flick to his defiantly on the word frivolous, but it was so fleeting he might have imagined it. 'Actually, the truth is I am going to build a home for foundlings. It breaks my heart when I see those lonely children huddled on the street begging for scraps because they have no one to care for them.' The passion in her tone humbled him. 'I have visited some of the orphanages in town and they horrify me. The children are treated like prisoners, as if they have committed some heinous crime rather than suffered the death of their parents. I want to create something different. Not a cold institution, but a home with a heart. My children will be taught to read and trained to earn a decent living when they are finally old enough to go out into the world. I don't want them having to resort to crime or the worst sort of menial work in order to eke out a living.'

It was all so worthy and he realised, with shame, something too close to her heart. Most people would see only her money and not the fact that she was an orphan.

'Well, I think that is admirable,' Joe said, obviously impressed. 'I should like to see it when it is built, Letty.'

'You must come and visit me, and I shall take you to see it myself.'

She was only being polite, but Jacob jumped at the invitation. 'We would love to. Can I come and visit you during the Season, too?'

Letty patted his arm affectionately. 'Of course. I shall have you escort me to all the *superficial* balls, parties and *soirées* I attend.' This time Jack was certain that her eyes flicked towards him with undisguised hostility before she grinned back at his brother. 'You can charm all of the young ladies.'

'As if an eligible young lady of the *ton* would look twice at him!' Joe scoffed just before he popped the last fluffy roast potato into his mouth.

'I believe I would cut quite a dash there,' said Jacob in his usual good-natured, slightly arrogant way.

'With your roguish charm, I fear for the hearts of the ladies, but then again I believe you would all cut a dash there. Three handsome brothers.' Another pointed look of disgust in Jack's direction as she deliberately cut him out. 'What young lady could resist you? One twirl around the dance floor and they would all be smitten.'

'Then I'm done for,' said Jamie wryly. 'My twirling days are over.'

'Ah, but, Jamie, you don't need to twirl. Once I casually drop into the conversation that you are a returned war hero, the women will swarm around you like flies around honey. The same goes for you, Joe. There is something about a learned doctor which ladies adore.'

'Will you introduce us to your dashing Duke as well?' Jacob said this without so much as a flicker of an eyebrow, but Jack was no fool. It had been a jibe designed to get a rise out of him. Ever since the night of the storm, all three of his brothers regularly pumped Letty for information about her Duke. Probably in a thinly veiled attempt to get him to show them he was jealous. He let the barb slide, as he had all the others. They could not understand why he resisted Letty— but then Joe and Jacob had been so young when their mother had died, so he doubted they remembered how living here, isolated in this desolate, crumbling prison, had ultimately destroyed her.

'I should be honoured to introduce you to the Duke of Wentworth. I am certain he would insist on meeting my brave rescuers without my having to prompt him.'

Jack forced himself to swallow the mouthful of food which had suddenly turned to chalk dust in his mouth. To hear Letty speak, the man was a paragon of virtue and the most perfect example of a proper society gentleman. Yesterday, he had endured the lengthy tale of how the illustrious Duke of Wentworth filled his splendid mansion with the most exquisite *objets d'art*. Soon, he would add Letty to his collection and Jack would hate him more than he did already.

'Then it's settled,' said Jacob decisively. 'We shall all visit you in Mayfair for the Season.'

The very last place Jack ever wanted to see Letty was in her natural habitat, with blasted Wentworth, surrounded by her own swarms of worthy flies he would enjoy personally swatting. With his fists.

'And who would run the farm, Jacob?'

Why had he sounded so churlish? His three brothers stared back at him with varying degrees of pity and despair as the atmosphere became strained. It was Letty who fixed things.

'Why, Jack, you would, of course. I doubt he has any interest in the *superficial* conversations of the privileged. I dare say, you three will have to visit me without him.' Hoisted by his own petard, he could do nothing but smile tightly and wish he was outside vigorously chopping wood. 'Shall we retire to the other room and swap presents?'

Letty sailed past him regally, apparently completely unperturbed by his curmudgeonly outburst, barely gracing him with a glance. Keen to regain the celebratory mood, his brothers tumbled out of the dining room behind her. Jamie punched him hard in the arm as he limped towards the door.

'Cretin.'

Jack supposed he deserved that, too. Letty was doing her best to behave as if nothing had happened, as Jack himself had implored, so why couldn't he? It had just been a harmless, meaningless conversation, with no firm plans set in stone. Why had he needed to throw his oar into the water and sour the mood?

Because he wanted her to believe he didn't care about her fancy Duke and was pretending nothing had happened, when *everything* had happened. Everything about the situation confused him, leaving Jack for once all at sea with no rudder to guide him. He set his shoulders and trudged into the great hall like a man on the way to his own execution.

Chapter Seventeen

❦

Nine days and approximately six hours until it's over...

Letty took her seat around the roaring fire and tried not to focus on Jack's blatant refusal to even consider maintaining their acquaintance once she was gone. At the very least, he could have pretended to care, although she already knew pretending was not something the man was capable of. If something was amiss or not to his liking, he was one for telling it like it was. Unfortunately, every time he told her what was what, Letty was always left feeling hurt by his brutal honesty. It was probably for the best. Her stupid, misguided heart would heal all the quicker knowing his was blissfully indifferent.

Joe walked towards her smiling, holding out a small gift wrapped in one of Jacob's newspapers. She decided there and then not to let Jack spoil her only family Christmas in almost four years. She grabbed it eagerly and undid the string which bound it. Two perfectly square cakes of perfumed soap sat within the wrinkled paper.

'I made them myself. I found a recipe for medicinal soap in one of my books and substituted the lye for lavender oil.'

Letty grabbed his lapels and kissed him on the cheek. 'I love them! Thank you. Before I go to bed I shall lounge in the bath for at least an hour.'

'You can have my present next.' Jamie reached behind his chair.

His present was bigger and also wrapped in newspaper. She unwrapped it and gasped at the beautiful watercolour in her hands. The detail was exquisite. 'Markham Manor...' Without thinking, Letty ran her fingertip lovingly along the painted edges of the quaint Tudor manor house and felt a surge of emotion. She was going to miss this place. It had become home in such a short period of time. But not as much as she would miss her temporary family. Jack's brothers had become her brothers. Losing them would be like a death and she would mourn the loss of them. 'I thought you might like something to remember us by.'

Tears formed in the corners of her eyes and Jamie stared back at her, alarmed. 'No waterworks, if you please, madam! I don't do emotional outbursts.' That was an understatement. Yet Letty knew his disinterested demeanour hid a deep well of emotions.

'You are a lovely man, James Warriner.'

He pretended to find her hug of gratitude distasteful. 'That's quite enough, thank you.'

'You're already wearing my present.' The youngest Warriner grinned. 'I already know you love it.'

'Yes, indeed. You certainly know what a lady likes.' All of the other brothers, including Jack, regarded them quizzically. Jack, she noted, also looked quite peeved.

'Jacob got me some hairpins.' Letty patted her coiffure for emphasis. 'Hence, I no longer look like a poodle.'

'Hairpins!' Jamie turned to his brother, outraged. 'Please tell me you didn't put Letty's safety at risk by buying them in the village.'

'Of course I didn't. What do you take me for? They came by way of that farmer's daughter I have been courting. Once I took them all out, I pretended to have lost the majority of them in the haystack we happened to be lying in. I would like it noted, I sacrificed *myself* for Letty's hairstyle.'

'And it was a very noble sacrifice, I'm sure. How you must have suffered...' Letty practically skipped over to the sideboard where she had hidden her gifts. 'I have made some things for you all, too.'

'Wait,' said Jamie pointedly, 'We haven't seen what Jack has got you yet.'

Much as she did not want to look directly at him, with so many eager onlookers, to do otherwise was rude. Jack met her gaze and appeared mortified. He stared down to his lap awkwardly. It was obvious he had not got her anything.

'You didn't forget, did you?' Joe asked slowly.

'Of course I didn't forget!' Jack unfolded his big body from the chair and edged towards Letty, looking likely to break into a run at any minute if given half the chance. Once he was in front of her, he frowned, appearing all stiff and, to her complete consternation, totally adorable. 'I wanted to give you something special. Seeing as you have worked so hard on behalf of myself and my brothers.' He still didn't look her in the eye. 'And...well...'

'Oh, spit it out, man!' Jamie rolled his eyes. 'I've never seen you so inarticulate.'

He shot his brother an evil glare, but he rummaged in his pocket and then unexpectedly took hold of her right hand. Letty watched transfixed as he slid a ring on to her finger. The band was gold; the square stone was a beautiful flat emerald.

'It's very old. Tudor, I believe. From Sir Hugo's day... Well anyway, I thought the emerald would complement your eyes...'

Her heartbeat suddenly speeded up as she stared at the lovely piece of jewellery, trying not to think about her body's immediate reaction to his touch or the fact she desperately wanted to tell him he had put the ring on the wrong hand.

'It's lovely. Thank you.'

He had noticed her eyes? What did that mean? And was he blushing? She was sure he was.

Letty had kissed the cheek of every man in the room except the one she most wanted to. All eyes, she realised, were now watching the pair of them closely. Too closely. Her breath became ragged and her lips tingled. To not kiss him would be poor form. But kissing him, after what had happened the last time, terrified her. Even a chaste kiss would serve as an uncomfortable reminder that he knew her passions were fired by him. Just thinking about doing it again made her limbs feel heavy and her head feel light.

She had also dithered a beat too long and Jack had taken a stilted step backwards. For some reason, even though she knew his true feelings, he appeared wounded by her hesitation. If ever there was a time for Violet's charming bravado, it was now.

'I shall treasure this, Jack.'

In one swift, decisive motion, Letty took a large stride forward and stood on her tiptoes, intending to bestow a light peck on his cheek, but his head turned towards hers and their lips brushed instead. The kiss was quick—but no less incendiary for it. Letty felt the power of it throughout her body as her nerve-endings positively exploded as if a fuse had been lit within her. Those first breaths afterwards were erratic. Jack stared back at her, stunned, and for one, brief moment, she considered kissing him again before she remembered she was currently supposed to be Violet. Charming. Detached. Superficial. As unaffected by him as he was by her. Except she might have begun the kiss as Violet, but it had been Letty's lips his had touched. Letty's heart which had soared. In a panic, she put some well-needed distance between them and her words tumbled out in a rush.

'I want you all to open my gifts at the same time, because, rather unoriginally, you all have the same thing.' Quickly, she distributed her packages and clapped her hands to signal the unwrapping could begin, all the while trying to ignore the shaky feeling in her legs and the steady, sure sound of her heart knocking against her ribs. Jack was too focused on untying the ribbons she had secured the tiny gifts with, so Letty assumed he was not similarly affected by the brief, intimate contact. He had probably done it on purpose to put her in her place for all of those petty jibes she had thrown at him over dinner. A reminder that he knew she was bluffing when she pretended he didn't matter. A way to regain the upper hand.

* * *

His fingers refused to work properly as Jack did his level best to undo the endearingly feminine bow and conceded he was having a bit of a moment. The emerald ring might as well have been a declaration of love! Good grief—what had he been thinking? And then he had had to touch her velvety skin and slip the ring on to her finger, and that felt like a declaration, too. A man only gave a woman one sort of ring... Oh, why had he done it in front of his brothers? The three of them now kept glancing at him knowingly and he would probably never live it down. There had been a ruby pendant in the box of old jewellery he'd unearthed. He should have given her that.

Not a ring.

But the ring, with its emerald the exact shade of her beguiling eyes, had called to him and, like a fool, Jack had listened. Then, because politeness, and only politeness, had dictated it, she had kissed him and instinctively he had turned to kiss her back, almost as if there was some sort of magnet pulling his mouth to hers. To all intents and purposes it should have felt like the platonic kiss she had meant it to be, except, the instant those soft lips had touched his, his skin had caught fire and his heart had literally swelled in his chest. Unfortunately, it was not the only swelling he was dealing with.

By accident, rather than design, the ribbon came apart at almost the same moment his brothers' did.

'Would you look at that?' Jamie actually grinned as he held up his gift. 'You're a fellow artist, Letty! The detail in this is astounding and the pattern is so personal to me.'

'Mine, too!' Joe displayed the medical motif. 'When

I finally qualify I shall carry this with me on all of my house calls.'

Jacob began to laugh at his. 'Letty, you are priceless.' He passed the square of fabric to Joe, who scrutinised the intricate stitching and began to laugh as well. 'Newspapers filled with gossip around every edge and a farmer's daughter in one corner! What did she make for you, Jack?'

In truth, he wasn't entirely sure what to make of it. The handkerchief was more elaborately embroidered than those of his brothers, but the golden lions around the edges in various poses all looked towards the magnificent male in the centre of the linen, who sat proudly staring out at him. He turned and searched Letty's face for clues and became more baffled when she refused to look at him. Was she blushing?

'I thought a lion would symbolise…um…the fact you are the undisputed leader of—'

Joe intervened. 'Our pride?'

'More like he's got too much stupid pride,' Jamie hissed in a poor attempt at a stage whisper.

'Lions are proud, noble and brave and so is Jack.' Letty's voice sounded a little squeaky, although she was smiling at everyone serenely. Jack didn't know whether to read anything more into her gift, or not.

Jacob leaned over to examine the handkerchief. 'Do lions usually have turquoise eyes?' Then he made a point of examining Jack's face and smiling slowly. The smile was apparently contagious, because it crept on to Joe's face next, then Jamie's, until the three of them were grinning like fools. 'Why, yours must have taken so many more hours to complete than ours!' It did beggar the question. If she had taken more care over his gift, did that mean she cared more for him? 'But I suppose Jack gave you an emerald when I only gave you soap, so I suppose his superior gift is fitting.'

Poor Letty appeared about to combust with embarrassment, she was so crimson, and, like Jack, she was clearly mortified by their reactions. They were reading meanings into Letty's gift which probably were not meant to be there, even though he now desperately hoped they were. In such situations, attack was always the best form of defence, although he could not think of anything to say which would not make the sudden disquiet worse. Instead, Jack glared at his brothers menacingly, letting them know purely by the ferocity of his glare that he would flay the skin from any man who dared to say what they were blatantly thinking. The boisterous male grins slipped off their faces smartly and the three of them stared at their boots like naughty children. The ensuing silence was so brittle it made Jack cringe. So he filled it, for her sake.

'Thank you for your lovely gifts, Letty. They were very thoughtful.'

She grinned again, making everyone, except him, feel better about what had just happened. She did it with such aplomb, she had almost convinced Jack she was oblivious to his brothers' blatant innuendo. Almost. But not quite. He was coming to believe Letty often hid her real thoughts behind an innocent, smiling façade which never quite touched her eyes. 'I thought we were going to play some games?'

In his head, he had just invented a new one, and it was called *How Quickly Can I Strangle My Brothers*. But he smiled and played along for her sake, and his. As the hours flew past pleasantly, Jack's fingers kept touching the square of linen in his pocket and hoping that proud lion was exactly how she saw him rather than the fortune-hunting cad everyone else would assume he was if he ever dared lay another hand on her.

When, inevitably, the time came to go to bed, his three brothers disappeared with alarming haste, although Jack was glad that they did. He was so confused he simply had to talk to her. Letty was almost through the door in their wake when he called her back.

'Letty—can we talk?'

She stopped and slowly turned around, but not before he witnessed her posture become rigid. Something about it did not bode well.

'Of course.' She clasped her hands tightly in front of her, almost defensively.

Like an idiot, he had started the conversation without a clear idea of what it was he was going to say. He wanted to ask about the turquoise lion eyes and if she liked her present. He wanted to know if her feelings for him were the same as his were for her. He wanted— *desperately* wanted—to know if there could still be more between them than the physical attraction he had stupidly dismissed it all as, even though he knew nothing good could ever come of it. 'I wanted to...' Her expression was unreadable, but her green eyes were stormy. 'The thing is...'

'Yes?'

Did she look hopeful? Eager? Letty stared back down at her hands, playing with the silly ring he had given her in a moment of mad weakness. In desperation Jack took her hand and she stared at it wide-eyed. She was definitely embarrassed by this unwanted conversation, too. Her cheeks were pink and he saw her swallow awkwardly at his clumsy attempt at…whatever it was he was clumsily attempting. It was probably better to let sleeping dogs lie. She was leaving in less than a week. Which was for the best. For her at least. Any declaration now was as ludicrous as it was futile.

What exactly did he expect her to do? Stay here when she had every luxury in Mayfair? Be content to live with a farmer? Kiss goodbye to her high position in society and be shunned by everyone she knew? Marry him when she had a duke waiting for her at home? There was wishful thinking and then there was fantasy.

'The thing is, I wanted to thank you for all of the effort you have put into today.' And inevitably, common sense returned.

'I see.' She stared at him levelly. 'Was there anything else you wanted to say?'

I think you are wonderful and I'm a fool. A stupid, penniless, unworthy fool. I wish I could turn back time and do it all again differently. This isn't just lust… I truly care about you.

Who was he kidding? He loved her.

'No. Nothing else…just thank you.'

Hell's teeth! He loved her. The room began to spin.

'Then I shall say goodnight.'

Please don't go. Not just now, but ever. Stay here with me.

'Goodnight, Letty.'

Chapter Eighteen

Five days left...

Tomorrow she would leave Markham Manor, yet even thinking about it hurt. Letty supposed she should be frightened about the potential for danger on the long journey or apprehensive about all the nastiness which would inevitably follow her return home, yet strangely both of those things paled into insignificance when compared to saying goodbye to this house and the men within it. She tried not to specifically link these feelings to Jack because she had already accepted the end of whatever it was they had. As each day passed and the time of her departure drew nearer, they conversed less and less. Yesterday, they had barely exchanged more than three sentences and two of those had consisted of 'Good morning' and 'Goodnight'. This, apparently, was something they were both responsible for. Today, Jack had left to begin his work long before Letty had come downstairs. If his most recent behaviour was anything to go by, she doubted she would see him until dinner. Their last dinner together.

Without thinking, she touched the gold band he had placed on her finger. Soon that would be the only thing she had left of him. It would always be her most treasured possession. His token of thanks which she had desperately hoped would be more. But, of course, the anticipated declaration of his affection had turned out to be nothing but a forlorn hope. Jack had not changed his mind about her unsuitability and Letty's heart had shattered.

Despite her mood, she wanted to mark the occasion, and to do it she was making chicken à la Braise again. The only twist, she hoped, was this time it would be edible. She had learned a great deal about the art of cooking in the last few weeks and was determined to do it properly. It was almost a badge of honour. A statement about how far she had come. The two sacrificial chickens were already roasting away nicely in the oven, completely devoid of feathers, and nesting in a rich, aromatic sauce made from reduced wine and herbs. Now she actually knew what *reduce* meant in a recipe, the final dish was definitely showing some promise. She plopped the last peeled carrot into the waiting pan of water to cook later, as vegetables, it turned out, did not need to be boiled to death for two hours. Then, with all the preparation done, she headed out into the hallway to freshen up and put on her homemade dress for the last time, too. Inside, Letty might be broken, but only Violet would be visible on the outside. She did not want their last memories of her to be of the real girl who didn't quite pass muster.

When the tears came, and they would, only Letty would ever see them. If this whole experience had taught her anything, it was that she was not prepared to settle for someone who did not adore her with the same depth and ferocity as she adored him. She was worth more than that. If Jack couldn't see it, when she had bravely let her guard down for the very first time, then perhaps, some day, someone else would. And perhaps, if her heart ever healed, if the big gaping hole shaped like Jack Warriner ever closed, Letty would move on with her life as well. Because she, Letty Dunston, thwarter of kidnappers, housekeeper, maid, cook, sheep rescuer and soon to be benefactor of London's most sympathetic foundling home, was worth it. So she would do her hair and dress prettily, and allow the *Tea Heiress* to sit at dinner in her stead one last time. When she got to Mayfair, she was determined not to bring her alter ego with her ever again. This was definitely Violet's last performance and Letty was glad to be rid of her, so something positive had come from this whole heartbreaking experience. She knew she had outgrown the confines of her old life and was more than capable of tackling the challenges of the new one. More than capable and now completely independent for the first time.

Rather bizarrely, she felt the vibrations of the approaching hoofbeats first. They resonated through the old wooden floorboards, sending tingles of alarm through her feet and legs as she realised those foreboding hooves came from more than the one horse. An entire team of horses was pounding up the driveway at speed, almost in synchronisation, which suggested a carriage.

Instinctively, she bolted up the staircase and camouflaged herself in a dark corner on the landing and listened as the carriage rattled to a stop outside the front door. Several pairs of boots jumped and crunched on the gravel before the threatening pummelling of a fist against the oak front door sent tentacles of fear whipping throughout her body.

'Open up! We know she's in there!' The tentacles wrapped themselves around her organs and squeezed like a vice. The Earl of Bainbridge's sinister tone did not brook any argument. He was coming in. Nothing was going to stop him. 'Go around the back. Check there are no other escape routes!'

Letty heard boots crunch away at speed from the front of the house. In moments they would reach the open kitchen door and swarm into her safe haven, defiling it. If they found her, she wouldn't stand a chance.

Panic glued her feet to the floor and caused her breath to saw in and out of her lungs painfully. Where was Jack and the others? Were they on their way to rescue her? Were they oblivious to the violation? Or worse, had they already been silenced?

The pummelling on the door began again in earnest. 'We know you are in there, Violet! Did you think you could escape me?'

The menacing words galvanised her. Bainbridge couldn't succeed now, not after everything she'd been through. She had to escape. She had to think. She had to focus on the practicalities.

Going back downstairs was suicide—however, staying up here, where there was no escape route, was almost worse. For a second she contemplated barricading herself into her bedchamber. The heavy wooden wardrobe would offer her some protection, if she could move it. But if she, a lone woman with a woman's physical strength could move it, so too could a group of angry men. Then what?

Blindly, she ran along the landing as the first voices appeared inside the kitchen, unsure of which way to turn. Then she saw the eyes. The bright blue eyes, identical to Jack's, staring out at her from the portrait. Sir Hugo's priest hole! Weeks ago, Jack had told her to hide there if the worst happened.

Her clumsy fingers struggled to release the hidden panel, yet the men were now noisily marching their way down the hallway, kicking open doors as they passed them. Searching for her.

Letty almost whimpered as the secret door finally swung open, but bit down hard on her tongue to stop herself. Stealth and silence were imperative. She slipped inside the tiny room beyond and forced herself to close the door slowly, even though she could already hear a pair of heavy boots on the stairs. With the door closed, she was plunged into blackness. Not so much as a crease of light bled through the ancient panelling, so she had to locate the sturdy bolt blind, with trembling fingers, and carefully, quietly, slide it until it locked.

The footsteps reached the landing.

'Pull apart every room. She could be hiding anywhere. Cupboards, under the beds, behind the curtains. You two check the attic! Leave no stone unturned.' Layton's cold, calculating voice issued orders rapidly. Letty could barely hear him. Her pulse was so noisy the sound of its drumming dominated the inside of her head, yet she knew her rapid breathing might betray her. Any sound she made might betray her. Carefully, she stepped cautiously backwards until she felt the hard press of brick against her ribs.

'Someone was here when we arrived. There's food cooking in the kitchen.'

Letty did not recognise that voice, but it was coming from only a scant few feet away from where she was. On the landing. She held her breath and stared into the darkness, praying she would hear the man's footsteps as he walked away. In the distance, the unmistakable sounds of the downstairs being ransacked, with no thought or care for the family's possessions, piled misery on to her terror. All the Warriners had done was help her, and now, everything they owned would likely be ruined by these monsters. If she survived this, she vowed to replace every stick of furniture damaged.

If she survived.

'Violet is definitely here.' The unmistakable sound of her uncle's voice. So he was here, too. She supposed he would be. Too much was at stake to risk not finishing the job properly. And this time, they would finish the job. She knew that with absolute certainty. They would kill her for sure now. 'Look.'

'It's just a handkerchief,' Bainbridge said dismissively.

'It's an embroidered handkerchief. My niece's work. I'd recognise it anywhere.'

The voices became more muffled as they walked away from her, the noise of the destruction of upstairs replacing it as wardrobes were ruthlessly, mindlessly emptied. Powerless to do anything other than listen and hope, Letty carefully lowered herself to the floor of the little priest hole, wrapped her arms tightly about her knees and silently pleaded for a miracle.

'Let's call it a day. It's almost dark.' Joe stood stiffly below him, stretching out his back.

It had taken all four of them to replace the roof on

the dilapidated cottage, but after two days of intensive work, largely because Jack had needed a proper challenge to stop his mind constantly wandering to Letty, it was almost done. One more tenant cottage finished would mean another tenant and another meagre rent. 'All right. You three head back. I will finish these last slates.'

'No. It's Letty's last night with us and whatever nonsense is going on in that stubborn head of yours, you owe it to her to be there for dinner.' Jamie glared up at him, his arms folded. 'We are all going back together. Now.'

'Fine.'

Jack feigned disinterest, although his gut was already clenching. Pathetically, he wanted to hide away from the grim reality of her going in the hope it would actually stop hurting. Fat chance of that. There was a pain in his heart so acute it kept making him physically flinch. But it was for the best because he had to think of her welfare before his overwhelming feelings. Reluctantly, he climbed down from the roof and helped the others pack away the tools. Their pace back was leisurely, in deference to Jamie's sedate speed, and he was grateful for that at least. In a few hours, he would watch her climb his stairs for the last time. This time tomorrow, they would set off to London. Less than two days after that, they would say goodbye.

The silhouette of Markham Manor loomed darkly in the twilight. It was odd that he should be thinking negative words like loomed again already, when for the last few weeks, the sight of his home had warmed him. It had warmed him, Jack recognised, because Letty had made it into a home rather than a responsibility. With her inside waiting for him, it no longer felt like a mill-stone around his neck, but more a place of light and hope. His feelings for the house would soon become as dark as the windows once more...

Something was not right.

Since Letty had taken charge of the house, those windows always glowed a golden welcome and tonight they were black. He began to run.

'What's wrong?'

'There are no candles burning. We left the gates un-guarded.' Jack had left Letty unguarded.

The closer he got to the house, the more the cold despair of dread settled in the pit of his stomach. They had been gone for hours. Letty could have been gone for hours.

Jack smashed through the back door and saw the carnage. The kitchen table was lying on its side, chairs scattered this way and that. All his worst fears were confirmed. They had come for her and he had not been here to stop them.

Behind him, he heard someone strike a match and the dim light highlighted that the wanton destruction went way beyond this room. Jacob thrust a lantern into his hand.

'Letty's a smart girl, Jack.'

She was. No matter what life threw at her, she always proved herself to be resourceful. She could have escaped. Or she could have hidden. 'Search everywhere.' Jack plunged into the chaos of the hallway and took the stairs two at time, heading to the one place he had told her to go.

'Letty!'

The he stopped in front of the secret panel. 'Letty,

sweetheart, it's me. Jack.' The deafening silence caused his throat to constrict, strangling his words. His fingers fumbled at the concealed latch and his heart only began to beat again when he realised it was locked. From the inside. Thank God!

'Letty, sweetheart.' He lowered his voice, trying to sound calm even though he had never felt so far from it. 'Unlock the door, darling. They've gone.' At least he hoped they had. In his haste to find her he hadn't checked.

Joe poked his head round the banister. 'There's no sign of them—not in the house at any rate. I've come to get Jamie's guns. We're going to check outside.'

He nodded, too petrified for Letty's safety to do any more. 'Did you hear that, sweetheart? There's no sign of them. Please. Talk to me.' *Please be in there. Unharmed.*

'J-Jack?' Her voice was so small, barely a whisper, but his heart soared at the sound.

'Yes, sweetheart. It's me. Unlock the door.' He needed to see for himself all was well. Touch her. Hold her.

'Are they really gone?'

'There is nobody here except me and you.'

He pressed his ear to the wood and heard movement. After an age, and a great deal of fumbling, she slid the bolt open. Jack yanked open the panel and watched her wince and cover her eyes against the weak light from the lantern as she knelt on the floor in front of him. She had been in the dark in there. All alone. Terrified. He could tell by the tiny quiver of her shoulders she was on the cusp of tears.

Automatically he dropped to the floor, crawling into the tiny space and gathering her against his chest tightly, tucking her head under his chin, needing to comfort both of them with the embrace. She burrowed against him, wrapping her arms around his neck, and he noticed her fingers were chilled, too. Jack pulled the edges of his greatcoat around her, rocking her as he tried to warm her skin, grateful at the reassuring, rapid beat of her heart against his.

'I thought they had taken you!' He ignored the crack of emotion in his voice; for once his manly pride could go to hell. She was safe. That was all that mattered. 'Are you injured? Did they touch you?' Because if they had, then they would have to die. It was as simple as that.

She shook her head against his shoulder. 'Th-they never f-found me. I came here as soon as I heard them. Oh, J-Jack, I could hear them pulling apart all the rooms. I thought they would never stop. Your poor house.'

'It's just a house, Letty. Things. None of them are important.' He kissed the top of her blonde curls reverently. The only thing of any importance was safe in his arms.

'I was so frightened. I thought they had hurt you.' An anguished sob escaped her lips. 'Are all your brothers safe, too?'

'Shh, sweetheart…everyone is all right.'

'I've put you all in such danger—I never should have stayed here. I'm so s-sorry, Jack.'

'This is my fault, Letty. If anybody should be sorry it is me. I left the gates open. I became complacent, so sure they were gone, I left you unguarded. If something had happened to you…' Emotion clogged his throat, preventing him from finishing the sentence, but Jack would have not been able to live with himself.

'You're here now. That's all I care about. You're here and safe.' Her slim body shook as the tears she had been bravely holding back came unabated. Jack didn't try to make her stop. After the ordeal she had just been through, she deserved the release and he needed the closeness. All he could do was hold her tight, smooth his hands over her hair and thank God she had had the wherewithal to seek the shelter of this ancient refuge, grateful it had finally hidden someone worthy.

How long they sat there like that, curled together on the floor, he had no idea, but it was long enough for his brothers search the estate and return to find them still there. Jamie wore a grim expression.

'We can't find them in the grounds. That doesn't mean they are not in them. It's just too damn dark to search properly. But the gates are secured and so is the house. Joe's guarding the front door and Jacob the back. If anyone tries to come in, both boys know to shoot first, ask questions later.'

'They know I've been here. My uncle found my embroidery and recognised it. They'll come back.'

A sobering thought. Jack exchanged a meaningful glance with his brother to silently gauge his opinion; the gloomy certainty he saw in Jamie's eyes terrified him. 'They won't be far away. Someone will be watching the house. More men will be guarding the lane. They will have seen us searching for them—but they are waiting now. To see what happens next.'

Jack felt Letty stiffen in his arms and pulled her closer. 'We won't let them near you, Letty.' This place was a fortress, perhaps they could hold Bainbridge and his men at bay. But even if they could, it was only a short-term solution. 'We need to get her out of here.'

'Agreed.' Jamie nodded, his jaw firm and his shoulders set for battle. 'I have a plan.'

Chapter Nineteen

Four tense days and twenty-three hours to go...

Just after midnight, Joe and Jacob set off to check the grounds. The light of their lanterns and the movement near the gates were designed to draw attention away from the three cloaked figures heading towards the barn. Jamie pushed bales of hay in front of the doors in case thin slivers of light from their single candle bled out into the darkness. Silently, Jack saddled two horses while Letty pushed their hastily procured provisions into saddle bags. Just before they extinguished the candle, Jamie pressed a pistol into her hand. The feel of something so deadly in her palm should have been frightening, but its cold weight was reassuring.

'Remember what I told you. Pull back the hammer, aim it at the head and squeeze the trigger.' She nodded her affirmation and put it into the belt tied around her waist. Jamie turned gravely back to his brother. 'Wait here till you see the light of my lantern. Once we are sure they've gone, we'll follow. Take care, Big Brother.'

With that he blew out the weak candle, pushed away

the hay bales and limped back towards the courtyard. She and Jack waited in tense silence, holding their respective horses by the reins. Not more than two minutes later they saw the glow of Jamie's lantern at the back door of the house. It moved slowly away from both his other brothers and from where they stood. Another decoy to fool whoever happened to be watching that the Warriners were either searching for Letty or for potential intruders.

'Let's go,' Jack whispered and led the way behind the barn, towards the dark, forbidding woods. Letty had to trust he would be able to find his way out of them and take them safely, directly to the Great North Road almost four miles away.

They walked the horses until the blanket of trees surrounded them. She let him boost her on to her mount, then waited while he hoisted himself into the saddle. 'Once we get to the river, we have to veer south, keeping the water to our right. That way we will bypass Retford altogether. The stretch of the London-bound road we should meet is fairly isolated. It should be easy to spot from the cover of trees if anyone is there waiting for us. If they are, we will simply remain hidden.'

He sounded so supremely confident, it went some way to allay the worst of her fears, bringing down her level of fear from completely petrified to merely terrified. If—no, *when* she got through this, it would probably take Letty weeks to feel anywhere near normal again.

But Jack's solid, calm presence did help. Ever since he had found her in the priest hole, she had drawn comfort from his strength. His house had been ransacked, the family's belongings ruthlessly strewn on the floor and trampled over. Yet Jack had simply cast his eye over the damage and shrugged. He tasked Joe and Jacob with clearing up the worst of the mess in the great hall so that they could all sit down and took Letty into the kitchen where he set the kettle to boil, keeping her busy by distracting her with mindless chatter while he made them all some tea. By the time it was ready and they carried it back into the hall, his brothers had almost put the room to rights and had hidden any evidence of the wanton destruction created by her would-be captors.

Then, the five of them had planned and prepared for the dangerous journey back to London. Too shaken to really participate, Letty had been grateful Jack had taken the time to seek her approval of every decision that was made, making sure she understood exactly what to expect. If they reached the Great North Road safely, they would travel to London under the veil of darkness, resting during the daylight hours so that there was less chance of anyone seeing her. It would take longer, and there were the added dangers of footpads to consider, but as those scoundrels would only want her possessions, of which she currently had none, they were a lesser evil than Bainbridge and her treacherous uncle. For safety's sake, any rest stops would likely not be in comfortable inns for the first day or two. Once they were closer to the capital, and as long as they had encountered nothing hostile on their route, they might be able to risk one of them. But it had to be a busy one, Jamie had cautioned, because people saw far less in crowds. London, Jamie claimed, would be the very best place to hide and Letty believed him. The circles she moved in were small and close knit. Those well-heeled, well-spoken paragons of society rarely ventured out of

Mayfair or the usual fashionable haunts. If they took a room somewhere like Cheapside, while the ugly legal necessities were dealt with, she sincerely doubted her peers, or more importantly her uncle, would be any the wiser.

Their horses picked slowly through the black forest. Letty made sure she was close on Jack's tail; it was too dangerous to risk even the dimmest of lights. After what seemed like an eternity, they heard the unmistakable sounds of rushing water. Jack stayed his horse so Letty could move up alongside him. He reached out one hand and gently cupped her cheek for a second. 'Are you all right, Letty?'

He had been doing that a lot since he had found her, she realised, taking every opportunity to touch her. Almost as if he needed to reassure himself she was safe and whole. Letty liked it. The gestures suggested he cared about her, and right now he was her whole world.

'I will feel a whole lot better when there is a good hour or more between me and the Earl of Bainbridge.'

His hand sought hers, held it, his thumb massaging her palm. 'I will not let him near you, sweetheart. I promise.'

And every time he called her sweetheart, her silly heart soared, even though he only ever used the endearment when she was upset or distressed. It didn't really mean anything. Any more than the emerald had meant anything more than what it was. A gesture of thanks. A small token. Yet Letty had been supremely conscious of the gold band encircling her finger from the second Jack had put it there. He let go of her hand and she automatically brought it to touch the ring, her index finger tracing the smooth stone. It had become a habit. A ritual. Soon, the small, old heirloom would be all she had of him.

Jack directed his horse south and she followed. Their progress was painfully slow as the forest closed in on them. Proud, tangled roots prevented the horses from building up any speed or momentum while low-hanging branches caught against her sleeves. With them came the dreadful memories of the last time she had been here, terrified and alone, yet determined to escape. In such a short time, she had now come full circle. The irony of the similarity was not lost on her, although this time Letty was not alone. She had Jack. And for the first time, he was bathed in moonlight. Ahead of him, she could see why. The trees had thinned and there appeared a valley cut through them. They had reached the road.

Jack slid off his horse and handed Letty the reins. She tried to remain calm when he retrieved the pistol from his belt and she heard the hammer cock with an ominous click.

'I am going to check we are alone. Stay here.'

He crouched down and manoeuvred his way deftly through the trees to step on to the lane, then for several heart-stopping minutes, he disappeared from sight. A twig on the ground snapped and she almost jumped out of her skin, until she saw him, smiling sheepishly, emerging from the undergrowth.

'Sorry. I should have said something. I didn't mean to scare you.'

'As I haven't stopped being scared for hours, a puff of wind would likely scare me. It was sensible you didn't warn me. Anything above a whisper has the potential to get us both killed. Is the coast clear?'

'I checked both ways. I never saw a thing. I think it is fairly safe to assume they will be watching the road closer to the house rather than here. We are at least four miles away from the village and there is not another one for ten miles.' She watched him haul himself effortlessly back into his saddle and nudge his mount down the small incline to the road. He waited patiently at the bottom while Letty did the same. 'It's pitch black and thankfully not raining. If ever there was a good opportunity to make some headway, it is now. If you're up for it, I say we push these horses for the next hour or so.'

They both set off simultaneously, varying between a trot and a canter until they approached the outer edge of the next village when Jack slowed and signalled her to do the same. 'Two fast horses clattering through the centre of a village in the small hours might arouse suspicion. Let's keep to the grass and avoid the cobbles.'

This formed the pattern of the next couple of hours. As they tore up the miles, Letty began to relax, although as the night time began to dissolve, she also realised she was exhausted. Jack found a road marker which warned they were only a few miles from Grantham. Even Letty knew it was too popular a stopping point on this road and would soon be filling up with early morning travellers keen to be on their way. Wearily, they turned their horses and plunged across fields instead, hoping they would find a suitably deserted place to rest in until the evening.

The big barn had an air of dereliction about it, perched as it was on a hilly pasture and well away from the rest of the farm buildings. As Jack had suspected, it was a spare hay store which was mostly empty, therefore they were unlikely to be bothered as the farmer's cows would all be closer to home in the dead of winter. Letty helped him to settle the horses at one end and fed them while Jack found water for the animals to drink. Once that chore was finished, they hungrily ate some of the food they had packed, swilling it down with milk.

Neither of them spoke, they were both dead on their feet. The hours of stress had taken their toll. Letty was so pale it worried Jack. The strain of her most recent ordeal was written all over her lovely face, yet she had not complained once on their long and arduous journey through the cold, damp night air. She needed several uninterrupted hours of sleep in a comfortable feather bed. Unfortunately, this ramshackle barn was going to have to do. It was about as far away from the luxury she was used to in Mayfair, but it was remote and almost watertight.

Letty packed away the uneaten rations in a saddle bag and fetched the blanket they had brought while Jack built her a nest to sleep in at the top of the haystack, away from view. If anybody did happen across them while they were sleeping, it would take a goodly while to find her and hopefully by then she would be prepared with her pistol. She smiled at him gratefully as he helped her to climb up and sank into the straw with a sigh. 'I can't remember ever looking forward to sleep more.'

Jack unravelled the bedroll and draped it solicitously over her. 'Where is your pistol?'

She retrieved it from her waistband and waved it at him. 'I know. I shall sleep with it close by.' He made to clamber back down from the stack and she frowned. 'Where are you going?'

'I shall sleep down here—near the door.' He wasn't particularly looking forward to lying on the draughty wooden floor, but with a bit of straw he supposed he could manage well enough.

'No. That will not do. You need your rest, too, Jack. I thought you were going to sleep up here. With me.'

The sudden surge of desire cut through his exhaustion very effectively, until he realised it was not a romantic invitation at all. 'That would hardly be proper, Letty.'

She giggled, the sound so unexpected after everything she had been through, clearly amused at his feeble attempt at behaving like a gentleman. 'Nothing about our association has been proper, Jack, so I hardly think we need to bow to propriety now. Come up here.' She patted the straw next to her and, to his consternation, his body took it as a signal. His groin tightened involuntarily.

'I shall be quite all right, Letty. If I am near the door, I can keep watch.'

'If you are near the door, you will freeze to death. Besides, I should feel much safer with you next to me than all the way down there.' If it made her feel safer, then perhaps he should sleep up there. With her. How exactly was he supposed to sleep, while his body was rampant with need and the woman he wanted more than anything else on earth was lying next to him? She saw his hesitation and inadvertently used it against him. Her eyes were wide and troubled and there was a definite, fearful catch in her voice. 'Please, Jack. I do not want to wake up in this strange place and wonder where you are. Don't leave me up here on my own.'

It was the tiny tremor in her voice which sealed his

fate. Underneath her façade of bravery, Letty was terrified, as anybody would who had spent several hours alone, locked in the darkness, listening to the men who wanted to kill you pull apart a house as they searched it. Compared to that experience, his unfortunate physical discomfort paled into insignificance.

With leaden feet, he grabbed his own blanket roll and climbed reluctantly to the top of the hay stack. There was hardly room for two, so he did his best to put some distance between them and stretched out next to her. Letty rolled on to her side and smiled sleepily at him, conjuring up thoughts of what waking up in the morning with her every day would be like. This close, even in the dampened early morning light in the barn, Jack could see the darker flecks of green which ringed her pupils. He supposed they gave her mossy eyes the depth which made them sparkle like emeralds. Her golden hair was almost the same shade as the hay she lay on, except the hay was coarse and lacked lustre; Letty's curls shimmered like the finest silk embroidery thread.

'I think we made good time last night. I hope your brothers are safe, too.'

'Jamie will see them off. And if they won't leave, he has a veritable arsenal in his bedchamber. I don't fancy Bainbridge and your uncle's chances against him.'

'The last thing I want is any one of them hurt on my behalf. I have developed quite an attachment to the three of them.'

But what about him? Had she developed an attachment to him? Jack wanted to ask so very much. Was there more to the precious lion embroidery, as there had been to his ring, or was he pathetically reading something into their relationship which was no longer there?

Jamie was convinced she was—how had he put it?—
mad for him. Mad being the operative word. Jack was
certainly mad for Letty. Today he had been ready to
commit murder on her behalf. The acute, visceral fear
he had experienced when he realised she had been in
danger had unmanned him. Seeing her so frightened,
curled up in the priest hole, yet utterly relieved she was
alive and unharmed, he had very nearly succumbed
himself and wept with joy. Afterwards, when she had
clung to him, he had almost told her exactly how he felt.
Only common sense and his own deeply held beliefs
that people under duress do not think entirely straight
had stopped the ardent confession spilling from his lips.
Despite the fraught circumstances, Jack suddenly decided he had to know if the hope in his heart, which
refused to die, stood any chance whatsoever.

'Letty… I was wondering…' Jack turned his body to
properly face her and noticed her shivering beneath the
thin blanket and completely forgot what he wanted to
say. 'Oh, sweetheart, you're frozen. Come here.'

It had been an unconscious, natural decision to pull
her into his arms. Sharing body heat and blankets made
perfect sense, the pragmatist in him knew that, yet he
had not fully thought the ramifications through. Letty
eagerly cuddled up, wrapping her arm around his waist
and hooking one leg snugly over his in order absorb the
maximum amount of heat from his body.

'Oh, that's lovely. You're so warm, Jack.' And getting warmer by the second, but there was nothing to be
done about it except grin and bear it. One arm curled
possessively around her back, while the other fumbled
for both blankets. He dragged one on top of the other,
then bundled them around the pair of them so that only

Letty's golden head poked out. She sighed contentedly and burrowed into the crook of his arm. 'I think we have discovered the perfect way to sleep outdoors. Perhaps sleeping in a barn isn't quite so bad after all?'

And perhaps he should just shoot himself now and put himself out of his own misery. Hours of potential torture stretched before him. By the deep rhythmic sounds of her breathing, Letty was not similarly overwhelmed with lust and longing. Her dark blonde eyelashes formed perfect crescents on her soft cheeks and her arm across his middle, scant inches away from the particular area which was causing him the most angst, was weighted with sleep. Stifling a groan, Jack pressed his lips to the top of her head.

'Goodnight, sweetheart. Sleep tight.' At least one of them would.

Chapter Twenty

Only two days to go...

Letty woke slowly, enjoying the weight of Jack's arm looped around her waist and the feel of his strong, broad chest pressed flush against her back. In the two nights they had been travelling, she had learned a few things about Jack Warriner's sleeping habits which utterly charmed her. Firstly, he talked in his sleep. The occasional word made sense, but most of the slurred mutterings which came out of his mouth were complete nonsense. Secondly, if she inadvertently moved away from him, he would instinctively roll towards her, curl his big body around hers and anchor her to him with a possessive arm across her middle. And thirdly, and perhaps not at all charmingly but quite thrillingly, just before he awoke the hard evidence of his desire nestled snugly against her bottom as it did now. All three things, he was blissfully unaware of she knew.

Yesterday, to spare his blushes, Letty had pretended to be asleep when he stirred and had remained like that until he had hastily released her and clambered down the haystack. This morning, she was severely tempted to see how he reacted when she didn't pretend, because his need to touch her constantly and call her sweetheart was not diminishing, no matter how many miles they put between themselves and her treacherous uncle. Something in their relationship had shifted and she was keen to explore what it was. Letty was beginning to hope Jack felt far more for her than simply lust—but the lust was a very good start.

Like the shameless harlot only he brought out in her, Letty wiggled her bottom against him until she heard him stir. Jack shifted slightly and pressed that intriguing part of him closer, so she wiggled some more. He sighed blissfully and nuzzled his nose into her hair affectionately, then, to her complete delight, the hand which had been thrown over her waist snaked up and firmly cupped her breast. It all felt very nice and very naughty. Too nice and too naughty to suspend the experiment any time soon.

She twisted slightly, to give him greater access to her neck and chest, and allowed her fingertips to stroke the exposed skin on his forearm while her wayward bottom continued to brush against him. When his thumb began to rub lazy circles around her nipple and his lips found her ear, Letty felt a momentary pang of guilt. The man was clearly still half-asleep and she was taking blatant advantage of him. How would she feel if he had tried to take advantage of her while she slept?

It was then that she smiled. Because if Jack had not been such a gentleman, Letty realised she would have been thrilled to bits. Boldly, she splayed her own palm flat on the hand which was currently lightly touching her bosom and shamelessly pressed it more firmly against her body, holding it in place as she shimmied her body around to lie flat on her back. Only then did she slide her palm under the hem of his shirt and caress the warm, smooth skin just below his ribcage. Jack mumbled some nonsense, but at the end of the incomprehensible sentence was one word which made her heart sing.

'Letty.'

It was half-sighed, half-groaned, yet it left her in no doubt he was thinking about her alone and not just any random woman, either remembered or imagined.

'Yes, Jack. It's Letty.' Her hand smoothed its way to his shoulders and her mouth was barely an inch away from his. She would not be the first one to succumb to a kiss this time. If it was going to happen, it had to come at his instigation.

'Mornin', sweetheart.' It was late afternoon, but she didn't bother to correct him, because his hand had found the undone top of her shirt and was burrowing underneath it decisively. She moaned when long fingers touched the sensitive bare skin of her needy breast, but that moan was stifled by his lips on hers.

As sleepy kisses went, this one was earth-shattering. It was soft, shockingly intrusive and delightfully intimate. His tongue tangled with hers as he rolled his weight on top of her and, in case he suddenly came to his senses and stopped his sweet torture, Letty wrapped one leg around his hip. Aside from holding him in place, this also served to cushion all that glorious hardness in the cradle of her thighs. Only two pairs of soft breeches separated their bodies. If Letty had had a wand or supernatural abilities, she would have used magic to instantly dissolve the unwanted barrier.

Jack had to be awake now, because surely no man

was capable of causing so much carnal pleasure in his
sleep. His lips strayed away from hers and trailed hot,
open-mouthed kisses down her neck, over her collarbone and deliciously over the covered swells of her
breast. His mouth tortured her nipple through the linen,
then with a growl, he grabbed the hem of the shirt at her
waist and hoisted it up, exposing both of her breasts. His
tongue swirled hotly around one aching tip before sucking it into his mouth. As Letty writhed in unashamed
appreciation, he swapped sides and hungrily worshipped the other one before seeking her mouth again.

Letty desperately needed to feel him properly. Skin
to skin. Heartbeat to heartbeat, so she clawed his shirt
up to his shoulders and yanked it over his head. She
arched against him wantonly, grazing her pebbled nipples against the solid wall of his chest and plunging her
fingers into his thick hair, moaning her encouragement
into his mouth. Everything blurred except the glorious
sensations he was eliciting from her body.

She felt his hand rummage between their squirm-
ing bodies for the buttons on the falls of his breeches.
Letty's fingers hungrily joined his to assist. It was
then that he pulled back, although not far enough to
detract from the intimacy of the situation. His hardness still pressed against her core, one hand still cupped
her breast, but his lips stilled and he lifted his head to
stare down at her, somewhat alarmed.

'We shouldn't be doing this.'

His breathing was laboured, his sleepy eyes darkened and stormy with desire.

'Why?'

'You have been through a terrible ordeal. You are
still overwhelmed with stress.'

To tempt him, Letty threw her arms back over her head. It brought her bare breasts into his eye line, one of them still covered by his big hand. 'Do I look stressed to you?' For good measure, she ground her hips against his and let him see the pleasure it brought her.

His thumb grazed her nipple once. Twice. He was not as immune to her as he had claimed. In that one moment, she could see how much he wanted her in the intensity of his deep blue stare. He closed his eyes and swallowed, clearly having an internal battle with himself.

'I want this, Jack. I want you.'

'I want you, too, Letty. More than anything...' He closed his eyes again and sighed. She watched a myriad of emotions chase across his expression before he severed all contact by rolling on to his back. 'But I won't ruin you like this. Not now. Not when so much is still unsettled and fraught and you have no idea how being with me will seriously impact on your life. But...' He sat up and stared down at her. She watched his eyes feast on the sight of her shamelessly sprawled on the hay, lingering on her breasts hungrily before he wrenched them away. 'When this is over, when you are home and safe, then perhaps we can discuss this again. I shall lay out all the pitfalls and all the reasons why I am not a good choice of husband, and then you can rationally decide what you want to do.' He located his shirt and hastily pulled it on. 'Things will be different then, I can assure you.'

Letty forced herself to stay exactly where she was, displayed for only his eyes to see her as nature had intended. 'Do you think my feelings will be different?'

'Yes. Until the dust has settled, your feelings are

bound to be confused.' His words might have upset her, except his hand had come down to rest on her belly. They both watched its progress as it edged up her body, gently kneaded her breast and then came to rest lovingly on her cheek. 'Passion isn't love.' Before she could argue, he jumped decisively down to the floor. 'I'll ready the horses. We leave in fifteen minutes.'

The weather matched Jack's mood. The rain had begun again shortly after midnight. Fine, misty rain at first, but then it came down with a vengeance. About an hour ago, it had turned to sleet. Another partially frozen droplet hit his neck and dribbled under his shirt, compounding his misery further. The only part of his body that had been spared a thorough soaking was his backside. However, the same saddle which had kept his posterior dry was now almost torture to sit on.

This leg of their nocturnal journey had been interminable. Partly because there was once again an atmosphere between him and Letty and partly because he could not seem to get the image of her sprawled in the hay out of his head. Jack might well be frozen to the bone, miserable and saddle sore, however none of these ailments apparently affected his rampant male parts one little bit.

Why had his sense of responsibility chosen to rear its ugly head when it had? A few minutes later and his lust would have been thoroughly sated and the dilemma he suffered would be moot. They would have had to have got married and that was that. Except, his heart wanted more than a wife by default. He would absolutely not be his father and trap her. He wanted Letty to choose him. Not because she was frightened, or lonely or unsettled or grateful, but because she had properly considered her decision and decided he was worth all the trouble. This last month had not been normal for either of them. Letty needed some normality to rediscover herself.

And once she did, then she would realise the concept of them as a couple was sheer folly. When the danger was over and she was back on familiar turf, he had to be prepared for Letty to see the potential misery of marrying a Warriner and making the considered decision that it was not worth it in the long run. In Jack's experience, hope in any form had always been the kiss of death. He needed to stop hoping, stop thinking they might stand a chance, and focus on getting her home safely.

He risked a glance sideways and saw she looked as miserable as him. The few strands of hair visible under the hat she wore pulled low were stuck to her face. Her long eyelashes were spiky from the rain and, more worrying now that the first light of dawn pushed forth, there was a distinct bluish tinge to her lips. She needed a warm bath, plenty of bedcovers and a roaring fire. The last time she had suffered exposure to the elements like this, she had been sick for days and he had feared she would die.

The last road marker had warned that they were only a few miles from Baldock, a busy little town where several roads merged with the Great North Road. Trusting Jamie's advice, this might be the perfect place to risk stopping at an inn. People apparently saw less in crowds and they could both do with a proper bed, hot food and dry clothes before they set off on the final leg of their journey. Tomorrow morning, with any luck, they would finally arrive in the capital, and once they got there, the next instalment of Letty's ordeal would begin. She would need all of her strength for that, so the risk of the inn was worth it. They would also benefit from having a brick wall between them when they slept. Two separate rooms would give them both some space. Letty would be able to think about their situation dispassionately and Jack would be able to avoid all temptation.

'We will find an inn in the next town.'

Letty nodded, her expression wretched, clearly too cold and too tired to comment, so they trudged on until they saw a suitably busy inn. The morning carriages were already loading in readiness of leaving and the tantalising scent of cooking bacon wafted in the air. Jack handed her some coins and sent her to the dining room to order them both some breakfast.

'While I sort out the horses and the accommodations, Letty, you should probably try and appear as inconspicuous as possible.' She nodded listlessly and walked off, and Jack went first to the stables.

A lad relieved him of the horses and led them inside to be rubbed down and fed. Jack went in search of the innkeeper, only to find his frazzled wife instead. 'I should like two rooms, please.'

'And I should like an ermine cloak and a husband who wasn't workshy and still abed—but we don't always get what we want. You can have one room or none at all.'

'But I need two.'

'We're full. The world and his wife are travelling back to London now that Christmas is over. I have one room spare, it's a fine one and plenty big enough for two. Take it or leave it, sir. If you don't want it, someone else will snap it up within the hour, I'm sure.'

Jack wavered for a moment. All manner of mischief could occur in one room as it had this morning when he was still half-asleep. Sharing a room with Letty, one in possession of a proper bed, was a temptation he did not need if he was to keep his vow of not ruining her...but on the other hand, Letty was frozen and exhausted. And the innkeeper's wife did say it was plenty big enough for two. There might be a place for him to make up a bed on the floor. If it came to it, he could probably bed down in the stables. Letty's health and wellbeing had to come first.

'I'll take it.'

He found Letty sitting hunched at a small table in the far corner of the crowded dining room. 'They only had one room.'

She shrugged and Jack couldn't tell if she was peeved at him, the lack of a second room or merely bone tired. 'It will have to do.'

'I've ordered a hot bath to be drawn. It should be ready in half an hour.'

'I wasn't sure what you wanted to eat, so I have ordered you pretty much everything.' She smiled then and the odd atmosphere began to float away. 'Personally, I could eat a horse.'

The meal turned out to be both enormous and delicious. The hot tea was even better and it revived them both. Thankfully, Letty was her usual cheerful self and made no mention of their earlier indiscretion. It suited Jack fine. Talking about what had happened would make him think about it and it was already proving to be near impossible to forget the glorious feel of her perfect bare breast squashed into his palm, or the way her body had fitted so splendidly against his and how she had writhed in pleasure... All at once, his breeches tightened again and remained ruthlessly so during Letty's third, painfully slow cup of tea.

By the time they had finished and located their room, the steaming bathtub was already waiting and, thoughtfully, the maid had also arranged a screen for privacy.

Jack had intended a swift exit as soon as he was sure Letty was properly settled, followed by a brisk and necessarily bracing wash from the pump out in the courtyard to cool his ardour, but the room was warm and the lure of proper armchairs to rest on was too strong, so he stepped inside. When he gave in to the urge to sit briefly in one of the chairs, his bones gratefully sank into the soft upholstery and his good intentions did not shout loud enough to drown out the sound of sheer contentment. The freezing pump could wait a few minutes more.

'Do you want to bathe first or second?'

More temptation Jack did not need—but, oh, how his aching body would enjoy the soothing relief of a nice hot bath. Now the chance to soak in a hot tub had presented itself, he was reluctant to turn down the opportunity. Besides, he was also reluctant to leave the wonders of the chair just yet.

'You go first.'

She disappeared behind the screen and Jack began to pull off his sodden boots. Letty's wet clothing came off piece by piece and she slapped them noisily across the top of the screen.

He really hadn't thought this through.

Now he knew she was completely naked behind the screen—and that was far too unnerving to contemplate for long. He needed to do something practical to distract himself. After he heard her sink down into the water with a throaty sigh, he retrieved the sopping clothes and arranged them near the roaring fire to dry. His own clothes stuck wetly to his body and he realised they were probably the reason his spine was aching with cold. He dithered as to whether or not he should take his off in readiness for his turn in the bathtub, then realised she had already seen him stripped to the waist, so the sight of his hairy chest was hardly going to come as a huge surprise. And he was cold, after all. He peeled off his shirt and breeches, wrapped a towel tightly around his waist and placed them next to hers to dry, trying to ignore the sound of splashing water as she soaped her naked skin only a few feet away.

The next ten minutes were the longest of his life. His imagination was out of control, his body was primed for action and the sounds of her bathing behind that blasted screen were possibly the most erotic noises he had ever heard. Who knew the sound of soap being rubbed on to a flannel would be so potent?

When she emerged swaddled in another towel, the skin he could see was all pink and it took all of his strength not to go to her, snatch away the towel and drag her into his unworthy arms. Her hair hung damply around her shoulders and down her back. She stared at him for a second or two, blinking rapidly, then smiled shyly as she padded past him. The back of the towel draped low, displaying the graceful lines of her back and the hint of the curve of her bottom. His big, calloused hands longed to be filled with it.

Feeling awkward, self-conscious and beyond aroused, Jack gratefully hid behind the screen to take his turn in the water. He undid the towel and stared down at his arousal mournfully. Was it ever going to subside or was he doomed to spend all eternity as stiff as a board? He should have washed at the pump. The cold water would have done the trick instantly. If he took a long bath, he reasoned, she would be tucked safely in bed by the time he finished. And if he stayed in it long enough, the water would chill and his rampant body might finally calm down. With any luck, it would take such a long time, she would already be soundly asleep by the time he felt settled enough to emerge.

Chapter Twenty-One

One final day remaining...

His skin was covered in goose bumps by the time he finally emerged from the bathtub. The dark, downy hair on his chest and abdomen clung wetly to the muscles beneath and his male nipples were puckered with cold. To say he made her mouth water was an understatement. A wet, half-naked Jack was even more appealing than any version of him she had seen previously. It took all of her resolve not to lick her lips at the sight.

He appeared surprised to see Letty sitting at the hearth drying her hair. Or perhaps he was simply stunned to see her shamelessly wearing nothing but a towel. Although it was tucked securely under her arm-pits, it was not long enough to cover her legs. His blue eyes flicked to them before he dragged them back to her face. When he spoke, his normally deep, commanding voice was a touch higher than usual.

'I thought you would be in bed.'

His eyes dropped to her legs again and she watched his Adam's apple bob in the thick column of his neck.

Had he not been naked under the towel, he probably would have bolted for the door. She bothered him. And judging by the interesting bulge under the waistband of the towel, he liked what he saw. As reactions went, it did a great deal to boost her confidence. However, that was not the sole reason she had waited for him to finish bathing. There were things they needed to talk about and Letty was not inclined to wait, as Jack had wanted, for the *dust to settle.*

'My hair is almost dry. Why don't you come and sit with me and keep me company?' There were things that needed to be said. Letty had several pertinent questions for him which positively demanded answers. She had had hours to mull over his words when he had put a stop to their intimacies this morning and his choice of phrasing had been telling. At no point had he mentioned *his* doubts about the pair of them, only *hers.* Why did he think she would suddenly change her mind about her feelings for him when she got back to London?

Jack walked stiffly to the chair, clutching the towel for grim death and doing his best to hide what was going on underneath it. When he sat down, he made sure the towel was suitably bunched to disguise his obvious arousal and stared back at her awkwardly.

'Tell me about your family.'

This appeared to flummox him, because his dark eyebrows came together and he suddenly appeared even more uncomfortable in the chair.

'What exactly do you want to know?'

'I want to know all of the terrible reasons why the world apparently distrusts the Warriners.' Because somehow, that was at the heart of his dilemma and the reason he held himself back from her. Letty had seen the effect she had on him. He wasn't immune to her charms, nor was he indifferent to her character. In the last two days, he had proved he would move heaven and earth to see her safe. Jack cared about her. She felt it.

'There are so many reasons, it would take days to tell you everything. All of them were a bad lot.'

'But you and your brothers aren't.'

'Mud sticks, I'm afraid. We have been ruthlessly tarred with the same brush. I have tried to allay people's fears over the last few years. So far, all my efforts have been in vain. As a family, we are universally disliked by all.'

Letty had heard versions of this comment frequently from all four of the brothers, yet they had been reticent about elaborating. 'Then start with your parents. What did they do to upset the world?'

She watched him take a deep breath and stare down at his hands. He didn't want to talk about it, she realised. He would use it as a barrier to stop him being happy— but it was not something he was keen on sharing. His fingers began to play with an edge of towel, alerting her to the fact he was uneasy about her potential reaction, but he met her gaze squarely. Almost defiantly. 'My father was a complete scoundrel. He drank too much and had a tendency not to pay his debts. He was untrustworthy and lacked morals.'

An interesting assessment, but severely lacking in tangible evidence. Letty already had the impression getting the whole truth out of this proud man would be tantamount to drawing blood out of a stone, but there was too much at stake not to ruthlessly squeeze the stone for every drop. 'What morals did he lack?'

Those disarming blue eyes narrowed. 'When my

father saw something he coveted, he did whatever he wanted to get it. Often, that meant he used foul means over fair.'

'Are you saying he cheated people?'

He nodded curtly. 'He was famous for it. Nobody would do business with him.'

'And now you suffer by default as nobody will do business with you either.'

'Nobody local will. I have found a butcher in Lincoln who will suffer my lamb and another merchant who will take the corn.'

'Suffer? Take? I've seen how hard you work and the quality of your stock, Jack. They are hardly doing you a favour.'

'Oh, they are. I assure you it's taken years to get anyone to do even that much.'

Years of listening to her father had given Letty a sound understanding of business. 'Do they pay you market price?'

'Almost.' The proud gleam was shining out of his eyes and those spectacular shoulders had risen defiantly. He knew he was being fleeced. Knew and accepted it because he had no choice. Further discussion on the topic would likely result in Jack's lips sealing up tighter than a drum, when for once he was talking, albeit with great reluctance.

'What other morals did your father lack?'

'He could be violent. He had a habit of punching people when he had a drink inside him. That also made him unpopular with the locals.'

It probably also made him wildly unpopular with his family. Letty feared she knew the answer to her next question already, but wanted to gauge his reaction to it none the less. 'Did he use his fists on you, too?'

He shrugged. 'Better on me than the younger boys or my mother.'

Poor, loyal, steadfast Jack.

'Is that why she took her own life?'

'Partly—but she was never happy at Markham Manor.' He raked an agitated hand through his damp hair. 'I am under-exaggerating. She *loathed* Markham Manor. She loathed my father. And because we all had the misfortune to be born the spitting image of him, she loathed us, too.'

Jamie had claimed Jack always had to be responsible. He absorbed other people's problems unconsciously, seeing it as his place to shoulder them as the head of the family. Hardly a surprise when his parents had let him down so dreadfully.

'Do you blame yourself for her death?'

He paused, as if giving it some thought for the very first time, then shook his head. 'No. I blame my father. Plunging herself into the river was far more appealing to her than living the life she had foisted upon her.'

'In what way was her life foisted upon her?'

Those proud shoulders deflated and his eyes became troubled. Darker. Bluer.

'My mother came from London. Like you. My father charmed her, ruined her and then took her away from the life she loved. They were ostracised from society. My mother never got over it.'

Another interesting insight into this complicated, stubborn man. 'You think the same would happen to me?'

He looked at her grimly. 'Don't you see, Letty? Everything about our situation has been fraught with danger from the outset. You have been through a great deal and do not know who to trust. But you trust me and perhaps you've fooled yourself into thinking those feelings mean more than gratitude. I cannot, in all good conscience, pursue whatever may, or may not, be between us until your life is normal again and you can see things clearly. It's not easy being a Warriner.'

His flippant dismissal of her emotions as being fickle and interchangeable galled. 'Oh, for goodness sake! I am neither that shallow nor that addled! I know my own mind perfectly well. And as for your claim about it not easy being a Warriner, perhaps you should try being the Tea Heiress for a few weeks. That is not easy either! We all have our crosses to bear, Jack.'

'I should imagine having a great fortune and society practically falling at your feet is a great chore!' he shot back sarcastically.

'Urrgh! How typical. Now *you* are tarring *me* with the same brush I have always been tarred with!' Gripping the edge of her towel, Letty stood up abruptly and stalked towards the window. She had hoped he would understand or think differently seeing that he actually *knew* her. But then again, why would he? Jack had always struggled to make ends meet. He had no concept of what being an orphaned heiress was like. If she wanted him to open up to her, then it stood to reason she should entrust him with the same honour.

'Do you know what it is like to be all alone in the world, Jack? I doubt you can even begin to imagine it, because you have your family. Three noisy brothers who are always there for you. You might fight, disagree, rub each other the wrong way, but there is always somebody for you to come home to. To talk to. Since my parents died, I don't have that.'

She turned and walked slowly back to her seat, all the while watching him digest the information. 'But the newspapers always talk of all the parties and balls you attend.'

It stood to reason he would compare what he thought to be true with her version of the truth. How best to explain it?

'I have a big house in Mayfair. It is filled with servants and fine furniture, I eat the best food, wear the nicest clothes—but it is a house without a heart, Jack. It intimidates people, so they rarely visit. And if they do, it is out of either curiosity or to gain gossip to pass on to their friends about the mythical Violet Dunston who resides within. Sometimes the house feels like a prison, except I am the only inmate.'

Letty sat down slowly and reached for his hand.

'You already know my uncle is not exactly the model guardian. At best, he has always been indifferent to me. He moved in and fulfilled his legal obligations, but we rarely spoke. Yes, I do go out to balls and parties. I rarely turn down an invitation, but that is not because I particularly enjoy them, it is because if I don't go to them, I never get to have a conversation with anyone. Except, they are never *really* the sorts of conversations I would wish to have. You were right when you called them superficial. Everybody believes I live this charmed existence. It never occurs to them that I am lonely or that Violet Dunston is a character I play in public. Nobody wants to see the reality of who I actually am.'

'You're lonely.'

This, apparently, was a grand epiphany because he

appeared both shocked and horrified in equal measure. Seeing his expression of pity, for her, made her want to weep.

'One never quite knows who to trust. Are they really my friends or is it the fortune which attracts them? Being one of my acquaintances has its benefits. I am famously generous.'

'I thought you had men lining up outside your door to marry you?'

Letty laughed without humour, because it really would be laughable if she was not on the receiving end of it. 'They do line up. It's terrifying. But it's not me, Letty, that they want. I sincerely doubt any of them truly see me at all. I sometimes wonder if the real me is completely invisible to everyone. It's the enormous pile of banknotes they see when they look at me which attracts them. You might think I have everything, yet I envy you your riches, Jack. You have three brothers who love you unconditionally, a noisy, cheerful house and a purpose every morning when you get up. I get up alone in the morning, make myself busy with trivialities which bore me senseless and go to bed alone again every single night. It is humbling to learn that I am of such little consequence to people that none of my so-called friends and acquaintances have even noticed I am missing. My uncle picked the perfect time. Christmas is a time for families. And I don't have one.'

'I never realised your life was like that.' His fingers had laced with hers somewhere during her monologue and it made her sadder, yet she did not want his pity.

'What do you see when you look at me?'

He was silent for ages, his thumb gently tracing lazy circles in her palm.

'I don't see a pile of banknotes or a superficial spoiled girl.' His intense gaze finally locked meaningfully with hers. 'I see the most beautiful woman in the world. I see a woman who never ceases to amaze me. One who rises to every challenge. One who is tenacious and kind, who can laugh at herself and stand up for herself. One who never gives up and who cooks chicken with the feathers on.' He smiled then, except it was not any normal, everyday smile. It was an intimate, knowing smile. 'I never see Violet. I only ever see Letty.'

Something finally fell into place inside her, some misplaced part which had been missing all of her life. With it came her own epiphany. He loved her. She could see it in those fathomless blue depths without him needing to say the words. The words were superfluous anyway. His feelings came out in every solicitous action, every noble deed. Not only that, but she loved him in return. She recognised that now. It was more than attraction and lust, or the need for him to like her. Her heart belonged to him and always would. Every sinew and fibre of her being wanted only to be with him. The knowledge gave her inner strength. New purpose to crack through the noble fortress he hid behind because it was *he* who felt unworthy.

She stood and let the towel slither to the floor, watched his eyes widen, then darken with desire as they raked her naked body, even though he remained rooted to his spot in the armchair. Feeling the weight of his stare, she turned and slowly walked towards the bed, feeling every inch the temptress she wanted him to see. When she reached the bed, Letty slid between the crisp, clean sheets and propped herself up seductively on one elbow, making sure the covers only covered her up to the waist.

'Come to bed, Jack.'

He sat as still as a statue, his eyes locked on her and his breathing erratic. 'No. I won't ruin you, Letty.'

Oh, bless him! she thought as she giggled at his ridiculously noble gesture. 'Don't you see, Jack? You *can't* ruin me. I could take a hundred lovers and it would make no difference. The majority of my suitors would overlook my lack of virginity in much the same way they ultimately overlook the real me. I'm Violet Dunston, remember. It's my fortune they want to take to bed. The lack of my maidenhead would hardly deter them—yet it would be such a shame to waste it on one of them when they wouldn't appreciate it. You would appreciate it, wouldn't you, Jack?'

She let him war with himself for a few moments, watched the interesting battle being fought in his expression. The responsible gentleman fought the human man with basic human urges. When he stood up, it was hard to discern which one of them had won. He strode towards her, suddenly appearing quite furious.

'I won't offer you marriage yet, Letty. I am not a fortune hunter.'

'I don't recall asking you to marry me, Jack. I'm asking you to come to bed. To make love to me. If anything, you silly, stubborn man, it is me who is intent on ruining you. In fact, if I do it properly, I will ruin you for all other women except me.'

Then he grinned. It was the same roguish smile which had dazzled her weeks before. 'You want to ruin me?'

'Indeed I do. I promise not to view it as a declaration

of marriage or even a promise of one. I am perfectly happy to wait and see if my feelings for you are real.' Which of course they were, except the idiot was too proud to see it. He couldn't accept that anyone would truly want him for the man he was. However, there was no point in arguing with him about it now. Not when his obstinate, responsible mind was made up. If she was going to get her way, then she had to give him another reason to willingly come to her bed. Fortunately, she did not have to make anything up. 'The truth is, I want you. I want that big, brutish Warriner body on mine. I want your hands all over me. I want to know what it feels like to be bedded by a man who doesn't care about my money. I want to give myself to the only man who sees the real Letty. And if you don't take me soon, all of this burning desire that consumes me will send me mad from the wanting.'

From the heated determined expression on his handsome face, her words might well have hit their mark. His mouth began to curve up slowly. It was all male and deliciously predatory.

'Brace yourself, Letty. You are about to be thoroughly ravished.'

'I am?'

She rolled languidly on to her back and stretched her arms out on the pillow like a cat enjoying the sunshine, but she could not hide her smug smile of victory. It slid off her face when he dropped his own towel on the floor and she caught her first glimpse of him completely naked. Every inch of him was firm, solid male.

Every single inch.

And, good grief, there was a lot of inches to accommodate.

He saw her reaction and gave her a very self-satis-
fied, confident smile. 'Try not to panic, sweetheart. If I
do it right, we shall likely both lose our heads and you
will have a splendid time in the process.'

'I—I will?'

His big body slipped under the covers next to her.
One strong arm snaked possessively around her hip
and tugged her until her body was flush up against his.

'You will. I promise. *This* Warriner always keeps
his word.'

Chapter Twenty-Two

‿‿‿‿‿‿○‿‿‿‿‿‿

Twelve glorious hours to go...

Jack did not disappoint. From the outset he assaulted
her senses with all manner of new sensations, each one
a revelation. Just being so intimately aligned, bare skin
to bare skin from head to toe, was an experience. His
body was solid and unyielding. He was hard where she
was soft. Flat where she had curves. Her hands enjoyed shamelessly exploring those masculine planes and
her eyes hungrily watched as certain muscles tensed
or jumped under her touch. Because she had to, Letty
placed her mouth on his chest, inhaling the intoxicating
scent of him as she ran her lips over his body.

Jack was doing some exploring of his own, except
his lips followed his fingers everywhere they went. He
started with her mouth, kissing her until her body ached
for more, then he tortured her by licking and nibbling
his way slowly down her neck and shoulders. He stayed
longer on her breasts, his clever tongue working her
nipples into such a state of arousal that she had to grab
his head and hold it in place. But even that did not ease

her body's urgent cravings and Letty found her hips straining to meet his, her legs falling open wantonly in invitation, desperately wishing he would put an end to the delicious torture and fill her body with his.

He knew what she wanted and denied it. Letty felt him smile as he twisted his hips out of her reach and placed soft kisses over her belly—which did nothing to satisfy her overpowering desires. There were other, better places she wanted his mouth. Her breasts, for example, still ached for his touch.

She tried to drag his mouth back to hers, but he would have none of it, preferring to trace the outline of her navel with his tongue, and she growled in frustration.

'You're a wretch, Jack Warriner.'

His returning laughter was muffled. 'Why am I a wretch?'

'Because…'

'If you cannot tell me, then how can I know what it is you want?' His teeth scraped her hip and began to nibble their way down the top of her thigh.

'You know perfectly well what I want…'

Those lips were torturing the sensitive skin on her inner thigh now. It was a vast improvement on having them on her stomach, but as pleasant as it was, it did absolutely nothing to lessen the ache between her legs. An ache which was causing her to writhe desperately on the mattress. His splayed hands rested on the very top of both thighs, so very close yet still so far away from where she craved them. Her hips bucked instinctively and he stared up at her with the most wicked smile she had seen yet. It was no wonder. From his position he could see all the secret parts of her which remained a mystery to even her own eyes and, heaven help her, she didn't care one whit.

'Jack…please.'

He smiled knowingly and dipped his head, and to her complete surprise, and utter mortification, placed a hot kiss *there*. Instinctively, Letty went to close her legs, only to find his hold on them made it quite impossible. She tried to sit up, but then his tongue touched something which sent ripples of pure pleasure through her entire body.

'Oooooh…'

The noise she made came out part-sigh, part-groan, and she quite forgot that she was outraged by the improper intrusion. When his tongue stroked her again intimately, Letty sank back on to the pillows and decided she did not want to fight him. Clearly the man knew exactly what he was doing, so who was she to argue? Within moments, nothing else existed other than his clever mouth on her most secret place and the mounting pleasure that tiny intimate movement was creating. Words would not form, only noises. Soft sighs, urgent moans. One hand plunged into his hair, the other gripped the sheets tight and her heels dug into the bed so she did not move a muscle, fearing if she did he would leave that one, delectable sweet spot she had not known had existed just a few minutes ago.

Jack could feel the tension build in her body and like the novice she was she fought against it. Her head thrashed from side to side, her hips strained against his mouth, while she hovered on the cusp. Gently, he eased his finger inside her to massage the inner walls of her body. Nobody else had touched her like this.

Just him.

If nothing else came of their relationship, he would always be her first and he was going to make sure she never forgot him. He was determined to spoil all other men for her, just as she had ruined him for any other woman. Letty was so warm and wet and tight it made him groan as he stroked her. His own body was screaming for release, but he wanted her to know what pleasure felt like before he stole away her innocence. Yet, it didn't feel like he was really stealing it from her. She was giving it to him, freely and with such trust it humbled him. When her hips began to buck, he sucked the sweet bud into his mouth and heard and felt her release joyfully. He shifted so that he could see her face. Her eyes were closed, her corkscrew curls were fanned over the pillow and her lips were parted in ecstasy.

She sensed his gaze and her eyes fluttered open and stared down at him. Jack had never witnessed anything so utterly perfect as Letty was right then. His heart stuttered and his breath caught, and his body throbbed with need. He should stop now. That was the gentlemanly thing to do. Slowly he sat back on his heels and sucked in calming breaths.

He watched, slightly unnerved, as Letty's small hands reached out to touch him. She traced his hardness reverently, her fingertips so gentle that Jack had to clench his teeth to stop crying out. Now would be the perfect time to rise from the bed and leave her, because if he stayed a moment longer his resolve would evaporate. He should leave her a virgin. That was the right thing to do. But against his wishes, his hand closed around hers, showing her how to hold him, and from then on he was lost. When he could stand the exquisite torture no more, he lay down beside her again and, like the trusting angel she was, she opened her arms in invitation.

Her lovely body was still trembling when he positioned himself between her legs and the happy, pleasure-filled smile she gave him, and the way her arms looped languidly around his neck let him know she welcomed this part of the act, too. Emotion clogged his throat. This beautiful, perfect, angel wanted him.

Jack Warriner.

What had he ever done to deserve such a gift?

'I love you, Letty.' The words tumbled out before he could claw them back. Her kiss-swollen lips parted and he just knew she was going to say the same words back. But he wanted them to be real, not uttered in the heat of the moment when her passions were inflamed. Jack placed his fingers gently on her mouth. 'Not now, Letty. Tell me in a month or two, when all the danger is over. If you still mean it.'

She sighed and kissed him deeply instead, pushing her hips against his in encouragement. He kissed her back, the tip of his arousal nudging her entrance, and then, with painful, tender slowness, pushed inside.

Her tight heat encased him. Jack's body urgently wanted to move, but he held back. He stopped when he met the barrier of her maidenhead. Only then did he break the kiss to stare down into her face. He did not need to tell her he did not wish to hurt her. She understood. Her hand came up to cup his cheek and she shrugged her shoulders.

'Just do it. I trust you to make it right.'

So he did. He pushed past the barrier swiftly, burying himself deep inside her and then stopped dead, feeling like a savage brute for causing her pain. It was Letty's hips which moved first, undulating against his, enticing him to continue and driving him mad with need.

When he moved, he intended to do so slowly, but it was Letty who spurred him on. She met his tentative thrusts eagerly, staring deep into his eyes, a beautiful, contented smile on her face. When she wrapped her legs around him and he saw her eyes flutter closed in pleasure, he quite forgot his oath to go slowly. The faster he moved, the deeper he plunged, the more Letty moaned her enjoyment. When her hands came down to grab his buttocks and he felt her pull them roughly, urgently towards her body, he gave up trying to fight it and let the desire take him. To his relief, she cried out first and her body pulsed around the entire length of him, and Jack finally lost his head and joined her, crying out her name in exultation as he pulled out and spilled himself beside her, protecting her even in the heat of the moment.

Knowing she had made good on her promise.

She had ruined him for all other women. He would never be able to look at another one again because no one else was Letty and he belonged to her.

They slept for a few hours before Jack could not resist the urge to make love to her again. Slower this time, because he knew it might well be for the very last time. When they next awoke it was already dark and way past the time they should have started on the road. He was tempted to ask her to stay until the morning, but knew what they had come to do could not be put off. If they made good time tonight, they would still see London in the morning and, as much as he feared what returning her home might do to them, it was long past time they banished the threat from her uncle and the Earl of Bainbridge from her life. Once that was dealt with, fate, no doubt, would have its rightful say and all Jack could do was hope and pray that, for once, it might take pity on him.

Jack lifted her on to the saddle carefully, his expression rueful. 'Are you sore, sweetheart?'

She was, a little bit, but it was a pleasant sort of soreness which reminded her of what they had done. The very last thing she wanted was to make him feel guilty for it. 'Not really. I quite like how it feels.'

'I shouldn't have woken you and—'

'Don't you dare apologise for our second time together. I thoroughly enjoyed myself.'

A smile played at the corners of his mouth as he hoisted himself on his own horse. 'It was rather spectacular.'

An understatement.

Intimacies with Jack Warriner were yet another revelation and not something Letty had any intention of giving up while he *waited for the dust to settle* and he decided they were meant to be together. Why was he so determined to be stubborn? What did she have to do to prove her feelings for him were as real as his were for her?

'It's insulting, you know.' Letty hadn't meant to think out loud, but decided not to be sorry for the sudden outburst.

'What is?'

'Your ridiculous insistence that I do not know my own mind.'

'You have been through such a terrible ordeal…'

Letty rolled her eyes in irritation. 'Oh, please! Not that speech again. It's becoming very tiresome. To be frank, Jack, I really haven't been through a terrible ordeal at all. Yes, I have had a few terrifying moments in the last month, I am not denying that, but overall, it has been a very positive experience.'

'The devil it has!' It was his turn to appear agitated now. 'Being kidnapped has been a positive experience?'

They turned their horses into a narrower section of the road, riding side by side while they bickered. 'Yes, it has. I have really enjoyed living at Markham Manor. I liked being part of the family and learning new things.'

'Like how to clean nooks and crannies and do laundry?' He was staring at her as if she had gone quite mad.

'Yes, I did, as a matter of fact. It made me appreciate my life more. I got a great sense of achievement from doing those chores and it made me happy to know I was helping you and your brothers.'

'So you do admit you are *grateful* to me, then?'

She was going to kill him. He was determined to twist her words to justify his own fears about them. 'Of course I am grateful. You saved me, sheltered me and took care of me. Who wouldn't be grateful? But *that* is not the reason why I gave myself to you. I was not *that* grateful, I can assure you. I was merely trying to explain why the past month has not been the dreadful ordeal you seem to think it was and you are determined to find reasons why I couldn't possibly love you, when I know quite well that *I do* love you. And a few weeks of contemplation in London is *not* going to change that.'

He pulled up his horse smartly and appeared to be quite annoyed with this statement.

'I've told you not to say anything like that until you are certain.'

But she could see the hope shining in his troubled blue eyes despite his words. If he hadn't been so much taller and broader than she was, and if they had not both been sat astride horses on the Great North Road, Letty would have grabbed him by those splendid shoulders and tried to shake some sense into him. Denied that satisfaction, words would have to do.

'I am certain, you stubborn fool! I have never been more certain of anything in my entire life.

'I.

'Love.

'You.

'There! I said it again. And I'm not addled, or suffering from misguided gratefulness or blinded by lust to the detriment of all else. It is *you* who is uncertain, Jack. And rather insultingly, you are uncertain of me!'

He went to interrupt, but she didn't give him the chance.

'You're convinced that after a few weeks, I will grow to resent you, like your selfish mother did your father and grow melancholy and perhaps fade away. What evidence do you have to support such a preposterous notion? I am not like her, Jack. I am not some silly, spoiled, weak-willed woman who cannot cope without the finer things in life. I can bake bread, for goodness sake, and round up sheep and thwart kidnappers all on my own. I am not now, nor will I ever be, the sort of woman who feels sorry for herself or throws herself into a river.'

When he opened his mouth once more to refute her, she gave him her parting salvo. Something, apparently, he had thus far not considered.

'You think my life with you will be hard. You believe I will be shunned and ostracised by society. If I am, it will be a blessing. I loathe society. I am sick and tired of pretending to be Violet and feeling lonely. But that aside, I think you are missing one very pertinent detail. I am *the Tea Heiress*. I have far too much money for anyone to shun me, and, in case it has not crossed your stubborn, proud, obstinate mind, *when* you marry me—and you will marry me, Jack Warriner, because *we* love each other to bits—you are going to be obscenely wealthy, too!'

Neither of them saw the four armed men at the side of the road waiting for them until it was too late.

Chapter Twenty-Three

Two precarious hours left...

'Hello, Violet. Did you miss me?'

The Earl of Bainbridge's face was suddenly illuminated when he struck a match. Jack glimpsed the yellowed whites of his eyes and the pistol in his gnarled hand before the match spluttered and died. Jack did his best to shield Letty with his body while he scanned the dark road for a way to escape. Dense tangled bushes flanked both sides of the road, too high for their horses to jump without momentum and too thick to be able to charge through. As he considered galloping back towards Baldock, a dark carriage rolled out behind them, blocking the *road* completely. Another man climbed out, the same sort of age as Bainbridge and clutching another pistol which he aimed directly at them.

'Uncle William. Have you come to do your own dirty work this time?' Letty glared at him defiantly, her delicate chin lifted and her fine eyes colder than Jack had ever seen them.

'You should have married Bainbridge, Violet. If you had, then we could have avoided all of this nastiness.'

'My father entrusted you with my safekeeping. He would be turning in his grave to know how you have betrayed me!'

'Perhaps if your father had distributed some of his wealth to me, then I would not have had to resort to this. But I did.'

Layton stepped out of the shadows, his white, jagged scar more apparent in the moonlight. Jack heard the click as he cocked the hammer of his pistol and pointed it menacingly at Letty. 'Get down from those horses.'

The cold calm delivery sent a chill down Jack's spine. Resisting the urge to pull his own pistol from his belt, he put his hands in the air.

'Do as he says, Letty.'

On foot, if he could distract Layton, there might be a way of slipping Letty behind the bushes so she could escape.

Unfortunately, as soon as her feet touched the ground, Letty decided to go on the attack. She made to lunge towards her uncle, but Jack caught her and shielded as much of her straining body as he could with his own. Being restrained did nothing to stop her resolve.

'Do you seriously think I will allow you to drag me to Gretna Green again and force me to marry *that* man?'

Her uncle frowned, his own temper dangerously close to the surface. 'I'm afraid that option is now closed, Violet, thanks to your intrepid escape. It will be easier all around if Bainbridge just kills you.'

'Are you too cowardly to do it yourself?' Good grief, now she was baiting the man. Jack shot her a warning look, hoping she would back down. Could she not see that while he was holding her back, he was unable to facilitate her escape?

Being Letty, of course she ignored him.

'Here I am, Uncle. Look me in the eyes and then put a bullet between them.'

'I have no taste for murder, Violet.'

'Yet you sold me off to a murderer quite happily! Does that alleviate your warped conscience in some way?' She gave a scornful laugh.

'I did what I had to. Now that I think about it, we should have done that from the outset. There was never any need for you to actually marry Bainbridge in the first place because, with you dead, all of your fortune automatically comes to me. But I wanted the deed done far away from London. There are too many curious onlookers there, all so keen to know the next thrilling instalment in the life of the charmed Violet Dunston.'

Jack saw Letty's eyes widen in terror a split second before he felt the cold press of a steel barrel against his temple.

'Step away from the lady, Mr Warriner.' Layton's voice was laced with malice. 'Or should that be *your lordship…* The people of Retford were very *eager* to tell us all about your family. A bad lot, by all accounts, cheats, thieves, debauchers—*earls* who would do anything to line their empty pockets with gold. It works in our favour.'

The bottom of Jack's gut sunk to his knees as he experienced a strange premonition of what they had planned. Whatever crime would be committed here tonight, the Warriners would be blamed for. 'Aren't you forgetting one thing? There are four of us. Or I am to commit your atrocities alone?'

Jack saw the moment realisation dawned in Letty's wide green eyes. So did the Earl of Bainbridge. His dry cackle of amusement was the only sound in the still, dark night. 'You picked a fine family to align yourself with, Violet. They have such a bad reputation I doubt anyone will question their guilt or their hand in your murder. Once the true horror of how they kidnapped you, demanded a huge ransom from your dear uncle, then tried to renege on the deal at the exchange by demanding even more money is known, no one will question it... Fortunately, your uncle had the wherewithal to come with armed men. Shots were fired. Your degenerate Earl was killed—and you, dear Violet, were accidentally caught in the crossfire. It will all be very tragic. Very fitting. One last, splendid story for the newspapers. We will arrange your funeral for the day his wastrel brothers are rounded up and hanged.'

Her eyes darted between Jack, the pistol at his head and the other men, the panic in her eyes clear to see. Eventually, they settled on Bainbridge, pleading.

'None of this is Jack's fault. I will do whatever you want—just let him go.'

She was trying to save him? Jack's temper surged forth. Of all the stupid, misguided, dangerous, selfless things to offer. If they got out of this alive, he might just kill her himself. But Letty wasn't anywhere near finished making sacrifices. Like a lioness protecting her cub, she placed her body in front of his. Jack heard the hammer of another pistol cock.

'Take that gun away from his head.'

When, miraculously, Layton complied and Jack

stepped away, he saw Letty had her gun pressed hard into the man's belly. She turned her head slightly, never taking her eyes off Layton and whispered, 'Run, Jack!'

Oh, for goodness sake! This was getting ridiculous. As if he would leave her? As if he could? He loved her, for pity's sake. When you loved someone you didn't abandon them. You tried to save them—

Just as she was trying her level best to save his sorry skin by sacrificing hers, he realised. A lioness to match his lion. There were certainly better ways to be confronted with the full extent of his utter, blind stupidity. Perhaps he wouldn't kill her after all. He would marry her instead—but first he had to find a way to get them out of here.

Before Jack could react, both Bainbridge and her traitorous uncle raised their own weapons and aimed them directly at him.

'What do you hope to achieve, Violet? You are outnumbered. Once your shot is spent, you will still have to watch him die.' The Earl walked towards him purposefully, his gun arm outstretched and his jaw set firm.

Despite Letty's brave façade, the impending threat made her waver. She tossed her pistol on the ground. 'Please! Don't hurt him. I'll marry you. I'll marry you willingly and then you will have all my money, just don't harm Jack.'

For the second time, a pistol was pressed against Jack's head, except this time he experienced the utter devastation which comes from defeat. She loved him and he loved her, yet now they were both doomed to die. Fate always had the last laugh at the Warriners in the end. Well, if he was about to die, he would do so bravely. Jack stood proudly, squared his shoulders and stared at Letty. Better her face was the last he saw...

But the blasted woman suddenly darted out of Layton's grasp and ran like a banshee towards the carriage.

'Take me to Gretna Green! Marry me to Bainbridge... I won't tell a soul.' Frantic sobs made her voice catch. 'Just leave Jack alone!'

It was her uncle who stalked towards her and grabbed her arm roughly. He tried to drag her back towards Jack, but she fought him, wrestling out of the confines of his arms and pushing him back against the door of the carriage. A sharp cutlass suddenly appeared out of the darkened window of the carriage and pressed against her uncle's neck.

Then came Jamie's calm but incredibly menacing voice.

'As I see it, Bainbridge, this whole sordid plot relies on this snake inheriting all of Letty's fortune. Once I kill him, even if you do kill her, all of that lovely money goes directly to the Crown, which leaves you with precisely nothing. Unless, of course, you can breathe some life into what will be left of his sorry carcase when I am finished with him.'

Jack saw the fear in Bainbridge's eyes and did not waste his chance. He reached under his greatcoat and retrieved his own pistol, taking great pleasure in aiming it at the old, wrinkled Earl and slowly dragging the hammer back.

'You are still outnumbered, Warriner!' he spat back defiantly as Layton and the remaining lackey aimed their own weapons straight back.

In the brittle silence another pistol clicked. Joe emerged from the bushes and poked his weapon into the lackey's back. 'And now there are three of us.' For a man who was more likely to heal a fly than hurt it, even Jack was convinced his brother meant business.

Jack's relief at his brothers' arrival was palpable, but the battle was still far from won. At best, it was a stand-off. Layton was only inches away from Letty—one false move and she might be hurt. He glanced at her and he saw nothing but determination and strength in her lovely eyes. For his benefit, she flicked her eyes to her abandoned pistol on the ground. It lay between them like a beacon, too far for either of them to snatch it up. Their only hope now was Jacob—but he had yet to make an appearance...unless he had stayed behind to look after the farm...

With a sinking feeling, Jack realised he might well have done. If he had been in charge, he might well have insisted someone stay behind to shoulder those important responsibilities. As if any of that was as important as Letty's life?

Jamie yanked back her uncle's head by the hair and pressed his blade against the whimpering man's neck. 'Drop your weapons now, or I will sever his treacherous head from his quaking, cowardly body.'

'Do as he says!'

It gave Letty some satisfaction to hear her uncle was terrified. However, it did not deter from the fact that all four of them were in a very precarious position. There were still two pistols pointed at Jack: Bainbridge's and Layton's. Only one would be required to kill him. Fortunately, all eyes were on her squealing uncle—not her. With one decisive lunge, she threw herself at the abandoned pistol, landing on the cold ground with a thud.

Layton instantly turned his gun towards her as she

scrambled to grip the weapon in her hands. Letty rolled on to her back and aimed right back at Layton. 'Now you are outnumbered.'

But only just. Jamie had a sword to her uncle's neck, Jack had Bainbridge in his sights, she had Layton and Joe had the remaining man.

'Then we have nothing to lose.'

Letty watched in horror as the Earl's index finger began to squeeze the trigger. She twisted to aim her gun at him, and pulled the trigger. The bullet tore through Bainbridge's leg, sending a spray of blood and flesh into the air, and at the same moment Jack knocked the pistol from his flailing hand.

Layton made a grab for her and Letty scrambled to her knees to try to crawl away. He fisted his hand in her hair and yanked her roughly back.

'Get your filthy hands off her!'

Jack went to attack, but stopped when he saw the man's pistol pressing into her neck. Behind her, Letty could feel Layton's laboured, frightened breathing and tried to remain calm.

She had to focus on the practicalities.

They were winning and Layton sensed it. A cornered animal was always the most dangerous.

'Go ahead, Mr Layton. Shoot me. It will be the last thing you ever do and we both know it.'

Beneath her, Letty could feel vibrations through the ground. Someone was coming. Layton realised it, too. His hold on her hair tightened and he gazed around him in panic. 'Murder is a capital offence, Mr Layton. If I die, you will be hanged. That is if my fiancé doesn't shoot you first.'

The hoofbeats came closer. Lots of them. In the distance there was the sound of voices, too. All she had to do was keep him from pulling the trigger until they arrived. 'You can't escape, Mr Layton. You are surrounded. Your accomplices have already lost.'

Her eyes locked with Jack's, warning him to stay back. The last thing they needed now was for Layton to shoot him in panic. His stormy eyes were furious, but he nodded curtly, he had delegated the responsibility for saving them to her and she loved him for that. Jack never relinquished control. Ever.

'If you surrender now, the worst you can be charged with is kidnap. If you are lucky, you will be transported.' She felt his fingers uncurl against her scalp and pressed her advantage. 'Throw down your weapon, Mr Layton. Don't let them see you holding a gun to my throat.'

The 'them' she was referring to trundled noisily towards them and Layton finally complied. He let go of her hair and threw his pistol down angrily just as Jacob arrived at the head of a large mob of men. His eyes took in the scene and he grinned down at her.

'I see I timed my arrival perfectly.'

He grasped her hand and hauled her up. A middle-aged man next to him stepped forward.

'Are you the Tea Heiress?'

When she nodded he appeared relieved.

'Miss Dunston, we heard you were in distress. Kindly point out the scoundrels who tried to kidnap you.'

Letty happily pointed at the guilty four, taking great pleasure in seeing them manhandled by the rescue party. Jamie kept his sword pressed against her uncle's throat while his hands were bound. Only then did he lower his weapon and climb out of the carriage. Two men took Layton by the arms, and he stood in quiet fury as he, too, was bound. Jack roughly hoisted Bainbridge by the shoulders and, in spite of his shattered leg, dragged him unceremoniously towards Letty and dropped him at her feet.

'I want to kill him.'

She threaded her arm through his and rested her head gratefully on his powerful arm. 'He will get his comeuppance. It's best to let the law deal with him. You can say your piece at his trial.'

Jamie limped beside them. 'With any luck, they'll hang. Did the fools not realise? When you mess with one Warriner, you mess with us all.'

Chapter Twenty-Four

Finally, midnight, 4th January 1814...

Letty and the four Warriners watched the locals make short work of securing the prisoners. Then they all returned to Baldock. The middle-aged man, it turned out, was the local constable and a great reader of the gossip columns. He gave orders for her abductors to be locked up in the local gaol and accompanied Letty and the brothers to the inn to hear their testimony. They all crowded around one big table, sipping steaming cups of tea, while he began with the formalities.

'I shall need your full names for the record.'

'Well, you already know my name is Violet Elizabeth Dunston. And this is my fiancé Jack Warriner, the Earl of...?' She turned to Jack in question as it occurred to her she didn't know.

'Markham.'

'Oh, that's nice. Your title is named after the house.'

'Actually, the house is named after the title. But that is neither here nor there.' He smiled at her indulgently before turning towards the constable. 'These are my brothers. Captain James Lionel Warriner, Joseph Lucas Warriner and Jacob Lawrence Warriner.'

More information Letty had not known. 'You all have exactly the same initials?'

'My parents were creatures of habit.'

'Does your middle name begin with the letter "L" also?'

Letty watched matching slow grins creeping up his brothers' faces and wondered why. She turned to Jack to see him smiling in amusement.

'Clearly it's a stinker if you are all grinning like idiots. Well? What is it, then?'

Joe answered for him. 'It's Leo. Like the constellation.'

'Leo?' Letty started to giggle, not caring that she snorted twice in the process. 'Leo the lion! Of course it is.' And never had a middle name suited its owner more.

The constable was extremely thorough. By the time they had all finished answering his questions, and writing down their personal version of events, it was almost two o'clock in the morning.

'What I don't understand,' Letty asked the brothers after he finally bid them goodnight, 'is how you came be in the exact right place at the exact right time?'

'You can thank Jamie for that,' Joe replied. 'We hid in the woods after you left Markham Manor and fooled them into thinking we had fled, too. When they headed to London in pursuit, we followed them. Jamie, apparently, can track anything. It was all very exciting and they never suspected a thing. We were less than a mile away when you decided to stop off at that inn.' He began to blush and Letty realised they had guessed what she and Jack had been up to in there.

Jacob, who clearly did not feel even slightly embarrassed, grinned. 'While the pair of you were *indisposed*, Jamie managed to get close enough to Bainbridge to hear what they were planning. Seeing as they were stupid enough to consider doing it so close to a town, we decided to let them ambush you in order to trap them. Catch the scoundrels in the act so that we had irrefutable proof of their guilt. I was sent to gather reinforcements.'

Jack appeared perturbed by this. 'How did you convince so many men to accompany you? Did you neglect to tell them your surname?'

'Oh, for goodness sake, Jack! Nobody in Baldock has ever heard the name Warriner. But they had all heard about Letty. Once they realised it was Violet Dunston who was the heiress in distress, they were surprisingly keen to offer their assistance.' Jacob screwed up his face, suddenly a little sheepish. 'I might have mentioned there would be a reward. Sorry, Letty—but I promised them five pounds apiece.'

Letty rose from her chair, grabbed his face and kissed him soundly on the forehead. 'I can afford it. It was good thinking on your part and I will be eternally grateful.'

She then marched to Joe and enveloped him a hug. 'Thank you, Dr Joe. For everything. You were very brave. And frightening. The ladies are going to love you.' The most studious Warriner blushed profusely and earned a ribbing from his younger sibling.

Letty finally stood in front of Jamie and felt a knot of emotion. For all of his inscrutability and curt comments, he hid a heart of pure gold. 'Thank you for saving me.'

'That's what families do, Letty—and I assume you

are about to become family and that my pig-headed oldest brother has finally come to his senses.' Jamie offered her one of his almost smiles. 'Consider it our birthday gift and wedding gift combined. And you can stop those tears right now before they fall, madam. I don't do waterworks.'

Letty felt Jack come up behind her before he curled his arm possessively around her waist. 'Now that we are not in such a hurry to get to London in the morning, shall we see if there is room for us all at this inn?'

'Inn? Haystack? I don't care so long as I am with you.' And she didn't. 'But I don't want to go to London. I want to go back home to celebrate my birthday—to Markham Manor.' Because there was nobody important in London apart from her solicitor and he could jolly well come to her. She would build her foundling home in Nottingham instead. It was equally as rotten and just as desperate.

Jack winced and heaved out a deep breath. 'With all of the worry and excitement, I completely forgot that today is your birthday. Now I feel bad. I haven't given you a gift.'

Letty grabbed his lapels and kissed him noisily. 'Yes, you did. You're my birthday gift. And don't let it go to your head, but for a girl who has everything, you, Jack Warriner, are the best present I have ever had.'

Joe and Jacob grinned. Jamie groaned.

'Seeing as you two are getting all soppy, I'm off to bed.' He tossed Jack a room key. 'Come on, boys. Let's leave the Earl of Markham and his beloved to it.'

Even though she knew they were creating a shocking spectacle, Letty could not bring herself to let go of Jack just yet. She needed to keep touching him to reassure herself that he was safe. And she didn't want to cry, even though the tears were so close to the surface. Her new life had already started and she was not going to spoil it with tears. They would fall, she knew, but not tonight. Tonight, she just wanted to enjoy being unashamedly with Jack. Her Jack. A farmer and, apparently, an earl.

'Why did I not know you had a title?'

'I've never had cause to use it.'

'I used to want a title. It was on my list of attributes for any potential future husband.'

'What other attributes did you want your future husband to have? I should be interested to know how I measure up,' he teased.

'Let me see…' Letty tapped her chin and pretended to consider it. 'He had to be handsome, which of course, you are. So that is good news. He also had to be witty, and whilst you are nowhere near as funny as I am, you can hold up your end—when you are not being stubborn and dictatorial, that is. I wanted him to be an excellent horseman. I like to ride and I needed my husband to have a fine seat on a horse. You ride well enough, but your seat is most excellent.'

She wiggled her eyebrows shamelessly and he grinned wickedly at the compliment. 'Aside from my superior posterior, is there any other criteria I will be judged against?'

'Of course! I am very particular. My future husband would have to be a connoisseur of the theatre—and I know you read plays when you can tear yourself away from those awful ledgers—and I suppose I could loosely class your portrait of Sir Hugo as evidence of your being a patron of the arts. I also wanted my husband to be the absolute envy of all of my society friends, but seeing as I am not altogether sure I have any *real* friends there, that hardly counts any more.' Letty wrapped her arms around his waist and stared up into his hypnotic blue eyes adoringly. 'Most importantly, my future husband *had* to be *hopelessly* in love with me. Which, it goes without saying, you are. And who could blame you. Just as I am hopelessly in love with you.'

His hands came to rest gently on her shoulders. 'You do realise absolutely everyone will assume that I have only married you for your money.'

'Not everyone. I know the truth. Your brothers know the truth. I don't care what anyone else thinks. Just as long as I get to marry my handsome, responsible, proud, stubborn Earl.' She walked her fingers up his broad chest suggestively before placing her palm flat against his steadily beating heart, secure in the knowledge it belonged to her, not the pile of banknotes which came with her. If it took her for ever, Letty was determined to banish all of his insecurities about his unworthiness away. 'Have I already mentioned how determined I was that my future husband would have a title? It was the one frippery I never had.'

With great deliberation, Jack took her right hand in his and slid the emerald ring off her finger. Then he took her left hand. He slipped the gold band slowly on to her ring finger, arranged the stone just so, then brought her hand up to his lips.

'Well, I am glad I can offer you that, at least. Once we're married you can call yourself Countess. No more Violet Dunston, the Tea Heiress. You'll be Letty Warriner, the Countess of Markham.'

Letty held out her hand to examine the ring's new

position and grinned. 'I quite like the sound of Letty Warriner—but I find myself surprisingly ambivalent to being a countess. It sounds so…superficial and privileged, don't you think? I believe, going forward, you should simply call me sweetheart.'

Jack kissed her long and hard until the walls of the inn swayed and her knees almost buckled. When he finally prised his mouth from hers, he stared down at her and smiled. It was his roguish smile. The one which always did funny things to her insides.

'Happy Birthday, sweetheart.' His deep blue eyes swirled with mischief and promise. 'If you follow me upstairs, I might be persuaded to let you unwrap your present.'

* * * * *

A WARRINER TO
RESCUE HER

For Ellen.

For always being there for my children with
either a ready bandage or unconditional love.

Chapter One

May 1814

The blood-curdling female scream shook him out of his daze instantly. Jamie pulled up his horse and glanced frantically around to see if he could locate the source. All he saw was familiar meadow and trees, and for a moment he thought he might have imagined it. With the warm sun on his face and the leisurely motion of his mount ambling aimlessly beneath him, it was quite feasible he had nodded off. He was exhausted, after all.

Constantly exhausted from his brain's inability to stop whirring when darkness fell, conjuring up memories from his past which haunted him even though he knew both men responsible for the pain were undeniably dead and therefore no longer a threat. Yet the ghost of them lingered in his mind, forcing him to stay vigilant and preventing him from snatching more than a few hours here and there, usually as the sun began to banish the darkness away. Or perhaps it was simply the darkness which frightened him as it had as a child?

After so many months, he was no longer sure. Just irritated with his own inability to move past it.

The second scream, no less curdling or high-pitched, raised all of his hackles, putting him on instant alert. With his soldier's instinct, Jamie raced his horse in the direction of the shriek, which happened to be towards the orchard near the huge wall which surrounded Markham Manor. The orderly trees were arranged in parallel lines with person-width paths of grass in between; aside from the gentle swish of leaves blowing in the summer breeze, silence reigned.

He cast his eyes methodically up and down the rows until he saw something—a dainty skewbald pony casually munching on the tiny, unripe apples that littered the ground around its hooves. As it was wearing both halter and a side-saddle, yet there was no sign of the rider, Jamie carefully lowered himself to the ground and wrapped his own reins loosely about a branch. At the best of times his temperamental black stallion was foul tempered; around other horses he was prone to be a brute. The pretty cream-and-dun pony, with her long fluffy mane and even longer eyelashes, would not stand a chance.

Jamie limped towards the abandoned animal slowly, conscious any sudden movement might spook the strange pony and send it galloping off to who knew where. 'Easy, girl...' At least he assumed it was a girl. If it were a boy the other horses would tease him mercilessly for that effeminate mane.

'Hello!' A slightly panicked woman's voice came from above. 'Is somebody there?'

'Hello?' He hadn't been expecting to address the sky. The sun pierced Jamie's eyes to such an extent he could not see a thing except blinding yellow light. The woman's exact location remained a mystery. Unless she was an angel sent to fetch him and drag him off to heaven, which he sincerely doubted. They had had their chance and failed miserably and if he was bound for anywhere it was probably hell. 'I can't see you!'

'I am in the tree... I wonder if you would be so good as to assist me, sir. I appear to be stuck.'

Surreal words, again unexpected. How did a woman come to be stuck in an apple tree? Jamie did his best to shield the worst of the glare with his hand and squinted through the tangled branches. Two wiggling feet dangled nearly six feet above his head. They were encased in half-boots and were attached to a very shapely pair of female legs, clad in fine silk stockings which were held up with rather saucy pink garters. His eyes widened at the garters. From this perspective they appeared to be completely festooned with flowers. Above them, about an inch or two of creamy thigh was also on display. The rest of the woman was hidden by leaves.

Thankfully, a passing cloud chose that exact moment to block out the worst of the sun, allowing Jamie to get a better look at the rest of the dangling woman. Her slate-coloured skirt, so incongruous in comparison to her choice of vibrant underthings, had inverted and appeared to be wrapped tightly around her upper body. One arm clung to a branch above, the other, and her head, were apparently trapped within the fabric. Her generous bottom was resting on a feeble branch which appeared likely to snap at any moment and, with nothing beneath her except the hard ground, his best assessment of her position was precarious.

'Try to remain still. I'm coming up!'

He supposed it was the gentlemanly thing to do, although Jamie had no idea if he was still actually capable of climbing a tree. Thanks to Napoleon, he could hardly walk, certainly struggled to run and his dancing days were most definitely over. Quickly, he tried to work out the best way to tackle the challenge. The last time he had cause to climb a tree, he had been a scrawny, nimble boy and he recalled it had been a simple procedure by and large. Thanks to his burly Warriner ancestors, and over a decade of growing, he was now an ox of a man. An ox of a man with a useless left leg.

However, that damned leg was not going to define him. If he wanted to climb a tree, he would climb a blasted tree! Putting all of his weight on his right foot, and using the strength of his arms, he managed to hoist himself laboriously upwards. It might have raised him less than a foot off the ground, but he had left the ground. He rearranged his good foot and heaved again. Two foot from the ground! What was that if it was not progress? Slow, laboured, feeble progress. Painful, humiliating, soul-destroying progress.

Oblivious to his grunts of exertion, or the supreme effort it took him to actually climb, the grey faceless bundle above his head decided this was the appropriate time for a conversation.

'I suppose you are wondering how I came to be stuck up this tree in the first place...' At this stage in the proceedings, how she came to be there was neither here nor there. All Jamie could concentrate on was putting one foot painfully above the other. 'It's a funny story really. My pony, Orange Blossom, has a fondness for red apples.' As she spoke, her legs and bottom jiggled, causing the fragile branch to quiver with indignation. 'And rather stupidly, I assumed... *Oooh!*'

The flimsy branch suddenly bent downwards as it split from the main trunk of the tree. Fortunately, she had the good sense to hook her legs around an adjacent branch and managed to halt her descent. Unfortunately, in doing so her dress had now ridden further up her thighs, displaying all of her legs quite thoroughly. As legs went, they were rather nice although now was really not the time he should be admiring them. As he had suspected, those saucy garters were festooned with pink-silk flowers. Her shapely derrière now hung between the two branches and directly over Jamie's head. In her panic, she was wiggling in earnest now in an attempt to free her head from its dull, muslin prison, her visible hand still clinging desperately on to a straining branch above.

Jamie began to inch closer to her struggling form. 'Madam, it is imperative that you remain still!' Because if she fell, it was his cranium which would bear the brunt and the closer he got, the less confident he was he was strong enough to catch her. If her bottom was anything to go by, she was not exactly petite. He pulled himself on to a sound-looking branch and locked one arm around it.

'Take my hand!' Perhaps he could swing her down to the ground? Unless, of course, she wrenched his shoulder out of its socket. Then he would have a crippled arm to go with his ruined leg.

He watched her wrestle within her tangled skirts until her other hand burrowed its way out and her arm made a frantic bid for freedom, but instead of grabbing his outreached hand as he had quite plainly instructed, she used it to attempt to cover her exposed legs with her inverted clothing. Tiny, hard, barely formed apples began to tumble out of the fabric and rained down around him. Two of the lead-lined fruits bounced off his head like miniature cannonballs and made him yelp.

'What in God's name are you doing, woman! Grab my blasted hand now!' For good measure, he prodded her arm to help her locate him.

More wood splintered somewhere close by and the faceless wench squealed again, her bottom lolling further between the branches and coming level with his face. At last, she swung her free arm around and grabbed his hand, but it was a moment too late. Thanks to weak, young wood and gravity, her advancing bottom had begun to gain some momentum and continued to slide on its journey downwards. Acting on impulse rather than gentlemanly manners, Jamie looped his good leg over another branch and tried to halt her descent in the only way now left open to him. Grabbing a handful of a rather pert, round cheek, he unceremoniously braced himself against it to stop her falling.

The headless woman squeaked in outrage and vehemently attempted to remove her posterior from his clenched hand by grasping at anything wildly to haul herself back up again. This frantic new movement proved to be problematic for both the tree and Jamie's tenuous grasp of it. The branch supporting his good leg snapped with a loud crack, sending them both careening helplessly downwards.

He landed flat on his back, with a resounding thud. A split second later the woman landed on top of him. Jamie was hard pressed to decide which event caused him more pain. If he'd had any breath left in his lungs, he probably would have screamed in agony. All that came out instead was a weird hiss, almost as if his entire body was slowly deflating. By some miracle, his eyes still worked. He knew this because he was currently drowning in a sea of hair.

He felt her brace herself on to her hands and lift her head up. Two brown eyes stared, blinking directly into his, far too close to allow him to see anything else. 'Are you all right?'

Hiss.

One hand came to the side of his face and she patted his cheek ineffectually, oblivious to the fact he was munching on a mouthful of her hair. 'Sir? Can you speak to me? Are you injured?'

Jamie flexed his fingers. When no pain shot down his arms, he brought them up to grab her by the shoulders and smartly lifted her upwards. 'Get your blasted hair out of my face this instant.'

She hastily scrambled off him and knelt at his side, peering down in concern. It was then that Jamie finally got his first proper look at her. Big brown eyes, with eyelashes so long they would give her pretty pony a run for its money, a heart-shaped face, obscenely plump lush mouth and a smattering of freckles dusting across the bridge of her nose. The hair which had threatened to choke him was neither red nor blonde. It hovered somewhere in between. But it was thick and heavy and really quite lovely. Even the way the twigs and leaves sprouted out of what was left of her hairstyle was strangely becoming. It was odd that splinters of foliage would suit a woman so.

He managed to lift himself up on to his elbows to

test his neck. He moved it from side to side before stretching out his spine. Nothing broken so far, which frankly, was a miracle after he had been effectively dropped from a great height, then crushed.

'You broke my fall.'

'I am well aware of that.' Jamie gingerly moved his bad leg. The fact it appeared no worse than it had before gave him some confidence. Carefully he raised himself to a sitting position and glared at the woman. She responded by grinning broadly and sticking out her hand. She grabbed his and shook it vigorously.

'My name is Cassandra Reeves. I am the daughter of the Reverend Reeves, the new vicar of this parish. I am delighted to make your acquaintance, sir.'

Well, he definitely wasn't delighted by the way the acquaintance had been made and, because he certainly did not feel like grinning, Jamie frowned instead. Her inappropriate cheerfulness was disconcerting. 'James Warriner.'

'Well, thank you for saving me. I really do appreciate it, Mr Warriner.'

'It's Captain Warriner.' Why he had the urge to make the distinction to her, he could not say, when nobody hereabouts ever called him anything other than either his first name or, sneeringly, '*one of those Warriners*'. Yet to become plain old mister again, when he was still technically an officer in His Majesty's army, was tantamount to accepting defeat. Until he resigned his commission, he would remain Captain Warriner for as long as was humanly possible. He might well have accepted his military career, as well as his life, was well and truly over—his shattered leg was never going to get any better than it was—but the rest of the world did not need to know he was finished. To be barely twenty-seven and rendered useless was a bitter pill to take.

'A military man? That explains it.'

'Explains what?' He was growling because his probing fingers could feel a tender bump forming on his scalp from the impact of one of the apple cannonballs she had fired at him.

'Your abrupt tone.' She screwed her face into a frown and put on her best impression of a man's deeper voice. *'"It is imperative you remain still..." "Grab my blasted hand now!"'*

Jamie stopped rubbing his head and stared disbelievingly at the woman. Was she pulling him up on his manners? Seriously? 'Had you grabbed my hand in the first instance, then perhaps I might have prevented you from falling out of the tree. Your dithering caused us both to fall.'

'My clothing was in disarray.' That, he knew. He had seen those garters and they were hardly the sort of garters he would expect a vicar's daughter to wear. 'It would have been improper to leave it that way.'

'Yet your nod to propriety proved to be remarkably ineffectual, did it not? Not only did it send us both crashing to the ground, it was a completely pointless exercise. Your skirts had been up for some time, Miss Reeves, and I am not blind.'

She blushed then, quite prettily, and those huge brown eyes widened with alarm. 'You might have told me. It was hardly gentlemanly for you to look.'

'Perhaps you would have preferred I closed my eyes and groped around in the branches blindly in the vain hope I might grab you on the off chance?'

'You did grab me, as I recall, and most improperly, too.' Her freckled nose poked into the air as she delivered this set down.

'You are absolutely right. I apologise sincerely for grabbing the only part of your body that I could reach as you careened towards me at dangerous speed. What I should have done was avoided grabbing you in the first place. That would have been the gentlemanly thing to do. It also would have meant that you would have plummeted out of the tree there and then, and thus relinquishing me from the noble task of breaking your fall.'

When he put it like that, Cassie was prepared to concede he had a point. She had practically flattened the man, the poor thing could barely breath a few moments ago. If only he hadn't seen her pudgy thighs. Or manhandled her massive bottom. And if only he wasn't so devilishly handsome then she wouldn't be feeling so self-conscious about her entire, ungainly body below the waist, as well as already feeling ridiculous for getting herself stuck up a tree in the first place. Captain Warriner's eyes were the absolute bluest eyes she had ever seen. Like the clearest summer's sky flecked with speckles of lapis lazuli. With all the dark, slightly overlong black hair and permanently frowning expression, he was exactly what she imaged a pirate to look like. Or a highwayman. Or a mythical knight sat around King Arthur's table. Very few men could carry off chainmail or a dashing pirate's earring, but she was quite certain Captain Warriner would. She would store his appearance away in her memory for when she needed inspiration for a handsome rogue...

But here she was, weaving him into one of her

stories and the poor man was still sat on the floor. Probably still winded and trying to pretend not to be. Why, he hadn't even raised himself from his seat on the grass.

'I am being unforgivably ungrateful, Captain Warriner. You have been extremely decent in trying to save me and I am truly sorry for squashing you when I landed. If it's any consolation, I did try to avoid you.'

Her fictional, fantasy pirate was still frowning. 'I already know I am going to regret asking this question, Miss Reeves, but how did you come to be stuck in one of my brother's apple trees?'

'I did not realise they belonged to someone, else I never would have taken the liberty.' Stealing was a sin, after all, and she was guilty of enough of them already to add one to the list. It was the Eighth Commandment. Cassie knew all of the Commandments verbatim. Forwards and, because her attention had a tendency to waver, backwards as well.

'Did you fail to notice the twenty-foot wall and giant wooden gates?'

As he was gesturing behind her with his hand Cassie allowed her eyes to turn to take in the towering stone barricade looming against the horizon. Now that he happened to mention it, she had noticed the enormous structure as she had ridden down the unfamiliar lane, but as the gates were wide open, she had assumed it was a public park. Both Hyde Park and St James's had gates, too, although granted nowhere near as imposing, so did the many parks she had frequented in Nottingham, Manchester, Birmingham, Liverpool and Bristol. But she was a very long way from those cities now and she supposed they had no real need for actual parks when lush, green countryside stretched out before you in every direction.

'I did not realise this was private property. I am used to living in big towns, Captain Warriner, where people take the air in big parks. I feel very silly now.'

He waved her explanation away impatiently. 'Anyway—the tree, Miss Reeves?'

She could tell by his expression he thought she was odd. His dark eyebrows were raised in question, but his eyes swirled with irritated bemusement. Cassie knew that look well. It was the way most people had always stared at her. Usually, it only hurt a little bit, because she was quite used to it—but for some reason having this dashing pirate view her in such a manner, when he had barely any time to get to know her, hurt a great deal. Clearly she was now irredeemably odd if an officer in the King's army had spotted it straight away, when Cassie had been trying so very hard not to be quite so odd since she arrived in Retford. To make matters worse, her reasons for being up the tree were, now she considered it, quite daft indeed. Further evidence of her unfamiliarity with country life.

'I was searching for apples for Orange Blossom. The ones on the lower branches were so very small and hard, I thought those higher up might be riper. Because they were closer to the sun...but I realise now, that it is far too early for any of the apples to be ripe. The ones I picked from the top were just as hard as the ones at the bottom.'

'This, I am also aware of. The majority of them fell on my head while you were trying to adjust your clothing.'

Could this day get any worse? She had made a fool

of herself, unwittingly trespassed and stolen unripe apples, then winded the most handsome man she had ever seen after flashing her fat legs at him. 'I am sorry about your head, too,' she said miserably, 'and for climbing the stupid tree in the first place. When the branch beneath my feet gave way, my dress got caught on something and I couldn't move. I shall be eternally grateful you came along. I might still be stuck there otherwise and I promised Papa I would be home by four to listen to Sunday's sermon.' Stuck inside again when she so loved being outdoors.

Captain Warriner merely stared at her, his magnificent eyes inscrutable, though obviously happy to end their acquaintance swiftly. Cassie stood up decisively and brushed the worst of the leaves and twigs out of her hair, chiding herself for her own ineptitude. Why did she always have to be so clumsy and so odd? People were always put off by her exuberance. As one pithy matron had said in the parish before the last one, Cassie was like a cup of tea with three sugars when only one was required. At little too much. Too loud. Too talkative. Far too passionate and prone to cause irritation in every quarter. Why couldn't she simply pretend to be like all of the other young ladies? Why did her silly brain put daft ideas into her head and why did her even sillier head listen to them? Ripe apples and pirates. Two classic examples of her wandering, odd mind.

'I suppose I should get going. Papa will be wondering where I have got to.'

Captain Warriner nodded, seemingly content to remain seated on the grass. 'Yes. Probably best.' He was a man of few words—either that or he didn't suffer fools like her gladly.

'Well, good afternoon then. And thank you again.' Cringing with awkwardness, Cassie untied Orange Blossom and began to lead her down the narrow path out of the dreaded Orchard of Embarrassment. A jet-black stallion, obviously as unimpressed with her shenanigans as his owner, glared at her in disgust.

You are a very silly human, aren't you?

Don't listen to him, said Orange Blossom loyally, *you meant well, Cassie.*

It was cold comfort. Captain Galahad still thought her odd. For some reason, it was imperative she did not leave him on such a bad impression.

'I am not normally this silly Captain.' Cassie spun around only to see him wincing, resting painfully on one knee, as he tried to stand. 'Oh, my goodness! You've hurt your leg.' She dropped the reins and dashed to his side to offer him some assistance. 'Let me help you up and then I will escort you home.' After causing his injury it was the very least she could do.

Those lovely blue eyes hardened to ice crystals. 'I'm not a blasted invalid, woman! I can get myself up off the floor and find my own way home!' To prove his point, he stood and stubbornly limped towards his horse.

'Please, Captain Warriner—allow me to assist you. Your poor leg!'

But he ignored her. He reached his horse quickly and grabbed the pommel of the saddle to steady himself. Then, with another wince, put all of his weight on his injured left leg so that he could place his right foot in the stirrup. He hauled himself upwards using only the power in his arms. Large muscles bulged under the fabric of his coat, emphasising his strength and excellent broad shoulders. He arranged himself comfortably before shooting her a scornful glare which could have curdled milk.

'Good afternoon, Miss Reeves. Next time you decide to go out for a ride, kindly remember *this* is private property.' He nudged the foreboding black stallion forward and the pair of them galloped off without a backward glance.

Chapter Two

~~~~~~~~~~~~~~~~

Jamie dipped his brush in some water and used it to soften the cake of blue paint to create the perfect wash. He preferred to work with watercolours rather than oils. Oil took too long and he was never completely happy with the effect. With watercolour, you could play around with the finish. He loved the translucency it created when he painted skies or water, yet with less moisture you could still create solid lines and definition, and mixed with gouache it could mimic oil paint when he needed texture. It was the perfect combination for recreating scenes from nature, his preferred studies, and definitely the most therapeutic.

He could paint a reasonable portrait if he put his mind to it, but his style was more romantic than practical, far too whimsical for a career soldier and most certainly not something he was ever prepared to discuss. Soldiers were not supposed to enjoy the shape and curve of a petal or the lyrical pictures drawn by clouds—yet he did. He always had. Right from the moment he had first discovered he could draw, somewhere around the age of seven or eight, Jamie had always created fanciful, dream-like depictions of all the beauty he saw around him. His father had always disparagingly claimed he painted like a girl. And as vexing his noxious father was something he had done thoroughly as a point of personal honour, the man's obvious disgust had only encouraged his talent more.

'That looks like the orchard.' His sister-in-law Letty peered over his shoulder, smiling. 'I always think things appear so much more beautiful once I have seen them through your eyes.'

'Hmm.'

It was as far as he was prepared to go in acknowledging her compliment and she knew him too well to push. He watched her move towards her favourite chair and carefully lower herself into it. There was no disguising the evidence of her pregnancy now, and every day it reminded Jamie of what he would never have. Not that he wasn't happy for his elder brother Jack and his wife. He was delighted for them. They both deserved every happiness. A man would have to travel a very long way to find two better people. A part of him was even excited at the prospect of being an uncle—but it was bittersweet. He had always thought he would have a family, although he had never spoken about it aloud because admitting such things was not manly, but he had always hoped he would have a large one. The promise of it had sustained him during his years fighting on foreign battlefields: little, dark-haired versions of himself running riot and driving him to distraction.

But the romantic part of his soul had refused to consider just any woman in those days. He had wanted the whole cake to eat, not just the icing. Fighting for King and country had occupied all of his time and he had stupidly assumed he still had plenty of time left to search for the woman of his dreams; that elusive soulmate who enjoyed nature's beauty as much as he did and who would want to sit with him while he painted because they adored each other. With hindsight, Jamie probably should have married a few years ago, when he was handsome and complete. He doubted any woman would consider the broken man who had returned from the Peninsula. And who could blame them?

Any decent young bride worth her salt would expect her new husband to be similarly brimming with vigour. Two working legs were a prerequisite, as was a sound financial future. Crippled soldiers had few career choices open to them and he could hardly expect a wife to be content to live under the benevolent charity of his brother for ever. He tried not to envy his three brothers. Jack was about to be a father, Joe was finally pursuing his dream of becoming a doctor by studying at medical school and Jacob was having the time of his life at university. Their lives were just starting while his had come to a grinding halt. A wife would definitely not want a man devoid of prospects.

Nor could he ask one to cope with his other *peculiarities*—peculiarities so evident he could hardly keep them a secret from a wife. Finding the right words to explain them to the unfortunate woman, without making himself sound dangerous and ripe for immediate incarceration in Bedlam, was almost impossible. No, indeed, marriage and family were lost to him until he could find a way to fix it all and as he had spent the better part of a year since his return home failing dismally, he did not hold out much hope a solution was around the corner. Mulling the fact was not going to change it. It was the way it was, yet the death of his dream still stung.

Jamie began to sweep the first layer of wash on to his paper, pleased with the hue he had mixed. It was exactly as he remembered the sky yesterday as he had stared mournfully up at it.

'What made you draw it from that perspective?' Letty was still scrutinising the picture and he supposed it was a little unusual to paint exactly what he had seen when he had been flat on his back, minus all of the hair covering his face, of course.

'I thought I would try something different.'

The lie seemed to appease her and she picked up her embroidery, but the truth was Jamie could not stop thinking about those damned pink garters. Or the way the wearer had pitied him when she had seen him struggle. At this stage he had no idea what colour to paint his complete humiliation. Black seemed fitting, but did not quite go with the sky. Maybe he would try to leave it out, in the vain hope he could erase the shameful memory from his mind by creating an alternative memory here on paper.

Their butler crept in stealthily and coughed subtly. Every time Jamie saw him it gave him a start. Six months ago they had not even had a maid—now, thanks to Letty, there was a veritable army running Markham Manor, all transplanted from her opulent mansion in Mayfair.

'You have a caller, my lady.'

A rarity indeed. Nobody called on the Warriners unless they were baying for blood or demanding immediate payment.

'A young lady. A Miss Reeves. She is enquiring as to whether Captain Warriner is at home.'

Jamie could feel the beginnings of nerves in the pit of his stomach, warning of further impending humiliation, but tried to appear impassive.

'Captain Warriner?' Letty was staring at him with barely contained delight. 'How very dashing that sounds.'

'Tell her I am not at home, Chivers.'

'Tell her no such thing! Have her shown in immediately, Chivers. And arrange for some tea.' His sister-in-law tossed aside her already forgotten sewing and sat eagerly forward in her chair. 'Why is a young lady calling for you, Jamie?'

He considered lying, but as the real reason for Miss Reeves's unwelcome visit was doubtless about to be unveiled there seemed little point. 'I tried to rescue her from a tree yesterday.'

'Tried?'

'Yes. And failed. Miserably.'

Further explanation was prevented by the arrival of his embarrassment. Just as it had yesterday, those red-gold curls refused to be tamed by her hairpins. Several very becoming silky tendrils poked out of her sensible bonnet and framed her pretty face. Her lovely chestnut eyes were wary as they darted between him and Letty.

Politeness dictated he should stand in the presence of a lady, but if he stood she would see more damning evidence of his infirmity and his pride was already bruised and battered quite enough. Letty, of course, sprang to her feet in an instant and gushingly greeted their guest.

'Miss Reeves! I am delighted to make your acquaintance. I am Letty Warriner, technically the Countess of Markham, although my husband is reticent about using his title. Do take a seat. I hope you will join us for tea?'

It was all a little over the top, in Jamie's opinion. Yes, a visitor was something of a rarity here, but the way Letty was behaving was a little too effusive. Especially as he was already counting the seconds until Miss Reeves left him in humiliated solitary peace.

'Tea would be lovely,' she said, flicking her eyes towards his briefly as she arranged her bottom on a chair. Jamie could still remember the feel of it in his hands. Firm. Rounded. Womanly. Which of course made him think about the incongruous garters again. 'I came to check on Captain Warriner's recovery. Because of my own lack of judgement, he was injured yesterday.'

Jamie stared straight ahead, but could feel Letty's eyes boring into him. 'Really? Jamie made no mention of an injury. Come to mention it, he also made no mention of the accident which must have led to the injury. All I know is what I have just been told. You were apparently stuck in a tree, Miss Reeves, and my *brother-in-law* tried and failed to get you down.'

She put unnecessary emphasis on the words brother-in-law, clearly making a point to their guest. A point which made Jamie uncomfortable.

He is single, in case you were wondering, Miss Reeves, and desperately in want of a wife. Try to ignore the fact he is lame, futureless and has the potential to kill if the mood takes him.

Miss Reeves blushed like a beetroot, a beetroot with distracting freckles on her dainty button of a nose, and wore a pained expression. 'Captain Warriner climbed the apple tree to save me, but I fidgeted too much and the branch snapped. I am afraid we both fell to the ground. The poor captain absorbed the brunt of the impact.'

An understatement. His ribs had damn near snapped in half.

Letty was grinning like an idiot. 'You fell on top of him? In the *orchard*?' And like a nodcock he just happened to be painting the same blasted orchard and things looked so much more *beautiful* through his stupid eyes.

Miss Reeves nodded. 'I feel awful about it.'

For his own sake, now was the opportune time to intervene, before Letty started to matchmake in earnest. 'As you can see, I am in fine fettle, Miss Reeves. You needn't have troubled yourself by coming all this way to see the evidence for yourself.' His sister-in-law shot him a pointed glance for his rudeness, but Jamie was unrepentant. The last thing he needed was Letty reading more into his choice of painting than he was comfortable with her knowing. Miss Reeves's fine eyes swivelled towards his leg, raised as always on a supportive footstool, and he inwardly cringed.

'But I can see your leg is still injured, Captain Warriner, and that is completely my fault.'

She thought his infirmity was a temporary affliction, and as tempting as it was to go along with the fantasy, his innate sense of futility kicked in. 'This is Napoleon's fault, Miss Reeves. Not yours.'

Now, please go away, woman!

'Napoleon?'

'Indirectly. It was his guns which fired the musket balls.'

'Balls!'

Her voice came out a little high-pitched and he simply nodded. He had no intention of telling her how they had had to dig three of the blighters out of his thigh while he was still conscious and he'd very nearly lost the whole leg, as well as his life, to infection afterwards. She blinked rapidly and Jamie could see her imagination filling in the blanks, those long lashes fluttering like butterflies as she did so.

Very pretty.

Somehow that made it worse. Pretty and pity made him feel less of a man than he usually did. However, under the circumstances, it was probably best to divulge the horrible truth and suffer her pity rather than give Letty false hope that this delightful armful of woman might enter into a romance with a dangerous invalid. 'They left me crippled, Miss Reeves.' And cripples were not attractive. Especially not to freckle-faced fertility goddesses with positively *sinful* hair and saucy garters.

Cassie had no idea how to respond to such a statement. Part of her was sorry he had suffered, another part of her was hugely relieved not to have been the cause of his injury and a bigger part of her kept remembering how very big, solid and manly his body had been sprawled beneath hers. Just thinking about it made her feel all warm and those deliciously *sinful* sapphire eyes were not helping. Once again those exuberant passions she was trying her hardest to suppress jumped to the fore. Fortunately, the arrival of the tea tray meant she did not have to respond and had a perfectly reasonable excuse for removing her bonnet before she began to perspire from her wayward, wicked thoughts.

'Do you take sugar, Miss Reeves?'

'Just one, please, Mrs...er...my lady.'

The pretty blonde woman giggled. 'To be honest, it confuses me, too. Perhaps we should simply dispense with the formalities. Why don't you call me Letty?'

'In that case, please feel free to call me Cassie.' She risked peeking at Captain Galahad, but he made no move to invite her to call him anything familiar. In fact, he looked quite irritated at her continued presence. His gorgeous eyes were distinctly narrowed, which made her babble. 'I am new to the area. My father has recently been appointed the vicar of this parish. We live at the vicarage.' A completely ridiculous clarification only an idiot would make. It would probably be sensible to stop babbling nonsense and wait to be asked a question. Unfortunately, once her nerves got the better of her, Cassie's mouth had a habit of running away with itself. 'I couldn't help noticing you are going to have a baby.' Was it polite to mention such things?

Whether it was or it wasn't, her hostess smiled and Cassie watched in wonder as the young woman's hand automatically went to her protruding stomach lovingly. 'Yes, indeed. But not until the autumn. I appear to have got very fat very quickly.' She handed Cassie her tea. 'Are you engaged to be married, Miss Reeves, or is there an ardent suitor on the cusp of proposing to you in the near future?'

A very sore point.

Cassie's odd personality, off-putting exuberance, unfortunate freckles combined with her father's ferocious temperament had all proved to be highly effective deterrents to the male sex. 'No to both questions, I'm afraid.'

I am doomed to sit on the shelf and gather dust; I only hope it is sturdy enough and wide enough to bear my weight.

'Well, I am sure it won't be long before some lucky gentleman snaps you up—you are uncommonly pretty, Miss Reeves. Isn't that right, Jamie?'

Captain Galahad grunted and appeared very bored. Clearly he disagreed. He was sipping his tea and practically glaring at her over the rim of the ridiculously delicate cup in his large, manly hand. Or perhaps he was glaring at his sister-in-law for asking him such an impertinent question? It was quite difficult to tell.

'Did you enjoy being a soldier, Captain?'

A safer topic might make their exchange less awkward, although this also seemed to annoy him because he frowned.

'It had its moments.'

'You will have to forgive Jamie, Cassie. He is a man of very few words and even fewer smiles. However, beneath that surly, unfriendly exterior he is actually rather sweet. He also paints the most beautiful romantic pictures of the English countryside.' This comment garnered another warning glare. 'Do you have any hobbies, Cassie?'

'I like to write stories. Children's stories.' It was the first time she had admitted that to anyone, but Letty did appear friendlier than the usual person she came into contact with.

'Oh, how lovely! What are they about?'

'As she is a vicar's daughter, Letty, I dare say they are morality tales,' the Captain said disparagingly, clearly disapproving of such things. Sensible men of action like him would disapprove of her whimsical nature and romantic fairy tales.

'Not at all!' There was no way of explaining without sounding odd, but as Captain Galahad was of that opinion already, Cassie confessed all. 'At the moment they are about my pony—Orange Blossom. Or rather how Orange Blossom views our life together. In my stories, she talks. All of the animals talk.'

And she was babbling again.

'I often weave the tales around my own personal experiences. For example, the story I am currently working on is called *Orange Blossom and the Great Apple Debacle...*'

Her voice trailed off when she saw Letty and Captain Warriner exchange a strange look.

'I suppose it all sounds very silly to you, but I have read one or two of my efforts to the children in my father's congregation; they seemed to enjoy them.' Cassie had also sworn the children to secrecy. If her father got a whiff of her vain and pointless hobby, he would forbid her from writing—or worse.

'They sound quite delightful. Maybe you should consider getting them published.'

Cassie already liked Letty Warriner a great deal. 'I doubt my scribblings are good enough for that. But perhaps one day.' After my father is dead and buried—because that was the only way he would allow such self-indulgent frivolity. Unless she ever did manage to escape his clutches just as her mother had done before her. The meagre savings she had secretly accumulated in the last twelve months would barely get her a seat on the post to Norwich and there were woefully no ardent suitors clambering at her door who might whisk her off from her dreadful life. Unless a miracle happened, she was stuck.

Miserably stuck.

Her father had no idea she wrote stories about talking animals. Or about anything at all for that matter and Cassie had no intention of alerting him to the fact. It had certainly never been broached in conversation, not that they ever had conversations. Such an atrocious sin would doubtless require a great deal of solitary repentance, so Cassie had kept it all hidden. Mind you, he also had no idea that she was plotting to run away either. The image of his stern face as he spun manically in his grave at her sinful, open defiance, despite everything he had done to curb her dangerous passions, popped immediately into her thoughts and threatened to make her smile. She hid it by sipping her tea.

Chapter Three

Jamie could see the light of mischief in his sister-in-law's eyes and did not like it one bit. If ever there was time for a speedy exit, it was now, but that meant standing like a creaking old man and then limping laboriously out of the room in front of Miss Reeves. He was torn between the devil and the deep blue sea. Staying opened him up to more mischief—of that he was in no doubt. Letty had a tendency to be tenacious when she set her mind to something and her mind was clearly set. However, leaving and displaying his infirmity was humiliating in the extreme, although why he was so keen to appear less useless in front of the vicar's daughter was as pointless as it was pathetic. She was only being kind, after all.

'I would certainly be interested to read *The Great Apple Debacle*. Will Jamie be in it?'

Pregnant or not, he was going to strangle Letty later, but for now he had to take the bull by the horns and direct this unwelcome conversation or else die of total humiliation. Unfortunately, that meant making conversation. Something he had never been adept at. 'What drew your father to darkest Retford, Miss Reeves?'

'The diocese sent him here. We were in Nottingham for a few months beforehand and they felt his talents might be better used in a rural parish...away from trouble.'

As Jamie had always thought Nottingham was a dire place, filled with poverty and crime, he completely understood. It was certainly no place for a lovely vicar's daughter. 'I dare say your father is relieved.'

'Hardly. My father prefers working in a city, although I cannot say I do. Of all of his parishes, this one is by far the nicest we have ever lived in.' Her face lit up when she smiled and her freckled nose wrinkled in a very charming manner.

'You say that as if you have lived in a few places.'

She nodded, the motion causing one of her burnished curls to bounce close to her neck, which in turn drew his eyes to the satiny-smooth, golden skin visible above the bodice of her plain dress, and, of course, the magnificent way she filled out that bodice. Jamie had always had a great deal of affection for a woman's bosom and Miss Reeves's bosom was undoubtedly one of the finest he had ever had cause to notice.

'Indeed we have. Why, in the last five years alone, we have lived in eleven different towns.' Her face clouded briefly and he realised this gypsy lifestyle was not something she enjoyed. He doubted he would enjoy being moved from pillar to post either. He had had quite enough of that on the campaign trail, although it was not the same. Moving about then had always been temporary and transient as he had always had a very solid place to call home. A place to go back to which remained resolutely constant. If Miss Reeves did not have that consolation, no wonder it made her unhappy. But then she was smiling again so maybe he was mistaken. 'I have lived in Manchester, Newcastle, Sheffield—and obviously London. We have moved there several times although always to different parishes in different corners of the capital. It is so vast; I never had cause to revisit the places we had already lived in. Also we have spent some time in Bristol, Liverpool and Birmingham.'

All industrial, overcrowded places, he noted. 'I think you might find Retford a lot quieter than the places you are used to. Nothing much happens here.'

'That is what I enjoy the most about it. I love all of the trees and nature, so does Orange Blossom, and it goes without saying the air is cleaner. I do so love being outdoors. I have spent hours aimlessly riding around every afternoon since my arrival. Hence I trespassed here yesterday without realising. I am sorry about that, too.'

'Trespassed? Of course you didn't.' Letty was smiling kindly. 'You are very welcome to ride on our estate whenever you want to. In fact, I absolutely insist you do. There are some very lovely spots in the grounds, especially close to the river at this time of year.'

Miss Reeves's eyes locked on his briefly and he saw her trepidation. He supposed he had been rude to her yesterday and, much as it pained him, Jamie felt the need to extend a tiny olive branch. 'The river is a very pleasant place to ride. Even Satan likes it.' Her eyes widened and he realised his choice of name for his horse was perhaps not really suitable in the presence of a vicar's daughter.

'You named your horse Satan?'

'In my defence, he can be truly evil. He has a troublesome temperament and can be hostile around people.'

'Much like his surly owner,' Letty added for good measure. Jamie chose to ignore it.

'Oh! I almost forgot.' Miss Reeves rummaged in her capacious reticule and handed him a package wrapped in string. 'I brought you a small gift. To thank you for attempting to save me and for breaking my fall.' The gesture was strangely touching. When was the last time someone, other than Letty, had extended the hand of friendship to a Warriner? Jamie turned the gift over in his hands before undoing the wrapping. Miss Reeves became flustered and her words tumbled out. 'Please do not get excited. I had no idea what you might want, but as you are a fellow horse lover I brought some carrots.'

She was blushing again. She apparently did that a lot. As promised, three orange spears were nestled in the paper and, despite himself, Jamie felt the corners of his mouth curl up. What an odd, useful and totally charming, gift. 'Satan loves carrots. Thank you.' If he had not been broken and useless, he might have suggested she accompany him to the stables to help him feed them to the bad-tempered beast. But he was, so he didn't. The thought of her politely accepting and slowing her pace while he limped along next to her made him feel queasy. Suddenly, his brief good mood evaporated. He covered the carrots with their paper and placed them on the arm of the chair and withdrew into himself.

* * *

For the next half an hour he remained almost mute.
Miss Reeves and Letty held up the conversation and,
if a response was required, Jamie grunted. To compound his discomfort, the subject of the 'Great Apple
Debacle' was brought up and he was forced to listen
to it regaled for Letty's entertainment. Miss Reeves
had a knack for storytelling. He had to give her that
even though she barely paused for breath. Listening to
her take on the unfortunate events of yesterday, combined with her self-deprecating wit and her insistence
on trying to see the whole sorry affair through the
eyes of her pony, was amusing. By the time she got
to the end, he came out appearing sensible and noble,
while she painted herself as silly and severely lacking
in common sense.

'It definitely would make an entertaining children's
story, Cassie, and if you do eventually consider getting it published, you should ask Jamie to do the illustrations. In fact, the painting he is doing right now is
hugely appropriate, isn't it, Jamie? And from such an
interesting perspective.' The innocence with which
this statement was delivered was astounding and he
gave Letty a tight smile which he hoped conveyed his
intent to murder her as soon as it was politely possible.

'It is just a study of the grounds and I sincerely
doubt Miss Reeves would have any desire to have my
amateur sketches in her book.' Jamie had the overwhelming desire to pick up his stupid, ill-conceived
picture and march out of the room with it. If only he
could still march.

'Nonsense—go and take a look at it, Cassie. Jamie is
merely being modest about his abilities. *Orange Blos-*

som and the Great Apple Debacle would make a wonderful picture book.'

To his horror, the vicar's daughter appeared to find this idea intriguing and clearly something she had never considered before his meddling sister-in-law had planted the seed. 'Pictures *would* be good.' She began to rise from her seat and walked towards him with cheerful interest. His only hope was she would not put two and two together and recognise the orchard. She peered at the painting, bending slightly at the waist to get the best possible view, and wafting some deliciously floral scent directly towards his nostrils. Violets. He had always loved violets.

'Letty is quite right. You are an exceptionally talented painter, Captain Warriner. Even unfinished, I can see this picture is outstanding. And quite charming.' He risked a peek sideways at her and saw her eyebrows draw together as she studied the details more closely. 'Is that the apple orchard?'

'Yes.' The inward cringe threatened to seep out and display itself on his face. Only pride kept his upper lip resolutely stiff.

'Isn't it peculiar the pair of you have both been inspired by yesterday's incident? *The Great Apple Debacle* is already a blossoming story and a half-finished painting.' Jamie sent his sister-in-law a glare which was a stark warning to stop. Typically, she ignored it. 'Have you worked out his perspective yet, Cassie?'

'You are painting it from your position on the ground, aren't you? Just after I flattened you.' Two mortified crimson blotches bloomed on her cheeks.

'It was an interesting view I had not considered before.' Come on, Jamie, old boy, brazen it out. 'From what I remember, the branches and leaves formed an aesthetically pleasing contrast to the sky.' That sounded suitably arty.

'I should probably be going.' She stood briskly upright, still blushing, and Letty heaved herself out of her own chair.

'I hope you will call again soon, Cassie. I should like to get to know you better and I am certain my brother-in-law would, too.' His sister-in-law shot him a pointed look. 'Come along, Jamie, let us walk our guest to the door together.'

Trapped, because Letty knew hell would have to freeze over for him to openly admit he was lame and in pain, he had no option other than to grit his teeth and use the strength in his arms to push himself out of his chair. It was only then he realised he had been stationary for too long and his shattered leg had started to atrophy. It screamed in protest, but Jamie ignored the hot shooting pains jabbing him mercilessly in his hip. Normally, he would wait a few moments for the initial discomfort to subside before he tested his weight on it. Had he not been such a proud man, he might have made use of the hated walking stick gathering dust behind his chair. But if he had to humiliate himself in front of Miss Reeves, he was going to damn well do it without looking completely decrepit and good for nothing. He forced himself to walk despite the agony, knowing full well he was going to regret the decision immediately and pay for his folly later. Hot molten bursts of pain stabbed his left thigh muscle, but Jamie shuffled in his best approximation of a normal man's gait towards the hallway, conscious Miss Reeves was right behind him.

Pitying him.

'Oh, I forgot,' said Letty unsubtly as they approached the front door, 'I need to have a quick word with Cook. If you will excuse me, Cassie—I have thoroughly enjoyed your visit. Please do call again soon and remember I absolutely insist on you riding in our grounds here at Markham Manor. Jamie will see you safely out.'

Yes, he would.

Reluctantly.

Then he would find his brother and demand he keep his troublesome wife in check.

Left alone with Miss Reeves, he limped awkwardly towards the door Chivers was already holding open. Out on the newly gravelled driveway he could see her pretty pony waiting patiently. The incongruous animal suited her. 'Thank you for the carrots,' he said stiffly, 'and for your misplaced concern for my well-being.' Miss Reeves gave him a weak smile and started towards Orange Blossom, turning at the last minute, her expression quite wretched and her words tumbling out in rapid, panicked succession once again.

'I really am sorry about yesterday. Getting stuck up a tree is a ridiculous thing for a grown woman to do—but unfortunately I am prone to act without thinking and often do things which are ridiculous. And I am sorry for not listening to you when you tried to save me, but I was embarrassed because you had seen my unsightly legs. I do not have the words to express how mortified I am to have caused you to fall and then for crushing you. I can be clumsy as well as inordinately stupid and ridiculous. And I am well aware I am ridiculous and more than a little odd. I do try not to be, but as you can see, it happens regardless. I am also aware

that at best you find me irritating. Everybody does—
and quite quickly. I am a cup of tea with three sugars
when one is quite enough. Too loud. Too talkative. I
am trying to be less enthusiastic about everything in
a quest not to irritate everyone I meet, so please don't
panic and think for a moment I would even consider
riding in your grounds again. I realise Letty meant well
in suggesting it and that you were only being polite in
agreeing with her. Nor do I intend to vex you further
by pursuing her idea of you illustrating my silly stories.
I am well aware of the fact you would like to be well
shot of me and the sad thing is I really cannot blame
you. Most of the time I irritate myself. I shall leave you
in peace henceforth, Captain Warriner.'

'I see.' Jamie was not entirely sure what he felt about
all that. There were several things he wanted to say,
and would have if his damn leg still worked, so he
stood awkwardly next to her long-maned pony. 'I suppose I should say good day to you then.' Even though
he didn't want to.

She blinked rapidly.

'Yes. Good day, Captain Warriner.'

She took the reins and then stared mournfully at
the ground. 'Would you be so good as to ask for a riding block, please?'

'No need.' Without thinking he placed his hands on
her waist and lifted her smartly off the ground to deposit her on her side-saddle. Judging from her wide-
eyed look of horror, he had overstepped the bounds of
propriety, but couldn't quite bring himself to care. She
felt good in his hands. Soft. Curvy. Definitely curvy.
'My apologies, Miss Reeves, I realise now that was
unforgivably inappropriate.'

'No…not really. I was taken by surprise that I could actually be lifted. It's never happened before. And I suppose propriety hardly matters when you have already seen my awful legs.'

Some devil inside him began to place her foot in the stirrup because he needed to touch her again, his fingers lingering too long on the silk-clad ankle above her half-boot.

'You have very nice legs.'

What in God's name had possessed him to say that? It sounded like flirting.

'And lovely eyes.'

Good grief! The words he was thinking had just spilled from his mouth when he absolutely *never* actually said what he was thinking to anyone. Her lush mouth fell slightly open and those mooncalf eyes widened. Now he was definitely flirting. Futilely flirting and had no idea what had got into him. To stop his suddenly talkative mouth from humiliating him again he chewed awkwardly on his bottom lip and stared down at his feet.

Please go now. I feel like a total idiot and wish I was dead.

'Thank…you. For the boost…' Miss Reeves blinked uncomfortably as her usually rapid flurry of words trailed off, her freckles disappearing in the rosy glow of her blush. How splendid. Now he had made her hideously uncomfortable with his clumsy, ill-advised, totally mortifying outbursts. 'Good day, Captain Warriner.' Then she smiled shyly and peaked at him through her ridiculously long eyelashes. 'And thank you for the lovely compliments.' She held his gaze for several moments before chivvying her pretty pony on.

Jamie allowed himself to watch her delightful bottom sway down the driveway and decided he felt peculiar.

Unsettled.

Slightly ridiculous.

Almost cheerful.

The good mood persisted even while he loudly castigated his meddling sister-in-law.

Chapter Four

Cassie spent the next morning accompanying her father as he visited some of his new parishioners. Those too old, too ill or too lazy to come to church were always graced with a fortnightly visit. Her father was nothing if not tenacious in his mission to bring the word of God into people's lives, whether they wanted to hear it or not—but at least she was outside. Spending any prolonged periods of time with her father at home was always fractious. She had heard every lecture and every dire final warning for a person to save his soul before Judgement Day and, because she definitely wasn't the world's greatest vicar's daughter, she had long ago stopped listening. Instead, she entertained herself by weaving stories in her head. Not the lofty novels of great writers, Cassie's wayward brain did not work in that way, but wild fairy tales. Feats of derring-do, mythical lands, pirates, princesses, dragons and, lately, talking animals.

If her papa had asked her opinion, which of course he never did, she might have told him his over-zealous, accusatory stance did more to dissuade the reluctant to come to church than encourage them. He was too much fire and brimstone and not enough love or goodwill for his fellow man. The Reverend Reeves was so blinded by his own confrontational fervour he never saw how he raised the hackles of others. Time after time, he had gone too far, upset too many well-respected and reasonable people, resulting in them having to up sticks and move to yet another parish. Usually another parish so far away from his previous one, nobody had heard of him.

Hence they were here in Retford. A tiny rural congregation which was so very different from the city parishes her father preferred, because, as he was prone to point out at least once a day, where there is deprivation and temptation, sin festered. In the fortnight since they had arrived, Cassie already loved the bustling, little market town. Her father, on the other hand, was not so enamoured, but determined to hunt for enough sinners to justify his presence. The wide-eyed farmer and his cheerful wife were probably not the sort of people he was seeking. But it made no difference. Her father was in full flow. As he had only just mentioned Sodom and Gomorrah, it was fairly safe to assume they would be here for at least another half an hour.

Cassie dived into herself. A technique she had mastered around the age of ten and one which effectively blocked out all of the outside world so she could focus on her latest story and allow her characters to speak to her. She had started it last night, whilst listening to Papa rehearse Sunday's sermon, and it was tentatively titled *Orange Blossom and the Great Apple Debacle*. Except, just as it had last night, the flow of the narrative kept being interrupted by thoughts of Captain Galahad, those aquamarine eyes and splendid shoulders.

Apparently, her affection-starved brain was determined to create a completely different sort of story involving him, his mouthwatering strong arms and a willing damsel in distress eager to fall into them so they could ride off into the sunset together. In her mind, the damsel was so thrilled to be going she did not even bother looking back at her hateful father as she headed triumphantly towards her new life. There was no point in pretending the damsel bore a passing resemblance to Miss Cassandra Reeves because she *was* Miss Cassandra Reeves. A bolder, braver version of herself, who batted her eyelashes coquettishly when the dashing Captain complimented her on her legs.

Really, Captain Galahad? Do you think so? Eyelash flutter. *Well, while we are swapping compliments, I think you have a fine pair of shoulders. Perhaps the finest I have ever seen. I do like a man with broad, strong shoulders...*

The word Warriner floated into her ears. The farmer's wife was quite animated with indignation.

'That family are the epitome of sin, Reverend. Debauchers, cheats and *vile* sinners every one of them. There's four of them Warriner boys and all four of them would sooner fleece you than be neighbourly. It's a scandal, I tell you!'

'Those Warriners sound exactly like the sort of people who could do with hearing the benefit of God's word. Perhaps I should visit them tomorrow?'

The zealot gleam was lit in her father's eyes all the way home. Cassie said nothing as she frantically sought a believable excuse as to why he probably shouldn't, then panicked when nothing suitable came to mind that would not result in him punishing her for speaking out of turn. As soon as they entered the vicarage Cassie busied herself with her normal daily chores, hoping he would forget, while her father disappeared in the direction of the church, appearing as preoccupied as he always was. With any luck, he would forget to visit the Warriners, as he so often forgot things that were not top of his list of immediate priorities. Fortunately, his priorities did tend to change like the weather and he had a memory like a flour sifter. Most of the time he forgot he even had a daughter, a very pleasing state of affairs as far as she was concerned as it gave her more freedom than most young ladies of her age. Cassie hauled the heavy kettle on to the stove to boil and got ready to prepare his luncheon.

Despite being well able to afford it, the Reverend Reeves never bothered with servants. Servants suggested he thought himself better than others, which hinted at vanity and vanity was one of the seven deadly sins. Something which was all well and good, but left the entire running of the house up to Cassie. Ungratefully, she supposed, she had come to believe her father kept her as a skivvy to ensure there was never any possibility of her meeting a nice young man and marrying him. She dreaded to think what sort of a rage he would fly into if he suspected she was desperate to leave. It did not help that his sour disposition and hot temper did not lend itself to finding willing employees. Far better to inconvenience his daughter, who slaved for free, and could barely scrape together a few coins for any luxuries whatsoever in the pathetic housekeeping allowance he counted out weekly like the miser he was.

Nevertheless, Cassie enjoyed two blissful hours of her own company, completely devoid of any fiery sermons or pertinent reminders about the need to continually spread the word of God to the seething cesspool of Earth-dwelling sinners. Or any veiled threats about the need for solitary penance to reflect on her wayward tendencies.

'Wool-gathering again, girl?'

His sudden reappearance at the open back door startled her. Without thinking, she touched the pocket of her apron to reassure herself that the key to the door was still there as he resolutely shut it behind him. Something which always created a cold trickle of fear to shimmy down her spine each time he did it. 'Not at all, merely thinking about what I need to do next.' Cassie put down the bread and dutifully pulled out a chair for him at the table. He sat heavily on a chair and began to load his plate with the food Cassie had placed on the kitchen table.

'I have had a most informative conversation with another parishioner.'

'Really?' Already she could feel herself glaze over, but tried to remain focussed, like a dutiful daughter who was not daydreaming about running away would have.

'I made some enquiries into that family we were warned about—the Warriners.'

Cassie felt the icy grip of fear stiffen her muscles, dreading what was coming.

'Yes. Indeed. A thoroughly bad lot. The eldest recently married an heiress, but in Nottingham there is talk he abducted the poor girl and compromised her into marriage.'

Letty certainly did not appear to be the unhappy victim of a kidnapper. Cassie had not met the woman's husband, but she had seen the great affection in his wife's eyes as she had talked about him and unconsciously rubbed the unborn child nestled in her womb like it was the greatest gift she had ever received. 'People do like to embellish gossip, Papa. Perhaps the Warriner family are merely the victims of such nonsense.'

'I fear not, Cassandra. There is too much evidence levied against them for there not to be strong foundations forged on truth. I have heard grave tales, far too terrible to sully your delicate ears, involving avarice, greed, debauchery. Suffice to say I am convinced they are in dire need of the Lord's guidance.'

Oh, dear. 'If they are as bad as you fear, Papa, then perhaps they are best avoided.'

'Nonsense. I have never shied away from the challenge, Cassandra.'

'Of course you haven't, Papa. In a few weeks perhaps you should call upon them, when you are more familiar with your worthier parishioners.'

Her father's response was as loud as it was instantaneous. 'These Warriners are in desperate need of my guidance, Daughter. I will go this very afternoon!'

There would be no stopping him, but there was still a chance Cassie could avoid accompanying him. At least then she would not have to witness the tender new shoots of her friendship with Letty and her only link to the Captain ruthlessly trampled on. Good gracious! A far greater issue suddenly presented itself. As soon as he visited them he would learn she had already done so and blatantly neglected to mention it.

'You came home a little earlier than I expected, Papa, and have rather spoiled my little planned surprise.' Cassie tried desperately to sound nonchalant. Her father hated liars almost as much as he hated thieves, murderers and fornicators, especially when the liar happened to be his own daughter.

He lifted his head and stared at her quizzically. 'I did?'

'Yes! I was about to make your favourite spiced fruitcake. Why don't we postpone our visit to that family until tomorrow?' By which time Cassie might well have thought of something to prevent her father from ever darkening their door.

'You would put cake above the saving of souls?'

'But, Papa—I was so looking forward to making it for you today.' Pleading to his better nature had not worked once in all of her twenty-one years, but still Cassie persisted. Her father smiled his benevolent I-know-better-than-you smile and took her hand, a gesture so uncharacteristic it took Cassie completely by surprise. 'I know what this is about.'

'You do?' Surely he had not been apprised of her unaccompanied visit to the family or, heaven forbid, her sinful behaviour in the apple orchard?

'Yes, and it does you credit. You are a God-fearing girl, Cassandra, and being exposed to the godless frightens you. But fear not. You shall be with me and that heathen family will see what a good example you are of my teachings.'

'But I would rather not do it today. Just this once, Papa, could we…?'

'No! You are a dutiful daughter Cassandra. Being dutiful means doing those things one might find unpalatable without complaining.'

'But…'

'Your mother was headstrong and weak-willed, Cassandra. Do I now see that unfortunate trait rearing its ugly head in you?' He was peering at her closely, looking, no doubt, for evidence to support his suspicion. Again her fingers grazed the heavy key in her pocket. For the moment it was still hers although that could change in a heartbeat. 'You must fight the temptation, girl!' Cassie schooled her features and tried her best to seem compliant, because being compared to her mother always kindled his anger and then her bedchamber door would be locked again.

'No, Father, I merely wanted to make you a cake…' Tears were prickling her eyes as she forced herself to try one last time to escape the ordeal of watching him castigate an innocent family whilst selfishly still avoiding the ordeal of being imprisoned.

'You will do as you are told, Cassandra.' He stared pointedly at the stairs until she capitulated with a terrified nod. 'We will leave within the hour.'

Jamie had spent most of the day riding Satan around the grounds. There was nothing out of the ordinary in that. He rode every single day, for goodness sake, because he enjoyed being out in the sunshine so it was hardly tangible proof he was being pathetic. Nobody apart from him knew he had lingered for the better part of an hour at the edge of the riverbank or that he had rode up and down every row of trees in the orchard until Satan's hooves threatened to carve out a deep trench in the ground. And certainly nobody had any idea he did so in the faint hope he would 'accidentally' bump into the delectable Miss Reeves again.

As if she would have been tempted to visit again after his clumsy, and doubtless unwelcome, attempt at flirting with her. Pretty girls who wore saucy garters and had the sort of figure which would make any man sit up and beg like a dog were not likely to be particularly enamoured of a crippled former soldier who was afraid of the dark. He sincerely doubted she had given him so much as a passing thought since she had ridden away from him. Unfortunately, Jamie could not say the same.

He had done a great deal of thinking about her. Aside from her acute physical attractiveness, and the garters that tormented him, there was something quirky, unusual and refreshingly unique about the vicar's daughter which appealed to him. Maybe because he was prone to being serious and she did, as she said herself, border on the ridiculous—but it was her ridiculousness which was so utterly charming. Jamie had never met anyone who imagined animals talked before, or who climbed trees and got stuck in them or who thought carrots were a gift. Or maybe all of this mooning had come about because Miss Reeves had been the first woman he had touched since his injury...

With a sigh, he limped out of the stable and headed into the house. It was a sorry state of affairs when you misguidedly counted an unfortunate accident as an amorous encounter. He found his brother Jack and Letty in the vaulted Tudor great hall they called the drawing room. His sister-in-law was sewing something which he assumed would clothe the baby one day and, like the besotted dolt he had become, his elder brother was watching her contentedly.

'Don't you have anything better to do than stare at your wife?'

'Not at the moment, no. I find I never tire of it. Don't you have anything better to do than gripe about it?'

Jamie shrugged, reluctant to admit that, no, he never had anything to do any more. His life was aimless because he was now pointless. His easel and paints lay within arm's reach, calling to him, but he resisted picking them up. It would only give Letty another excuse to ask him how his orchard picture was coming along. Instead, he picked up a newspaper and made a great show of reading it.

'Ahem.' The butler appeared on stealthy feet. 'You have visitors my lord. The Reverend Reeves and his daughter would like an audience.'

It was all Jamie could do not to sit bolt upright and neaten his unruly, windswept hair. She was here. Again. Very probably only to see Letty—but that was all right. At least she was here.

And he was pathetic.

'Miss Reeves passed me this note while her father was not looking, my lady, I got the impression she wanted you to read it before I showed them in.'

Chivers handed Letty a letter, which was unsealed and appeared to have been hastily folded. She opened it, scanned it quickly, then scowled. 'Well, I am not altogether sure what to make of this.'

Deliberately, Jamie slowly folded the newspaper in case he seemed too eager to hear what Miss Reeves had to say and schooled his features to appear bored,

rather than slightly panicked and yet nauseatingly eager
to gaze upon her again.

Letty read the missive out in hushed tones.

Dearest Letty and Captain Warriner,
Please accept my sincerest apologies for the
clandestine manner of this note, however, my
father would be very angry if he learned that I
had visited you unchaperoned or that I had been
climbing the trees in your grounds.

I would be eternally in your debt if you pre-
tended this was our first meeting. I know I am
asking you to lie for me and appreciate that you
are under no obligation to do so and that my re-
quest is odd, to say the very least.

I should like to say sorry in advance for what
is about to happen. None of this is of my doing.
Cassie

'I suppose we have to honour her request?' Letty
folded the note slowly and looked towards first Jack,
then Jamie for guidance. They both shrugged in response. It was a peculiar letter to be sure. 'Show them
in, Chivers.'

Like the others, Jamie stood. Miss Reeves had already seen him limp so there was no point trying to
hide it, and if she had brought her father in tow then the
man would expect to see proper manners. Meeting her
father suddenly made him feel nervous, as if he were a
potential suitor keen to make a good first impression.
Where had that ridiculous thought come from? He was
not suitor material. He was not anything material any
more. Not until he was fixed. If he ever got fixed.

*Stop getting ideas above yourself and just be pleased
she has graced you with her company again. You have
to take whatever crumbs are thrown at you, old boy.*

For some reason, he expected to see a jolly, rotund
man with his daughter's friendly open expression.
The sour-faced, reedy fellow who walked in, ramrod-
straight and unsmiling, was nothing like her. Worse
still, the effervescent Miss Reeves was apparently un-
available for this visit. The pained, slouched woman
who dutifully walked behind her father was a shell of
the vixen he had been thinking about incessantly. Behind her father's back, she screwed up her face and
stared at him mournfully, almost apologetically, then
did the same to Letty. Judging by the stern expression on her father's pinched face, he was not pleased
to be here.

Odd.

Being the ranking man of the house, his brother
stepped forward with his hand outstretched in welcome. The Reverend curled his lip in what appeared
to be disgust and limply returned the handshake as if
Jack's hand was somehow offensive. As a greeting, it
was definitely not particularly friendly and Jamie felt
his hackles rise at the insult.

'We are honoured to meet you, Reverend Reeves.
Miss Reeves.'

Jamie's eyes never left her as his brother spoke and
her expression became more wretched by the second,
yet she refused to meet his gaze and stared dejectedly
at the handkerchief she was worrying in her fingers.

'Allow me to introduce my daughter Cassandra.' She
stepped forward, looking completely dejected. 'Stand
straight, girl! Stop slouching.'

The vicar's voice was clipped and cold and his daughter withered beneath his steely glare. Instantly, for that alone, Jamie decided he hated the man. The sort of man who would openly chastise his daughter in front of apparent strangers was not the sort he was inclined to think charitably towards. The Reverend Reeves was a bully, like his own father had been, and like all bullies needed standing up to. He bit back the urge to give the man a set down on her behalf, fearing it would only make this increasingly awkward situation much worse and might enlighten the imperious vicar of their prior acquaintance. Definitely not what she needed.

To her credit, Letty never faltered. His sister-in-law stepped forward and smiled benevolently. 'My dear Miss Reeves, I am so glad you have come to visit us here at Markham Manor. You and your father are most welcome. May I introduce you both to my husband, the Earl of Markham, and his brother, Captain James Warriner?'

Jamie stepped forward and received his own version of the vicar's limp handshake and bowed politely to the woman who had dominated his thoughts for the last few days.

'It is a pleasure to meet you, Miss Reeves.' She smiled somewhat nervously and blushed bright pink as soon as her eyes guiltily flicked to his.

'How do you do, Captain Warriner. Your lordship.' Then she stepped back behind her father and stared back at her crumpled handkerchief as if her life depended on it.

It was all very peculiar, yet for reasons unexplained they were pretending to be complete strangers. It was

obvious she was frightened of her father. Jamie knew
how that felt. His own sire had been a nasty piece of
work by and large, and one not averse to using his fists
when the mood struck him, usually after dark when
it was least expected. He had wielded the element of
surprise perfectly. And the old Earl had not been particular about his choice of victim. His sons, his wife,
servants, complete strangers. Was the reverend also
a man like that? The prospect was as unsettling as
it was galling. Surely a man of God would abhor the
use of violence? But then again, already this man had
openly criticised his daughter in front of strangers, so
perhaps he was capable of worse and Miss Reeves appeared cowed in the man's presence. It all looked far
too familiar for Jamie's liking.

Letty ordered refreshments and invited the vicar
and his lying daughter to sit, and did the very best impression of a woman making polite small talk he had
ever seen. Throughout the arduous pouring and serv-
ing of the tea, the reverend wore a mask of haughty
superiority and barely said a word. His daughter said
nothing, seemly content to watch her fingers tightly
twist her handkerchief into a tangled ball, her lovely
brown eyes limpid.

Jamie had just brought his cup to his lips when the
good reverend cleared his throat and began to speak in
an overly loud voice to no one in particular.

*'"The Lord knoweth how to deliver the Godly out
of temptations, and to reserve the unjust unto the day
of Judgement to be punished."'* The vicar paused for
effect and stared directly at his elder brother. 'A stark
warning from the gospels which is pertinent for this
family, I believe.'

He watched Jack's dark eyebrows come together in confusion while he tried to come up with a suitable response to what was undoubtedly meant as the most grievous of insults. As usual, his brother resorted to diplomacy, although those who knew him well heard the steel embedded in his words.

'Perhaps the Warriner family of old, sir, but I trust you are not suggesting those of us who stand before you today are the *unjust*?'

Jamie felt his own eyes narrow and would have intervened if he had not seen Miss Reeves stare at him, her sorrowful expression completely wretched. He held his tongue reluctantly.

The vicar was unrepentant and glared back at his brother as bold as brass. 'The whole of Nottinghamshire is rife with stories about the Warriner family. Cheats, liars, debauchers—*fornicators*! But fear not!' One bony finger pointed heavenward. 'It is not too late to save your miserable souls.'

Had the man come here to preach at them? How dare he? Jamie had had quite enough. 'If your intent was to come here and grossly insult my brother and his wife, Reverend, you have succeeded...'

His brother stayed him with a placating hand and a warning glance. 'Reverend Reeves, it is true the Warriners of old were a thoroughly bad lot—and I include my own father in that generalisation—however, I can assure you that his sons have chosen to tread a very different path.'

The bony finger pointed directly at Jack in accusation and wiggled menacingly an inch away from his brother's chest. '"*Enter not into the path of the wicked, and go not in the way of evil men.*"' Almost as an afterthought he added, 'Proverbs,' in case they had the urge to look it up in the Bible to check the validity of his unwarranted sermon.

Miss Reeves, Jamie noticed, had now completely covered her face with her hands and was bent over in the chair, almost as if she were trying to become part of the upholstery. It was obvious she wanted no part in her father's zealous tirade, but felt powerless to stop it. Jack tried to reason with the vicar again. Clearly he had far more patience than Jamie gave him credit for as he'd have sent the man packing smartly. His fingers itched to grab the man by the lapels, toss him on the newly gravelled drive and to hear the satisfying thud as he slammed the door on him. But he and his elder brother were vastly different in character, therefore, Jack still persisted. 'As I have just said, Reverend, my brothers and I have chosen a different path to our ancestors and I can assure you none of us are cheats, liars, debauchers or—'

"'Behold, the day of the Lord cometh, cruel both with wrath and fierce anger, to lay the land desolate. And he shall destroy the sinners thereof out of it."' The vicar's eyes were wide and he was practically quaking with righteous indignation. 'Isaiah!' His finger jabbed Jack's ribs for emphasis and Jamie saw his brother's expression harden although he still did not pull the obnoxious preacher up. 'Repent, Mr Warriner! Before it is too late and your souls are banished to the fiery torment of hell!'

'Oh, this is beyond the pale!' Jamie briskly limped towards the vicar, snatched the teacup out of his hand and clattered it noisily on the table. 'My brother is an earl, Reverend Reeves, not a mister, therefore when you next address him it had damn well better have the words *my lord* at the end of it, else you will have me to answer to. And, whilst we are quoting the Bible, *he who is without sin, let him cast the first stone!*' He grabbed the vicar by the elbow and unceremoniously hauled him towards the door. 'John! Chapter Eight, Verse Seven, I believe. Now, good day to you, Reverend Reeves! Take your unsolicited sermons elsewhere.'

'Do you refuse to hear the word of God, sir?'

'I refuse to listen to a sanctimonious, judgemental, self-righteous diatribe from a man who is little more than a gossipmonger.'

'Gossipmonger!' This, apparently, was the highest of insults as the vicar began to turn alarmingly purple. 'I have it on the highest authority that—'

'Highest authority? Whose?'

The vicar's mouth opened to speak, then closed again, giving Jamie his answer.

'I see. Hearsay? Gossip? History? Surely that is not what the Bible condones, Reverend?' Jamie continued to walk the man to the door where Chivers stood waiting, still holding his elbow firmly.

'Jamie.'

His brother's calm voice penetrated his roiling temper. He understood the implication.

Stand down. We have to be above this.

He glanced at the wide-eyed Miss Reeves and saw the horror in those chocolate-brown depths and realised that his coarse physicality probably frightened her. Freckled-faced vicar's daughters, as a rule, would not be exposed to such aggressive behaviour. Or at least he hoped she wasn't.

Jamie let go of the man's arm and forced his next

words to be cold and final. 'I believe the Gospel of John, Chapter Seven, Verse Twenty-Four, also tells us, *"Judge not according to the appearance, but judge righteous judgement"*. Righteous judgement. Based on actual facts rather than salacious rumours. Something, Reverend Reeves, you appear to be incapable of. Show him out, please, Chivers.'

The well-trained butler tried to manoeuvre the outraged vicar towards the hallway.

'Cassandra. Come along, girl. Let us leave this house of sin!'

Jamie turned to see her stand, those beautiful brown eyes awash with tears. She sailed towards him miserably, wringing a handkerchief in both of her hands, and as she came level she never even looked at him. Whether that was out of embarrassment for her father's behaviour or complete disgust at Jamie's flash of temper he had no idea, but she continued towards the door in the wake of her father. Hunched. Afraid. Subservient. It was a horrible thing to see.

Chapter Five

No matter how much Cassie willed them, the words would not come. She was too distracted to write to-night, not when her cheeks still scalded with shame and her heart was heavy with bitter regret. She had hoped she had finally found a friend in Letty and did not dare put a name to what she had imagined between herself and Captain Galahad. But alas, like all of her brief and transient attachments, her interlude with the Warriner family was dead and buried. Unlike her, she doubted they would be holding a wake to lament its passing.

She closed her journal and carefully hid it under her mattress, sitting down on the bed afterwards and simply staring at nothing. Even by his usual standards, her father had been scathing. He had not even given the poor Earl a chance to defend himself against all of the slander laid at his family's door and that was un-forgivable. She had almost said as much to her father as they made the depressing walk back to the village. Almost, because the moment she had asked where he had acquired all of his salacious evidence against the family, he had pinned her with his penetrating stare and shaken his head in outrage.

'Do not dare to side with those heathens over me, Cassandra. Where my information comes from is no concern of yours. *"Honour thy father"*, Cassandra!'

As always, he omitted the end of that particular biblical quote. *'And thy mother.'* Her name was never brought up unless it was to compare Cassie's unfortunate wayward tendencies with the legendary wanton wickedness of her father's absent wife. The wife who scandalously took a lover and then shamelessly ran away with him when Cassie was but a babe. She had no memory of the woman apart from those planted in her head by her father. Memories which should haunt her, but threw up more questions than answers. Answers she would never get, from questions she did not dare ask. However, she envied her mother the escape, understood it and yearned for her own one day. In fact, it really could not come soon enough.

'I was not siding with them, Papa, merely questioning the validity of the charges made against them. They did seem to me to be very pleasant.'

Her father pinned her with another outraged stare, as if she had gone quite mad and needed to be incarcerated in a lunatic asylum. 'Have you learned nothing from my teachings, Cassandra? Appearances can be deceptive!' Then, as he often did, he looked up towards the heavens to seek forgiveness for the silliness of his only daughter. 'Help her, oh, Lord, to develop the fortitude and character you granted to me rather than the weakness cursed upon her by her mother.'

As she supposed it was meant to, this swiftly put a stop to any further impertinent questions. If she pushed too far, he would lock her in her bedchamber again for days on end, forced to pray and endure hour upon hour of his sermons behind the closed door while the inherited badness was exorcised from her soul. It was an ever-present threat; over the years those interminable hours in cloying solitary confinement had made her fear locked doors and crave a constant link to the fresh air of outside. Even in a blizzard, her bedchamber window remained steadfastly open. Just in case. 'Honour they father, Cassandra.'

Cassie watched the satisfaction in his cold eyes as he spied her fear. 'I always do, Papa.' A lie that would probably doom her to an eternity in hell. She obeyed him, sort of, and hated him at the same time. There was no honour in that.

They had walked the rest of the way in complete silence. Despite the utter humiliation, she admired James Warriner's loyalty towards his family. He had stepped in to defend his brother without a moment's hesitation and then he had not thought twice about manhandling her father out of the house. Cassie had never seen her papa so flummoxed before or so effectively silenced.

The Bible quotations he threw back were also to be commended. If her father would listen to her, which of course he never ever did, she was sorely tempted to tell him a man who could correctly quote chapter and verse from the Good Book, without the need to first check the Good Book for reference, was hardly ungodly. Captain Warriner knew chapter and verse and wielded them with the same deathly precision her father did. Yet to better effect.

Then the Captain had practically lifted her father off the floor with those impressive strong arms of his, forc-

ing her papa to do a funny little tiptoe dance as he was
removed swiftly from the Warriners' drawing room.
Cassie would have enjoyed that particular part of the
awful memory had she not been completely mortified
by everything which occurred beforehand. She would
have laughed at the ridiculousness of the spectacle.
Perhaps she would be able to find the wherewithal to
laugh if she ever managed to escape.

It was funny, but in her mind her father had always
been such a towering, terrifying man. A man to brook
no argument. Up against her dashing, serious pirate
he was little more than a weed stood next to a mighty
oak. Solid. Strong. Dependable. And oh-so-handsome
Captain Warriner made her want to swoon. Perhaps,
as her father was wont to point out, she was her mother's daughter after all if she was so easily impressed
and overwhelmed by the sight of a gorgeous man. A
gorgeous man who probably wanted to wring her by
the neck now. So far, she had inconvenienced him,
squashed him, forced him to lie on her behalf and allowed him to be grossly, unforgivably insulted in the
comfort of his own home.

Now, to compound her misery and right the wrong
which he had perceived had been done to him, her father intended to vilify the poor family further from the
pulpit. Cassie had already endured an hour of it over
dinner, scathing, hateful words which blackened the
Warriner name and cast fresh aspersions about their
characters, and that was only the first draft of his sermon. There would be more fire and brimstone by Sunday. No mercy would be shown. Cassie's only hope was
that the family did not attend the service. She had not

noticed them sat in the pews in the fortnight she had been in Retford, although that was hardly a surprise when she rarely paid attention in church at the best of times if her father was preaching the sermon. However, she had a feeling she would have seen Jamie. The sight of his fine shoulders in his Sunday best combined with his dashing good looks would have brought her out of even the deepest of daydreams. And those penetrating, soulful eyes... But there was nothing to be done about it now. Those eyes, quite rightly, would only regard her with wariness in future.

With a sigh, she blew out the candle on her nightstand and swung her legs into bed. She doubted she would sleep, but as *Orange Blossom and the Great Apple Debacle* had come to a shuddering halt in her mind at least she would be comfortable while she stared listlessly up at the ceiling.

As bad ideas went, this one ranked as one of the worst Jamie had ever come up with. It made no difference how well trained he was in covert reconnaissance, lurking in the bushes outside a lady's open window at midnight was not really something any decent gentleman should do under any circumstances. As a Warriner, with the absolute worst of reputations, the repercussions for both himself and poor Miss Reeves did not bear thinking about. Nobody would believe he was there out of necessity because his conscience needed to know that she was safe and well. In fact, he had needed to know so badly he had even braved the darkness to find out, skulking in the bushes for the right opportunity to present itself.

But he had lurked for the better part of an hour al-

ready, waiting for her awful father to finally leave his
study and head to bed, and now that he was sure the
man must be fast asleep, regardless of the impropriety, he simply had to see her. Properly see her, to speak
to her, rather than the fleeting glimpses he had seen
of her moving about her bedchamber from his hiding
place in the foliage.

At least she was still awake. The dim light of her
candle did little to illuminate the darkness, but it was
some light. There was also a full moon which offered
a little more and a reassuring sprinkling of twinkling
stars to alleviate the paralysing fear which came from
total blackness. In view of the clandestine manner of
his visit he had had to leave his lantern hidden down
the lane with Satan, which was beyond unnerving.
Without thinking, he checked the waistband of his
trousers and settled his hand on the solid comfort of
the handle of his pistol. Just in case.

In case of what, he would not be able to articulate
to anyone. He certainly had no intention of using it on
either her father or any locals who might happen to dis-
cover him in his current precarious position. Except,
the incessant feeling of unease was his constant companion during these dark hours, and he could never let
down his guard even though he understood the threat
was gone. No matter how many times he gave himself a
stern talking to, Jamie knew all too well that bad things
occurred at night when he had least expected them,
so it made perfect sense to him that he should always
face it armed, even though the only danger nowadays
came from himself.

The light from her window suddenly died and fear
clenched his gut as the darkness choked him. The

rational part of his mind reasoned with the irrational and he remembered his mission. Irrational fears had to be ruthlessly ignored until he knew Cassie was safe. Stealthily, Jamie crept out of the bushes and limped towards the vicarage. Her window was tucked to the side, offering him some camouflage. Fortunately, she had also left it open.

'Miss Reeves.' The rustling leaves stole his voice although he dared not speak any louder. Jamie chose the smallest of the stones in his hand and tossed it at the glass, then waited.

Nothing.

The next two stones tapped the window in quick succession. After half a minute of standing poised, Jamie decided there was nothing else for it. A handful of gravel pelted the darkened window as hard as he dared without shattering the glass. Finally, his perseverance was rewarded by the sight of her face peeking through the new crack in the curtains. He waved like an idiot, watching her eyes widen with alarm, and suddenly wished he had given up on his foolhardy plan an hour ago. As if the poor girl would actually want to see a broken, useless former soldier stood below her like Romeo. What the hell had he been thinking?

She flung open the curtains and pushed the window open further. Her head followed. Only then did he realise her hair was unbound. It hung down above him like a silk curtain, momentarily distracting him from the dark or from immediately explaining his presence and making him wish he was Romeo. If there had been a trellis, and if he hadn't been lame, then he would have eagerly clambered up it then. Just to touch her hair.

'Captain Warriner?'

She issued one of those weird whispered shouts which had no volume and appeared completely flabbergasted.

'I apologise for the bizarre way in which I have sought you out, Miss Reeves, but I wanted to talk to you and could think of no other way to do it without raising the ire of your father.' The words were out before he realised how stupid they were. If her father disapproved of her speaking to him in public, properly chaperoned and in broad daylight, his response to seeing his only daughter clandestinely speaking with him in her nightclothes at midnight was hardly going to go down well. The sanctimonious old fool would probably have an apoplexy. He could tell by her expression she thought much the same.

'I was just thinking about you.' A sentence to warm his cockles, dashed by her next. 'And how you manhandled my father out of your drawing room.'

Jamie winced. While he was not sorry he had removed the fellow, he was sorry he had upset her in the process. Very probably frightened her with his sudden aggression. 'Of course, I apologise for my quick temper, Miss Reeves, but you have to understand that—'

'My father was inexcusably rude and deserved nothing less.'

Her head disappeared back inside, leaving the window wide. After an unnaturally long pause she still did not materialise. 'Miss Reeves?' It was very hard to whisper with force so Jamie cupped his hands around his mouth in the hope it might direct the sound better. 'Miss Reeves?'

He heard the tell-tale sound of a bolt being drawn and whipped his head towards it in alarm. And there she was. Stood behind him in her nightgown, a dense shawl wrapped around her shoulders and her lovely hair falling about her face in tousled waves. Bare toes poked from beneath the hem of the garment, reminding him that only the thin linen and one woollen shawl came between her skin and his eyes. Her eyes were downcast and something peculiar happened to his heart, almost as if it had lurched in his chest at the sight of her so upset.

'I cannot tell you how sorry I am about what happened, Captain Warriner.'

He exhaled and continued to scrutinise her. Cassie found herself shifting uncomfortably from foot to foot, then when she could stand it no more she stared down at her feet to watch them dance nervously. When his big, warm hand came to rest gently on her cheek she almost jumped out of her skin.

'Are *you* all right?'

She had been expecting shouting or curt, brittle words of outrage, not concern. Cassie risked peeking up at him and saw the same concern etched on his face. Almost as if he was worried about her.

'Yes. I am quite well, Captain.' Aside from the strange warmth spreading across her skin from where his palm still touched it. His hand dropped to his side and he sighed.

'Your father is an interesting character.'

A very tactful way of phrasing it when, in her opinion, her hateful father did not deserve it. Making a decision she hoped she would not regret, Cassie pulled his arm gently and led them both well out of earshot of the house towards the bushes. Only when she was certain their voices would not carry, did she stop and turn to face him.

'You are being unnecessarily kind. My father is a zealot, Captain Warriner. He is rude, sanctimonious and utterly self-righteous.' And she had never criticised him out loud to another living soul before. Cautiously she glanced up at the sky just in case the Almighty had a mind to smite her for her disloyalty. Then again, if she was about to be consumed by the fires of hell, she might as well continue, because she was so mortified at what her father had done. 'I tried to stop him from coming, but he never listens to me. In actual fact, I am not sure he ever listens to anyone. His overbearingness and forthright opinions are the reason why we move from parish to parish. The bishops try to reason with him, then when they fail to enlighten him to the error of his ways they find a more affable clergyman to replace him.'

As there were no ominous rumbles of thunder or lightning bolts in the star-kissed black sky she dared wonder if the Lord might have similar opinions of the Reverend Reeves. Despite her misgivings, Cassie felt strangely unburdened to have shared what she had kept locked inside her for so long and so relieved that he had come here, of his own volition, to see her that she was decidedly lightheaded. Captain Galahad's dark eyebrows were raised, but other than that his expression was inscrutable in the shadows. Then just one side of his mouth quirked upwards.

'I am sorry if I embarrassed you by throwing him out.'

'You are not angry at me?' Because people usually were. When her father had pushed too far and grievously upset someone, more often than not it was Cassie who they railed against as her father refused to hear them.

'*My* father was a nasty, lying, violent drunk, so you have my sympathy, Miss Reeves. I know how unfair it is to be judged by the sins of a father. Did you think I came here to reprimand you?'

'I asked you and your family to lie for me.'

'After meeting your father, and hearing his condemnation of both my family and you, I can understand why. I doubt he would have been very pleased you had already taken tea with us, what with the Warriners all being cheats, liars, debauchers and *fornicators*!' He imitated her father at the last word by pointing a quaking finger towards the sky, then he smiled and that smile turned her insides to mush. When it slid off his face and his brows pulled together again, Cassie felt bereft. 'I did not like the way he spoke to you. He reminded me too much of my own father. I saw your fear, which in turn has made me wonder if your father is violent towards you, too, Miss Reeves.' There was steel in his tone.

And just like that, he became Captain Galahad again, ready to rescue her or defend her if needed, like a true literary hero would. Cassie was in no doubt he would if she asked him to, something she should not have found thrilling, but did. However, she barely knew him and feared her father's retribution too much to confess the truth.

'My father is not a violent man, Captain Warriner.' At least not in the strictest sense of what violence meant. He preferred to use repentance rather than beat her, although she would prefer a sound thrashing any day than his cruel choice of punishment. He had a violent temper. An unpredictable and violent temper which terrified her. Even when not in a temper he was fearsome. Changeable. He had verbally assaulted her on at least a daily basis for as long as she could remember. He was cold, distant, frequently spiteful and disappointed by her. Sometimes, she had genuinely believed he might lend his unpredictable anger to his fists, but in each instance he had chosen to lock her in her bedchamber instead. Manhandling her was not the same as beating. 'He believes violence is a sin.'

'I am relieved to hear it.' Although he didn't look entirely convinced he believed her. 'If that changes, you will tell me.'

It was a command rather than a question. A lovely command which made her pulse flutter. Nobody had ever offered to defend her before. Or thrown stones at her window in the dead of night to see her. And now, without even considering the gross impropriety of the situation, she was stood before him in her nightgown, enveloped by the intimacy of the night and charmed by the stars. Despite her best efforts not to, a hot blush bloomed on her face and she stuttered a pathetic response which she had intended to sound glib, but which came out a trifle desperate instead.

'Th-thank you for your consideration, although I dare say we shall be summarily moved on to yet another unsuspecting parish shortly so you will be relieved of the obligation.' The reality of the statement made her voice wobble. Always moving was so unsettling. One day, when she had squirrelled away enough of the pitiful coins she was able to save from her meagre housekeeping budget, she would find a permanent home and never go back. It was a dream which sustained her and demoralised her at the same time. At the rate she was going, she might have enough to rent a squalid room somewhere in a decade. Until then, she had to make the best of things, which in turn meant being at the mercy of her father's tempestuous and nomadic lifestyle.

'My offer stands, regardless of your location.'

Cassie wanted to hug him. Feel the contact and the strength in those big arms and perhaps experience what is was to be close to another human being. Just this once—but such nonsense was not acceptable. Not in a nightgown at any rate.

'Again, I thank you for your consideration, but your concern is not necessary. My father is not a violent man, Captain Warriner.' Just a cruel one.

He said nothing, but those blues eyes saw too much, making Cassie suddenly uncomfortable with her need to tell him everything. As a diversion she walked a little way in front of him and stared up at the moon while she waited for either him to speak or to come up with a safe topic of conversation herself. Already she knew he would not be the first to break the silence. Her pirate was a man of few words. 'You know your Bible, Captain.' A topic too close to her father, but the best she could manage in her current state.

'By accident, Miss Reeves, I can assure you. Religion did not form much of my education growing up. We Warriners are all cheats, liars, debauchers and fornicators, remember.'

His expression was serious although his eyes shone with mischief. An unexpected bubble of laughter escaped and lightened Cassie's mood. 'How does one learn the Bible by accident?'

'I spent six months as a guest of Napoleon in his dankest gaol. My only company was an old and mouldering King James Bible.'

'You were a prisoner!' Instantly Cassie felt nauseous. Six months of incarceration did not bear thinking about. The most Cassie had endured was a week, although that week had felt like an eternity, leaving her feeling weak, exhausted and completely dead inside. 'How did you cope?'

She could tell her question had made him uncomfortable because he looked away. 'I did a great deal of thinking and repeatedly read that book from cover to cover.' He came to stand beside her—just a few inches of air separated his arms from hers and the proximity felt intimate. 'I read it backwards once. Just for something to do.'

'I know the ten commandments backwards.'

His mouth curved slowly into a smile which made his eyes twinkle like the starlight. 'Why am I not surprised, Miss Reeves?'

'Perhaps we are kindred spirits?' Why had she said that? Aside from the fact that she really wanted them to be. Silly fool that she was. 'What I meant is we have things in common.'

'Dreadful fathers and a tendency to do things backwards?'

'Yes. I suppose. And we both enjoy creative pursuits. You paint beautiful pictures. I write silly stories. We also both love to ride.' What was she trying to achieve? Did she hope he would want to carry her off into the sunset after a few scant meetings? While she would happily clamber on to the saddle with him, because already she knew him to be kind, brave and honourable as well as being ridiculously handsome and delightfully broad, Cassie forced herself to remember she was an odd, silly and slightly ridiculous specimen of womanhood and one who had caused him nothing but grief. Friendship, perhaps, with a man who probably thought her peculiar, but had still come to see her this evening to offer his protection. She was confusing pity with more. 'Forgive me, Captain Warriner. I babble. I don't mean to, but it happens regardless, and here I am again—babbling when I should plainly shut up.'

'And I remain silent when I should speak. Perhaps we balance each other out.'

Her heart was beating too fast. Words like that gave her too much hope. 'Perhaps...' And for once, no words fell haphazardly out of her mouth. Instead a deep crimson blush began to crawl up her neck and her mind refused to work coherently. 'I should go. My father might wake up.'

'Of course.'

Awkwardness returned between them then, cloaking them in silence. In unison they moved towards the vicarage. Like a gentleman, he walked with her to the back door and stood stiffly as she opened it. 'Thank you, Captain Warriner.' Even though it had been several minutes since his palm had unexpectedly cupped her cheek she still felt it there, almost as if he had branded her with his touch. Marked her as his. Her flesh hummed. 'You have been very kind.'

He nodded and stepped back, looking as uncomfortable as Cassie felt, before wordlessly turning to limp slowly back up the narrow path. She was about to close the door before he quietly called out.

'I ride along the river every afternoon. I should enjoy some company, Miss Reeves, should you feel inclined to ride there one day.'

Chapter Six

Jamie had made Satan pace the same stretch of river-bank for the better part of an hour before he had forced himself to face facts. She wasn't coming. Not that he had seriously expected she would. He had spouted the invitation to her retreating back because he could not bear the thought of that being their final goodbye and she had merely gazed back at him with wide eyes and a nervous smile before softly closing the door.

Why had he been foolish enough to hope when there were so many reasons why she wouldn't come? Firstly, she hadn't said that she would. Surely that spoke volumes. Secondly, proper young ladies—vicars' daughters—did not meet gentleman unaccompanied and out in the open countryside in case something untoward happened. Unless, of course, they wanted something untoward to happen. Yesterday's clandestine meeting had only come about because he had instigated it and she was too polite to turn him away in light of her father's disgraceful behaviour. Only an idiot would read more into her motives than that. And thirdly, why would a lovely specimen of womanhood like Miss

Reeves waste time in the company of a crippled invalid in the normal order of things? If she was inclined
towards a tryst, then the lucky fellow would be robust
and in possession of two working limbs.

As depressing as it was, you couldn't argue with
logic. Beneath him, Jamie could feel the frustration
of his horse at the inactivity. Satan wanted to gallop
while Jamie was content to wallow in a bit more self-
pity—something which was hardly fair on the horse.
Out of decency, he swung himself off the beast, un-
packed his painting equipment from his bag and began
to remove the halter and saddle. The big black stallion
would appreciate an hour of freedom to fly across the
land. It had been weeks since the petulant animal had
escaped the stable and gone wandering. Satan was determinedly wild at heart, yet Jamie knew full well he
always came back of his own accord when he had had
enough. The horse bolted the moment the last strap was
unbuckled, just in case his owner changed his mind,
leaving Jamie alone with his miserable thoughts. He
limped towards the bank, set up his little easel, then
began the ungainly process of sitting on the ground.

'Hello!'

Any elation he felt at seeing her trotting across the
field towards him was cancelled out by the utter humiliation of knowing she had seen him clumsily manoeuvre his broken body to do something which most
people did without any prior thought or preparation.
Clearly he was doomed to be infirm for ever in the
pretty dark eyes of Miss Reeves. Even worse, without
a horse he couldn't go riding with her as he had suggested, where at least he would give off the illusion of

sprightliness. On a horse, Jamie was his old self. Without one, he might as well be old.

Out of politeness he gave her a cursory wave, wishing now she hadn't come, and busied himself by organising his paints to give off the impression he was occupied. Behind him, he heard a swish of petticoats as she climbed off her own saddle, a saddle which any normal gentleman would have helped her out of. However, getting back up was now out of the question. There was a finite amount of humiliation he could stomach in any one day and he had already surpassed his limit.

'Where is Satan?'

'He wanted to run, so I let him have his legs while I waited for you.' Good grief, now he had admitted he had been awaiting her arrival. Pathetic.

'I can't see him.'

Jamie risked looking up at her and was pleased to note she was too busy scanning the horizon for his temperamental stallion to see his reaction. Lord, she was lovely! Her skin was slightly flushed from her ride, the apples of her cheeks a little pink, lips very pink. In profile, the thickness and length of her lashes was obvious. One slippery burnished curl had escaped her bonnet and shimmered in the sunlight against her neck. The plain, pale grey muslin dress was too drab for her colouring, but from his angle on the ground showed off her splendid figure to perfection; hugging her bosom tightly, then falling in soft folds which caressed her rounded hips. Above those hips he already knew she had a narrower waist. And below were lovely legs. The memory of those garters came flooding back and his cravat instantly became tight and uncomfortable around his neck.

'He will come back when he is ready. I am afraid you and Orange Blossom will have to ride alone.' Something which she would undoubtedly prefer.

Jamie's eyes followed her as she led her own pony down to the water's edge to drink, then briskly marched back up the bank to where he sat. In one fluid movement, she plonked herself down next to him, legs outstretched, and wiggled her feet. 'I am more than content to sit here and while away the time. That is if you can bear my company and my babbling while you paint.'

Of course *he* could bear it. He just did not want to feel so blasted awkward in his own skin. 'I fear you will be bored.' But she was untying the ribbons of her bonnet.

'How could anyone be bored with this stunning view?'

Never were truer words spoken, except his view and hers were completely different. She gazed out to the horizon. Jamie gazed at her. As soon as she lifted the hat from her head, more glowing tendrils fell about her face which his fingers itched to touch and unfurl to fall around her shoulders like it had last night. He had dreamt of that hair when sleep had finally come. That hair. That nightgown. The freckles. Those bare toes poking out to tease him. Oblivious of her impact on him, he watched in fascination as she removed several pins, holding them between her lips, and deftly secured the errant locks back in their proper place, then sat back to rest on her hands before smiling at him.

'I know I should keep my bonnet on because freckles are unbecoming. But they seem to spring up all over the place regardless of whether I wear it or not, so I have decided to embrace them. And I do adore being outside in the open.'

'Hmm.'

He was such a wordsmith! He had had little to charm a woman before his injury. All of the easy charm and talent with the ladies had gone to his youngest brother Jake. Jamie thought the words—he could just never say them.

I adore your freckles, Miss Reeves. I should love to kiss every one of them.

Tree trunks had more talent for flirting than he did. Dead tree trunks covered in fungus and filled with woodlice.

She closed her eyes and tilted her face up to the sun. In doing so, she offered him an unobscured view of her neck and décolleté. There were a few random freckles trailing down her throat, dusting her collarbones and the hint of her breasts visible above the demure neckline of her dress. Jamie swallowed hard, trying not to think of potential freckles on the rest of her breasts and failing spectacularly.

'You can paint while I prattle on, Captain Warriner. You do not even need to pretend to listen. I don't mind. In fact, it would probably be more prudent to ignore me as I tend to talk nonsense most of the time. Most people do.'

Jamie tore his eyes away from her exposed flesh, picked up his brush to start and realised he had forgotten to fill his jar with water. Should he ask her to do it and thereby admit to his infirmity or go to fetch it himself and display it? The latter was too awful to contemplate. He wiggled the jar instead. 'Would you mind?'

'Oh, yes, of course.' She grabbed the jar, stood up and hurried down the bank. 'I suppose getting up and down is difficult with your leg?'

And there it was. He was thinking carnal thoughts about her while she was busy pitying him.

'I am not an invalid, Miss Reeves!'

His voice came out harsh thanks to the anger and shame boiling in his gut. Anger that he was a blasted invalid and they both knew it, and shame that it was, quite rightly, the way she saw him. He watched her wince, but didn't apologise for his outburst. Nor did he look up to take the proffered jar of water when she returned with it up the bank, forcing her to place it next to him on the ground. She sat down heavily while he focussed his efforts on trying to mix a wash and wishing he had not created such a tense atmosphere with his curmudgeonly reaction, when the poor girl had only just arrived and she was only trying to be nice.

'I have a knack for saying the wrong thing, Captain Warriner. I am sorry. Yet again. All I seem to do is have to constantly apologise to you. I am certain you must be already regretting inviting me here.'

Jamie risked a glance sideways and was dismayed to see her bereft, unsure expression. His fault. 'It is I who should apologise for my outburst. You should not be sorry for mentioning the obvious and I need to learn to accept my condition.' Just saying it made him furious. He doubted that would ever stop.

'How did it happen?'

His first reaction was to tell her to mind her own business. He did not talk about it. Ever. The awful memory of that night still haunted him. Except he still felt bad for snapping at her and wanted her to stay a while longer, even if she was only there out of pity or good manners. Unfortunately, the whole truth would likely send her running for the hills.

'I managed to break out of that gaol I told you about last night.'

After he had snapped Capitaine DuFour's neck with his bare hands, stolen his keys and then his horse. He could still hear the definitive crack when the bones had broken. Was still horrified at the surge of elation he had felt when he had killed the man in cold blood.

'The guards shot me as I rode away.'

Three bullets had ripped through his leg, one shattering his thigh bone, a fourth went straight through his body above the same hip, leaving an impressively symmetrical pair of scars on both the front and back of his body. He'd almost bled to death before Satan delivered him to the British lines. Fortunately, he was still conscious and had vociferously forbidden them from amputating the mess. For the next month he had lain useless in the makeshift battlefield hospital, snatching sleep where he could with a pistol under his pillow to prevent them from removing the damn thing while he fought the infection and prayed the splints would achieve a miracle and make him whole again. He still slept with a pistol under his pillow. Just in case. But for altogether different reasons, although he was coming to suspect they were linked. Like DuFour and his father, those surgeons had preferred to sneak up on him while he slept—until he almost shot one of them and they left him well alone.

'The surgeons did the best they could to patch me up, but the damage was extensive. There's nothing to be done about it, I'm afraid.'

She blinked and appeared horrified. 'You poor thing.' He saw the pity and hated it.

'How is your story coming along?'

'I brought it with me, if you would like to hear it.'

Jamie nodded, eager to avoid any further discussion about his useless leg and useless life, and watched her scurry back to her pony and retrieve a small journal from her saddle bag. When she returned and sat back down next to him she was blushing. 'Please bear in mind it is meant for children, so I have used some artistic licence with the actual events...and with the characters.'

'I thought the characters were us.' Although he supposed children would be as unimpressed with a limping, broken soldier as she was.

'They are. After a fashion. But I have changed some things.' She stared down at her hands for a moment before opening the book and he wanted to tell her that she did not need to feel bad for wanting a proper hero for her tale, but kept his own counsel. Saying that would merely alert her to the fact he knew she pitied him and Jamie was not certain he could hide his devastation at that. To cover it, he picked up his brush and palette and began to mix some paint and waited for her to begin, dreading it at the same time. He had rather liked being noble and brave when she had regaled the events to Letty—but now he was to be replaced with a better version of a dashing hero, Jamie was not so keen to hear about him.

'"*Dear Reader, My name is Orange Blossom and I am a pony. My owner is a silly young lady called Miss Dolt, who does silly things—so silly that I simply have to share them with you...*"'

'Wait—you cannot call yourself Miss Dolt. It's insulting.'

'But as I am the one doing the insulting and I am insulting myself, I fail to understand your objection.' Cassie watched his annoyed expression with interest, smiling at him to convey the fact that she was perfectly comfortable with poking fun at herself. She was ridiculous after all.

'Dolt suggests you are stupid.'

'I did get stuck up a tree. What's that if it is not stupid? Besides, it is a book intended for children so I want the character names to conjure an image of the protagonists in their minds. Something which sets the characters apart from one another. Miss Dolt is a friendly name and I want her to be comedic.'

'I still do not like it. There are other friendly names which might conjure an image, too. Nobody wants to read about a stupid heroine. Comedic, yes. Definitely intrepid. Making your heroine appear like an idiot might upset the little girls.'

He might have a point there, although she was surprised a surly soldier would concern himself one way or another about the feelings of little girls. 'What do you suggest, Captain Warriner? Because I can hardly call her Miss Reeves. I would prefer to remain anonymous.' Or risk being locked in her bedchamber for ever.

He scrunched up his face as he pondered, staring at her intently with his head tilted slightly to one side. 'What about Miss Freckles. You did say you wanted to embrace them and if freckles are considered so unfashionable, it might bolster the confidence of all of the little girls who also have them. She can be intrepid but silly sometimes.'

'Miss Freckles does have a good ring to it. And it is such a pretty word even if the freckles themselves leave a great deal to be desired.'

'I happen to like freckles.'

For a moment Cassie was certain he had paid her another unexpected compliment, but instantly he busied himself with applying paint to his paper and she could tell he was more interested in his work. Feeling somewhat disappointed, she idly crossed out the word 'dolt' and replaced it with 'freckles' and added intrepid to the description before reading it out loud again. It worked. Aside from that, it also gave the characters more scope. Now that the heroine was intrepid, she and Orange Blossom could go on all manner of adventures which a completely silly girl would never be able to cope with.

New name decided, Cassie continued to read to him. However, the Captain seemed so absorbed in his work she became certain he was not listening. Which was just as well, because she had reached the part where he saved her from the apple tree.

'*"Captain Galahad charged in on his magnificent jet-black stallion. He was a handsome pirate with sapphire eyes, a single gold earring and a stormy expression..."*'

'Captain Galahad?' His brush stilled and he appeared surprised as he scrutinised her. Cassie tried to brazen it out despite the burning red circles on her cheeks.

'Of course. He is a hero, after all, come to save the intrepid but silly Miss Freckles.'

'Hmm...'

He focussed back on his work with the exact stormy

expression she had pictured when she had written him. Whether he was angry at being likened to a pirate or if he simply thought her as silly as she had written herself, Cassie couldn't say and she was suddenly nervous about reading the next bit. Decisively, she closed her journal. 'I suppose that's quite enough nonsense for one day.'

His brush paused again. 'But I want to hear what happens next.'

'You know what happens next. You climb up the tree to save me and I cause us both to fall out of it, flattening you in the process.'

'But I should still like to hear how you have written it.'

Cassie saw Orange Blossom gazing at her knowingly from the edge of the water. *I bet you wish you weren't quite so gushing about your pirate now, Cassie?*

Yet the Captain was still watching her intently, clearly waiting for the next instalment. In a smaller voice than she'd intended she read the damning passage again.

'"*Captain Galahad charged in on his magnificent jet-black stallion. He was a handsome pirate with sapphire eyes, a single gold earring and a stormy expression. 'She was fetching me apples,' I said, 'and then she got herself stuck.' He saw her dangling feet and knew what had to be done. 'Try to remain still. I'm coming up!' He dismounted briskly and started towards her. The Captain was the bravest of men, who had fought many battles and slayed many dragons...*"'

'He's slayed dragons?'

'Of course. All of the best heroes have slayed dragons. I thought it would make the tale more exciting as well as being a good way to explain how you got your limp.'

His square jaw hung slack for a moment. 'Captain Galahad limps?'

There were frequent moments in life when her silly mind and traitorous mouth got her into trouble. This was one of them. It was now blatantly obvious that she was writing fanciful prose about how much she admired his physique. Unless she could quickly weave some equally fanciful words which would convince him otherwise. 'He was seriously wounded saving the kingdom from a dragon called Napoleon—but he rallied…obviously.'

And now she was making it worse and glowing like a tomato, while he was staring at her in total bemusement. Cassie felt more hideous words bubble up and knew that if she didn't take decisive action then she would babble more of the truth and look even more foolish. She avoided his eyes and began to read quickly, not daring to look back at him until she was certain he was engrossed in his painting again. Not long after that she ran out of words.

'So that's where I am up to.'

He nodded with uninterest and continued to paint, so Cassie sat quietly and stared at the beautiful parkland and wondered if he would even notice if she tiptoed away. Usually, when she wasn't being odd she had a talent for blending into the background. After what seemed like an age he sat back to admire his work, then one corner of his mouth curved up into an almost-smile. From her position, she could barely see the edge of the picture.

'Can I see?'

He shrugged and twisted his small easel around. She couldn't quite believe what she saw. It was a scene from her story. Exactly as she imagined it in her mind's eye. Only funnier. Captain Galahad, complete with rakish pirate earring, was stood at the base of a tree staring upwards with his hands on his hips. Two female feet were sticking out of the leaves and witty caricatures of Orange Blossom and Satan were stood side by side, watching the humans with complete astonishment. The colours were bold and the composition ideal for children to enjoy.

'Oh, my goodness! It's perfect. You have painted it exactly as I imagined it.' It did not take a great deal of imagination to visualise a few lines of her prose written underneath the picture on a page. 'I do believe your sister-in-law is correct. It would make a wonderful picture book. Now that I have seen this I want to see the rest of the story.'

'I suppose I could cobble together one or two more.'

He was frowning. Did that mean he was merely being polite in offering? 'I do not want to inconvenience you, Captain Warriner.'

Inconvenience him? It was not as if he really had anything else to do with his time. Jamie had thoroughly enjoyed creating the whimsical picture. He had also thoroughly enjoyed listening to Cassie read it to him. She did have a talent for comedy and the little children's story definitely captured his interest.

Initially he had been intent on painting the river, but once her voice transported him into her idealised, fairy-tale version of reality, the picture where he was the bravest of men who slayed dragons had practically drawn itself. The finished article amused him immensely and had also inspired him to finish the orchard painting as soon as he got home. Only now he knew that Miss Freckles would be falling towards him in a shower of apples while the two exaggerated horses looked on in alarm.

Miss Reeves's delighted reaction to it had thrilled him too. All at once he had felt useful again. Even if the something responsible was not particularly important in the grand scheme of things, it was important to her and at the very least his pointless talent for drawing had finally served a good purpose.

'I wouldn't have offered if it was an inconvenience, Miss Reeves.'

In his head he had intended to say this with a charming smile. Adding, *And perhaps you would care to meet me here again tomorrow so I can show you my efforts.* However, it came out tinged with belligerence instead.

'Be here tomorrow afternoon.'

Her stunned expression quickly turned to amusement. 'Yes, sir!' Then she saluted him. 'What time should I ready the troops for inspection?'

Jamie felt himself smile. He could hardly blame her for poking fun at him because he deserved it. She was being nothing but friendly and his clumsy, curt remarks probably did make him appear horrendously stiff and humourless. To show her he really wasn't, he flipped out his pocket watch. 'Have them standing to attention at two on the dot, Corporal Reeves.' He was rewarded with a grin that made the gold flecks in her eyes sparkle.

'I was hoping to be a lieutenant at the very least.'

'With hard work and discipline there is always the chance of promotion.'

She leaned closer and nudged him in the arm playfully, giving Jamie a waft of her subtle perfume, then frowned as she caught a glimpse of the time. 'Good gracious! I should be home by now. My father will be wondering where I am!'

She jumped up and scurried down the bank to retrieve her horse, hastily stuffed her journal in the saddle bag and came towards him. 'Would you mind helping me on to my saddle, Captain?'

Of course he didn't mind. It was an excuse to touch her again. Jamie tried to stand as gracefully as possible, which was impossible. When Miss Reeves thrust her hand out to help him he was mortified. Those little gestures of pity reminded him he was broken. 'I can manage!' If only his blasted leg hadn't frozen solid.

'Oh, for goodness sake, Captain Warriner, stop being so stubborn. I have happily asked for your help to get on my pony, so surely I can return the favour?' She saw him set his jaw, offended, and rolled her eyes. 'What did you say to me in the tree?' She mocked his deep voice again. '*"Take my hand!"* Or are you too proud?'

Reluctantly, he did and she hauled him to his feet, then went about the business of organising her pretty pony's reins. Jamie limped towards her and was about to cup his hands to boost her into the seat as she had asked, when the urge to show her he was still a man asserted itself. Damn over-familiarity or impropriety! He might well need assistance getting up, but once he was up he was still as strong as an ox and capable of doing all of those things everyone thought he couldn't.

He slid his hands around her waist deliberately, pulling her gently towards him, then lifted her off the ground. He softly deposited her on her side saddle and then, as he had the first time, he eased her feet into the stirrups. Only this time his fingers lingered longer on her ankles, feeling oddly privileged to know that under her proper vicar's daughter skirts she enjoyed the whisper of silk against her skin. If he slid his hand a few inches upwards, he was certain he would find those incongruous, naughty garters that in all probability only he knew about.

She stared down at him oddly and he knew he had overstepped the mark. 'I really must get home, Captain Warriner.'

Jamie released his hold on her ankle and patted the haunch of her pony. 'Until tomorrow, Miss Reeves.' She blinked twice, then snapped the reins. Quick as a flash, she and her delightful freckles were gone.

'Where have you been, girl?' Her father stood in the kitchen, his face already contorted with anger.

Cassie chided herself for being so careless as to lose track of time. Her father was a man of strict routines. She might not exist to him for most of the day, but the times he remembered her were chiselled indelibly in stone. Four o'clock he expected a hot meal on the table and a pair of ears to listen to him practise his sermon.

She and Orange Blossom had galloped home, slowing only when they turned into the lane which led towards the vicarage. If he had witnessed her riding with abandon he would forbid her from riding and sell her little pony to the slaughter man, exactly as he had threatened. The Reverend Reeves never made idle threats when it came to disciplining his wayward daughter and Orange Blossom had been her only friend in the world for so long her father knew exactly how to hurt her.

For her own good, of course. Always for her own good lest she turn into her mother. Her eyes darted to the clock on the mantel. She was only ten minutes late—yet in less time he had been known to work himself into such a temper he was practically delirious with it. She would have to tread carefully.

'I was talking to some of your new parishioners in the village, Papa. Listening to their ills and offering comfort. Those duties kept me a trifle longer than I wished.' Cassie headed quickly to the fire to see to the bubbling stew she had placed there earlier. It gave her an excuse not to meet his eyes or to allow him to see she was fibbing. Instinctively her eyes flicked quickly to the door. The key was in the lock. A good sign.

'Liar! I saw you as you rode down the lane. You were smiling!'

'The weather is beautiful, Papa, and Retford is such a lovely village I cannot help smiling at all of God's creation.'

'You went to meet a lover, didn't you, Cassandra? A clandestine meeting with a man! Did you disgrace yourself like your mother, girl?'

Instantly, every muscle in Cassie's body tensed while she forced herself to appear normal. She had been having a clandestine meeting with a man, of sorts, so her father's accusation was dangerously close to the mark. Only the illusion of calmness would help alleviate his fears and placate him so she tried to centre herself as she grabbed a cloth, wrapped it around the handle of the pot and carefully carried the steaming vessel to the table. Sometimes, gentle calm worked.

'I saw Mrs Sansam in the village today, Papa. She told me to tell you that she very much *enjoyed* your sermon last Sunday.'

Sticking to the truth, finding things he could easily confirm when he went searching for sign of her sins, was always best. Mrs Sansam, with her bushel of lively children, was always so busy keeping them on a tight leash Cassie reasoned she would have little concept of time. The fact that they had spoken in the early afternoon rather than just now would hardly register if her father questioned the woman tomorrow. Despite his claims of vanity being the most dreadful of sins, her father adored getting praise for his sermons. The tiny compliment was already softening the tension around his jaw.

'Mrs Sansam is a good woman. Godly. She does this parish credit.' People who fell into line were always a credit. Rebellious traits, like imagination or humour, were evidence of ingrained sin caused by ungodly wilfulness, so Cassie hid those parts of her character in his presence, pouring them all into her stories instead.

'I have offered to watch her youngest two children tomorrow, to give her some peace.'

'Peace? Nonsense. Children are a blessing from the Lord, Cassandra.'

Funny, she was *his* child and had never felt like a blessing—more of a curse left to him by her mother when she had made her dash for freedom. As the years had passed, Cassie had developed some empathy for the strange woman she did not remember, yet who kindled her father's daily wrath. To remain shackled to him till death was tantamount to torture. Like her face-less mother, Cassie had the dream of escaping one day. For years she had assumed that would happen when a nice man offered to marry her. However, for that mi-raculous event to happen she would need to stay in one place for enough time to actually meet a nice man in the first place. Something, thanks to her father, much easier said than done.

Older and wiser, Cassie now realised how dread-ful her life might be if she married the wrong man in haste. If she found one with any of the same traits of her overbearing father, then all she would be doing was jumping out of the frying pan and diving into the fire. What she wanted for herself was a pleasant life where she did not have to continually pretend to be something she was not, which meant setting up on her own some-where. Hence she had begun to squirrel away every spare farthing—aside from those she had spent on a few fripperies she could not resist.

'You are right, as always, Papa.' His mind was mov-ing on, she could tell. The mask of fury was being re-placed by the dour expression of a man who believed he was listened to. 'I also thought I would take a small basket to the elderly couple we met last week—you know the ones. The husband is blind. It must be very difficult for his wife to leave him alone to go to the market.'

Cassie tried not to let the palpable relief show as her father sat down at the table. He never sat when he was angry, so the brief, sharp fury she had witnessed upon her arrival must already be dissolving. He believed her.

This time.

Although who knew if she would be so lucky next

time. Although she had never gambled—because gambling was a heinous sin—she had often thought gauging her father's mood would be a great deal like playing hazard. One never knew how the dice would fall and she never knew what might send him into a rage.

'Whilst it is to be commended that you pity those unfortunate souls, Cassandra, and fitting that you should offer them some charity, as I have taught you, try to remember the Lord took that man's sight for a reason. Perhaps he was a sinner and to live for evermore in darkness was his penance.'

Hogwash. But her father put a great deal of stock in the concept of penance.

'Yes, Papa.' She ladled the rich stew into his bowl and then did the same to her own. After her father said grace they ate in silence. The Reverend Reeves believed meal times were for quiet contemplation rather than social discourse. When he'd finished, he sat back to watch Cassie clear away the table. Only then did he retrieve his latest sermon from his study to read to her as she washed the dishes.

As was expected, she listened in silence. Except she wasn't listening. The drone of his voice was easily shut out while she weaved the fanciful stories in her head. And thanks to Captain Warriner's wonderful illustration and desire to create more for her never-to-be-published book of children's stories, she now had a greater incentive to think about her characters than ever before. She couldn't wait until bedtime in order to write the next instalment. In it she would have to find a way to convey Miss Freckles flattening the handsome pirate when they fell out of the tree without alluding to the scandalously splendid pleasure of being in such close, intimate proximity to such a fine figure of a man. Captain Warriner had such strong arms…

'The Warriner family have long been an evil stain in this parish!'

Her head snapped up at the sound of her father's fervent, practised tone.

'The previous Earl was a drunkard and a cheat, swindling many of you out of money and worse. Now his sons are a plague. An infestation of vileness without shame or conscience. Only recently, the new Earl kidnapped his bride and forced her into marriage. Under your noses he kept her prisoner in that den of iniquity—one lone, terrified woman in a house occupied by four vile men. Four soldiers of the Devil himself. Despoilers. Debauchers. *Fornicators!*'

Her stomach clenched as Cassie listened to more of his outrageous vitriol. Grossly unfair words which her father would have honed and rehearsed before he delivered his sermon in a few days. Words which would find their way back to Markham Manor and wound the people within. The good people within. So far she had met only three Warriners and knew they were good people in the same way you could smell a storm in the air. It was a gut feeling. And now, after all the trouble she had already caused him, Cassie would have to apologise to James Warriner once again. She only hoped he meant what he had said to her under the stars last night and that he would not judge her by the sins of her father.

Chapter Seven

❧❧❧❧❧

Jamie had painted well into the night like a man possessed. Or besotted. Miss Freckles had quite got under his skin. Both the real one and the fictional. Now his saddle bag was stuffed with two more colourful illustrations from the start of the tale, as well as the finished *orchard* painting which was no longer a view of the sky through the trees from the floor. Miss Freckles was hurtling towards the ground, arms and legs waving frantically in the air, big brown eyes wide with alarm and her lovely gingersnap hair in disarray. For good measure, he had added the leaves and twigs to her hairstyle he had found so becoming. He had been tempted to also show a hint of the saucy pink garter, but decided against it on two counts. One, such things were hardly appropriate for the eyes of children and, two, he did not wish to enlighten the vicar's daughter to the fact that he was secretly lusting after her. Jamie sincerely doubted she would be thrilled with the latter.

Horrified more like—yet achingly polite lest she inadvertently insulted a cripple. He would prefer to walk on hot coals before he witnessed that—or limp on hot coals, which was probably more fitting. The most tragic thing about the whole situation was the limp was merely the tip of the iceberg. There was a whole hornets' nest of other issues which he would rather never have to admit to. Ugly scars down his left thigh and above the left hip. The unsightly muscle wastage which came from the infirmity. Those were not things he would want to show a lady.

But even if he did find a woman who could overlook such distasteful physical flaws, because they might not be so obvious if he insisted on making love to the poor thing in the dark, then there was the fact that he was terrified of the dark and therefore prone to react in a manner which shamed and frightened him in equal measure. The fear paralysed him and took away all reason, then he would lash out. Unless he had a pistol in his hand and a light on somewhere close by. Or a big, fat full moon to illuminate the sky. He could cope with it then. Just about. However, even the most forgiving of women would find the prospect of making love to a man with a pistol clutched in one hand, just in case his father or Capitaine DuFour miraculously rose from the dead to come and beat him senseless again, petrifying.

Then there was also the disturbing habit of his trying to attack anyone who tried to wake him up. Granted, he had only done it the once but, as he had almost strangled the life out of his brother Jacob in the process, it had been a memorable event. Significantly memorable enough to mean that nobody ventured into his bedchamber unannounced while he slept and Jamie certainly could not entertain the notion of ever sharing his bed with another. Not when he had hands strong enough to snap a neck in two. It had taken less than a few minutes to send DuFour to his maker and the sadistic Frenchman had been in possession of a thick and meaty neck. Very definitely a man's neck. A delicate female throat would snap like a dry twig in summer before Jamie had remembered blasted DuFour and his damned father were already dead.

If he married and miraculously got to enjoy some conjugal rights, he would have to order the poor woman swiftly out of the bedchamber as soon as he had done the deed in case he nodded off. Something he had happily done back in the old days after a vigorous bit of bed play. Since his return, the only thing his bed was good for was hiding an astonishing variety of weapons under the mattress. Weapons he had no real cause to use, but which were necessary to put his whirring mind at ease. Just in case. Good grief, he was pathetic!

All in all, the chances of him finding a woman who was prepared to contend with all that, who was also happy to take on a man who no longer had a career or a means to earn his own living, or the ability to turn his hand to something new, were practically non-existent. Because what professions were there for a hardened, embittered former soldier, highly trained in the art of cloak-and-dagger reconnaissance and that one, memorable silent assassination? *The Vicar's Daughter and the Silent Assassin*—now, there was a title for a book. Unfortunately, and quite rightly, the sorry pages within it would send the whimsical Miss Freckles screaming for the hills.

He spied her in the distance, waiting by the river, and began to slow Satan's furious pace. She spotted them and waved. Even from this distance she looked lovely. Her bonnet had already been discarded, he noted. The drab-coloured dress only served as a foil to her vibrant hair and delectable figure.

Jamie knew it was delectable. His hands had easily spanned the trim waist twice now, felt the womanly curve of her round bottom, traced the delicate bones of her ankle. He had seen the silky and creamy soft skin above it. He thought about that illicit glimpse of her skin constantly. What he needed to do was stop thinking about her as a woman, because as a woman she was so far out of his reach it was pointless even fantasising about it. But as a painter he could be an acquaintance, a useful acquaintance with skills she could utilise, justifying the powerful need to see her. Which was bizarre as he usually preferred to keep his own counsel and avoid people like the plague.

The preposterousness of his own thoughts made him groan aloud. Useful acquaintance indeed! What on earth was the blasted matter with him? He would do better to remember that she was a vicar's daughter who had been raised to do good deeds for those in need. To her he was probably just another parish invalid she was charitable towards and had to help up from the ground. He needed to put a stop to all of those fanciful, frustrating and fruitless thoughts before they did damage. Lusting after the vicar's daughter was as pointless as it was pathetic.

Cassie heard the approaching hoofbeats and steeled herself for the inevitable before turning around. The sight of him astride his magnificent horse quite took her breath away. The pair of them were well matched. Both dark and brooding. Both a tad menacing and oozing an aura of untamed, unbridled power. Both staring at her as if she were peculiar.

Which, of course, she was.

The Captain pulled his massive horse to a halt and dismounted carefully. Cassie could see the intense concentration this took etched into his brow line and wondered if he was trying to disguise the fact he was in pain. If he was, he certainly wouldn't appreciate her commenting upon it; she had seen the flash of anger when she had offered to help him yesterday, almost as if he was embarrassed to be seen to be weak. Not that she would ever consider him to be weak. The man could lift her off the ground, for goodness sake! Something beyond impressive when there was so very much of her. His big body had absorbed the impact of her falling on top of him from a great height and he had still managed to move afterwards. She might have inadvertently killed a lesser man.

Because she was certain he was self-conscious about his limp, she turned towards Orange Blossom and stroked her mane, and worried about exactly how, and when, she was going to bring up the dreadful topic of her father's impending sermon. Especially after all of the other chaos she had caused him in their eventfully short acquaintance.

You can't tell him yet, her pony cautioned with her eyes, *it will spoil the precious time you have with him. There will be plenty of time to spoil his day afterwards.* And spoil it she would.

'Hello.'

The deep yet soft timbre of his voice made her insides melt like butter.

'Good afternoon, Captain Warriner.' Two piercing

bright blue eyes met hers, disarmed her, and Cassie heard her voice wobble. 'I trust you are well?'

'Yes. I brought these.' All business, he thrust a small pile of paper at her. More of his pictures. Then he turned abruptly back towards his horse to retrieve his painting equipment. Clearly he did not wish to waste time engaging in the sort of inane, odd chatter which Cassie was famous for.

She glanced down at the pictures in her hands and experienced a tight knot of emotion at the beauty of the pieces. Not at all what one would think would emerge from the brush of such a serious and brooding man. The first showed her climbing up the apple tree, a clearly disapproving Orange Blossom staring at her in exasperation. The second depicted the moment she had got stuck. Miss Freckles' arms were poking helplessly from her inverted skirts, the bottom half of her body and her modesty shielded with dense leaves. But it was the third painting which was the most astonishing, partly because Cassie had seen the bulk of the painting before as it was the Captain's unfortunate perspective of the orchard after she had sent him tumbling out of the tree and partly because it was unsettling to see close up his view of her.

In the other pictures, her face had been so small that there were no discerning features. He had made her look pretty, which was flattering, but not drawn in the same intensely personal way that she had been in this picture. Was this truly how he saw her? The falling Miss Freckles had big, brown eyes framed with very becoming, thick lashes. The detail on the irises was phenomenal. He had used several different shades of brown to replicate a real eye, yet amongst all that dark were shimmering flecks of gold. Her O-shaped, startled lips were pink and plump, a lesser, subtler pink emphasised the apples of her cheeks while the dusting of freckles across her nose, hopefully much darker than her actual freckles, gave the face a special charm. The hair was quite splendid. Thick, wavy and a clever mixture of yellow, copper and red tones. Curls and leaves framed her face. The finished woman was quite beautiful. So beautiful Cassie could not take her eyes off her.

'This is wonderful.' Her focus slowly shifted to him and once again he was frowning.

'Hmm.' He stalked towards the softest patch of grass overlooking the river and set up his easel. 'We should make a start on the next instalment to maximise the afternoon.' Cassie watched him limp back towards his horse. 'I shall find somewhere sturdy to tie up Satan first.'

'Poor Satan. Why don't you leave him be and let him wander where he chooses while we work? It seems such a shame to tie him up on such a lovely day.'

'I don't trust him with your pony.'

'If I remember rightly, Orange Blossom and he got on famously last time they were together.' To prove her point, the pony was already ambling towards the stallion. Satan appeared to be quite pleased with this state of affairs and walked towards her while the Captain looked on, frowning. The two horses sniffed each other, then began to chew on the grass simultaneously. Something which appeared to surprise him.

'Well, I suppose we can keep an eye on them.' He did not seem convinced.

'I wrote the next segment last night if you would like to hear it?'

He nodded and lowered himself carefully to sit down on the riverbank. 'It would help to give me ideas for the subsequent illustrations. I believe you left off where Captain Galahad had just begun to climb the tree.'

'I thought it would be amusing to have the two horses introduce each other next and perhaps make this a tale about the start of the friendship between them. The moral being sometimes good things can come out of a dire situation.'

'And there must always be a moral to a fairy tale,' he said dispassionately and Cassie realised he was poking fun at her.

Smiling, she opened her journal. 'I am a vicar's daughter Captain Warriner. There must *always* be a moral.' She quickly located the place and began to read aloud. '"*My name is Orange Blossom—how do you do?*"

"*I am charmed to meet you, Miss Blossom. My name is Stanley...*"'

'What?'

'Satan is hardly a suitable name for children. It might confuse them into thinking your horse is a thoroughly bad lot, when I want him to be friendly.'

'But *Stanley*? Surely there are better names. Satan is a magnificent, haughty and temperamental beast. The name Stanley hardly conveys those traits.' Now he appeared affronted. 'What sort of a name is that?'

'It does have many of the same letters as Satan for a start. And to me it does convey temperamental. My father's shortest tenure as a parish priest was in Stanley near Durham. The temperamental parishioners had him removed in three weeks.' Although, in their defence, her father had insulted the beloved patroness

of the parish because she had a penchant for a dash of
red trim on her gowns. Cassie had been sinfully en-
vious of those gowns and the daring splash of colour.
One day, when she was free, she was going to dress in
all of the colours of the rainbow which were currently
forbidden by her overbearing father. Naming a horse
after that town felt like a tiny act of defiance against
him. Another small insignificant rebellion he would
never know about, like the ostentatious and highly dec-
adent garters she had bought from some travelling gyp-
sies just before she left Norwich and the three pairs of
clocked silk stockings she had found cheap in a market in London almost a year ago. Vain fripperies which
probably made her the worst daughter in the world
bought with some of her precious savings. Yet Cassie
could not find the will to regret either purchase. Those
hidden fripperies made her feel pretty and went some
way to making her miserable life just a little bit more
bearable while she waited for the opportune moment
to make her dash for freedom.

Jamie let her have the name as it seemed to please
her and he was prepared to concede Satan was not really the sort of name to grace the pages of a child's picture book. For an hour he listened contentedly while
she read the latest part of the story while he drew a
caricature of himself, halfway up a tree being pelted
with apples. When her voice trailed off and she lapsed
into silence he risked a sideways peek at her and was
surprised to see her looking troubled.

'What's wrong?' Because he got the distinct impression something was. She inhaled deeply and squared
her shoulders before facing him and in that moment

he was sure she was going to say they could no longer continue to meet like this. He supposed she had already been more than charitable towards him. The severing of their odd little acquaintance was always inevitable.

'I am not sure quite how to tell you.'

'I am a big boy, Miss Reeves. Whatever it is, just say it and be done with it.' He would shrug as if it was of no matter to him, when it was. Her rejection, regardless how inevitable, would still hurt.

'My father has made your family the subject of this Sunday's sermon. I'm so sorry.'

Jamie let out the breath he had not realised he was holding. Relief made him smile. 'Is that all? Why, I am sure the congregation will adore it. They love nothing more than to malign us Warriners.'

'You don't understand, Captain Warriner. I have heard parts of it and he makes foul accusations.'

'Let me guess—we are all liars, cheats and fornicators? Believe me, worse has been levied at us in the past. I am plagued with troublesome ancestors.'

She buried her face in her hands and shook her head. 'I think his sermon goes much further. He is claiming your sister-in-law was kidnapped for her fortune.'

'She was.' Her head shot up and her lush mouth hung slack and Jamie chuckled. He had heard this tall tale repeatedly embellished in the last few months. Why bother with the facts of the event when the fiction offered better scandal? 'My brother found her bound and gagged in the woods. He hid her from her abductors until it was safe for her to return to London and claim her inheritance. During that month they fell hopelessly in love. If you want to know the honest truth, they were each both nearly killed trying to rescue the other one. It was sickeningly romantic, if you are inclined towards that sort of thing.' Which he was. Deep down where nobody else could see it.

Unfortunately, the truth made her appear more wretched. 'I don't know how to stop him. He doesn't listen to me. Aside from the lies he is perpetrating about your brother, he also has written awful things about your father and grandfather.'

'Which will all probably be true. Both men were hideous. We are quite used to being gossiped about.'

'And he has written about you, Captain.'

'He has. Does he paint me a rogue, too?'

'He calls you the Earl's henchman—someone to be feared.'

Feared? At least he was not being referred to as an invalid. 'Capital. I quite like the idea of being considered fearsome. Perhaps it will make your father think twice before he decides to come and lecture my family again.'

'But you will be vilified from the pulpit. Everyone will hear it and judge you.'

'Then perhaps we should all attend church on Sunday. To give your father's sermon some added gravitas. He can malign us to our faces and earn a great deal of respect from his new parishioners to boot. It might even serve to secure his tenure here for a long time. The locals will respect a man who calls out the dreaded wild Warriners. Excitement is thin on the ground here in Retford. The people hereabouts must grab their entertainments where they can. And if it is at our expense, so be it. Please do not let it trouble you.'

Jamie wanted to cup her cheek tenderly with his hand and smooth away the lines of anguish around her mouth with his thumb. Seeing her so distraught gave him a strange ache somewhere in his ribcage.

It's all right, Freckles, don't be sad.

The damning words threatened to blurt out of his mouth. To avoid humiliating himself by acting on the impulse, he set about cleaning his brushes to give his hands something else to do.

'I must say you are taking this well.'

He shrugged. There was no point in getting upset about it. 'The situation was the same long before my birth, so I accept it for what it is. My brothers, Letty and myself all know it is nonsense. I have never really cared what other people think.' Except he suddenly cared what she thought. 'Do you believe all of the gossip, Miss Reeves?'

Her beautiful brown eyes locked with his and held. 'You strike me as a very decent man, Captain Warriner.' That gaze never faltered and he found he could not tear his own eyes away. Around him, all the sounds of nature were amplified. The river water, birds, even the gentle swishing of the grass in the breeze was heightened as he lost himself in those dark depths.

Neigh!

The agitated sound of a horse came from behind and Jamie experienced a rush of irritation. Blasted Satan! Was there ever an animal more spiteful and ill tempered? To pick on that pretty little pony was beyond the pale and to do so when he was having such a splendid moment with Miss Freckles was unforgivable. Except when he turned around, Satan was not intimidating Orange Blossom. The pair of them were rubbing noses and necks quite excitedly.

A little too excitedly.

Judging from her quizzical expression, the innocent vicar's daughter had no idea that all sorts of inappropriate shenanigans were on the cusp of taking place.

'Satan.' Jamie kept his voice low and intimidating while he tried to scramble off the ground before his button-nosed companion received an education. If he could get to the beast before...

Too late.

Satan reared up on his back legs, displaying his ardent intent to the world, while the dun-coloured minx his horse desired batted her eyelashes at him and swished her fluffy tail out of the way. In a split second, his stallion and her pony were doing what nature had engineered them to do and there really was nothing Jamie could do about it. He could hardly try to prise them apart. There was no telling how Satan would react to such an imposition. If he were in his horse's shoes, Jamie doubted he would be very pleased to be thwarted either.

'Oh, my!' Miss Reeves, her eyes like saucers, watched open-mouthed as his horse had its wicked way with hers. Then she turned away abruptly and resolutely stared at the river. 'It feels impolite to watch.'

At a loss as to what else to do, Jamie listlessly stared at the gushing water, too. 'I am dreadfully sorry.'

'Oh, please don't be. Orange Blossom is a shameless flirt. She must take half of the blame for what is occurring.'

More fevered horse noises came from behind them.

'The weather has been quite lovely so far this month, don't you agree, Captain Warriner?'

'Yes, it has. Quite lovely.' Apparently they were now going to make small talk whilst listening to the passionate equine grunts behind them. Jamie sincerely hoped Miss Reeves would not have any questions about what their lusty mounts were up to.

'I cannot remember a time when I have enjoyed the month of May more.'

It was then that the ridiculousness of the situation overwhelmed him and he found his lips twitching. 'I am sure Satan would agree with you.' The bark of laughter escaped then, closely followed by another. Then she began to snigger next to him and before they knew it, they were both clutching their ribs and brushing tears from their eyes, because really what else could they do under the mortifying circumstances? After what seemed like an eternity, peace descended.

'Is it safe to turn around?'

Jamie glanced behind him and saw a smug-looking Satan standing proudly with the flirty Orange Blossom nuzzling his neck affectionately. 'I believe their business is concluded for the day. At least I hope it is.'

'I hope it is, too. I need to get home. But it seems unnecessarily cruel to split them up now, don't you think? They do appear to be very fond of each other.'

Fond of each other! Such a whimsical explanation for what had just occurred, as if the two horses experienced more than the primal urge to mate, and so charmingly just like her to view it that way. 'Then I shall accompany you down to the end of the lane, Miss Reeves, so our lovestruck horses can spend a little more time in each other's company.'

Deciding to abandon his easel until later, Jamie followed her back towards the animals and lifted her swiftly on to her saddle before hauling himself on to Satan. They rode in slightly uncomfortable silence for a few minutes, far too close as apparently their horses could not bear to be too far apart, and Jamie searched his mind for something to talk about which would break the strained tension. In the end, it was Miss Reeves who spoke first.

'Well, at least we have our ending now.'

'We do?' Surely she was not suggesting they finished a children's books with the exuberant joining of two horses!

'Isn't it obvious? The book will have to finish with a wedding now that Satan has compromised Orange Blossom.'

'You want our horses to get married?' What a ridiculously charming and splendidly brilliant idea. Already he could picture Satan in a jaunty beaver hat while his bride would have flowers woven into her mane. He would be best man and Miss Freckles would be the bridesmaid, and they would leave the church under an arch of crossed carrots held in the guests' hands like swords, delicate confetti rose petals fluttering in the air.

'Of course! Orange Blossom has been thoroughly ruined, Captain Warriner. A wedding is only proper. The silly and intrepid Miss Freckles inadvertently instigated their love story when she foolhardily climbed up that tree. It is the perfect happy ending.'

They reached the end of the lane and both dithered, not that Jamie minded. 'My father will be angry if I am late home again. He is a stickler for timekeeping and quite rigid in his schedule. Will I see you tomorrow? Unless you are already quite fed up with all of the trouble I bring to your door, Captain Warriner.'

'I always ride by the river at two. We soldiers are creatures of habit.'

She beamed at him and Jamie felt his heart warm at the sight. 'Then I shall bid you good afternoon, Captain Warriner.'

She nudged her pony forward and Jamie realised he did not want her to go. 'Miss Reeves!' She turned around, pretty eyes questioning, the late afternoon sun picking out the copper fire in the single tendril of hair poking out of her plain bonnet. 'Seeing as our horses are betrothed, perhaps you should call me Jamie. Everyone else does.'

'That would be nice. Until tomorrow… Jamie.' Except when everyone else said his name it did not make his heart stutter. He sat still until he saw her disappear around the curve of the lane, needing to see her for as long as possible. Only when the lane was deserted did he say the words which had almost tripped out of his mouth in her presence. 'Until tomorrow, Freckles. I shall count the hours.'

Cassie could not remember ever spending a pleasanter afternoon in her life. Aside from the shameless behaviour of their two horses, she and Jamie had whiled away the better part of two hours simply talking and working. For once, she had not felt even slightly ridiculous or odd because she was convinced his mind saw exactly what hers did. When she thought up her silly stories, she could see them unfold in her head like a play, hear the conversations and the noises in the scene and be transported away to that place. Jamie's paintings were exactly as she imagined that place to be. Whimsical. Childlike. Utterly charming. It was such a shame they would not be able to publish them because she was becoming increasingly convinced they were creating an excellent children's book while they sat companionably on the riverbank.

She dried the last dish and went to sit dutifully at the table where her father was scratching away on his sermon, the quill moving frantically as he scribbled whatever fevered prose were currently occupying his thoughts. A quick glance at the paper and she saw the word Warriner written over and over, and her stomach sank. He was still on his misguided quest for revenge. Even though Jamie had told her he was ambivalent, her father's intentions still bothered her. It did not sit right to stand by and watch them wronged. He saw her interest.

'With each new day I learn of new horrors from that family. I now know the father pushed the mother to suicide and no doubt his spawn helped, too. She threw herself into the river rather than spend another day in hell.'

Poor Jamie. To lose a parent in that way could not have been easy, especially as he had made it plain his relationship with his father was fraught. 'What a tragedy for the children, to be forced to grow up motherless.' Something she could empathise with.

'If only she had had the sense to drown her foul sons like unwanted puppies at the same time, then the world would be a better place!'

'Surely you cannot mean that, Papa.' Sometimes, his cruelty astounded her. 'They were just children.'

'Who have grown up to be replicas of their evil father! A man who was rarely seen in public sober. A man who shamelessly cheated my parishioners at any given opportunity. Refused to honour his debts. A man prone to violence! Already we have borne witness to the violence those boys are capable of. Did you not see the way I was assaulted by that man?'

It had hardly been an assault, more an assertion. Jamie had removed her odious father from his presence justifiably, nobly defending his brother. And he had offered to defend her whenever or wherever she needed him. Another nod to his innate sense of honour. How to explain such a thing to her father? Like a coward she decided not to. He would never understand. He took her silence as acquiescence.

'They abducted an innocent woman for her fortune, Cassandra, lured her into their life of sin and now live off her like parasites.'

'I have heard a different version of the tale, Papa, so I am inclined to think all is not as it seems. For every person who claims the Warriners abducted the woman, there is another who says they rescued her from her kidnappers and gave her sanctuary. I am told the Countess married the Earl because she loved him.'

'Who are these liars you put such stock in?' His voice had the calm, icy edge to it which she had learned to fear the most. 'Tell me their names, Cassandra.'

'We are new here, Papa. I do not know their names yet.'

'And now you are protecting these sinners!'

'No, Papa. Please believe me, I do not know their names yet, but they are good people.' Jamie was good, she felt it in her bones and her heart.

Without warning, his arm shot out and he grabbed a hank of her hair in his fist and pulled it hard. 'Liar!'

'I am not lying, Papa. Please believe me!' But Cassie

knew it was already too late. One wrong word and his tenuous hold on his unpredictable temper was lost.

'Your mother was a liar, too!' He was already dragging her to the stairs, his palm now securely anchored in her hair. His strength, combined with her now powerless position, made fighting against him agony. Yet as she fought she also realised her punishment was inevitable. He never backed down when he was like this.

Never.

Cassie forced her feet to move in the direction he wanted in the hope that he would at least acknowledge her lack of rebellion at her impending imprisonment. Such behaviour might lessen her sentence. Panicked tears gathered in her eyes as fear coursed through her body. How she reacted now would determine the length of her penance.

'I am sorry, Papa. I was wrong. I should never have doubted you...'

'Oh, Lord! Help her to see the error of her ways.' They were at the foot of the stairs. The tears were already streaming down her face as the familiar, paralysing terror began to stiffen her limbs and quicken her heartbeat.

'I'm so sorry, Papa.'

'Cleanse her of the wantonness of her mother. Teach her to be meek and to obey your commandments...' Cassie's scalp burned where his fist pulled, his knuckles and fingernails digging painfully into her skull as she climbed each step cowed behind him, powerless to stand straight. 'Teach her to honour and obey her father!' She tried to placate him even though she knew it was futile. It was always futile. He was already lost in the scriptures and talking to the heavens.

"'For the sons of Israel walked forty years in the wilderness, until all the nation who came out of Egypt perished, because they did not listen to the voice of the Lord...'"

When they arrived at her bedchamber, he threw her to the floor as if she were something fetid and rancid he desired to be well rid of, still chanting manically and slammed the heavy door behind her. As the silent sobs racked through her body and she heard the key turn ominously in the lock once again, Cassie curled her arms around her knees and tried to take her mind to a happier place.

A place where horses talked and handsome pirates came to save her.

Chapter Eight

ᕤᕚᕦᕤᕚᕦᕤᕚᕦ

She didn't come. For two days Jamie had sat miserably on the riverbank waiting like a lovesick puppy and for two days he had gone home with his metaphorical tail firmly between his legs. A churning, angry disappointment whirled in his gut as he sat in the drawing room early on Sunday morning.

What a blasted fool he was. He knew better than to build his hopes up when he had known he would ultimately be disappointed. He had confused her interest in his artistic talents as something more, which he knew was unlikely in the extreme and completely impossible given his circumstances, yet he had still convinced himself there might miraculously be something else going on.

The affinity he had thought they had shared, the strange sense of oneness which had overwhelmed him whenever they were together, was clearly one-sided. Why, she hadn't even felt the urge to send word she wasn't coming, almost as if he were of no consequence at all, and that galled. Had she forgotten they had arranged to meet again? Was he so instantly forgettable now that he was no longer a full man?

Wallpaper.

Something one noticed if it was right in front of your face, but forgotten when a more interesting diversion presented itself. He did not want to think about the interesting diversion she had been distracted by. There were plenty of fine young bucks in Retford, any one of them could have tried to turn her pretty freckled head. The surge of jealousy at the prospect came like a bolt out of the blue, rousing his temper at the imagined diverter and his own, physical limitations. He was not the sort of man to turn a young girl's head any longer. It was all so blasted unfair!

But then they had shared a special moment when they last met. He was sure of that. His instincts told him there had been. A perfect moment where their eyes had locked and words were not necessary because it was just them and everything else had become insignificant.

Jamie groaned at his romanticised interpretation of what might have been, for her at least, an awkward moment. The impromptu noise caused his younger brother Joe, home from medical school for a short visit, to regard him curiously.

'Is there a particular reason why you keep sighing and moaning?'

Jamie felt himself frown as he turned back to his painting and tried to concentrate on adding the detail to one of the carrots in the bridal arch he was painting. 'My leg aches.' Symptoms of any sort always distracted Joe.

'Are you using the liniment I mixed for you?'

'Yes.' He wasn't.

'Then why is the bottle still full on your nightstand?'

'Why are you poking around my bedchamber?' Not that Joe, or any of his brothers, would comment on the ready arsenal of weapons placed strategically about the room and tucked under his mattress. They knew he would not discuss those things even though he was heartily ashamed they were still there. 'Stay out of my room.'

'Then take your medicine, you stubborn fool, and I would.'

Jamie grunted and pretended to work, effectively ending the conversation. Or so he thought.

'Letty tells me you've met a young lady. A pretty girl, by all accounts. She says the pair of you have spent a great deal of time together—cosied up by the river.'

'Hardly.' This needed to be nipped in the bud before *he* became the main topic of conversation around the dinner table later. 'She is the daughter of the very reverend we are being forced to see this morning. The one intent on vilifying us from the pulpit with his sermon.' A sermon Jamie was annoyingly looking forward to in the hope he might catch the eye of Cassie and remind her he still existed, and hopefully satisfy himself that there were no young, limp-free bucks on the horizon.

'We, of all people, cannot judge her by her father, Jamie. Letty says the pair of you are working on a children's book together. Based on your eventful first meeting.' One glance at his brother's amused face told him that he and his meddling sister-in-law had been doing a great deal of speculating about the silent assassin and the vicar's daughter.

'No, we are not. I merely did a couple of illustra-

tions for her as a favour.' But Joe was already rising
from his seat and walking knowingly towards him,
obviously eager to catch him in the middle of another
'favour'. The most whimsical, romantic and damning
'favour' of all of the ones he had created thus far. He
quashed the urge to cover his easel with his arms to
hide it from his brother's view, but knew he would be
sentenced 'guilty as charged' if he did and ribbed mercilessly. Better to brazen it out.

Joe stood at his shoulder and peered at the painting,
grinned and then fished in his pocket for his spectacles before bending at the waist to scrutinise it further.

'Are those horses getting married?'

'Miss Reeves has an odd perspective of the world.'
One that matched his.

'Is that Satan?'

Jamie gave one curt nod and dipped his brush in
the orange paint.

'And the other pony, the pretty one, does that belong to your vicar's daughter?' She was not *his* vicar's
daughter. Never would be *his* vicar's daughter.

'Yes. That is Orange Blossom.'

His brother's index finger pointed at the pretty
bridesmaid, her coppery hair festooned with pink flowers which exactly matched the ones Jamie had seen on
her blasted garter. 'And this must be Miss Reeves. She
does look pretty. I can understand what you see in her.'

He ignored that comment to focus on painting the
carrot. Miss Freckles was beautiful, not pretty. Heart-
wrenchingly beautiful, sweet and funny.

'Why are you sporting an earring?'

Jamie did not have to look at Joe to see he was grinning from ear to ear. 'He's not really me. Cassie calls him Captain Galahad. He's a pirate. Apparently.'

'Cassie? Hmm. First-name terms. Very *familiar* first-name terms.'

The anger was swift and irrational. 'Stop it, Joe! Don't try to make something out of that which is plainly not there. Miss Reeves asked me to do some illustrations. That is all. There is nothing else between us.'

'If you say so. But you have been meeting down by the river every day. All alone.'

'No, we haven't! I met her twice. I have not seen her since Thursday. Clearly she has had better things to do than entertain a cripple on her afternoons off.' Jamie instantly regretted the words as soon as they spewed from his mouth. They said too much about how he was truly feeling. He experienced the overwhelming urge to punch his well-meaning brother in the face at the sight of the pity which suddenly suffused his expression.

'I doubt she cares…'

Jamie threw down his brush. 'Don't say it, Joe! Don't offer me platitudes or blasted pity. It is not welcome.' He stood up and limped towards the window, staring out sightlessly on to the garden and tempering his voice lest this awkward exchange continue any longer. 'I'd have thought the carriage would be here by now, seeing as Letty is quite determined to sit in the front pews.'

There was a beat of silence before his brother decided to retreat from the treacherous path the conversation was leading to. 'I will go and check.'

He heard Joe leave the room quietly—only then did he allow his forehead to rest listlessly on the glass. When he saw her this morning he would need to appear unaffected by her rejection and impervious to whatever her awful father said. He would not stare at her, try to catch her eye or give any indication that he had desperately missed her these last few days. As always, his true feelings would remain hidden deep inside where nobody could see them and he would endure the pain silently. If only his brother could mix a liniment for his aching heart.

The Norman church was already half-full by the time the Warriner carriage pulled up in front of it. They made their way slowly towards their rarely used seats at the front, Letty stopping to chat to the one or two people who were beginning to warm to her and ignoring the way a great majority of the congregation felt the urge to whisper speculative asides to one another. Thanks to his years in the army, Jamie had been spared this usual reaction by the locals, therefore it irritated him perhaps more than it did the others. Few people even acknowledged them, which was beyond insulting when Retford had always been their home, yet the infamy of his father and grandfather before him had been so well deserved Jamie understood it even if he did not approve. But his father had been mouldering in the ground for eight years, during which time not a single Warriner had put a foot out of place, so he wished people would simply move on.

Jamie scanned the pews for any sign of Cassie, but she was not there. Neither was her fire-and-brimstone father. No doubt he preferred to make a grand entrance. He struck Jamie as the sort. A grand, ecclesiastical entrance which would signal the start of his retributive sermon. Like his brothers, Jamie staunchly faced the front defiantly in the hope they would see the vicar falter at their unexpected presence.

Out of the corner of his eye he saw a small wooden door open to the side and witnessed the object of his torment emerge. Except Jamie's plan to avoid outright looking at the woman failed instantly. Because something was not right. Her face was pale and drawn. Dark shadows sat under her red-rimmed eyes. There was a tightness about her mouth and jaw he had not seen before and her gaze was downcast. Cassie appeared smaller, slumped and almost broken.

'Well, that explains things,' mumbled Joe to his left, 'Your lady has been too ill to leave the house.'

'Hmm.' Jamie didn't agree, but held his tongue. Whilst it was conceivable she had been ill—people got ill all of the time, after all—mild illness did not usually crush a person's spirit and for some inexplicable reason he knew Cassie's was damaged. There was no light in her eyes. No laughter. No joy. None of the things he associated with her and which drew him to her like a moth to a flame.

Jamie willed her to look across the aisle and meet his eyes, but she did not. In fact, it seemed as if she was completely unaware of the congregation at all, which only served to increase his concern. He could hardly stride over there and ask her what was wrong. Not here, where her father would hear of it, so he searched his mind for a solution. How exactly could he speak to her now when the whole town was there to bear witness?

'Here we go.' Joe nudged him and refocussed Jamie's attention back to the pulpit. The door from the vestry had been dramatically thrust open and the Reverend Reeves strode out in his billowing black cassock.

An overly large wooden cross attached to a leather cord dangled from his neck and he clutched an old, worn bible in one hand like an amulet to ward off evil.

Jamie had the satisfaction of seeing the slightest hesitation in the man's gait as he spied them, although he doubted the rest of the congregation would have noticed it. The reverend placed his free hand flat on the lectern, briefly closed his eyes and inhaled deeply as if he was receiving divine strength from the Lord before speaking. Jamie recognised the reading. It was from Genesis. The tale of the fall of Sodom and Gomorrah was an obvious choice for a man intent on besmirching the Warriner name, yet he found his teeth grinding in annoyance just the same. Around him, the congregation were held spellbound by the vicar's demonic delivery.

The man had a way with words much like his daughter did, Jamie had to give him that, although what he was saying was too much for some. Around him he saw people wince at the odd word while anxious mothers held the hands of their children in case the sermon frightened them. Nothing so dramatic had ever been seen in the tiny market town before.

The cleric paused. His eyes travelled along the row of the front pew, taking in each of the four people present quickly, before returning to burn hot with hatred directly at Jamie. He directed the next words to him, so it stood to reason Jamie stared back unmoved.

'This week I attempted to take the word of God to Markham Manor. It pains me to tell you that it was not welcome. Like the inhabitants of Sodom and Gomorrah, the Warriner family prefer to fester in avarice and sin!'

As he had promised Jack faithfully he would not react with his usual quick temper, Jamie feigned mild amusement instead. Nobody apart from the vicar could see it and, as he had hoped, it riled the man. His eyes bulged manically and an unpleasant foamy clump of spittle gathered in the corners of his mouth—something the congregation did see and it alarmed a few more people. And who could blame them? Foaming at the mouth was not something country vicars should do.

The army had taught him that disgust, fear and dissension were contagious, therefore as weapons they were invaluable. All it took was one person to begin to turn against the Reverend Reeves and others, like sheep, would be encouraged or emboldened to follow. For the vicar's eyes only, he stifled a minute yawn which had spectacular consequences. Arms began to wave, fingers began to point in accusation and the man began to shout quite unnecessarily. From the pews, it all appeared very aggressive. Unfriendly. Distasteful.

This was followed by a long diatribe about his awful father which Jamie was inclined to agree with. The old man had been spectacularly hideous and spiteful. Yet as shocking as it sounded second-hand, the congregation did not truly know the half of it. Not every scar on his body had been caused by Napoleon. He still bore the faint stain of the belt marks across his back which had been generously bestowed courtesy of his father. Painting was for girls. And perhaps Jamie was not quite a man. Therefore, it stood to reason the bad had to be beaten out of him. Something Jamie had endured defiantly for years.

Night after night, once his father had consumed enough brandy to feel up to the task, he would climb up the narrow wooden staircase that led to Jamie's room. His heavy boot would always make the top stair creak. The signal that hell was about to be unleashed for Jamie's own good. When the bedchamber door opened, the belt would be wrapped around his father's fist, in case his disappointing son was left in any doubt of what was to come. Then he would stride to the bed, drag him out by the hair and use that belt or that fist on him until he was satisfied Jamie had learned his lesson.

He had learned a lesson, but not quite the one his odious father had intended. He had learned that the best way to fight back was to refuse to comply. He hid his fear deep inside and never cowered while the violence took place. Each time his father battered him senseless, Jamie would paint something prettier the very next day as an act of rebellion. If his paints were taken away, he used the charcoal embers from the fire to draw, or pieces of chalk dug up from the ground, using art to fortify him and show his father that his spirit could not be crushed no matter how hard his father could hit. Then one day, shortly after his fifteenth birthday, Jamie had fought back. The brandy had numbed his father's reflexes and he had never anticipated that his artistic, girl of a son would ever retaliate, so it came as a shock to find his own belt wrapped tightly around his neck while the artist almost choked the life out of him.

In truth, the animalistic burst of violence had shocked Jamie as well. One minute he had been sound asleep and the next he was choking the life out of his father. How this state of affairs had come to pass he still did not know, except he assumed the man had attacked him in his sleep and in a daze Jamie had allowed the savage which was caged inside him to escape and wreak havoc. Only at the very last minute, when he saw his father's eyes bulge and his face turn purple from lack of air, did he find the ability to step back. But it had taken everything he had to do so and left him oddly unsatisfied not to have finished the deed.

He learned he had tremendous physical power and the ability to separate his mind from the job which needed to be done while that power was unleashed. Both things he had harnessed and used to great effect as a soldier later on, and perhaps that night had been instrumental in his decision to join the army. It gave the terrifying savage inside him an outlet in which to channel the violence. Or perhaps that had simply been to prove a point to himself as well as his father. I might well paint flowers, but I am a man. And one to be reckoned with.

His dear papa had never returned in the night again, nor used his fists on Jamie from that day onwards. He gave his disappointing son a wide berth, which suited Jamie just fine. They didn't converse or sit in the same room and his father never again so much as referred to him, let alone tried to disparage him. And Jamie had openly continued to paint. Still continued to paint. So his father had never won. Neither would the Reverend Reeves. Jamie stared back at him dispassionately, doing his very best impression of a man bored senseless and totally unmoved by the hate spewing from the vile reverend's foaming mouth.

All at once, he felt a warmth spread up the back of his neck and sensed she was watching him.

Cassie had not expected Jamie to be sat in the church. Not really. And after three nights of incarceration she had been too traumatised to give anything much thought other than her palpable relief at being free again to pay much attention to the congregation. Her father had only released her a few minutes beforehand with the terse instruction to 'get ready, girl!', so she had hurried to take her seat in the church in case he changed his mind and locked her in again.

The aftermath of each new punishment always left her drained and befuddled, a state which got worse each time and took days to shake off, to such an extent that the effort of putting one foot in front of the other was almost too much. But as soon as her father had begun his litany of the Warriner family's many flaws she suddenly had the overwhelming sense that he was there. For reasons Cassie did not understand, his presence soothed her. It did not matter that he was glaring at her father with barely disguised disgust or that he would, in all likelihood, never want to speak to her again after the sermon. He was there. That was all that mattered.

As if he sensed her watching him, he turned slightly and his intelligent bright blue eyes sought hers. It was a look which spoke volumes. She could see his concern for her clearly, saw the question about her whereabouts and knew instinctively he wanted to speak to her. She also watched his gaze flick back towards her father furtively, in case her father noticed the meaningful, silent exchange between them and she was grateful for that, too. Jamie understood there would be repercussions if her father got wind of any sort of relationship between them, even though he could have no earthly idea of exactly what those repercussions entailed, but she felt enormous relief knowing he would never approach her here.

Cassie offered him a tremulous smile to show him everything was all right, when it really wasn't, and then directed her focus back to her father. Like the dutiful daughter he wanted her to be, hoping this was not a temporary freedom and that he would leave her unpunished for another few weeks. Her eyes wandered to an enormous statue of the crucifixion behind her father and, to blot out the sound of the terrible words filling the church, she prayed that she would miraculously find enough money to run away from her tormentor, rent a little room somewhere and never fear the sight of a lock again.

As soon as the sermon finished the church was silent. It was obvious nobody could quite believe her father had said such dreadful things about the family while they sat there in front of him. In many of the faces she saw outright sympathy for them—and felt some relief that her father might perhaps have made things inadvertently better for Jamie and his family. The way the Warriners all sat proudly without saying a word actually made the tension worse. Everyone was waiting to see how the family would react. Her father included. Cassie knew him too well not to notice he was nervous, too.

The Earl of Markham stood and solicitously helped his pregnant wife to stand. She beamed at him and threaded her arm lovingly through his before they both walked the short distance to the altar.

'Thank you for the sermon, Reverend. It was most… enlightening.'

This caused a flurry of incredulous and slightly impressed whispers from behind and her father to snarl. Ignoring it all, he then led his wife proudly towards the door, the pair of them chatting pleasantly to each other as if nothing untoward had just transpired. Behind them, Jamie followed, walking next to a man who was the spitting image of him. One of his brothers, no doubt, although which she had no idea. As the rest of the congregation stood and began to gather themselves ready to leave, visibly deflated to have been denied a grander spectacle, Cassie watched Jamie whisper something to his brother and slip stealthily out of the church. Clearly he had had quite enough and had no intention of hanging about, not that she blamed him. Not after so much of her father's hateful words had been directed solely at him. The devil's own henchman. Who painted talking horses who were going to get married.

Miserably, Cassie made her way out into the churchyard to talk to her father's parishioners. Papa was quite particular about her properly fulfilling her duties and while she was still forced to live under his roof she had no choice but to live by his rules. Normally, she quite enjoyed talking to the parishioners. It was a tiny piece of human contact in a week filled with coldness. But today she was in no mood to care. She would be stuck here and, judging by the eager faces of some of them, nobody was in a great hurry to get home today. Not when the entertainments might not yet be concluded.

Outside, she could see no sign of Jamie. Several people immediately crowded around her and began to speak with incredulity that her father had been so bold. A few congratulated her on his performance, to which Cassie could not pretend enthusiasm. Never in her entire life had she been so ashamed of being Edgar

Reeves's daughter than she was today. He had gone too far and he had lied. For a man who claimed lying was the most grievous of sins, they had spilled from his lips like a fountain, all because Jamie had had the good sense to throw him out. Cassie had seen how he had directed his poison towards Jamie and at times she had almost allowed her complete abhorrence to show on her face. If she were braver, she would have stood up and demanded her father should stop, except she could not face another minute staring at the same four walls. Walls which crept closer and closer with each passing minute, which suffocated her with their proximity and terrified her by with their impenetrable sturdiness.

'Good morning, Miss Reeves.' The other brother had sidled up next to her and was smiling kindly. 'My name is Joseph Warriner.'

Cassie glanced towards her father and saw him engrossed in an impassioned conversation with quite a crowd, oblivious of her existence. 'I am pleased to meet you, Mr Warriner.' And then in a tiny voice she felt compelled to add an apology. 'I am so sorry for all of the things my father said.'

He brushed it away with a smile and a casual flick of his hand. 'We have heard worse, Miss Reeves, I can assure you. But that is neither here nor there. I have been sent on a mission by Jamie. He has told me to tell you that he has finished the pictures and that they require your approval. He said you know where to find him.'

At the same moment her father looked up to locate her, Joseph Warriner had already swiftly moved on and, to all intents and purposes to the eyes of the world, they might never have spoken at all.

Chapter Nine

It was another two days before Cassie was able to go out alone without fear of retribution. She might not be under lock and key but that did not mean her father was ready to give her all of her freedom back. There was all manner of laborious tasks which he suddenly needed doing, which would also help to purge her soul of badness, and he insisted she accompany him on visits to every parishioner who had not heard his epic denunciation of the Warriners in church, which meant she was forced to hear it regurgitated again and again. Fortunately, fate, or rather the Bishop of Nottingham, intervened and her father was summoned urgently to the diocese.

Cassie left it an hour before saddling Orange Blossom and riding into town. As soon as she could confirm that, yes, the post had left and, yes, the Reverend Reeves had been on it, did she hurriedly turn her pony towards the Markham estate.

She saw Jamie the moment she passed through the giant open gates. He was sat astride Satan, winding his way up and down the rows of trees in the orchard, looking every bit as ferocious and wild as his mid-night-black horse.

'Cassie! Are you all right?'

He manoeuvred his horse alongside hers smartly, searching her features for any sign that she was not.

'I couldn't get away sooner. My father needed me at home.' But those eyes of his saw too much and she could tell he remained unconvinced. For a moment she was tempted to tell him the truth about exactly why she had been absent for almost a week, then instantly decided against it when she remembered how he had manhandled her father out of his home and how intensely he had offered his help if ever she needed it. If Jamie took her father to task on her behalf, no matter how tempting the fantasy of it was, she would ultimately be forbidden from ever seeing him again and would probably spend the better part of a month imprisoned in her bedchamber. Maybe longer. Her father would definitely move to another parish, as he had in the past when questions were asked about her welfare by well-meaning parishioners, and then she would lose Jamie and this lovely place in one fell swoop. It was not worth the risk. Far better to keep her punishments private until she could escape them for good. 'And I have been ill. A bad summer cold.'

'I see.'

Cassie knew he did and she was certain he saw everything, which made her nervous. 'I am eager to see what you have painted. I have finished the story.' Scribbling away into the small hours in the two days since she had been free because picking up a pen, even moving from a spot, was too terrifying with the door locked. The only way she could survive it was to climb into herself and live in the imaginary world in her head. 'Perhaps we should ride down to the river so I can read it to you?' Without waiting for his agreement, Cassie set Orange Blossom into a gallop, partly to escape his disconcerting gaze and partly to exorcise the demons of her incarceration. It was good to be out in the open again. Walls, doors and especially locks always put her on edge. There was nothing between her and river except half a mile of meadow, fat, woolly sheep and an infinite cloudless sky.

Bizarrely, she was smiling by the time they reached the bank, something which surprised her so soon after her ordeal. Racing Jamie and Satan had been a pointless exercise because they had easily passed her as she had known they would. Jamie's horse was all muscle and power, much like his owner, so he practically flew. Her pony did her best, but they ended up trailing in the wake of the lightning-quick black stallion and his impressive, able rider. Seeing Jamie race across the fields, his big body crouched low over his horse with effortless grace, was quite something. If she needed further proof she was her mother's daughter, even though she knew she shouldn't, Cassie's eyes feasted on the sight of his rear, his broad shoulders and the flash of bare skin visible between the collar of his shirt and the soft, black hair curling gently at the nape of his neck. Not that she had ever been particularly competitive, but losing this race had turned out to be such a pleasure it felt like winning.

'What kept you?'

He had already dismounted and was stood nonchalantly, leaning against his panting mount, examining his fingernails as if he had been stood there for hours.

Smug, male satisfaction at his victory was written all over his handsome face. All of that thick, dark hair was delightfully windswept, making him appear boyish and young and far less burdened than she had ever seen him. Playfully, she ignored the jibe and spoke to her pony instead. 'We had to let them win, didn't we, darling, otherwise the boys would have sulked all afternoon.'

'You didn't let me win. I won fair and square and we both know it.'

'A gentleman would have let Orange Blossom win.'

'That is not in my nature, I'm afraid. I grew up with three very competitive brothers and I like to win.'

'Did you win often?'

'All the time.' When Cassie turned he had moved to stand beside her, waiting to help her down from her saddle. Instantly, her pulse jumped at the prospect of feeling his hands on her waist again and the power in those strong, capable arms as he lowered her to the ground. No sooner had she let go of the reins, than she enjoyed the sensation of those warm palms searing through the fabric of her gown just under her ribs. Because she needed to touch him, too, Cassie placed her hands on his shoulders, ostensibly to steady herself although she did not need steadying. They were as firm and as hard as she had imagined. Jamie was a solid, impressive specimen of raw, powerful maleness.

Who smelled divine.

As he helped her down, Cassie had wanted to bury her nose in the exposed skin of his neck and simply inhale him. Errant, wanton thoughts like that would only serve to get her into more trouble, so she quickly stepped out of his reach as soon as her feet touched the grass to rummage in her saddle bag.

'I brought us some cake and some lemonade.' She pushed them into his hands and tried to ignore the odd expression she saw flit across his face. Confusion? Bemusement? Discomfort? A picnic, even like the tiny one she had prepared, was something courting couples did. Under the watchful supervision of a chaperon. Immediately, she recognised it as what it was and realised she was being far too forward and slightly pathetic. Worldly-wise and eligible men like James Warriner would hardly find anything appealing in a frecklefaced, odd sort of a vicar's daughter who largely lived inside her own head. He was here on sufferance or out of a sense of duty, because he was kind beneath all the surliness and she was being overpowering again.

To avoid making him uncomfortable she would need to clarify. 'I did not have time to have luncheon,' she lied, avoiding his eyes. 'And it seemed rude to pack food for only myself to eat. I hope you don't mind.'

Embarrassed and horrified at her own lack of forethought, Cassie pulled out the pork pie, wrapped cheese, rosy-red apples, fresh bread and butter she had also lovingly packed—because the way to a man's heart was through his stomach and because she was a fool who had wanted to do something nice for him without fully thinking through how it might be perceived. In truth, Cassie had so been looking forward to spending time with Jamie again, the notion of a cosy picnic had seemed perfect. She really should have considered the obvious message it sent.

Jamie remained silent while he helped her arrange it on the stupid embroidered tablecloth she had also brought with her, then watched warily as she handed him a delicate china plate festooned in brightly painted flowers. Her secret plates, procured one day on impulse and hidden in her bedchamber. This was their inaugural outing, yet another thing which marked this encounter as special.

'You really did think of everything, didn't you? It might have been quicker if you had simply eaten lunch rather than prepare all of this.'

The blush which had been threatening to bloom for a good five minutes suddenly exploded like a crimson firework on her face and neck. She tried to cover it by sawing off a slice of bread. 'Yes, I suppose so. However, in my defence, it is such a lovely day I wanted to enjoy the sunshine.' If she kept her bonnet on he might not notice. Her hot, irritating bonnet. Which if she kept it on much longer would have to remain on for the duration as her hair would become plastered to her heated head. But if she kept it on, then her face would glow in that unsightly, deep pink way and, horror of horrors, perspiration would trickle down her cheeks. There was nothing for it, the bonnet had to come off.

Hastily, her fingers went to the ribbons at her neck and wrestled with them. Nerves made her clumsy and she knotted them hopelessly.

'Here. Let me help.' Which, of course, was the very last thing she needed, but because she had worked herself up into a state she had no choice. Cassie lifted up her chin and tried to stare up at the solitary wispy cloud, the empty sky, a random fly buzzing in the air, anything to avoid looking at him. So close she could see the shadow of stubble on his chin. Could count every eyelash. Sniff him like a dog in season.

'I have altered the story so that Orange Blossom and Stanley fall hopelessly in love whilst you try to save the intrepid and silly Miss Freckles from the apple tree.' Oops. It was meant to be a fairy tale—most definitely not about him, although it was. 'I mean Captain Galahad saves Miss Freckles, but then as you are Captain Galahad…what I mean is Captain Galahad is largely based on you. Not that you are a pirate, of course. I mean I know you were in the army and not on a pirate ship. I suppose those two careers are vastly different.' Her voice was getting higher pitched with panic and the disconcerting sensation of feeling his fingers accidentally brushing the sensitive skin at her throat as he worked the knots in her ribbons.

He was touching her skin.

Good gracious, it felt good!

'Did you enjoy being a soldier? What made you join the army in the first place? Because you are an artist, so one would assume you would have become an artist rather than a soldier? Did your father insist you join the military? I know second sons have a tendency to either take a commission or join the clergy. Although I can't really see you as a vicar. Even though you do know your Bible. Would you have liked to be a vicar, do you think?'

'Which of those multiple questions would you like me to answer first?' Those glorious blue eyes locked on hers for a moment and he was almost smiling, which was devastating, until Cassie realised he was smiling because he probably thought she was an idiot. A babbling, blushing, ridiculous idiot.

'I know you think I am silly, Captain Warriner, I am well aware of the fact I tend to babble.'

'I thought we had agreed that you would call me Jamie.' The stubborn ribbons finally came free and his hands finally left her skin. 'And I sympathise with the babbling. When I am nervous I tend to grunt, which makes me appear rude when I do not mean to be.'

'You get nervous?'

'Have you heard me grunt?'

Yes, she had. Quite a bit. And he was smiling again as he broke off a sizeable chunk of pork pie, then popped it into his mouth. After a moment he stopped chewing and appeared stunned. 'This is delicious! Surely it did not come from the local bakery? If it did, they have certainly improved their standards since the last time I went in there.'

'I made it.' His obvious admiration for her efforts made her feel proud. 'We don't have any servants at the vicarage so I do all the cooking.'

As well as the cleaning, washing, listening to endless sermons, visiting parishioners. Being a dutiful daughter. Wishing she was somewhere, anywhere, else and having to resort to making imaginary worlds to pass the endless hours of drudgery.

'Until Letty married my brother, neither did we. When I came home from the war I became the cook for a short while. I can't say I was very good at it. I can roast a chicken and boil a carrot. At best, my food was edible. My brothers were hugely grateful when I was relieved of the duty.'

Would it be considered rude to ask why Markham Manor did not have servants? Surely the Earl was not a skinflint like her father? Cassie nibbled on her food and tried to think of a polite way of asking. After half a minute he burst out laughing. It was a wholly masculine sound which she felt inwardly all the way down to her tingling toes. 'I quite admire your restraint, Cassie. I can see you are burning up with curiosity and ruthlessly suppressing the question. Shall I put you out of your misery?'

She nodded sheepishly, supremely aware of other tingles in the most outrageous places, and watched him lean back slightly as he made himself comfortable, turning his face to soak up the sun and stretching his bad leg out. The sudden urge to scramble on his lap made her breath hitch.

'We were broke, Cassie. Poor as church mice and everyone hereabouts knew it. Nobody would extend credit to the Warriner family because we were a bad risk. I am not sure my father ever paid a debt in his life, but he certainly racked up a great many of them. All of them had to be settled after his death, which took more years than one would imagine. We couldn't even afford labourers to tend the fields. Jack, Joe and Jacob worked them from dawn till dusk and I sent back my wages to supplement them while I was away. When I came back I became the cook and housekeeper all rolled into one. Obviously, I could not draw a salary when I couldn't fight for His Majesty, so the purse strings were even tighter. They were grim days indeed.'

'But they are over now? Your fortunes have been restored?' Cassie swept her eyes over the well-tended fields. Markham Manor appeared to be thriving.

'I forget you are new to this area and therefore do not know all of the scandalous gossip. It is technically Letty's fortune. She was an heiress. A very wealthy heiress. And one everyone believes had to marry my brother because he had either kidnapped her or compromised her.'

'How unfair. It is obvious they are in love.' The emotion had positively shone out of both of their eyes when they had proudly left the church after her father had grievously slandered them. His cruel words had not mattered because they had each other, a state which made Cassie long for her own happily ever after. However, mentioning love in any shape or form made her self-conscious in front of this man. To keep sane whilst locked in her bedroom, Captain James Warriner had featured in a great many happily-ever-afters. In all of them he had rescued her, declared his secret, undying love for her, then ridden off with her into the sunset.

'In love—like Orange Blossom and Stanley? Tell me the ending of the story, Cassie. I should like to hear how two horses fall hopelessly in love beneath an apple tree.'

So she did. Reading her story from the very beginning to the end. He smiled in all the right places and occasionally chuckled. The deep, throaty rumble continued to do odd things to her insides and made her breathing a tad erratic, forcing her to inhale slowly and purposefully to avoid appearing vexed.

'"*...and Stanley nuzzled my mane as we walked off into the sunset, ready for our next adventure with the heroic Captain Galahad and the intrepid but silly Miss Freckles...*" The End.'

'I would have thought Stanley would have kissed his bride, seeing as that is the tradition.'

Jamie would have kissed his bride. Quite thoroughly and at the first available opportunity. Then he would have taken her somewhere quiet and kissed each and every one of her freckles.

'You cannot have kissing in a children's book. It's not proper. Besides, horses can't kiss—they nuzzle, which I always think would be a nicer way to show affection than kissing at any rate.' Her button of a nose wrinkled in disgust, which amused him greatly. But then she was a vicar's daughter after all, so all talk of passion in any form was something she was obviously unfamiliar with. Unless it was between horses, of course.

'Clearly you have never been kissed.' And he would give his back teeth to be the first one to kiss her.

'This may well shock you, Jamie, but, yes, I have.' She giggled conspiratorially while a knife wedged through his heart at her surprise admission. 'It was wholly uninspiring and quite messy. I fail to see what all of the fuss is about.'

'Then the gentleman who kissed you clearly didn't do it properly.' Thank goodness! The relief was palpable. The idea of his Freckles feeling passion in another man's arms was abhorrent.

She snorted prettily and swatted his arm, something she did quite a lot and which he enjoyed immensely. Usually. 'Gentle*men*, Jamie. There has been more than one. Although in truth, they couldn't really be classed as gentlemen. Scoundrels would be more appropriate a term, with the benefit of hindsight, of course, although I must confess I suspected as much at the time. Which is odd, because from the books I have read, the kiss of a scoundrel is supposed to be the best sort—yet I found them quite dull, really.'

More than one! And by her own admission the hid-

eously unworthy men who had dared to steal those
kisses were scoundrels to boot! The dagger of jealousy
had him furious instantly. 'You allowed scoundrels to
kiss you? Willingly?' If any of them had dishonoured
her he would hunt them down and take pleasure in tear-
ing them limb from limb. 'Did the wretches do more
than kiss you?'

This she found immensely funny. 'Of course not. I
am a vicar's daughter. But I confess I was curious to
know what the process entailed, so when the opportunities presented themselves I allowed a few kisses.'
She shrugged as if it was of no matter, when it most
definitely did matter. It mattered to him. 'I suspect I
am one of those women who does not melt into a puddle at the merest touch of a man. Odd, really, when I
had always thought I would be prone to swooning...'

'Then all I can say is not one of those scoundrels
knew the first thing about kissing!' Jamie sounded belligerent and didn't care. He still could not quite believe his ears. Of all the conversations to have with a
vicar's daughter...

'Of course they *knew* about kissing.' She spoke to
him slowly, as if he were a silly child who needed the
simplest of concepts explained to him. 'All scoundrels
know what they are doing when it comes to romancing
a woman. Seduction *is* their stock in trade.'

Romancing a woman! Flowery words, heated, stolen glances. Trysts! *Seduction!* Jamie's world turned
red, then white as anger turned to incandescent, irrational, unquenchable rage. How dared they? If anybody
should have been the one to induct her into the art of
kissing, it should have been him. Unlike those charming scoundrels he appreciated her. Respected her. He

definitely wanted her. Infinitely more than any of those faceless seducers could ever imagine. But then, if he were to hazard a guess, none of those vermin were broken and lame and scared stiff if their candle blew out in the night. He'd bet his horse on the fact that they were very nimble on their despicable, conniving feet and thoroughly embraced the promise brought by the dark. Not a single ugly scar would mar their good-for-nothing bodies, so it stood to reason her lovely freckled head would be turned at the splendid blasted sight of them!

And she had kissed them.

Them!

Knowing full well they were scoundrels from the outset, because she had wanted to be kissed. Not him, of course. He was vastly inferior to those two-legged charmers in her gold-flecked eyes, more was the pity. His kiss would not be dull or messy. It would be spectacular and she *would* swoon. Jamie would make damn sure she swooned.

Before he could think better of it, he hauled her against him and pressed his mouth to hers. She gave a tiny squeak of surprise, while he shamelessly poured all of those boiling, jealous feelings into a kiss that positively burned. Jamie didn't care.

It needed to burn.

He had to sear his mark on her and banish the memory those faceless, unworthy scoundrels from her lips. Brand her as his, enlighten her to how spectacular a kiss could be if done correctly, by someone who was just as much of a man as those charming rogues who made seducing beautiful women their stock in trade. Despite his crippled leg, damaged mind and ruined prospects, he was still very much a man... Except somewhere along the way he got lost in it all.

He forgot that this was a kiss borne out of fury and frustration at what might have been, if he had not gone off to war and come back a shadow of his former self, and rejoiced when it turned into something important. Passionate, affectionate and filled with the promise of more.

The white-hot rage which had consumed his mind only a few scant moments ago evaporated like the early morning mist, replaced instead by something indescribable, almost like an exquisite rainbow bursting behind his eyes. But one unlike any he had ever witnessed before. One which assaulted all of his senses, not only his sight. She smelled of violets and cut grass and sunshine. Tasted of ripe strawberries on a hot summer's day. Felt perfect in his arms. Warm, soft, womanly. Desire ripped through him and Jamie welcomed it, feeling vibrantly alive and whole again for the first time in over a year. A proper man again and one who was quite capable of pleasuring a woman.

This woman.

He desperately wanted her bare skin against his, from the tip of her button nose to the ends of her pretty pink toes, to slowly unwrap her like a treasured gift and worship her with his eyes, mouth and fingertips. He wanted to peel her out of her proper vicar's-daughter dress and lay her bare to the sunshine and find out once and for all if there were other freckles on her body. Secret freckles that only he would know about. Freckles he would brand with his kisses, too, before he made her his in every way possible. Here on this riverbank, in broad daylight, before he took her home with him for ever.

His greedy palms smoothed down to her hips and then back up again to cup her face before they plunged into her silken hair. Of their own accord, his fingers found the pins that held it and plucked them out, filling his hands with the tumbling mass as he began to ease her slowly backwards on to the grass. And throughout it all, all he could hear was the rapid beating of his own heart as it rested deliriously against hers, as if it was meant to be there.

Always.

Which frankly scared the hell out of him.

And probably out of her, too.

Jamie abruptly ended the kiss and sat up, his chest rising and falling rapidly and his breeches considerably tighter than they had been a few moments ago. He had no right to be kissing her possessively. Or in anger. Or kissing her at all for that matter, despite the sight of her lying rumpled on the ground and looking positively ripe for the picking. Cassie had certainly made no flirtatious overtures or given any hint that such impertinence was welcomed. Theirs was a platonic relationship based on their mutual desire to complete her storybook. Why, she hadn't felt the urge to visit him in almost a week, even after he had passed on a message through Joe at the church days ago telling her explicitly that he would be here. Waiting. Where he had waited, like the besotted fool he was, for three interminable days. Therefore, it stood to reason that the turbulent feelings choking him were one-sided. One-sided and doomed to be unreciprocated.

Yet as fruitless as it all was, the last thing he wanted

was to frighten her away. Meeting Cassie by the riverbank, talking to her, painting while she read to him or wrote were already the brightest, shiniest, most important parts of his day. To think he might have ruined what they had with one, irresponsible, irrevocable moment of jealousy terrified him more than the yearning in his heart as he gazed at her. Her clothing was in disarray, her lips swollen from his onslaught and her eyes screwed tightly shut, blocking out the hideous, maimed sight of him while he had foisted himself upon her like an animal, oblivious to everything except the overwhelming need to take her.

Poor Cassie. His inappropriate, unwelcome personal desires were his alone to contend with and they shamed him. He had to fix it. Perhaps make it seem as if it had not meant the world to him. Lie if need be.

At first, Cassie was unaware the kiss had ended. Her eyes remained closed, her mouth eager and every nerve ending in her body positively vibrating with need. It had been a wonderful, impromptu surprise and a revelation. Who knew both of the scoundrels she had fleetingly kissed before Jamie had done it completely wrong? Or that, as she had always suspected, she was prone to swooning after all?

His mouth had been all urgency and passion, his strong arms had held her tightly, not that she had had any desire to escape. Far from it. From the outset she had instinctively burrowed against him, shamelessly flattening her suddenly aching breasts against the firm wall of his chest and replicating the movements of his lips against hers. His teeth. His tongue. When he had pushed her backwards, she had surrendered gratefully, running her palms brazenly over his shoulders and moaning her appreciation loudly into his mouth...

Which probably accounted for why there was at least a foot of fresh air between them now and he was blinking down at her in horror. Like her wanton mother before her, Cassie had gone too far and disgusted him with her enthusiastic and newly awakened passion. Hadn't her father warned her almost daily that a good man would never condone a woman who would lustily give of herself for her own satisfaction?

Well, now she had tangible proof. Jamie was mortified at her scandalous behaviour. Passion had no place in an honourable life or a marriage. The act of marital congress was for the creation of children and any unseemly, sinful urges of the flesh should be mercilessly ignored or she would end up like her mother. Shamed. Shunned. Her soul destined for eternal damnation. Five minutes in the arms of Captain Galahad and she would happily have burned in hell and not given a damn.

'I believe I have proved my point. Your scoundrels knew nothing about romancing a woman.'

The coldness of his words were a slap in the face. He had done this to prove a point? Not because he had wanted to. Not because she tempted him or appealed to him in any way, but because he had wanted to teach her that her scoundrels were not quite as skilled at the art of seduction as she had been led to believe. And that he was better.

He held out his hand and hoisted her up, refusing to meet her eyes, then turned away from her. That blatant rejection stung and she felt her cheeks burn with shame. Like a needy fool she had allowed him to take all of the liberties she had denied those other would-be seducers and would have allowed him to take so many more had her pawing, mauling hungry passion not repulsed him.

Or perhaps he was not repulsed, merely uninterested and unaffected by it? She was hardly the sort of woman who sparked besotted admiration in the male sex. She was an odd, freckled vicar's daughter. Three sugars when one was enough. By his own admission he was vastly competitive. There might be a chance the kiss was simply a way to gain one-upmanship over those men from her past, just as he done with his own brothers growing up.

Would he stoop so low?

It went against everything Cassie thought she knew about him.

Whilst such a convoluted explanation appeared unlikely, already Cassie could see the heated moment was forgotten as far as he was concerned. Jamie was blithely munching on an apple and rummaging in his saddle bag. When he produced some sketches and handed them to her as if nothing had transpired between them at all, she seriously considered the notion he had done it to win. While it hurt, it did give her the opportunity to appear as unaffected and worldly-wise as he apparently was. A kiss was nothing to him. Simply a physical act which could be mastered with practice. Something he was instinctively good at, like riding or painting. Something he could use to prove a point.

'I should like your thoughts on the wedding picture.'

She did her level best to act as composed as him, something which was inordinately difficult on account of all of the riotous loose hair tangled about her face. Evidence of his petty victory. Cassie tucked as much of it as she could behind her ears and pretended to study the picture rather than weep pathetically and drown in the ocean of tears which were forming behind her eyes.

As always, the painting was perfect. His attention to the tiniest of details was impressive and endearing. Stanley was staring at Orange Blossom with pride and adoration, looking smart in a beaver hat set at a jaunty angle, her pretty pony had wildflowers and leaves woven into her long mane, while scarlet rose petals thrown by the wedding guests floated about their heads as they wandered beneath a formal, whimsical arch of crossed carrots.

Behind them stood Miss Freckles and Captain Galahad. Miss Freckles was clutching a posy which matched the bride's headdress and was beaming at the happy couple. But it was the Captain who caught her eye and made her heart bleed. Because in this painting he was not watching the bride and groom. His piercing bright blue eyes were slanted towards Miss Freckles with an expression which almost matched the black stallion's. Bemused adoration.

The tableau mocked her and she wanted to rip it into tiny shreds that matched the cheerful painted confetti and throw the whole lot in his arrogant, smug point-proving face.

'It's lovely.' *And I am dying inside.* 'And we are done.'

'Yes. *Orange Blossom and the Great Apple Debacle* is finally finished.'

As endings went, this one was quite tragic and he was missing the point entirely. 'I am going home, Captain Warriner. I shan't bother you again.'

He paused, his half-eaten apple hovering inches

from his lips, and frowned. 'If it is the kiss you are worried about, you needn't. I merely wanted to show you that those scoundrels you put such stock in were not worthy. I meant nothing more than that.'

Cassie found herself scrambling to her feet and striding towards her pony, hurt, irritated and insulted by her brooding companion's blatant ambivalence, when he had just kissed her until she was insensible and that kiss had been so profound.

To her.

To him it meant nothing. He had just said so.

Yet he had asserted his dominance and power over her. Whilst the way he had gone about it was wholly different from the way her father exercised his dominance, he had used those kisses to put her firmly in her place. Something which made her angrier the more Cassie thought about it. What was it with men that they had to be in charge? And why did they have to break a woman's spirit to do it? To think she had been considering a happily ever after with a man who would stoop so low to prove a point. Ha! She still had her original escape plan to revert back to. One where she created her own happy ending. Devoid of domineering men who hurt her feelings and made her feel insignificant! She might have to tolerate her father until she could escape, because he was her father, more's the pity and she had nowhere else to go. But she certainly did not have to tolerate Jamie.

When he made to stand up to assist her on to her pony as he usually did, looking confused by her obvious overreaction, she wanted to slap him. The prospect of his hands on her body again so soon after it had betrayed her so wantonly was out of the question. 'Do not trouble yourself getting up. I do not require your superior help in this matter as well. I could get on my own pony before you came along and I dare say I shall manage well enough going forward. You see, there is a tree stump over there.' To prove the point, Cassie marched Orange Blossom swiftly towards it while he struggled to get himself off the ground and deftly used it to put her own bottom into her own saddle much quicker than she had ever sat on her saddle before. 'Good day, Captain Warriner. Thank you again for lending me your painting talents. And I am glad I could facilitate another petty win for you and feel I must congratulate you in your exemplary seduction skills. Kindly keep them to yourself in the future.'

Chapter Ten

Well, he had made a spectacular hash out of that. Even Satan was staring at him incredulously.

Could you have been more boorish or offensive, you stupid human? You ravished the poor girl, failed to apologise for groping her and made it sound as if you were teaching her a lesson for having the audacity to be delightful enough to inspire men to kiss her. What a thoroughly charming creature you are!

To add insult to injury, Jamie could now apparently hear his horse speak! Or maybe it was his own disgusted voice in his head? Either way, he couldn't argue with the sentiment.

What had started as the perfectly pleasant afternoon he had longed for had deteriorated rapidly into one of the worst days of his life, thanks entirely to his legendary quick temper and a rampant case of jealous lust. The only day he could remember which had turned out to be worse was the one in which he had been shot four times and almost died from the injuries—although as he watched her lovely bottom disappear in the distance, that cute freckled nose defiantly poking up in the air in outrage at being treated so abominably, he would have swapped the shame he currently felt for those destructive, life-changing bullets in a heartbeat.

If there had been a convenient brick wall close by, he would cheerfully smash his stupid head against it. Maybe he would go and find one, do it anyway and be damned. He doubted it would hurt more than his heart did. Who knew it was possible to grievously insult a woman in so many different ways in such a short space of time.

Jamie began to snatch up his things in utter disgust at his own ham-fisted behaviour. Seeing the remnants of the lovely picnic she had prepared still strewn across the grass only served to further sour his mood. The poor girl had departed in such a hurry she had left it all behind. Even her leather-bound journal, the one in which she wrote her precious stories, sat discarded on the tablecloth. He picked it up and began to flick through it. The moment he saw the name Captain Galahad, a fresh wave of shame washed over him, his fingers tracing the flamboyant, sloping handwriting lovingly. Her words. Words which summed her up perfectly. Cheerful, funny, vivid. Generous of spirit. Thoughtful. And he had behaved with such thoughtlessness he wouldn't blame her if she never ever wanted to see him again.

He rode home listlessly and was grateful when he collided with nobody when he arrived. The drawing room was empty and silent, so for ages he sat miserably and stared out of the window. It went without saying he owed her the most enormous, grovelling apology it was possible to give, no matter how humbling or mortifying it was likely to be. He needed to explain why he had kissed her in the first place—or a watered-down version of why he had kissed her. One which kept his growing affection for her a closely guarded secret—and then allow her to decide if she still wanted to cut him out of her life afterwards.

What was he thinking? For her to cut him out of her life he had to be in it in the first place, which he was entirely sure he was not. For almost a week she hadn't given him a passing thought bar today, preferring to fill her afternoons with other, more enticing activities, than sit and talk to him. A humbling realisation indeed. Jamie rubbed his hands over his face and caught the lingering scent of her perfume. His fingertips smelled faintly of her, from where he had plunged them into her hair and greedily run them all over her body. When he closed his eyes he could conjure her at that exact moment. Tumbled on the ground, hair fanned out around her head, the gold-and-copper strands standing out in stark contrast to the rich green grass, her lush mouth swollen from his kiss. So lovely just thinking about it made his heart quicken. There seemed no point in stifling the urge to paint her, because when she sent him packing later, he would at least have that perfect image to remember her by.

With her father away overnight, Cassie was not in any hurry to go to bed. Not when she could sit and write at the kitchen table by the light of a proper lantern without fear of discovery or retribution. In her haste to leave Jamie she had left her journal behind, so she was forced to used loose pages of foolscap until she could find some manner of retrieving it while deftly avoiding him. Besides, she did not need her journal to write. Loose pages would suffice and she still had every intention of filling them. Opportunities to write at a table were few and far between, and too splendid an opportunity to waste. Hours and hours free to indulge in her passion for writing. Just her, her writing equipment and the whimsical stories in her head.

Utter, utter bliss.

Unfortunately, no matter how much she willed them, no words came out of her pen because all she could think about was *him*. The glorious feel of his lips on hers and the bitter sting of his reaction afterwards. Both events befuddled her mind in equal measure and effectively chased away the fantasy world she loved to write about.

Why was she wasting so much thought on him anyway? He was not the first person to reject her and she very much doubted he would be the last. And anyway this relationship, like all the others she'd had in the past, would be transient. They would move away from Retford sooner rather than later, or her luck would turn and she would be able to claim her independence, therefore it was probably for the best she did not allow herself to become too attached to him. Although she already was. At least this way she would have time to get over him before she left rather than mourn his loss afterwards. It was also better that she was positively fuming at the audacity of the man.

Proved my point!

Of all the outrageous reasons to kiss her. Well, he had certainly proved it and now she had to prove her own point and that was James Warriner could go to hell. She wouldn't care. She wouldn't! All Cassie had to do was what she always did. Pick herself up, dust off her dented pride and pretend it did not matter, even if it did.

Tea was undoubtedly the answer. A nice, hot cup of tea in which she would shamelessly dunk a vast number of the sugar biscuits she had baked a few hours ago to take her mind off *him* then as well. *He* had spent far too much time occupying her thoughts. Enough was enough. Cassie decisively grabbed the empty kettle from the hearth and went to fill it from the jug, only to find the jug empty. With a huff, she strode out of the back door to go to the well and fetch more.

A dark head suddenly popped out of a bush to her side and she screamed. The instinct for survival kicked in and she instantly threw the metal jug at the intruder as she darted back towards the house and heard the decisive clunk as it hit him smack in the face.

'Ow!'

She knew that voice.

'Jamie?'

'That was a blasted good shot, woman. Do you play cricket?' He was whispering and rubbing his temple as he emerged limping from the leaves. 'Because you have a very strong arm and excellent aim.'

Cassie's heart was beating so fast she put her hand to her chest to try and calm it down. 'What in God's name do you think you are about, James Warriner? You gave me the fright of my life. What are you doing in the shrubbery?'

'I came to return your journal. You left it by the riverbank.' He began to pat down his pockets and then groaned. 'And apparently I have left it back at the house. Sorry. I shall fetch it back to you tomorrow.'

He touched his fingers to his eyebrow and she saw

a stain of something dark there. Blood. Instantly she felt guilty for throwing the heavy jug at his head, but really…he had rather brought it upon himself.

'I think your forehead is bleeding.'

'It's only a little graze and I dare say I deserve it. My behaviour this afternoon was… What I mean to say is… Well, frankly, I'm not entirely sure quite what came over me earlier, but I am heartily ashamed of myself, if it's any consolation, and I came here to offer you a grovelling apology for being an overbearing brute. I wish the whole sorry episode should never have happened.' Sorry episode? Cassie's teeth began to grind afresh. 'And I think it would be best if we pretended it had never happened. Let's go back to being friends again. I've been stood in this damn bush for close on an hour waiting for your father to go to bed so that I could throw myself on your mercy and beg for your forgiveness.' He was still whispering even though there was no need.

'My father was summoned to Nottingham. The Bishop is not very happy with him. I don't expect him back this evening.' Why was she telling him that when she was justifiably still furious at his scandalous behaviour? 'Not that it matters. I am not speaking to you. You kissed me to prove a point!'

'Not my finest hour, I will grant you. I also behaved like a total cad afterwards.' He bent down and picked up the jug, then handed it to her. 'You can throw it at me again if you want. I promise I won't duck.'

He looked charmingly boyish and contrite. Too charmingly boyish and convincingly contrite that part of her resolve to continue to be furious at him began to waver. The thin trickle of blood next to his eyebrow chiselled away a bit more.

'Perhaps you should step in so I can take a look at your cut before you go.' Her tone was brittle because she was nowhere near ready to accept his apology. The only excuse for kissing a woman senseless was desperately wanting to kiss the woman in the first place. Especially when the kisses were as lethal as his were. Throwing them around willy-nilly to prove a point was irresponsible and calling them a 'sorry episode' was just plain insulting. If he hadn't been wounded by her hand, she would have given him his marching orders smartly. But he was injured and, although she could not muster up any guilt to have been the cause of it, it was her Christian duty to help him.

He followed her meekly into the kitchen and stood awkwardly by the door while she fetched some witch hazel and gauze. Cassie laid the things on the table and motioned snippily for him to sit. She watched his eyes dart about the sparse kitchen, taking in the plain walls whose only decoration were the large, rough-hewn crosses which had been nailed on all four sides. It was such a miserable, depressing kitchen, but matched the rest of the miserable depressing house. 'My father disapproves of unnecessary fripperies. When you move as often as we do, you learn to keep material possessions to a minimum.' And now she was making excuses when she shouldn't care what he thought. Except she knew he loved colours and...well, there weren't any. 'We can't all live in a grand house, Captain Warriner.'

'I notice I am back to being Captain Warriner again.'

'I think it's for the best.' He didn't flinch when she began to clean the wound, but those deep blue eyes stared into hers mournfully, somehow making the simple matter-of-fact act something intimate.

'Would you like me to beg?'

The idea had its merits. 'No, of course not.'

'But you are not ready to forgive me either.'

Cassie stepped away and began to clear away the witch hazel. 'I accept your apology, Captain Warriner, and wish for you to leave immedia—'

There was a great deal of scraping as he pushed the chair back and began to lower himself to his knees on the floor. She saw him wince with pain although he tried to cover it.

'What on earth are you doing?'

'I am about to beg. I believe to do it justice, one should be on their knees. If your father has a hair shirt lying about somewhere, I shall happily put that on, too. Or I could flail myself with birch twigs.' He shuffled towards her on his knees, which had to have hurt him a great deal although he bore it stoically, a sad puppy-dog expression in his handsome face that did not quite hide the discomfort he was feeling. 'Or you could flail me with birch twigs. Or that jug.'

'Please stand up. I have caused you enough injury for one night.' Cassie held out her hand and helped to hoist him up, regretting it instantly when he stood too close and towered over her, forcing her to tilt her face to look into his. And he was still holding her hand. It was so disconcerting, she snatched it away and she took a step backwards to put some well-needed distance between them. Distance he closed instantly.

'Please forgive me for being such an insufferable buffoon earlier. There is no excuse for my crass, boor-

ish behaviour and I will do anything to hear you say
you forgive me.'

'Anything?' A smile began to tug at the corners of
her mouth as she found herself being charmed by him
regardless. Her father had never apologised to her once
in his life. Cassie rearranged her features into a frown
and promised herself she would remain impervious. 'I
believe I shall need tangible examples before I commit
to forgiveness, Captain.'

'I could brush your pony down every day for a
month. That would take for ever. She does have a ridiculously long mane.'

'Only a month? No, thank you. I like to brush her
myself and Orange Blossom likes to look pretty.'

But she would be guaranteed to see him for another
month. Weak, pathetic, needy fool.

Cassie folded her arms in a show of strength. She
would not be charmed by him. Not now. Not ever.

'I have asked you to leave, Captain Warriner, yet
you are still here. Please go.'

'I could take you shopping and buy you whatever
you wanted, then carry all the packages afterwards. I
hate shopping. Every minute will seem like an eternity.'
She wanted to giggle, but took another step back instead, but it escaped loudly from her silly mouth when
he stepped towards her again, an arrogant and mischie-
vous gleam in his eyes. Her pulse began to flutter and
tiny butterflies appeared in her tummy. The interac-
tion between them now felt like a game and one she
was apparently happy to lose.

Fortunately, she could hear Orange Blossom's voice
from the stables. *Don't stand for it, Cassie! He kissed
you to prove a point, remember?*

'Tempting, but, no. My father disapproves of unnecessary fripperies. Besides, forgiveness should never be bought.' She backed up and found her bottom pressed against the wall. There was nowhere else to go and despite her disappointment in his behaviour she really didn't want to. This felt like flirting, not that she had ever really flirted before to have anything to hold in comparison, but there was something quite wonderful about having this surly man pleading in such a wholly delightful manner.

'What if I promised to illustrate every one of your stories for ever?' He was watching her intently. Ready words failed her. Would he really do that? And if he did, wouldn't it be marvellous!

'I suppose…'

'Wait!' His playful expression was replaced by a frown. 'Listen.'

It was the unmistakable sound of a carriage. And it appeared it was heading towards the vicarage. The pleasant butterflies turned into tentacles of panic which wrapped themselves around her gut and windpipe.

'It's my father! He cannot find you here, Jamie!'

Chapter Eleven

Necessity meant he had to react quickly. The sudden movement, combined with his ill-advised drop to his knees, made his leg muscles tighten and almost give way. Jamie pushed through the pain with gritted teeth to move stealthily towards the window. The Reverend Reeves was indeed currently alighting a shoddy-looking carriage, and one which had very effectively blocked Jamie's escape route. Poor Cassie looked rightly terrified.

'Is it him?'

Jamie nodded and scanned the lower floor for an exit or a suitable hiding place. The lack of furniture rendered the latter redundant.

'Oh, my goodness! Oh, my goodness!' Her panicked face was white, her dark eyes round with fear. 'You cannot be here! You cannot be here!' She had started to yank at his sleeve.

'If I leave now he will see me! Which way is your bedchamber?'

'You cannot go there!'

'Would you rather he found me here. With you? Alone?'

That seemed to bring her up short. 'Turn left on the landing! Hurry!' An instruction which was completely unnecessary when Jamie had just heard her father bid the driver goodnight. He was no more than two stairs up when she called him back. 'Here—take these and hide them.' She thrust the paper, pen and ink bottle into his arms. 'He cannot know I write.'

There was no time to ask her why. Questions would have to wait—unless her father discovered him and shot him, in which case the point was moot. Ignoring the screaming pain in his leg caused by climbing at a speed it was no longer capable of, Jamie miraculously managed to dart into the moonlit bedchamber at the same moment the vicar came through the door.

Carefully, he tiptoed towards the wardrobe and silently placed her writing materials inside, hiding them under some clothing in line with her odd instruction. Her father did not know she wrote stories when those stories were her essence, just like his painting was his? How did one keep a secret like that? At some point he would have to ask her.

Jamie lowered his backside slowly on to her bed and gently removed both of his boots, as he had so many times before when he was somewhere where he shouldn't be. Although on all of those occasions he had been spying on the enemy, not creeping around in the bedchamber of a vicar's daughter. He placed his boots quietly on the floor by the bed and fleetingly considered how lovely it would be to do this every night before he climbed under the covers. With her.

Cuddle up contentedly with her in his arms. Kiss her freckles goodnight.

Probably strangle her as she slept innocently beside him because the blind terror of the darkness had rendered him insensible and unleashed the coiled violence which lurked inside him. A very effective way of shattering a romantic fantasy!

It dawned on him then that if her father discovered him bootless in her bedchamber he would assume something untoward would have occurred, until he realised there would be no pretty way of dressing this up and explaining his presence if he was discovered. The absence of his boots would hardly make a difference. Her father had the lowest opinions of the Warriner family so it stood to reason he would think the worst. Debauchery. *Fornication!*

If only.

But poor Cassie would be ruined by his foolish actions and then probably forced into marrying him. Bizarrely, the idea of being caught so thoroughly in the parson's trap with Cassie did not make him the least bit nervous. Thinking about the abject disappointment such an arrangement would have on her did. Already he cared too much about her to see her life ruined like that, or worse, putting her in the path of danger caused by his hands.

He really should not have risked coming here again. At night. Something so clandestine was bound to cause trouble—but he had been pulled here by his own guilty conscience, eager to make amends and put their blossoming friendship back on to an even keel and bluff his way out of stealing that kiss. He certainly should never have taken her up on her offer to come in so she could tend to his wound. That had been madness. Although he had been lured in by the hope she might accept his apology and because he had desperately wanted to spend some more time with her. Alone. Potentially, he had made the mess worse than he had this morning, something he doubted he would ever forgive himself for. Especially if he *had* ruined her.

On stockinged feet, he crept back to the door and opened it a crack to listen. If Cassie was in trouble, they would face the music together. There was no way he would remain hidden like a coward to leave her to bear the brunt of her father's anger. If he took one look at his daughter's guilty, panicked face and put two and two together then they were done for. But there was no noise coming from the austere little kitchen at all. Which was an even greater worry.

Jamie crouched low and eased his head and shoulders out of the door to spy over the landing. The Reverend Reeves was stood all alone in the centre of the kitchen, his eyes scanning a letter of some sort. Cassie was nowhere to be seen. A painful minute ticked by and she burst through the back door clutching the exact same jug she had tossed at his head with such precision only a few minutes earlier.

'Here we are, Papa! More water. Now I can make you tea. Did you have a good trip? Was the bishop well? Would you like some supper? I could cut you some ham or cheese. Which would you prefer?'

She was babbling, a sure sign of her nerves, and he willed her to breathe for both their sakes.

'Shut up, girl! What is the matter with you? The last thing I want to hear after a long journey is your nonsense. You are such a silly girl, Cassandra—I keep hoping that you will outgrow those irritating traits you inherited from your mother, but, alas, with each year you grow more and more like her. She never knew when to shut up either. Make the tea and do it quietly.'

Jamie had not warmed to her father when he had first met him, even before the man had opened his mouth and insulted his family. However, hearing the way he spoke to Cassie at home made his blood boil. He watched her face fall and her shoulders slump, as they had the last time he had witnessed her with her father, before she meekly did exactly as the foul man had asked.

While the kettle boiled, she sawed off slices of meat, bread and cheese despondently and piled them on a plate, her eyes darting furtively back towards her father to see if he had any suspicions that something was amiss, but the man was too engrossed in his correspondence to care. When she placed the food in front of him, the dour vicar never even acknowledged it, not with a slight gesture or with any words of thanks, but he clasped his hands together and loudly thanked the Lord for what he was about to receive.

Clearly his only daughter, the one who cooked and cleaned and slaved for him, was invisible. Something which Jamie should have been grateful for, seeing as there now appeared less of a chance the Reverend Reeves would notice Cassie's guilty behaviour, but which made him sad for her sake regardless. It was no wonder she had made so many flippant remarks about how irritating she was, or how he could ignore her while she 'prattled on', or that she was odd and ridiculous. Her father had drilled those beliefs into her with his callous disregard and cruel words. He understood first-hand how demoralising that could be.

Jamie was forced to watch her sit dutifully opposite him while he ate, then clear away the plate while her father immersed himself in his Bible. Then she sat with him again and was completely ignored for another twenty minutes before the old man rose and announced his decision to go to bed. After watching them for so long, Jamie was not surprised when Cassie was left with the task of blowing out all of the lamps and closing the windows. His daughter was little more than a servant to him, except he doubted she received the same benefits a real maid would enjoy. Like wages.

As the vicar climbed the stairs, Jamie slunk back into the bedchamber and softly pushed the door to. It was then he noticed the darkness. The moonlight had disappeared, lost behind a dense wall of clouds, and he felt the stirrings of the blind panic which only solid darkness could create.

His heart was racing already. Cold beads of sweat erupted on his forehead and trickled down his neck. His palms were hot and moist.

Not here!

He could not lose control here. Not while Cassie's security depended on his silence. Better to focus all of his energy into his current predicament, the one which could have dire consequences, rather than give in to the irrational fear which was already clawing at his belly mercilessly. Instinctively, he touched the trusty pistol tucked into his belt and fought for calm. All he could do was wait it out until the pious reverend was snoring, then leave the same way he came in. Until Cassie came into the room, there would be no candlelight and until the clouds floated past he wouldn't see the moon, so Jamie needed to take his mind off the dark.

Something which was nearly impossible when his

heart was racing so fast he could barely breathe. He had to slow it or suffer one of the paralysing attacks of nerves which rendered him hysterical.

He had to breathe.

He clawed at his cravat and carelessly tossed it to the floor, loosening his collar. Already his behaviour was nonsensical. Just once he needed to bring it under control. For Cassie.

Months of rotting in that foreign gaol had taught him to focus on something pleasant when the panic engulfed him. Something not linked to his fear, something his mind could hold on to when he lost control of his own emotions and his own mind. It had been a technique born out of necessity then and one he had not used in months because he had a ready supply of candles at home and had therefore not needed it. But under the circumstances, it was worth a try. The reverend was none the wiser as to his presence here. Jamie would be damned if he would allow his own irrational hysteria to alert the man to it.

He lay down on the mattress and began to slowly inhale a lungful of cleansing air. It smelled of Cassie. Violets. Cut grass. Sunshine. Slowly he blew it out again and closed his eyes to the darkness, trying to picture her as he had painted her this afternoon. Tumbled on the ground, her glorious hair fanned out about her head. Lips swollen from his kiss. The sun was shining. It warmed his back as he lowered himself on top of her. He inhaled again and the tight bands of panic began to loosen around his ribs. He was kissing her, his beautiful Freckles, and she was kissing him back and there was a rainbow. A glorious, vibrant rainbow...

* * *

Cassie felt quite peculiar for all manner of reasons, the biggest being the fact there was a man in her bedchamber. As scandalous, outrageous and terrifying as that was, underneath all of those frightened emotions was a quiver of excitement. Because the man in her bedchamber was Jamie. They would be alone there together for a little while before he could slip out quietly into the night. They would have no option but to sit together on the only surface available to sit on—her bed. Something she should not find so thrilling, but she did. More proof she was a thoroughly bad daughter, not that she needed any.

Once all of the lights were extinguished, Cassie took the stairs slowly with a single candle in her hand and her strained nerves bouncing all over the place. She pushed open her bedchamber door and immediately saw him stretched out on her bed, filling the narrow mattress with his big body. A pertinent reminder he was all male. Gloriously male and scarcely a few feet away from her father across the hall. He rolled on to his side and appeared immensely relieved to see her. When he smiled her mouth dried. The collar of his shirt was open, displaying a tantalising V of skin she had not seen before, and his dark hair was rumpled from her pillow. A pillow she would have to sleep on when he was gone. Cassie doubted she would ever wash that particular pillowcase again.

He waited until she closed the door before whispering, 'Is he asleep?'

Cassie shook her head. 'He usually reads for an hour or so.'

'Then I suppose you are stuck with me for an hour.'

Her lips tingled. 'I suppose so.' She was stood awkwardly in the middle of the floor, clutching the candlestick for all it was worth, wondering what it would be like to stretch out next to him on that mattress. Like a lover. He mistook her posture as wariness and shuffled to sit.

'Fear not, Cassie. Your virtue is safe with me.' More was the pity. As she was undoubtedly her mother's daughter she might easily be convinced to part with it where he was concerned. He patted the mattress next to him. 'You might as well sit.'

She did. Reluctantly. Instantly feeling the heat emanating from his body just a few inches away from hers. Even though all disappointingly proper, it was an oddly intimate position to be in. Several painful minutes ticked by in necessary silence, reminding her of how potentially dire their current situation was. Too close for comfort, they listened to the sounds of her father readying himself for bed, neither of them daring to so much as breathe loudly in case it alerted him to Jamie's presence.

If he was found here, then she genuinely feared her father's reaction. Aside from the fact he now loathed the Warriner family unjustly, he had a particular axe to grind with Jamie and venomously hated him above all of the others. It also did not bear thinking about the way he would respond to finding a man in her room. It would confirm all of his worst fears and suspicions. Her mother was a disgrace in his eyes and Cassie was already almost one although she had never done anything to deserve the comparison. Briefly kissing two scoundrels in two separate churchyards hardly counted. Having experienced a proper kiss with Jamie, she now realised how innocently chaste the previous two had actually been.

Her only foray into proper wanton abandon had been with the man currently sat next to her. If she were being honest with herself, even here, with her father across the hallway, if Jamie decided he had made a mistake earlier and really needed to kiss her again she would happily fall into his arms and let him.

The silence next door had stretched for almost five minutes, suggesting her ill-tempered father was finally ensconced in his bed, when Jamie shifted his position to lean a little nearer.

'I feel I owe you another grovelling apology for putting you in this predicament, Cassie. I can see now my coming here was a dreadful idea.' He was speaking close to her ear, something which apparently had the power to scramble her wits and make her forget that her father was so close and that she was potentially in the worst trouble of her life.

'So long as my father remains ignorant of your presence, it doesn't matter. Fortunately, as I am sure you heard, he rarely notices me.'

'I preferred it when my own father was oblivious of my existence. Things were always easier when he left me alone. Does your father's lack of interest bother you?'

If only he knew. 'It used to bother me a great deal. Now I find it gives me certain freedoms which would otherwise be denied me. Like riding every afternoon for hours on end unchaperoned.' This conversation was dangerous because she desperately wanted to confide in him about the awful times her father did notice her.

Jamie seemed to understand her situation, almost as if he empathised. He was very open about his own father's many shortcomings, even sharing the fact the man was violent towards his sons. Cassie knew if anyone would know what she was going through, it would be Jamie. 'My father can...'

They both stilled at the sound of footsteps across the hall. Her father was rummaging for something in a drawer. His shoeless feet padded back towards his bed, the bedframe creaked slightly as he obviously lowered himself into it. Jamie crept towards the door, opened it a crack and then shook his head as he closed it again.

'The light is still on.' In two, stealthy strides he was back at the bed and once again sat directly next to her. 'I am afraid you are stuck with me a little bit longer.'

For several seconds they were both so quiet the only thing she could hear was the soft sound of his breathing. Sitting here like this, so close to him and yet not close enough, was unsettling and exciting. Cassie needed to do something to take her mind off such thoughts and, since her own confession had been cut off, she was not entirely sure she should be that open about her situation just yet, just in case Jamie tried to come to her aid and inadvertently made her situation worse—something which would be very difficult indeed when she only had a pitiful stash of farthings in her wardrobe and nowhere near enough to be in a position to leave. 'Tell me about your father, Jamie.'

'He was a nasty piece of work and a tyrant to all four of us boys, but he used to single me out especially. Painting, in his opinion, was something only girls did. Especially the sort of painting I do. My father was keen for me to grow into a proper man. I think he genuinely thought if he beat me hard enough then he could make it go away.'

'Then I can only assume he failed in his endeavour, seeing that you still paint. And quite beautifully.'

'It turns out I have a stubborn streak,' he said with an undisguised touch of irony which made her smile. 'My painting became my one act of open defiance. I remember reading somewhere the only way to deal with a bully is to stand up to them. I was not big enough to fight fire with fire, so my pictures were a way of telling him he could not control me. The angrier it made him, the more I drew. A small, petty victory over the man I hated most in the world.'

Like Cassie's pretty secret plates or her pretty pink garters. All of her writing. 'Do you still paint out of defiance?'

He paused for a moment, those dark brows drawn together while he thought about it, giving Cassie the opportunity to gaze at his profile in the candlelight unhindered. His skin golden. Those spectacular eyes as blue as the deepest ocean. After a moment his mouth slowly curved upwards. 'No. Now I do it because I need to. We both know my efforts at conversation often leave a lot to be desired, but I can talk with my paints and say things I would never dare to say out loud.'

'Like what?' He was staring down at his hands where they rested on his knees, suddenly awkward in his skin and all the more endearing because of it. Not so tough and brash underneath it all perhaps?

He groaned and shook his head, smiling sheepishly. 'It doesn't matter.'

'It matters to me and it matters to you. Tell me.'

'If this conversation ever leaves this bedchamber,

Cassie, I might have to hunt you down and wring your pretty neck.'

Pretty? In whatever context the compliment warmed her. 'Go on, Captain Warriner—you cannot leave it unsaid now as I will hound you until you confess all. What can you say with paint you would never dare say out loud?' She nudged his arm playfully and wondered if he was blushing. In the dim light it was difficult to tell, but as he was hiding his eyes behind his floppy hair and his shoulders had dropped, she was certain he was embarrassed. Eventually, he scraped his hands over his face before slanting her a look of surrender.

'To me, the world is a beautiful place. Trees, flowers, animals, even clouds fascinate me. I love the patterns and shapes. Appreciate the colours and proportions. All things which horrified my father, who might have been more accepting if I had painted grand battle scenes or epic pictorial commemorations of classical literature, like the great masters. But I would prefer to paint a marigold than a masterpiece.

'Or a pair of talking horses getting married under an arch of carrots.'

'So much more interesting than a battle scene for sure.'

'Did you really mean it when you said you would illustrate all of my stories?'

She heard him exhale. 'I did.' No doubt he regretted the offer now. 'If you will forgive me for my appalling behaviour this afternoon and my monumental folly in coming here tonight, I will illustrate all of your flights of fancy gratefully.'

'You would do all that solely for my forgiveness?'

'Not entirely. I have a selfish reason to want to do

it.' Cassie's pulse began to race at the words, hoping he was about to make a declaration of some sort, because in these last few minutes he had opened up to her in a way he never had before. Shared confidences. Sat so close to her they were practically touching when he could have moved to the opposite end of the bed quite easily. Quite properly. Yet right now, they were cosy.

Close.

At his instigation. And it felt so right. If he felt it too...

'The thing is...'

He regarded her shyly and her heart leapt.

'I find I actually enjoy painting your whimsical stories. I think I might have a knack for illustrations.'

Cassie deflated as her silly, fleeting hope was crushed, not that she would allow him to see it. Of course he was not as overwhelmed by their intimate predicament as she was. He had only kissed her to prove a point, after all, and she had forgiven him for it. Sort of. 'You do have a knack for illustrations. I am sure all manner of people would pay handsomely for your skills.' She risked peeking at him and could see her words had pleased him even though his had disappointed her.

'I doubt there is much money to be had from drawing caricatures.'

'I believe Hogarth and Gillray would disagree with you. They made a fortune from their talent for caricature and satire. You have a good eye for the amusing and funny details, Jamie. Like Hogarth. A wedding arch of carrots is very funny.'

'But I only thought of the carrots because you had painted such a vivid picture in my mind with your witty words. Maybe our combined talents could earn us both a living? Your stories and my illustrations do make a pretty good picture book, if I do say so myself.'

Cassie sighed and shook her head. 'Alas, I can never publish them. I daren't. My father would never allow it. He disapproves of common entertainments and works of fiction in general. If you are going to make a career out of drawing, it cannot be with me.' Although it would be a splendid way to earn her own independence.

'You write in secret.' It wasn't a question. He had probably worked out as much when she had begged him to hide her equipment.

'I do. It is a guilty pleasure I allow myself, but not one I could ever seriously pursue, as much as I might want to. At least not while I live under my father's roof.' Was that too blatant a hint that she was open to him rescuing her? Probably. It made no difference. Jamie failed to pick up on it, or if he had, he was letting her down gently.

'Many writers publish anonymously or use a pseudonym to disguise their real identity. Perhaps you should acquire a *nom de plume*. *Orange Blossom and the Great Apple Debacle* by the intrepid Miss Freckles.'

She could not help smiling at the thought. 'Illustrated by Captain James Warriner.'

'It would never sell with the name Warriner attached to it. We are far too untrustworthy a family.' He was smiling, too, and somewhere during their exchange he had leaned a little sideways so their shoulders were lightly touching again. It was playing havoc with her pulse.

'Then you also need a—what did you call it? A *nom de plume*?'

'It's French. Literally translated it means a pen name. But as I don't work with a pen but with a brush, mine would be a *nom de pinceau*. A brush name.'

'You speak French?'

Of course he did. Fluently. Had he not he never would have been able to blend in so well in the French lines or gather the essential intelligence and reconnaissance he had been sent in alone to retrieve. A whole hornets' nest of things he really did not want to talk about. 'Only a little.'

'I suppose you had to, fighting Napoleon and all. Do you miss being a soldier?'

'No.' The word came out without Jamie having to consider it, yet as he said it he realised it was true. He missed being able to walk properly, that went without saying. He missed not earning a salary. He sometimes missed the respect which came from being *Captain* Warriner, decorated soldier and all-round reliable fellow in the King's Army. But he did not miss the dangerous and unpredictable existence of being in a war. The knowledge came as a revelation. For as long as he could remember, being an officer had defined him, then not being able to be that soldier had cruelly defined him. Now, here on her bed, talking in whispers with a beautiful freckled woman who was slowly driving him out of his mind with longing, he was not entirely sure what he was any more. An artist? Cassie had certainly given him something to ponder. The idea of earning a living from his art excited him more than anything had in a very long time because one did not need good legs to draw and he loved doing it.

That idea and Cassie, of course. As he sat beside her in her bedchamber, the single candle picking out the copper in her hair and the gold speckles in her eyes, his mind was wandering away from the problem of her father in the next room and on to other more carnal thoughts. One man. One woman. Hundreds of glorious freckles.

And one bed.

Beds were for sleeping in and for making love in, and right at this minute he was desperate to do the latter. Painfully desperate and becoming more so with each passing second. The enforced intimacy created by having to whisper and huddle together in order to hear the other was not exactly helping. He shivered every time her lips dallied near his ears. Several times he had been sorely tempted to just close the short distance between them, kiss her and be damned. He had even rationalised how he could worry about all of the ramifications and obstacles later. Once the deed was done.

If she was open to the idea, of course.

He was resourceful and wily after all, Napoleon's bullets had not robbed him of those skills, so perhaps he could find a way to figure it all out.

She licked her lips, drawing Jamie's hungry eyes to them and reminding him of the way they had tasted only a few hours before. The lingering memory of her soft mouth pressed against his was not helping to cool his ardour. His was a scant few inches away. He could close the distance in a heartbeat. Without thinking Jamie found himself drawing closer, then stopped short. He had promised her that her virtue was safe with him after his ungentlemanly behaviour earlier. If he stole another kiss, she might never trust him enough to forgive him again. Yet the air between them positively crackled with promise and she hadn't backed away.

Did that mean she might be open to the idea, too? 'Cassie, do you think…'

What?

Do you want to spend your life leg-shackled to a cripple who might attack you in the night because he has mistaken you for the sadistic Capitaine DuFour? But it will be all right, my darling Freckles, because you will have your own bedchamber, preferably one a good half a mile away from mine because I cannot be trusted. I also sleep with an arsenal, don't you know. And I just might, if I am in the full grip of my irrational and ferocious panic, take that pretty neck of yours in my bare hands and snap it as I did le Capitaine's. Like I almost did to my brother's. It took the other two to pull me off him then, as I was so insensible I was like a wild animal. A rabid dog. A monster.

No.

He wouldn't do that. Even though she was staring right back at him and he could have sworn he saw matching need mirrored in her eyes. 'Do I think what?' Her voice was breathy. Or was he imagining it?

Seductive.

God help him. Or perhaps he was mapping his own desires on to her and seeing things which were just not there.

'Do you think your father might be asleep yet?'

She sat a little straighter and he saw the confusion in her face. 'He might be. Do you want me to check?'

Jamie nodded and grabbed his discarded boots from the floor. The sooner he could escape her intoxicating presence the better. For both of their sakes. She scurried to the door and poked her head out, then motioned the coast was clear. Boots in hand, he started down the stairs, trying to ignore the ominous darkness which awaited him. It would be all right. Satan was hidden a short way down the lane, tethered to some branches and stood next to his lantern. Even if it was no longer alight, Jamie had oil and flints in his saddle bag and could soon remedy the situation. And the moon was probably out again, or at least he hoped it was, and he had his pistol tucked into his belt.

He was halfway down the staircase when the vicar woke up. 'Cassandra? What are you doing, girl?'

Jamie froze and waited anxiously. 'I left a light on downstairs, Papa. I am going to put it out.'

'You are such a stupid girl! Can I not trust you with even one simple task? You'll burn the house down one day.'

'Sorry, Papa. I shall try harder in future.'

Noisily, and for effect, she clomped down, too, giving Jamie a chance to get to the back door and open it without too much fear of being heard. She hovered close by, her fingers nervously wringing the edge of her skirt as her eyes kept darting back towards the top of the landing in case her father followed.

The worst part was, Jamie did not want to leave her. He did not want to be denied her company or leave her at the mercy of her dreadful father. He had the overwhelming urge to ask her to come with him. Then what? It was a silly, futile hope. 'Will you be all right?'

'Yes. Believe it or not, to me he appears in good humour. When he is angry he is a lot less affable.' Although she had intended those words as a joke, they set alarm bells ringing in Jamie's mind.

'Will I see you tomorrow?'

'If you want to.'

'Of course I want to. We have another storybook to create, don't we?' Lord, how he wanted to kiss her goodnight.

'Then I shall see you tomorrow, Jamie. In our usual place.'

Our usual place. How splendid that sounded. 'Goodnight, Cassie.'

For the next fortnight they met every day for two blissful hours, Cassie writing a new adventure for Orange Blossom while Jamie translated her words into whimsical pictures which delighted them both. Sometimes they rode idly along the riverbank, sometimes they shared stories over the home-baked delicacies she brought them, and sometimes they sat in surprisingly comfortable silence, gazing up at the clouds and the ethereal patterns they made in the sky. It was almost sheer perfection. Almost, because the spectre of that one, passionate kiss hung over them. Unspoken about and yet so prominent in her mind at least. When the Reverend Reeves was once again summoned to the diocese in Norwich, Cassie suggested they spend the whole day together to work. By midday, they had done precious little actual work as they had ridden over the entire length and breadth of the Markham estate talking. Jamie had an idea about dragons which she knew would make a good story.

It was Jamie who suggested they deposit their mounts at his brother's stable for a well-earned rub down and some oats, so they set up his easel and her pens on their favourite spot by the river beforehand, intending to stroll back horseless after they had eaten some lunch with Letty. The beautiful Countess of Markham was thrilled to see her and made no mention of her father's outrageous sermon. Even when Cassie tried to apologise, it was cheerfully waved away. 'Who cares about such nonsense? Jamie tells me the pair of you are actually going to try to get your storybook published. How exciting!'

'We might. One day.' They hadn't seriously talked about it since the night in her bedchamber.

'Cassie is concerned about putting her name to it as her father would disapprove.' Jamie made a disgusted face at the mention of her father before taking another bite of his food.

'And Jamie is convinced attaching the name Warriner to anything is doomed to see it fail. I need a *nom de plume* and Jamie needs a *nom de pinceau*—which is apparently French for paintbrush.'

'Whatever names you choose,' Letty replied knowledgably, 'they must be memorable in order to stand out on the cover. No Smiths or Jones for surnames. And no Johns or Janes for the Christian names either. You need something with a bit of dash—it is a great shame you will not use your own name, Cassie, because Cassandra is the perfect name for an author.' She dipped her spoon in her pudding and licked it thoughtfully before grinning. 'Why don't you amalgamate both your names? Seeing that you are now a partnership.'

'I'm not sure I follow.'

Letty ignored the stern look Jamie shot her and continued to speak to Cassie as if he did not exist. 'What I mean is, as you are both keen to maintain your anonymity by using pseudonyms, why not create just the one. Cassandra James—the talented new author and illustrator of humorous storybooks for children. People in London will fall over themselves to buy them. The pen name will be a delightful nod to your real selves. A marriage of sorts.'

Despite the obvious attempt at matchmaking which had Jamie scowling across the table, Letty's idea did have merit. *Cassandra James.* It was a lovely name and she enjoyed the sound of the syllables. *Cassandra James.* It was almost musical. However, it was not just the *nom de plume* which excited her. The idea that they could publish a book, and one that people would actually pay for, opened up a world of possibilities. A way to fund her future independence in a quicker way than squirrelling away the odd coin from the frugal housekeeping money. Such a possibility seduced her. 'I rather like it, Jamie. But it is up to you. Do you feel uncomfortable with the idea of being published as a woman?' Because if he didn't, Cassie now knew she needed to find a way in which he would be happy to have the book published. It was her ticket to freedom.

He shrugged as he wiped his hands on his napkin. 'My vile father always said I painted like a girl—pretending to be one for the eyes of the world will have him spinning in his grave. I rather like *that* idea.'

'Right, then. It's settled. *Orange Blossom and the Great Apple Debacle* by Cassandra James it is!' Letty tossed her own napkin on the table. 'I happen to know a publisher in London. My father invested heavily in his fledgling business years ago so he owes my family a favour. Even if it is not the sort of thing he publishes, he will be able to point it in the direction of someone who does. Give me your story and paintings and I shall send them to him this very afternoon. By the time I have finished, books by the talented Cassandra James will be famous.'

Her excitement was infectious and Cassie suddenly wanted to go along with the idea before she had time to think about it and decline. How marvellous would it be to see her story as an actual book, and one perhaps which hundreds of children might enjoy? Aside from the potential money it might make, it would also be another guilty little act of defiance against her overbearing father, yet another reason to do it. 'Do you have my journal, Jamie?' He still hadn't brought it back to her and she was hoping he hadn't mislaid it.

'Yes.'

'Splendid. Chivers!' Letty was already ringing the bell. The butler appeared through the door as if he had been stood outside poised for such a request. 'Chivers, I will need to send an express to London this very afternoon. Can you get someone to fetch Mr James's charming horsey paintings, which are piled by his chair in the drawing room, please?'

'Have you been rummaging through my things again, Letty? I've told you a hundred times, do not touch my painting equipment.' Jamie looked pointedly at Cassie as if he were greatly put upon. 'There is no privacy in this house. Something which has got worse since my brother married this witch.'

'I did not see Miss Reeves's journal there, Jamie. Where, pray tell, is that?'

The Countess was grinning again and Cassie swore she heard Jamie actually grind his teeth. 'Oh, I think you know, dear Sister-in-law. Let us not play *this* game again.'

'Honestly, I do not know.' Although it was obvious she did. 'Come along, Jamie, Chivers hasn't got all day. Tell him where to find Miss Reeves's small, *brown* leather-bound journal.'

The butler's eyes were darting between the pair of them like a spectator in a tennis match. Letty was grinning and Jamie was scowling. A good ten seconds of impasse ticked by until Jamie grunted what sounded like. 'Nightstand.'

Poor Chivers appeared confused. 'I did not catch that, Mr James.'

'Yes, do speak up, Brother dearest.'

'It's on my blasted nightstand, Chivers!' He stood up, looking charmingly annoyed. 'Come along, Cassie. We have *work* to do.' Then he limped away as smartly as his injured leg would allow.

Cassie thanked Letty for lunch and hurried after him down the hallway. Instead of exiting towards the back door in the kitchen, Jamie veered down another passageway. 'Where are we going?'

'I need to fetch some more paint. I am running out of blue.' He opened an ancient-looking door and disappeared down a narrow staircase. With nothing better to do, Cassie followed his retreating back and was surprised to find herself in a rabbit warren of a cellar. There were literally doors everywhere. He grabbed a burning lantern before he opened one. Inside was an artist's store cupboard which even Michelangelo would envy. Hundreds of tubes of paint, brushes and jars were cluttering the shelves. As he began to rummage for the exact shade he wanted, he quickly turned towards Cassie. 'I could probably do with more paper as well. Would you mind grabbing some from the cupboard next door? It's piled to the left as you walk in. Be careful. It's a bit of a mess.'

Cassie did as he asked, pushing open the heavy oak door expecting another cupboard—except it was hardly a cupboard. More a cavernous room. Piles of paper and easels of varying sizes were stacked haphazardly against one wall. Everywhere else was evidence of Jamie's art. Beautiful pictures were piled on or against every available surface. It was like Aladdin's Cave.

Cassie couldn't help herself. To have such an unexpected opportunity to see his work, to witness firsthand the things he could paint but never say, was a tantalising insight into a man she was becoming inordinately fond of despite her better judgement. Shamelessly she began to flick through them, amazed by the level of intricate detail he could create using just a brush and his own extraordinary talent.

He really did see beauty in everything and his choice of composition was staggeringly romantic. Vivid sunsets, delicate butterflies, intricate cloud formations. Birds, deer, trees and plants. All of the prettiest things nature had to offer, except people, and all painted with the gentle, loving care of a man who could not say it, but felt it all so deeply. She could see as much clearly with every detailed, considered and romantic brushstroke. It was obvious he truly loved creating such beauty.

Another part of the feeble dam she had constructed around her heart washed away on a wave of affection so strong, it staggered her. Leaving Captain Galahad behind when she inevitably left Retford was going to be the hardest thing Cassie had ever had to do. He was the only true friend she had ever had—yet there was no point in trying to pretend otherwise, he was so much more than a friend. At least, she wanted him to be more than a friend and occasionally she thought he might feel the same way as well.

There were those oddly charged moments when she caught him staring at her, for instance, when he would quickly look away, but not before she had seen his blue eyes swirling with some undecipherable emotion. The way his hands lingered on her waist or ankle when he helped her on to her pony. The way he glared at his sister-in-law every time she hinted there was something between them, which she did at every available opportunity and each time Jamie became flustered, grunting one-word responses. By his own admission, a sure sign he was nervous. And then there was the way he painted Miss Freckles. The tiny caricature was so pretty, with her wild hair and big brown eyes, Cassie wondered if that was how he saw her. The real her.

It was obvious that the fictitious Captain Galahad was hopelessly in love with the intrepid but silly heroine they had created. It positively shone out of his painted turquoise eyes as he gazed across the paper at the woman who appeared oblivious to his feelings. Miss Freckles, she noticed, never gazed at him with the same adoration. Her eyes were always turned towards Orange Blossom or Stanley or whatever scrape she had currently dragged him into, almost as if he was insignificant. Perhaps that was how he felt. He was so sensitive about his limp after all and had felt the urge to prove himself better than those scoundrels enough to kiss her that one time…

That thought brought her up short. Was Jamie's art imitating life? Was there a chance he had deep feelings for her, too? Things he could never say with words—only paint? And perhaps his kiss—because it had been a very heartfelt and passionate kiss, regardless of his claim to the contrary—was tangible proof? Maybe he had concocted the whole story about proving a point to cover up the real truth? Unless she was being ridiculously fanciful again. If she were really as intrepid as Miss Freckles, or even the shameless flirt Orange Blossom, she would be bold.

She might be bold enough to instigate another kiss to find out if he was truly immune to her charms as a man proving a point would be. She could sneak into the cupboard next door, slide her arms around his waist and whisper something seductive close to his ear.

I was wondering, Jamie, if you would allow me to conduct a little experiment...

Which, of course, she wouldn't. Cassie was ultimately a coward despite being her mother's daughter. The trouble was, the more time she spent with Jamie, the less guilty she felt about her fanciful daydreams involving him, her and the magnificent sunset they rose off towards together. She supposed she should try harder to stop thinking such wanton thoughts, seeing that they would only confirm her father's worst fears for her rotten soul and get her into a mountain of trouble, but the simple truth was where Jamie was concerned she couldn't find the motivation to care.

A vibrant study of a flower caught her attention and she pulled it up level with her eyes to get a better look. In the centre of the fat pink rose was a bumble bee, the wings appearing almost translucent and, if she was not mistaken, every fuzzy hair on its striped back individually defined using the finest of brush strokes.

No doubt exquisite, but the pale glow from the lantern outside was too weak to see them properly. Cassie took a step backwards to try to catch some of the light on the picture, her hip grazing against something hard in the process. Whatever it was, it moved. She heard it slide to the floor on a whisper. Then the door violently slammed shut behind her and her heart literally stopped beating in her chest.

Chapter Twelve

Jamie found the blue he needed, then remembered he should also stock up on some black paint as well, as he was going through it at a rate of knots getting Satan the deep, opaque colour that did his temperamental horse justice. He stuffed everything he needed into his pocket and left the little storeroom.

'Cassie, did you find the paper?'

The passageway was empty and silent, and he assumed she must have headed back upstairs without him. He could hardly blame her; he did climb stairs pathetically slowly. More like a feeble old man than one supposedly in his prime—but his damaged thigh muscle found that particular movement the most challenging of all, so he supposed stairs would always be his nemesis. The flash of temper which always accompanied any reminder of his infirmity was tinged with self-pity. Obviously Cassie, despite her inordinate patience with his blasted physical limitations, occasionally felt constrained by him. Hence she had skipped up the stairs smartly rather than wait for him to hobble along with her.

The fresh dose of self-pity mixed with the awkward self-consciousness which his brother's meddling wife had sowed with her thinly veiled hints about his relationship with Cassie. When you put those two states together, he found his previous buoyant mood significantly deflated. He had been so looking forward to spending a whole day with her, rather than the few stolen hours she managed in the afternoons. Riding, chatting, laughing. He was always happier with her by his side, even if he was just a friend. He had managed to convince himself that was better than not having her in his life at all. But as usual the truth crept in when he found himself looking at her longingly and wondering *what if*?

Jamie returned the lantern to its hook and scowled. In all honesty, maintaining the charade of being happy with their state of affairs was proving more and more difficult with every passing day, not helped by unsubtle hints from his family suggesting it was quite apparent he wanted more. Today, over lunch, had been positively cringeworthy. Letty's well-meant and playful words had wounded.

Partnership! Marriage of sorts! As if he could seriously contemplate a marriage of any sort in the state he was in. The final humiliation had been having to admit to keeping Cassie's journal on his nightstand like a lovesick milksop, another glaring clue to his intense feelings towards her. Although only he knew he had taken to sleeping with it tucked beneath his palm, a little part of his freckle-faced temptress to help ward off the demons of the darkness which still lived inside his own broken head. At least he hoped only he knew.

What was worse was that he really only had himself to blame. He knew damn well his relationship with Cassie could only be platonic—yet he still hoped and yearned for a miracle. Hoped that one day he would miraculously wake up fully healed and nimble, the hated limp gone and his irrational nocturnal behaviour gone with it. But miracles had proved to be decidedly thin on the ground as far as he was concerned. Annoyed, Jamie stomped loudly on the first step and then stopped abruptly when he heard a strange noise. It sounded like sniffing—or perhaps sniffling.

Definitely sniffling.

Quiet, almost imperceptible sobs which he might never have heard if his military training and years of covert missions had not made him acutely aware of the slightest sound out of place.

'Cassie?' He started back the way he had just come, wondering if she might have got herself lost in the cavernous and winding cellar. It was highly plausible. Jamie and his brothers had played hide and seek down here for hours when they were children. 'Cassie, are you still down here?'

He heard another snuffle and realised it came from the paper store. If she was in there, why didn't she answer him? 'Cassie!' The shout went unanswered.

Unless she couldn't answer him. Perhaps something had fallen on her or she had tripped? There were all manner of easels and canvases in that room, things which he had been meaning to properly tidy up since he returned home from the Peninsula and could never quite find the incentive to. Thinking of Cassie hurt sent a chill through him as he grabbed the lantern again.

'I'm coming, Cassie!' He tried the handle repeatedly before acknowledging it was futile. The blasted door wouldn't move, which meant something was wedged behind it. Very probably an easel because he had carelessly stacked them next to the door for his own selfish convenience. If one of the bigger ones had knocked her on the head, she could well be out cold.

Or worse.

Jamie put his shoulder against the ancient oak and put his full weight behind it, enough to open the door a crack to see inside. She was on the floor and, by the looks of things, hunched up in a ball because she was in agony. If she had broken a bone because of his slapdash organisational skills, he would never forgive himself.

'Stay still, Cassie, I'm coming to get you!' He began to push at the door again repeatedly, slowly shifting whatever piece of his equipment which was blocking it. 'Where are you hurt?' No response, but he could now see her shoulders quivering in the dim light cast by the lantern he had placed on the floor. She was sitting. Curled into a ball, her arms tightly wrapped around her knees, face buried in her skirts. Clearly something dreadful had happened.

'Cassie! Where are you hurt?'

The door was open enough for Jamie to squeeze through. He rushed towards her and crouched down to touch her shoulder, his heart racing and fighting for calm. If he had hurt her, even inadvertently… 'Cassie?'

She looked up then, an expression of complete terror etched on to her lovely face, eyes wide. Even without the aid of the lantern Jamie could see she was as white as a ghost.

'Jamie?' Her fingers came up to claw at his lapels where she clung on for dear life. 'Oh, thank God!'

He ran his hand gently over her face, her shoulders,

arms, then along her legs to ascertain the extent of her injuries. 'Where are you hurt?'

'Not h-hurt.'

He might have been relieved at this statement, but her breath was sawing in and out rapidly, and for a moment he thought she might pass out, but then she shuffled closer and collapsed against him, wrapping her arms about his neck and hugging him desperately while she dissolved into hysterical sobs, practically panting with the exertion, which alarmed him. Because in a rush, he suddenly understood what ailed her. Jamie knew only too well what a blind panic looked like and how all-consuming one could be, and for whatever reason, the quivering woman in his arms was in the grip of one.

'You need to breathe, Freckles.' He smoothed his hand over her hair and forced his tone to be matter of fact, forced his own ribcage to rise and fall slowly as he inhaled and exhaled for her. 'Breathe with me… in…slowly.'

He felt her struggle to emulate him with some difficulty, but at least she was listening. She could hear his voice over her terror.

'And out…slower. That's right, darling, and again…'

With no clue as to what was wrong and with Cassie in no fit state to tell him, all he could do was gather her close so she could feel the motions of his chest and rock her in his arms, telling her over and over again that everything was all right, because he was here and he would sooner die than let anything bad happen to her.

Cassie began to focus on the rhythmic beating of his heart, the gentle rise and fall of his chest and the feel of his hands idly sliding up and down her back. Focussing on Jamie, on being held by Jamie, helped to banish the paralysing terror which controlled her. He was so strong. So dependable. Strangely she knew with him she would always be safe. Instinctively, she buried her face in his neck and tried to focus on each breath. His own was so measured it served to slow hers. This in turn began to calm her frenzied pulse and painfully loud heartbeat.

'It's all right, Freckles,' he soothed and instantly it was. 'I have you, my darling. Nothing can hurt you now.'

Such beautiful endearments, the sort a man might whisper to his sweetheart.

Or croon to a hysterical woman in order to calm her down.

As her wits returned, Cassie began to wonder how she would explain her bizarre behaviour to a man who held his own emotions so very firmly in check. A man who had fought Napoleon, stoically fought pain every single day since and one who had endured six whole months of incarceration rather than the few minutes she had been accidentally shut in a storeroom.

Accidentally being the case, as she knew full well she was in Markham Manor and not the vicarage, her father miles away in Norwich. However, when that door had slammed she lost all sense of place and reason and did what she always did when the key turned ominously in the lock. The brave man holding her probably thought she had gone quite mad, which for a moment she had, but it was a madness which was transient and only possessed her when she could not get out. She doubted Jamie would understand such nonsense. Not when she barely understood it herself.

He sensed she was more in control and spoke quietly into her hair. 'Are you all right, Cassie?'

As tempting as it was to lie in order to save face, she couldn't bring herself to do it. Not to him. 'The door slammed shut.'

'An easel fell down and jarred the door. Did it hit you as it fell?'

'No. I am well.' A glaring, blatant lie. Her heart was beating a rapid tattoo in her chest, her lungs burned from the after-effects of her frantic, desperate breathing.

'You are not well—you are shaking.' Something she probably would not stop doing for at least half an hour and which effectively called her out on her lie. How to explain without truly explaining and appearing more ridiculous than ever?

'I have a fear of locked doors, of being trapped inside places. I know it's irrational, but when it happens I freeze. The panic seems to strangle me and I can't... I c-can't—' Bitter tears of shame began to fall, choking off her confession.

'Breathe.'

Cassie nodded, surprised he could finish her sentence. 'It's silly.'

'Fear is not silly, Cassie. It is real and visceral, regardless of whether the cause is imagined or not. Did you have a bad experience as a child? Were you locked in somewhere and couldn't find a way out?'

It was yes to both answers, although she could never tell him the whole truth. For as long as Cassie could remember her father had shut her in a room when he thought she had been bad. When she was younger she would scream and cry, kicking and scratching at the door for all she was worth. This had only served to increase his anger, especially when her 'infernal racket' brought well-meaning neighbours to their door, daring to question his disciplinary measures.

They had moved at least twice as a direct result of such visits and although those people had only been trying to help, their interference had caused the punishments to be longer and her father's tone more threatening. Silent penance, her father explained repeatedly from the other side of the bolted door, proved to him she was thinking carefully about her actions and trying to hear the guiding words of God. Screaming and even audible crying showed him she still did not understand what it was to be a dutiful daughter. Bringing criticism and meddling to his door undermined him and incurred not only his wrath, but the wrath of the Lord as well, because she was a sinner. Like her mother before her.

Unfortunately, as the years passed, her father became frustrated by her inability to learn her lesson so the penance needed to take longer. And longer. The only thing Cassie could do to mitigate those interminable days in petrifying isolation was to be, at least on the surface, the dutiful daughter her father wanted her to be. Back down. Agree. Keep quiet. Suppress all aspects of her wild character traits in his presence. Deflect, fib—outright lie if the need arose. Do whatever it took to spare herself the agony of being imprisoned again.

'I believe I must have been trapped somewhere once, although I do not remember it.' Lying to Jamie, although necessary, did not come quite so naturally. Cassie stared at her hands rather than let him see the truth.

'It must have been a bad experience indeed to still affect you all these years on.' His hand was still stroking her hair so gently. 'However, the human mind is a powerful thing. It can twist or warp reality cruelly.'

'And we both know I have a mind prone to ridiculous flights of fancy. No doubt I have concocted this silly fear like I do my stories. Weaving fiction into reality and believing my imagination over fact.' Laugh it off, Cassie. Make him see it doesn't matter.

However, he stared at her quietly, worry and some other odd emotion clouding his handsome face. When he finally did speak, it was just above a whisper, almost as if what he was saying was some great secret he was sharing.

'When I was a boy I had a morbid fear of the dark. My mind would play all manner of cruel tricks on me when night time came.'

'You did?' Picturing Jamie scared of anything was difficult. 'Did you have a bad experience, too?'

'I had a father who liked to wake me up with a sound beating in the dead of night. I suppose, after a while, I came to associate the two things as one. The dark and the violence. I think, because I was so confused at being awoken so horrifically, I grew to dread closing my eyes if it was dark. Sleeping became difficult, just in case he came in and I did not hear him.'

'Did he leave you alone if you were awake?'

'No. He still came—with his belt and his anger— but I was prepared for it then, steeled in preparation for whatever onslaught he had planned, so it did not seem as bad.'

'I know what you mean. The door slammed so quickly, I was unprepared. I feel such a fool.'

He must have seen her eyes flick nervously towards the partially open door before they dropped to her hands in shame at being so obviously vulnerable. 'Come. Let us get you out of here so you can compose yourself properly without the fear of the door slamming again.'

He used the wall to lever himself from the ground, then took both of her hands in his to help her up. Once she was upright, one of his arms came reassuringly about her shoulders as he led her from the room and well away from any doors, and still he did not let go of her. His solid warmth comforted her and restored her at the same time. When they were stood in the dim passageway he surprised her. Instead of leading her up the stairs or offering her platitudes, he simply tugged her head to rest on the hard wall of his chest and held her tight. Bizarrely, it was exactly what she had needed him to do.

Cassie lost all sense of time as they stood there, because time did not matter when being close to him mattered so much more. Needing to be closer still, Cassie burrowed her hands beneath his coat to rest on those broad, reliable, loyal shoulders. He might not be shimmying up an apple tree this time, but he was still rescuing her. Saving her from herself and the peculiar workings of her odd mind. Gradually, her erratic pulse began to slow, the vice-like band of terror around her organs loosened as she matched her breathing to his. Slow and steady. In and out. Feeling warm, protected and, rather peculiarly because she had never experienced it before, loved.

Cassie tilted her face up towards his and their eyes locked. She wanted to kiss him, partly as a thank you, but mostly because she needed to. Kissing him would certainly banish the last remnants of any lingering fear. Cassie doubted she would be capable of thinking about anything other than the wonderful sensations his mouth had the power to elicit from her body. She licked her lips and saw his eyes drop to them. Beneath her palm his steady heartbeat was definitely faster, his breathing no longer as slow and steady as it had been only a few moments ago. When he began to lower his face to hers Cassie hoped he might kiss her.

When he hesitated, looking anxious and perhaps a little nervous, she wondered if he was waiting for some signal from her that he should proceed. Tremulously, she reached up and laid her hand on his cheek, watched his eyelids flutter closed, heard the slow exhalation of breath. 'Jamie... I...' His lips were now inches from hers, his intense blue eyes almost black. Hypnotic. She pressed her upper body brazenly against his, marvelling in the power and strength there, before inching closer still so her hips were almost pressed intimately against his. 'I was wondering if...'

'Tea is the solution, I think, and cake of course. Let us go and fetch some and sit outside to drink it. Tea and fresh air!' He stepped back, severing the full body contact and taking her determinedly by the arm. 'You have had a fright and need to settle your nerves.' He took the stairs quickly, too quickly, she thought, because she saw him wince once or twice in his haste to escape the intimate confines of the dusky cellar and her unwelcome amorous overtures. He abandoned her swiftly at the top, calling for the butler and Letty and his brother in quick succession. Because he certainly did not want to kiss her. Not when he could have tea in the garden instead.

Chapter Thirteen

The incident spoiled the rest of the afternoon. Jamie appeared on edge, smiling far too frequently and determinedly keeping them both busy, ostensibly to take her mind off her ordeal, but more likely to cover his embarrassment at openly rejecting her feeble advances. It was also obvious he was not prepared to discuss it either.

Cassie had tried to broach the subject twice and both times he had changed the subject with as much subtlety as it took to smash a hazelnut with a hammer. It was clear he wanted to maintain the status quo, remind her to adhere to the defined parameters of their unsatisfactory platonic relationship and pretend the sensually charged moment in the cellar had never happened. Just as he had after he had kissed her to prove a point. Then he had tried to divert her using one of his illustrations, now he was trying to divert her again by plotting out the next part of the new adventure for Orange Blossom and Stanley.

But for once, no words or ideas came from her odd brain. His overly friendly, overtly courteous behaviour was so out of character as to become irritating, especially as she was still smarting and humiliated in equal measure at his clumsy withdrawal and the even clumsier aftermath. If she hadn't been so grateful he had rescued her from the locked room so quickly, she would have grabbed him by those splendid broad shoulders of his and shook him in sheer temper.

Even so, Cassie found herself reluctant to leave him until the evening after Letty insisted she stay and have dinner with them. Being with Jamie, even this awkward façade of Jamie, was infinitely more appealing than going home to the unwelcoming, sparse vicarage which had the audacity to be her home. The fact it felt only marginally better without her father in it did nothing to hasten her return. Since meeting Jamie, and spending a brief amount of time with some of his boisterous family, she had come to realise what a true home really was and it certainly wasn't anything like hers.

A true home was a place of laughter and camaraderie. The Warriners were a noisy, nosey sparring riot of a family who passed insults across the dining table alongside the potatoes. However, the unbreakable bond and loyalty they had for one another was as plain as the freckles on Cassie's face. Their conversations were so natural. Nobody watched what they said or feared incurring the wrath of another, because despite all of the banter, they clearly loved one another unconditionally.

Cassie's relationship with her father was so diametrically opposed to theirs as to be laughable, except laughter was not tolerated in her house. Not that there was a great deal to laugh at. Nor was industry, imagination or freedom and it all seemed more stifling now than it had a few short weeks ago. Too stifling if she experienced the overwhelming urge to turn somersaults every time her father was called away. Even with him gone, her home lacked heart. Was it any wonder she sought to escape it either by riding outdoors or inventing a better place to live in her mind?

She stared at it mournfully after settling Orange Blossom in the tiny stable. At least she would be spared the ordeal of her father tonight. The Bishop of Norwich had insisted the Reverend Reeves would also have to attend a meeting of the diocese tomorrow after their necessary conversation today, so the earliest she would encounter his miserable face was late afternoon at the earliest. With any luck, a freak torrential rainstorm would flood the roads and prevent him from returning for a month. By then, a publisher might have bought her book, giving her enough money to pay for lodgings somewhere, to finally escape from her father's sermons, rages and punishments. And Cassie did not care if thinking such errant thoughts made her a bad daughter either, she was in far too much ill humour to worry about eternal damnation as well.

She spied the Bible lying on the kitchen table the second she stepped into the house. Unless he had forgotten it, its presence could only signal one thing. He was home and, seeing as the clock on the side stated quite clearly it was nine o'clock, there was every possibility she was already in a whole heap of trouble.

'Cassandra. You are home.'

The words came from above, but she could not see him on the landing. His voice was calm. Cold.

'Yes, Papa. As I was not expecting you, I took the opportunity to visit some of your parishioners. You remember Mrs Sansam, don't you? I promised to watch her children for her.'

Already the fear was seeping into her limbs, making them seem leaden and stiff as she hoped he might believe the lie if she got it in quick enough.

'Come upstairs, Cassandra.'

Cassie was sorely tempted to run, where she had no idea, but knew fleeing would confirm her guilt and only briefly put off the inevitable. Deflection might work better. 'Of course. In a minute. I am going to put the kettle to boil first. You must be wanting a cup of tea after your long journey tonight.' If he had only recently come home, then maybe he would be open to explanations. If he had been home for hours...

'Come upstairs now, Cassandra. I have something I should like to show you.'

He did not sound angry, she reasoned. Cold was normal, so was terse. Perhaps there was nothing to fear this time. And perhaps hell had frozen over. Resisting was futile, especially as she had no idea what she was resisting against. Better to find out, then temper her response accordingly.

'What is it, Papa?'

Cassie made a show of slowing removing her bonnet in case he was watching, putting it away neatly and swinging the kettle over the hearth as if she had absolutely no qualms about his request whatsoever.

'I have an issue with the laundry. Hurry up, girl, I have not got all day.'

There was something about the way he delivered this, with its impatience and frustration, which put her at her ease. As it was the way he always spoke to her and because it was about a domestic task she relaxed. He was always highly critical of her efforts, no matter how hard she scrubbed and cleaned. No doubt his preaching tabs were not starched enough or one of his black coats had not been sufficiently brushed, showing a laxness in her duties which was reminiscent of her mother.

Cassie climbed the stairs and entered his bedchamber, only to find it woefully missing an irritated vicar. Dread settled heavily in her gut as she realised he was in her bedchamber—a place he usually avoided unless he was camped outside her locked door reading the scriptures and praying for her infected soul.

With the certainty which came from years of his abuse, she realised she had walked into a trap. This was a new and terrifying development. It smacked of another level of distrust. In that moment, Cassie understood he had not just arrived home. He had arrived home hours ago. His suspicions would have been raised by her initial absence, but as the afternoon wore on and she had not made an appearance, his temper would have bubbled. Creating more force behind it. Waiting to erupt with potentially explosive consequences. If ever there was a time to run, Cassie knew it was now.

Behind her, she sensed him and slowly turned. He was blocking the top of the staircase, almost as if he had known she would bolt, his eyes narrowed with hate and malice. One snowy white cravat dangling damningly from his clutched fist.

'What is this?'

It had to belong to Jamie, although why it was there or where he had found it she had no clue. He must have lost it on the night he had hidden in her bedchamber. Cassie could already feel the guilty blush creeping up her neck and the icy terror in the pit of her stomach. If he ever found out she had had a man in her bedchamber, then it would confirm all of his worst fears about the state of her tainted soul.

'It must be one of yours, Father. I have no need of a cravat.'

'I would not be seen dead in something as fine as that one—this linen is of the best quality. An unnecessary frippery bought out of vanity. Which begs an interesting question, Cassandra, doesn't it? If it is not yours, and it is very definitely not mine, whose is it? And, more importantly, what was it doing under your bed?'

He did not give her the chance to answer. The back of his hand hit her soundly across her cheek, causing her head to reel back. Cassie clutched her face, stunned. He had never struck her before; it was another terrifying new deviation in his behaviour.

'I swear to you, I do not know!'

'Liar! His initials are on it! You are a disgrace, Cassandra! Like your mother before you!' The hand lunged out again, this time violently grabbing her hair above her ear and yanking for all he was worth, pulling her head down and dragging her like a yoked animal. The heels of her boots scraped along the floor as she resisted, because this time Cassie knew she had to resist and she had to leave for good. There could be no coming back from this. She could feel the fury emanating from him. Violent, boiling fury—much worse than any she had encountered before. But he was too strong. Too angry. His nails dug into her scalp so fiercely he had to be drawing blood. Even with Cassie exerting all of her strength, he still managed to easily drag her the few feet to her bedchamber.

'Do not fight me!' He practically threw her to the floor.

A floor covered in every belonging she possessed. Automatically, she used her legs to push herself away from him, still reeling from the unexpected and horrendously violent assault.

'Did you bring your lover here? Did you let him raise your skirts and spread your legs in my house?'

'No, Papa, there is no lover! I swear it! I would never—'

'Liar!' The arm still gripping the cravat swung and hit her hard on the cheekbone. The blow was so severe it blurred her vision for a second. 'You have dishonoured me under my own roof just like my treacherous wife. She denied it, too, then left me! But like her you prostitute yourself in harlots' clothes!' He snatched up a pair of her silk stockings which he had placed on the bed and then rummaged in his pocket to produce her pretty floral garters. He flung the garters at her. 'Do you deny those are yours, girl?'

Tears of desperation had begun to silently trickle down her face. 'I just wanted something pretty...'

'Something pretty to lure men to your bed! How many have there been? And do not lie to me—I have found your stash of coins. The money they left on your nightstand after they had paid to fornicate with you.'

His fist plunged into her hair again and he used it to force her eyes to look at his. The maniacal gleam in them was beyond anything she had witnessed there before. The raw hatred glowering down at her. 'I have never lain with a man, Papa! I promise you. I am still a virgin!'

He yanked her to her knees and wrapped one hand

tightly over her windpipe, not forcefully enough to choke her, but enough to convince her he still might do so. The other anchored her in place with her hair.

He began to chant to the sky. 'Lord, what shall I do with this filthy girl? Leviticus tells me *"The daughter of any priest, if she profanes herself by harlotry, she profanes her father; she shall be burned with fire."* Do you want her dead, Lord?'

Cassie began to feel light-headed as his grip around her throat tightened. She clawed at his hands ineffectually, fighting for her life. 'Please, Papa.' The words came out in a barely audible whisper. 'Papa…'

'Never call me that again! I have no daughter.'

Both hands came about her neck and squeezed. As her bedchamber began to fade away, Cassie thought about the only two things she cared about. Her pretty little pony and her handsome pirate. When she closed her eyes there was a sunset and she was riding towards it.

Free at last.

'Cassie is lovely.'

Jamie's elder brother said this a little too casually over the breakfast table as he popped a crisp bit of bacon into his mouth. The fact Letty was missing this morning was also a little too convenient. She had taken her breakfast on a tray in bed when she never took her meals alone. It all smacked of an imminent elder-brother chat. Jack had even dismissed the footmen. No doubt some great, earth-shattering wisdom was about to be imparted unless Jamie could sidestep it with indifference.

'I suppose she is.'

'You suppose? What an odd turn of phrase. Especially as you continually look at the girl exactly like a man besotted looks at a girl.'

'I am not besotted.'

I'm in love. Hopelessly, desperately, miserably in love and I have no idea what to do about it.

'I wish everyone would stop trying to pair us off.'

Usually, this belligerence would garner a witty riposte, but Jack simply stared at him for several moments, then sighed. 'I know you believe no woman will want you now that you are lame, but...' He paused at Jamie's warning glare and sighed again. 'I doubt she cares.'

'I care.'

'It's just a few scars and a limp, Jamie.'

'No, it's not and we both know it. You all know I am not...' What? Safe? Sane? Jamie threw up his hands in exasperation. 'You all know I'm not *right*, Jack. I thought it might have gone away by now, but it hasn't. It's as bad as ever. I am dangerous, Jack.'

'That was months ago and Jacob was unhurt.'

'Only because you and Joe were there to pull me off him. I almost killed him. My own brother.'

'In your defence...'

'There is no defence!' Jamie slammed his palm on the table so hard the crockery rattled. The savage had possessed him and he had not been able to distinguish the face of his youngest brother from either his father or DuFour. In his mind, at that time, all he could see was both of them and both of them had to die.

'In your defence,' his brother continued, undaunted by the quick display of temper, 'you had only just arrived home. You were still so sick. You were in constant pain, confused with the laudanum, and it was obvious to anyone with eyes in their head you were exhausted. And not just physically exhausted. For a long time, you were almost dead inside. Monosyllabic. Isolated. You have come a long way in the last six months. You *will* get better.'

For almost a year Jamie had hoped he would—but the irrational fears showed no signs of abating. If anything, they were now so ingrained he could not remember a time when they weren't present. His peculiar nocturnal madness had become normal. 'Until it is gone, I cannot consider any sort of relationship with a woman as anything more than platonic.'

'Perhaps if you talked to someone about it? You're so stubbornly tight-lipped about it all. Maybe if you opened up and told one of us what happened in that gaol in France…?'

'No, Jack! Not now, not ever. I want to forget about it!'

'Clearly you are doing a magnificent job then. How many pistols do you sleep with? One? Two?'

Jamie scraped his chair noisily as he shot up from the table. 'Stay out of my room, Jack.'

There were three pistols. One under his pillow, one in the drawer of his nightstand and another hidden down the side of the mattress with his dagger. The French cutlass he had taken from Dufour's corpse was stashed under the bed. Despite his outburst, his brother appeared nonplussed as he blotted his mouth with a napkin and then dropped the linen square on to the table before rising as well.

'For what it's worth, your Cassie looks at you in exactly the same way as you look at her.'

'She's not *my* Cassie.'

His brother chuckled and shook his head. 'I recall a similar conversation between us a few months ago, Jamie, during which you rightly pointed out that Letty was *my* Letty and I was just too stubborn to see it. And guess what? You were right and I shall be eternally grateful to you for it. Once I stopped being a stubborn fool, Letty turned out to be exactly what I needed.' He walked to the door, then turned. 'Has it occurred to you that Cassie might be exactly what you need, too?' The words *stubborn fool* did not need to be said. 'Tell her, Jamie. All of it. I suspect she will surprise you.'

Chapter Fourteen

Jamie spent the rest of the morning and a great deal of the afternoon thinking about Jack's advice and his tangled feelings to no avail. He waited for hours on the riverbank for her to trot along on her pretty pony and felt even more wretched when she didn't materialise.

He still did not know what to do. He wanted to her to be *his* Cassie more than anything, but he couldn't trust himself—or more importantly the savage inside him—not to harm her in a fit of blind panic and really did not have any desire to saddle the poor girl with an invalid for the rest of her life. That was no life for a vibrant, generous and whimsical creature like Cassie. Once the bloom was off the rose, something was doomed to happen sooner rather than later when she understood how truly broken he was inside and out, he would see the quirky sparkle in her eyes turn into the flat gaze of patience as he inevitably slowed her down and disappointed her. Seeing that would destroy him.

However, a tiny part of him refused to give up hope. The more he thought about it, the more he became certain that Cassie had wanted him to kiss her yesterday afternoon. And he almost had. His damned conscience had reminded him of the fact she had only minutes before been a terrified bundle in his arms—which had made him hesitate and ignore the desire he thought he had seen swirling in her eyes. Kissing her then had felt like taking advantage. Then all the usual doubts clogged his mind and suffocated the impulse. He had practically run out of the cellar and no matter how much he had tried to behave as if nothing had happened he suspected he had made a royal hash of things. Again. She had left with her button nose in the air and a look of irritation in those lovely gold-flecked, big, brown eyes, leaving him stood at the end of the lane without a backward glance.

Really, there was nothing else for it. Much as he would rather squirt lemon juice into his eyeballs and insert red-hot needles under his fingernails, there was no escaping the fact his brother was right and they had to talk. It was the mature thing to do. The decent thing. They would have an honest and frank conversation about exactly what was going on between them in order to obtain some clarity. Jamie needed to know if she considered him more than a friend and he would have to find a sensible, matter-of-fact way of telling her that he was well on the way to being hopelessly in love with her and so consumed with lust he could barely look at her without drooling. Or toned-down words to that effect.

Just thinking about it made his toes curl. He was going to have to lay himself bare before her, tell her about the ugly scars on his body, admit to his physical limitations and his private feelings. Tell her about his irrational fear of the dark and his propensity for extreme violence in the grip of a blind panic. In all probability, she would ask uncomfortable questions, so he would have to confess that, yes, he had killed a man with his bare hands—which would dredge up all of the horrors of that dank French hellhole he had been incarcerated in. Kick the blasted hornets' nest he had been doing his level best to forget about and then wait to see if she decided he was worth all of the bother or if he had misread everything and she was perfectly content with simply being his friend.

As he lay listlessly on the bank, staring half-heartedly at the wispy clouds in the early summer sky, Jamie did not hold out a great deal of hope his woeful charms and buzzing hornets' nest were going to be enough to woo the fair maiden by the end of his sorry tale. His only hope was she dismissed the pathetic belief that she was open to being more than platonic friends at the start of the conversation and thus rendering the rest of the mortifying conversation unnecessary.

He heard his horse snort and sighed. 'You're back then, are you? I hope you had a better afternoon than I did.' Disgruntled and bored with his master's long swim in the ocean of self-pity, Satan had flown across the fields as soon as Jamie had removed his reins. The bad-tempered beast had been gone for over an hour. But when he turned his head, Satan was not alone. Next to him stood Orange Blossom.

Instantly his heart soared at the prospect of seeing Cassie and Jamie sat up, but as his eyes hungrily scanned the area for his first sight of her it came to dawn on him that she wasn't there. Like Satan, Orange Blossom was devoid of both reins and a saddle, suggesting she had escaped from her stable or—

the more likely scenario—Satan had broken in to the pretty pony's stall to fetch his lady-love. That he had chosen to bring the minx back here with him, because Satan certainly did not have any issues with going after what he wanted, made Jamie feel inadequate.

'Have you brought her here to rub my nose in it? I suppose you are feeling very smug, aren't you? You have a wife.' Satan snorted and looked down his nose at him. 'Please tell me you didn't kick down the Reverend Reeves's stable door in order to free her, Satan. That man loathes me enough already. I could well do without further ecclesiastical censure caused by your charming talent for demolition.'

Jamie executed an ungainly manoeuvre to get himself upright and stretched, only to find the soft muzzle of Cassie's pony nudge him in the ribs.

'I suppose you are annoyed at me, too, aren't you, Orange Blossom? Is she still angry at me?' He stroked her mane idly. 'I made a hash of things again yesterday. The truth is, I really have no idea what to do for the best. Cassie deserves a man who isn't broken, don't you think? Someone she doesn't have to pity. A real Captain Galahad. Brave, strong, dashing. Not a curmudgeonly, limping former soldier who sleeps with a light on and cannot find the words to say what he feels.' The pony nudged him again, slightly harder this time. 'Do you want me to take you home?'

Because taking the pony home would give him an excuse to see her. Aside from Satan, most horses did not wander the land freely so it stood to reason that Orange Blossom might be a little anxious at being without her rider. And if Cassie's father was home from Nottingham already, then he could hardly assume anything untoward when Jamie was merely being neighbourly.

Good afternoon, Reverend Reeves, I came across this pony whilst I was out riding and thought I had best return it home. It belongs to your daughter, I am told.

Perfectly plausible. She would have to come out eventually to settle her pony back in the stable and Jamie would be hiding there, waiting for her. If the vicar was still away, which he hoped was the case, then Jamie would be able to converse to Cassie openly. Either way, he would see Cassie.

They could talk.

Good grief—his toes were curling inside his boots again at the prospect, but it had to be done. The thought of walking around for all eternity wondering what to do was going to send him madder than he already was. Before he could talk himself out of it, Jamie saddled Satan again, but put the reins on Orange Blossom. He hauled himself on top of his mount, then led both horses across the fields decisively.

To begin with, he thought nobody was home. The vicarage was silent. Every door and window locked and the curtains tightly pulled closed. Something about that bothered him, but he could not quite put his finger on why until he remembered he had never seen them closed before. On his two previous visits, Cassie's bedchamber window was always wide open. Of course, he now knew why. She hated being locked in. A fear he could empathise with wholeheartedly, although to her credit Cassie did not lunge at him with a cutlass between her teeth and try to strangle him. Hers was a quiet, gentle type of blind panic. Civilised. Devoid of a lurking, murderous savage. Unlike his.

Jamie took a deep breath and tried to focus on the task in hand. The hornets' nest could wait until he saw her. To see her window closed must mean she was not there. It made sense she would be out searching for her pony and, having lived in some of the unsavoury places she had lived in during her lifetime, it also made perfect sense she would lock up the house before she left it.

Jamie considered his options. He could return the pony to the stable and leave. An unsatisfactory solution which denied him the chance to see her. Or he could go off and search for her—and perhaps waste hours doing so. The only reasonable alternative was to sit close by and loiter until she came home, and in case her father caught him there he would keep Orange Blossom with him. A readymade excuse for his distasteful presence, and one he could also use on Cassie if she made it plain she did not wish to see him.

In view of the fact he was not supposed to be skulking around, Jamie walked both horses to the front of the house and left them munching on the lawn while he eased his backside on to the low wall closest to the building. Really, he reasoned, what happened next was down to her. He intended to ask her outright about it straight away.

Did you want me to kiss you yesterday?

Too blunt.

I was wondering, should I have kissed you yesterday?

Pathetic.

Cassie, yesterday there was a moment when I was convinced you wanted to be kissed. Like a fool I let it pass. Was I right to do so?

Jamie groaned aloud. His toes would cramp up before this awkward debacle was concluded, in fact...

He heard a chair scrape on wood close by and realised the only place the noise could have come from was the vicarage. Somebody was home, which meant he could hardly remain sat in their front garden rehearsing all of the cringingly bad sentences he intended to say. Jamie stood up, straightened his coat, smoothed down his wayward hair, then smartly rapped his knuckles on the front door.

More wood scraped against wood and footsteps made their way to the door, but did not open it. 'Who is it?' The Reverend Reeves's tone was wary and unwelcoming, something which did not bode well when he could have no idea who his visitor was.

'Captain James Warriner. I should like to speak to you, Reverend.'

'Go away. You are not welcome here.' Well, it had started well. Things would undoubtedly get much worse before this conversation finished.

'I appreciate that, Reverend Reeves, however I come here with a purpose. A neighbourly purpose.' When this was met with stony silence Jamie knocked again. 'I have something for you.' He bit back from telling the man he had Cassie's pony in case the man told him to take it to the stable without opening the door. He could hardly argue with such an obviously sensible request. 'It is important.'

The bolt slid noisily open behind the door and it finally opened a crack. Half of the vicar's face came into view. He appeared quite dishevelled. His hair was sticking up on one side of his head, the shoulder seam of his cassock torn, but it was his eyes which began to bother Jamie. They were quite manic.

'Go away, Warriner. Whatever you have I do not want.'

'I found this pony wandering riderless—I believe it is your daughter's.'

'I have no daughter!' This was spat with venom— a worrying amount of venom—then the vicar tried to close the door.

Jamie wedged his foot inside.

'This is your daughter's pony, sir! Your daughter Cassandra…'

'Do not speak her name in my presence!'

Foaming spittle was gathering in the corners of the man's mouth again, not that Jamie needed to see it to know something was amiss. Jamie was instantly, loyally furious.

'Where is she?' He angrily pushed at the door with his shoulder, ignoring the resistance from the other side. The Reverend altered position to brace his full weight against it to close it, allowing Jamie to see the whole of the man's face for the first time.

Four deep scratches marred his left cheek. More were visible on his neck and on the backs of his hands. Not scratches, perhaps. Claw marks. Human claw marks. And was that blood on his shirt?

His neck prickled with fear. 'Where's Cassie?'

The vicar refused to budge, still denying him entry. 'Did she open her legs for you, Warriner? Did you use her for your pleasure or to get petty revenge on me for daring to speak the truth about your sins?'

Every instinct Jamie had was positively screaming. Something was very, very wrong.

He stepped back, then lunged at the door with a primal grunt of exertion. As he had intended, the odious vicar fell backwards as the full force of the impact knocked him off his feet.

Wasting no time, Jamie strode into the stuffy kitchen. 'Cassie! Cassie where are you?'

There was no reply, and her father was already scrambling to his feet. He threw himself in front of Jamie as he stalked towards the narrow staircase. '*Get thee behind me, Satan*!'

The bitter taste in Jamie's mouth, his palpitating heart and the way every hair on his body had suddenly stood to attention were warning signs he had grown to trust. They had kept him alive in the Peninsula and he was damned if he would doubt them now. He grabbed her father sharply by the lapels. 'Get behind me!' Unceremoniously he shoved him back to the floor and took the stairs two at a time.

'If you have so much as harmed one single hair on her head, I will kill you!'

When her bedchamber door refused to open Jamie felt the bile rise in his throat.

'You locked her in, you bastard! The thing she fears most in the world! Give me the key!'

Below him, the Reverend Reeves walked towards one of the plain wooden crosses nailed to the wall and closed his eyes, his body rocking back and forth as he began to chant in a monotone. 'The Lord is my rock, and my fortress, and my deliverer; in him I will trust. He is my shield, and the horn of my salvation and my refuge. Thou savest me from violence…'

'The *key*!' Jamie no longer existed, he could tell. Wherever the Reverend's mind had gone, it was no longer in this building.

Chapter Fifteen

❧❧❧❧

'I will call on the Lord, who is worthy to be praised, so I shall be saved from mine enemies…'

The man was quite mad. Clearly lost in his own fevered recitation of the scriptures, trying to reason with him was only wasting time. Wondering about the sort of life Cassie endured with him did not bear thinking about. Not yet at any rate, because he still had to find her.

Jamie threw his shoulder repeatedly at the door with a strength he had not known he possessed. As he did, he called to her and each time she failed to answer he rammed the barrier between them harder. For the first time since his injuries, Jamie was thankful those bullets had torn through his leg. Because his weakened leg had forced him to rely more on his arms, and those arms, these shoulders, were now stronger than ever. The door really did not stand a chance. Once the ancient wooden frame began to splinter he was able to break through in a matter of seconds as it all gave at once under his relentless onslaught.

'Cassie!'

Although daylight outside, the room was dark. The heavy curtains were pulled tight and it took his eyes a moment to focus properly. The tiny bedchamber had been ransacked. The blankets and sheets from the bed hideously tangled and strewn over the floor. Her clothes were scattered around, ripped and torn as if some ferocious beast had rampaged through the room and gone at them with its bared teeth. All around him was carnage, yet he could still not see her.

Jamie clambered over the mess to search on the other side of the bed and there she was. On the floor. Slumped against the solid leg of the headboard. Most of her hair covered her face, but he saw enough to feel sick. Gagged. Hands bound tightly behind her back, whatever held them together had also been lashed securely around the bedpost. One sleeve of her dress hanging limply where it had been torn from the bodice.

Whatever rage he felt for her father was temporarily forgotten in his rush to help her. Jamie ignored the protest in his thigh as he dropped to his knees beside her.

'Cassie?'

He smoothed the bulk of her hair from her cheek and saw the bruising. Her cheekbone was covered in an angry raised mark. Her lovely eye swollen from another blow to her face and she wasn't moving.

'Oh, my darling, what has he done to you?'

Instinctively his fingers went to her neck and located her pulse. It vibrated strong and steady beneath his touch, easing some of the tension clouding his mind. He wrenched the knife out of his boot and carefully cut through the bond which held her to the bed. It wasn't rope or cord. Whatever it was, it had the distinct texture of silk. Those binding her hands were harder to remove. The ribbon, and he was certain it was ribbon, was covered in some raised decoration which made slicing through without harming her skin problematic. Jamie had to lean her heavy head against his upper body in order to do it. When they finally came free, he glanced down at the tangled mess in his hands and recognised part of it instantly. Her floral garters, and if he was not mistaken the other restraint was made out of a single silk stocking.

Jamie gathered Cassie close and began the arduous task of trying to stand with her in his arms. Unconscious, she was a dead weight, but his arms were strong and he was damned if he would fail her.

Something hard and angular caught him unawares on the back of the head.

'She needs to repent!'

Jamie almost dropped her. Almost. Instead he managed to lower her carefully to the ground just as another blow caught him across the shoulders. He twisted around in time to see the crazed vicar coming at him again, brandishing one of the austere wooden crosses from the kitchen. He allowed his assailant to attempt to strike him again, lunging for the makeshift weapon and using its downward momentum to destabilise the man. Jamie wrenched the crucifix from his hand and tossed it out of harm's way, before heaving himself awkwardly to his feet to go on the offensive.

As he topped the man by over six inches, he did not bother crouching to take him down. Instead he stalked towards him menacingly, grateful for the burning fury and hatred which coursed through his veins and rid him of any guilt at what he was about to do. This time he welcomed the savage inside, happily opened the cage and let it out to wreak chaos. This man deserved nothing less.

His palm shot out, gripping Cassie's father firmly about the throat, then marched him back against the wall to loom over him.

'You hit her.' And he wanted to kill him.

'She is just like her disgraceful mother!'

Jamie felt his palm squeeze tighter of its own accord and didn't care.

'You tied her up. Gagged her. Locked her in!' Dear God, he hoped she had not been imprisoned for long.

'She prostituted herself for money!'

'You're a monster!' He could feel the vicar struggling to breathe and still he didn't care. 'A raving madman!'

'*She's* the monster. She is possessed by the devil himself. I saw the evidence of it with my own eyes! Pages of blasphemy where animals talk! Harlots' clothing. Wanton lust. In my house! With *you*!'

Behind him, Jamie heard the magnificent sound of Cassie moaning. She was coming to. It distracted him and her father used it as an opportunity to wrench his neck free.

'I know it was you who fornicated with her. JW! *JW!* It was on your cravat. I did not put it together till now. James Warriner. Debaucher. Fornicator!'

The need to smash the man's head against the wall was instinctual, because this man had hurt Cassie and therefore he needed to die.

'And don't forget, Reverend, I am the devil's own henchman. This face will be the last thing you ever see and it will be laughing as it chokes the life out of you.'

Both of Jamie's hands wrapped around his neck. One violent twist and he would have the satisfaction of hearing and feeling it break.

An execution.

Justice. And Jamie would be the executioner.

She moaned again and without thinking he turned to her. Saw her eyes. The pain and fear in them and knew he couldn't allow her to see him as the monster he truly was. With a growl of sheer frustration, he smashed her father's head against the wall. The older man's eyes rolled back in his head and his knees gave way. But the man was still breathing as Jamie left him on the floor.

'It's all right, Freckles. You're safe now, darling.'

Feeling choked with emotion, shaking like a leaf in a gale and still desperately fighting to control the anger, Jamie went to her, helped her up and supported the bulk of her weight as he led her from the bedchamber. She swooned slightly at the top of the stairs, clutching at his waistcoat and collapsing against him. He didn't trust his leg to carry her like a lady. If it gave way on the staircase, then the fall would add to her injuries. Thinking about her in more pain because of him made his stomach lurch. All he could do was bend down and fling her over his right shoulder like a sack of flour, and let his undamaged right leg bear the brunt of the lifting as he carefully picked his way down.

She hung limply behind him, but he did not stop. He took her to where he had tied Satan and deposited her gently across the saddle, then he hauled himself up behind her, positioning her damaged body to sit safely in the cage of his arms. His temperamental horse

appeared to understand the gravity of the situation and
set off a fair lick in the direction of home. Next to him,
Orange Blossom galloped alongside. Even though it
was not possible, Jamie could almost see the worried
expression on the pretty pony's equine face.

Only when he was certain he had put enough distance between Cassie and her crazed father did he stop
to remove the tight gag in her mouth. The task made
Jamie's heart ache with regret, because he recognised
what her father had cruelly used to silence her. It was
his cravat. Letty's tiny embroidered initials—JW, in the
distinctive pattern which was reserved only for him—a
damning reminder of his part in her fate.

Cassie had a vague recollection of the events which
had ultimately brought her to this soft, comfortable bed
in Markham Manor. Obviously, she wished she did
not recall exactly the dreadful things her father had
subjected her to. The beating, the choking and being
practically shackled to her bed were memories which
would always haunt her. It was her dramatic rescue
which was a little hazy. Flashes really. Jamie's voice
calling out to her. His look of complete disgust as he
threw her father to the ground. His arms around her
as they galloped away, when ironically, the sun was
setting. It might not be the happily ever after she had
often imagined, but it was a definitive ending of sorts.
After what her father had done this time, Cassie was
determined never to go back.

It really did not matter that the only possessions she
had escaped with were the torn clothes on her back.
Everything else had been violated by her father. Her

writing had been shredded before her eyes, the pretty fripperies she had hidden for so long were used to tie her up. The few plain dour dresses she had owned meant nothing to her and almost seemed like the uniform of her father's oppression. The only thing she cared about was her pony and Orange Blossom had had the great good sense to accompany Jamie back to Markham Manor. As soon as they were all safely ensconced inside, those enormous imposing gates were ceremonially closed, meaning she was safe from harm in a virtual fortress. Never had a bolted door given her such palpable relief.

Of course, everyone had made a huge fuss over her. The physician had been fetched by the Earl himself. Her injuries were declared to be temporary. Nothing which a good night of bedrest and several hearty meals could not fix, and now that the awful after-effects of her latest incarceration were waning, Cassie felt like a fraud lying here, in one of Letty's fine night rails, being waited on by a family who had shown her nothing but kindness and for whom she had caused nothing but trouble.

There was a light tap on the door before his dark head popped in. 'I just wanted to check you were comfortable.'

Cassie beckoned him in, feeling an overwhelming surge of love and gratitude for this man who had come to her rescue yet again. He took a few steps towards the bed and stood awkwardly. 'Come. Sit.' She shuffled her bottom across the mattress and patted the space she had created. With trepidation he did as she asked, his posture stiff and barely meeting her eyes. 'What is wrong?'

'I feel dreadful. What you were subjected to—that ordeal—it was all my fault. He found my cravat, didn't he?'

Technically, yes, but Jamie did not deserve to absorb the blame. He deserved the truth. 'This time it was your cravat. Last time it was because I spoke out of turn. The time before it was because the points of his shirts were not properly starched. Once I was locked up for three days because he caught me humming when I was scrubbing the kitchen floor. The slightest thing will send him into a rage, Jamie, and they now occur with such alarming frequency I doubt it matters what is the cause. I have come to believe his moods send him half-mad and then he finds everything about me offensive.'

'Half-mad?' His hand had found her hand and he was lacing his fingers through hers. 'I hate to say this, Cassie, as he is your father, but he is a lunatic. I wish you had told me about all this before today. I could have helped you.'

'I have learned through bitter experience to keep my father's behaviour a secret. He could be relentless if others interfered, and in my defence I was trying to help myself. I had a plan to escape. I knew that now I am of the age of majority he could not drag me back once I left, but I did not want to be at the mercy of the streets either. In many ways, the life some of those poor wretches endure is a life more brutal than mine. At least I had a roof over my head and food in my belly. Most of the time my father is oblivious of my existence, so I was able to carry on until I had made all of the preparations to escape properly. Once and for all. To that end I had been saving a little money each week. A pitiful amount really, but I hoped eventually

I would have enough to afford to rent lodgings before seeking gainful employment somewhere.'

'You still should have told me.'

'When you move around as frequently as I do, you assume all friendships to be transient and I did not want to burden you with my problems.'

'You are not a burden, Cassie.' The hand holding hers squeezed tighter and he stared down at their intertwined fingers. 'I asked you if he was violent towards you and you denied it.'

'Until yesterday he had never struck me. My father believes silent penance in solitary confinement is a far better punishment.'

'Which is why you are afraid of locked doors.'

Cassie sighed and rested her head against his strong shoulder. 'Something, I am sure, which made the punishment more fitting in his eyes.'

'You cannot go back there.' His arm came about her shoulders and gathered her close. His chin rested comfortably on the top of her head.

'I know.'

Her father had almost killed her. If there was a next time she might not be so lucky. For several minutes they simply sat there, Cassie burrowed against his chest, his free hand idly stroking her hair. For the first time in the hours she had been here, she felt totally relaxed. Content. Sleepy. He felt her stifled yawn.

'You are exhausted. I shall leave you to rest.' He began to remove his arm to rise and she lazily wrapped her arms around his middle. Now that he was here she couldn't bear him to leave.

'Don't go yet. I know this is silly and irrational, but I would feel safer knowing you are here. Just for tonight.'

* * *

There was nothing safe about him in the night. But a lamp was burning low on the nightstand and Cassie was clinging to him as if her life depended on it. Added to that was the desire to comfort her after everything she had been through and to know for himself she was all right. Being here would ease his own mind on that score. The red marks around her delicate neck troubled him. To know her father had attempted to strangle her, that she would have had to watch his crazed face as she was robbed of breath was too close to home and unsettling. He suspected what she had told him already about her father was merely the tip of the iceberg.

The Reverend Reeves had effectively tortured his daughter for years. It was testament to her strength of character that she was not a meek and terrified creature all of the time. Jamie did not need to be told this episode had been the second one in as many weeks. The pinched, strained expression she had worn in church that day matched the one he had seen on her face when she had accidently been trapped in the store cupboard. The remnants of it still stained her lovely face now, hours since he had carried her from that dungeon, and it was obvious it had taken its toll. Angry bruises stained her skin. Bruises he wanted to avenge because he could not undo them. If she needed his comfort, right at this minute he did not have the heart to deny it.

'I am not going anywhere, Freckles.' He would sneak out once she was sound asleep and lock himself in his own bedchamber. A bedchamber, which by his own insistence, was as far away from Cassie's as it was possible to be within the constraints of the house. Without dislodging her from her comfortable position against his shoulder, Jamie swung his legs up on to the mattress and reclined on the fluffy pillows behind his head. Instantly, she burrowed against him, the lower half of her delectable body fortunately covered in blankets. She snuggled closer still, her silken hair falling over her face and his waistcoat, touching all the way down his side from that shoulder to the middle of his booted calf, yet the tough leather nor the covers formed a satisfactory barrier. Every nerve ending was alive.

Bizarrely, it was not lust which pulsated through him, it was something quite different. A sense of wonder, of rightness and the primordial need to hold her close. Protect her as if she were his woman.

So he did. Muttering reassuring platitudes against the crown of her head, allowing the golden tendrils of her hair to run through his fingers. Enjoying, just this once, the heady feeling of being with the woman he loved, cuddled up together.

Like lovers.

The bright slice of daylight shining through the gap in the curtains was a revelation. As was the feel of a delightfully rounded womanly bottom under the palm of his hand. He must have nodded off. A foolhardy and dangerous thing to have done considering his propensity for violence, but also a miraculous one. Cassie was still in his arms, the majority of her body sprawled atop his. One leg hooked proprietorially across his and her face was buried under a sea of hair. One errant strand tickled his nose and he blew it away rather than wake her by moving. Her breathing was the heavy, rhythmic sort of a person not inclined to rise any time soon and if anyone deserved the rest, it was Cassie. Besides, his hand was perfectly happy resting on the curve of her hip as if that particular curve had been carved by a master craftsman to be the perfect fit for his meaty paw.

A quick glance towards the nightstand confirmed the lamp still burned, although its glow was pointless now. It was definitely morning. What time in the morning he was blissfully ignorant of, but as he could not hear any sounds of servants mulling about, if was fairly safe to assume it was early. With nothing better to do, Jamie tried to piece together the events of the night to ascertain at what point of it he had been taken by Morpheus.

He remembered clearly holding her for at least an hour because it had been a perfectly splendid way to spend an hour. He had stroked her hair, then he had a vague recollection of burying his nose in it. After that was a huge gaping blank. Which meant he had inadvertently spent many hours snoozing contentedly with this woman in his arms. And she truly was a glorious armful. Clearly she had long ago fidgeted out of the bedcovers. The only thing separating her bare skin from his touch was the soft, gauzy nightgown. He had touched Cassie's waist before, but without the layer of stays and petticoats, it was deliciously soft. Jamie suddenly became aware of the feel of her breasts flattened against his chest. The flash of lust was instantaneous and made him suck in a breath, causing the sleeping woman to stir. She burrowed and wiggled against him and he bit down on his bottom lip to avoid groaning out loud.

Lust and wiggling was a heady combination indeed.

Hot blood rushed to his groin, adding to his sudden discomfort.

She wiggled again and sighed into his neck.

Good grief! She was going to kill him. There were worse ways to go, he reasoned, than burning up with the flames of unspent passion. Under his palms he felt her body stiffen, then her freckled face emerged out of the sea of hair and she blinked down at him, startled.

'Hello.' The smile she bestowed upon him made his heart melt.

'Hello, yourself.' Thank goodness his aroused state had not affected his ability to talk normally, but by God she was beautiful. All mussed from sleep, hair all over the place and that face so close to his he could count every freckle. Jamie had never seen anything quite so lovely in his life.

'I slept well.' She had braced her head on one hand, the elbow of which was propped happily on his chest and showed no signs of moving. It should have felt awkward, but didn't.

'Glad to hear it. Sleep cures all ills, or so I am told.' She shifted slightly, reminding him of those breasts pressed intimately against his chest and making his body throb with need.

'You stayed.'

'You asked me to'

'Thank you.'

It was the sleepy eyes that did it, he would recall later, she was looking at him dopily through those long lashes and he was seduced by her beauty and completely burning with desire. For her. Of their own volition, his arms wound possessively around her ribs and tugged her until her mouth fell within kissing distance of his. Then it was completely natural to close the small distance and press his lips to hers.

Later, he would also recall the way she melted against him, which encouraged him to roll her over on to the warm, rumpled sheets and kiss her some more. And Cassie kissed him back, coiling her arms tightly about his neck and plunging her fingers into his hair. She felt the evidence of his desire and it did not repulse her. In fact, it apparently did quite the opposite. She arched against him, sighing into his mouth. Jamie could not have asked for a better response. Cassie in the throes of passion took his breath away.

At some point his hand found the hem of her nightgown and his hands dived underneath, running his greedy palms over the creamy, soft skin of the thighs which had haunted his dreams since he had spied them in the apple tree. They ventured further, lingered for a while on the ripe cheeks of her bottom before they were filled with her full breasts and he went to heaven. Of course, by then he was lost. All that mattered was the woman in his arms and the way she was making him feel.

Having never woken up with a man before, Cassie did not know what to expect. But as soon as she had begun to wake, she had been aware of his big body beneath hers. Initially, she felt safe, such an unusual emotion when she was used to living with her father, under constant threat of another of his cruel punishments that a constant sense of unease felt normal. Only when she was out in the open, riding Orange Blossom, did that state wane. It had never completely gone before, yet it was gone now and it was wonderfully liberating. So liberating she was giddy with it and wanted to giggle. Maybe that was because she knew she could never return, even though she had absolutely no idea how she was going to support herself in the short term, but it probably had a great deal more to do with who she had woken up with. Jamie looked positively delicious all rumpled. Cassie had immediately wanted to run her fingers through his hair and bury her nose in his neck. As it turned out, they were doing something infinitely better.

Yes, she should have rolled off him the moment she realised she was shamelessly sprawled across him, however, he had seemed perfectly content with their intimate position. He had instigated the kiss, tugging her close and then brushing his mouth over hers, and that kiss had been so achingly perfect, so charged with emotion, it had brought tears to her eyes. It was very different from the first kiss they had shared, the one tinged with anger and done to prove a point—this time Jamie made her feel precious and special. The fact he was taking his time over it was also interesting. Each time his lips touched hers, her body reacted. Tingles, shivers, an unfamiliar awareness of her womb and her breasts, an awareness which grew when he began to use his teeth and tongue as well as those intoxicating lips.

When it heated and became more, she welcomed it, loving the nearness and the intimacy of his weight above her. She could feel the evidence of his desire pressed against her belly, yet it was not close enough for her needy body. When his hands touched her bare skin it had come alive, the secret parts of her crying out to be explored and caressed. Cassie heard herself moan when he found her breasts and grazed the pad of his thumb over her aching nipples.

That guttural noise had an interesting effect. He shifted position and tugged her nightgown up her body to see her nakedness with his own eyes. Those bright blue windows to his soul had darkened with passion as they lazily took in every part of her from the pointed tips of her breasts to the triangle of hair at the apex of her thighs, before coming back to lock with hers. 'You are beautiful, Cassie. I hoped there would be more freckles and now I know for sure.' His finger trailed slowly down one breast to rest on one of the blemishes before it traced the outline of her nipple. The grin he gave her was totally wicked, possessive and wholly male, and instead of feeling ashamed that she was bared before him her arms and legs became heavy and her body craved more of his touch. When he bent his head to kiss her, it was not her lips he sought, he kissed that freckle and, heaven help her, she wanted more. So much more.

Shamelessly, she wriggled closer until his tongue began to trace the edge of her nipple and still it was not enough. Shockingly, she wanted to ask him to kiss all of it, thoroughly, and to touch her between her legs. Too shy and too frightened, Cassie kept angling her hungry nipples towards his mouth, yet each time his tongue came close to where she wanted it, he would change course and kiss another part of her breast. When she felt him smile against her heated skin she relaxed and accepted the sweet torture he was subjecting her to, waiting for his tongue to find the throbbing tip. He sucked it into his mouth and did wicked things to it, and like the true wanton she was, Cassie moaned and grasped his head in her hands, clamping him to her body so that the sensations would not end.

But they did, thank goodness, because he worshipped the other breast with equal devotion. Needing to feel his skin on hers, Cassie clawed at the hem of his shirt, yanking it up towards his head while he went in search of more freckles. It got caught. Twisted. And he laughed and tugged it over his head for her. It gave her the very first look at the shoulders which she longed to touch properly. Broad and beautifully muscled, strong arms and a chest which made her mouth water. Her hands immediately went to it, explored the dips and planes, marvelled at the solid feel of it. The smoothness of his skin. The tantalising roughness of the dark hair which dusted it before narrowing and disappearing beneath the waist of his breeches. And this time, when he lowered himself on top of her to kiss her deeply, there was the joy of feeling him. Jamie. Her hero and knight in shining armour. His naked skin on hers. Almost no other barriers between them.

Almost. Because he was still wearing his breeches. Emboldened by everything they were doing, Cassie set her fingers to work on the buttons of his falls, giving up to feel the long, thick length of him beneath the fabric and rejoicing when she heard the guttural sounds coming from his throat this time. One of his hands came down to assist her with the buttons, until between the pair of them they had managed to get a few undone before she pressed the flat of her hand against him again through the fabric. An open invitation that she was determined to be thoroughly ruined. In case he missed it, Cassie finally found the courage to tell him what she desired. 'I want you, Jamie. Right now.'

Beneath her palm, his arousal twitched, so she slowly traced the outline through the taut fabric with the tip of her index finger to torture him as he had spectacularly tortured her. 'I want to see you naked and kiss every inch of you.' Shocking words, yet the truth nevertheless. She had never wanted anything more. His hand came on top of hers and he closed his eyes, pressing her palm firmly against that part of him. The part which would join their bodies. The part her body craved so much she could not hide the urgency in her voice. 'Let me see you, Jamie. I need to see you!'

He sat back on his heels sharply and stared down at her, his dark brows now drawn together in a frown, his chest rising and falling as rapidly as hers. Whatever trance of passion had bewitched him no longer held him now. She could sense his withdrawal and didn't understand it.

'I'm sorry.' Before she could stop him, he was off the bed and hastily buttoning his breeches back up. 'I can't do this.'

'Why not?'

'I can't.'

'But I want you to.' Surely he could see that she wanted him to?

'No. It's not right. I can't explain.'

He was shaking his head in agitation, unaware his rejection was like a knife to her heart. All at once, she no longer felt beautiful and tempting, but ashamed and exposed. She dragged a blanket to cover her nakedness and watched, devastated, as he snatched up his shirt and hurried to put that on, too. All the while, he resolutely refused to look at her. He was halfway to the door when he stopped and turned around, looking every bit as wretched as one would have expected a disgusted man to be. 'For what it's worth, I am sorry. I never should have let things go this far. Forgive me.'

Then he was gone and Cassie was left staring at the closed door, wishing she had not allowed her true nature to surface and shock him. The evidence of her wantonness was everywhere. The limp and crushed nightgown was in a puddle on the floor. The sheet knotted from her shameless writhing, her hair a riot of tangles to match. And even now, even after he had spurned her so vehemently, beneath the blanket her breasts still ached and her secret area yearned for his body to join with hers.

She did not need her father's words to confirm the truth. She was her mother's daughter after all.

Chapter Sixteen

He avoided her for the rest of the day, riding the grounds aimlessly rather than face up to what he had done and tell her what was wrong. To say he was ashamed of himself was an understatement. Every muscle and sinew had been clenched in mortification since he had abandoned her naked on the bed. But he had panicked.

Let me see you, she had said, and in one fell swoop he had remembered it was daylight. Broad daylight. And he was broken—something which around Cassie he had a tendency to forget.

The early summer sun was already streaming through the gap in the curtains to highlight his deformity. Every hideous gnarled scar would be illuminated and he would have had to watch the wondrous sight of her passion-filled dark eyes cloud with distaste at the unpleasant spectacle. In daylight there could be no hiding it—which in turn meant he would undoubtedly have to talk about it. Then he would have to explain why half of the French garrison had been shooting at him and that he had murdered a man in cold blood when not completely in control of his faculties. Because he had been asleep when DuFour had come, and just as he had when his father had woken him with violence, the terrible uncontrollable savage which lay waiting inside him, the beast Jamie tightly controlled, had sprung forth and taken over.

Even if the sight of him did not horrify her, if they had continued what had so naturally started, Cassie would be ruined. They would have to marry. Whilst he would happily marry her right this minute, he had to consider the hornets' nest which she would have to contend with as his wife. There were so many things she did not know about him, things a wife would need to know before she said her vows. It hardly promised to be a casual chat.

Before this goes any further, you might find the following information useful, my darling. I cannot abide the taste of cheese and I have a tendency to break people's necks in my sleep.

Separate bedrooms, obviously, but he would have to explain why. Not just what he had done, but what he was capable of. The danger he would pose to his future wife and future children. His irrational and pathetic fear of the dark. That ridiculous arsenal of weapons he slept with. Any one of which could kill her in an instant. He never wanted to put her in harm's way again, let alone directly from his murderous hands. All of that had to be properly discussed, rationally, and understood before he could act on his desires.

Properly discussed rather than the ham-fisted hash he had made of it this morning. God only knew what she had to be thinking. She had looked positively wretched and on the cusp of tears when he had left her so abruptly. He could not make her his, and potentially create a child in the process, without being honest. Although in bringing her home with him, he had ruined her anyway, so the poor girl was very likely stuck with him whether she wanted to be or not. Yet how did one begin such a dreadful conversation?

With heavier feet than usual, Jamie limped back into the house. It couldn't be put off any longer. He found Cassie in the drawing room with Letty and Jack, looking withdrawn and more than a little alarmed at his arrival.

'There you are!' His brother was annoyed and rightly so. He had brought Cassie home here last night and then disappeared as if she wasn't his responsibility, when she so clearly was. 'I was about to send out a search party. Where have you been?'

'Riding.' He did not need Jack to make him feel any worse when his mood was already trawling the depths of despondency. 'Cassie, might I have a word?'

'Can it wait?' Her voice was shaky and her eyes were darting every which way except at him.

'Not really.'

'Oh, for pity's sake, Jamie, leave the poor girl alone!' Even Letty sounded irritated with him and who could blame her? 'Cassie has been through a dreadful ordeal, not helped by your silly disappearance this morning, and besides I have ordered tea, which the three of us are going to enjoy. You can join us, if you can bear to grace us with your presence, or you can scurry off again and hide. I dare say it will make no difference to any of us regardless.' Her attention went back to her sewing, but by the way she was jabbing the needle in the fabric, Jamie could tell his sister-in-law was imagining it was his thick head. He was tempted to offer her his actual head in the hope it might make both of them feel better. 'What were you saying, Jack? Before your idiot brother came in and interrupted us.'

Just like that they closed ranks around Cassie and Jamie was forced to sit ignored, in painful isolation, feeling like the worst sort of cad. The object of his misery said little, although once or twice he caught her looking at him before she blushed furiously and resolutely stared at her hands. All Jamie could do to pass the time was stare angrily at her bruises and castigate himself for his part in her misery.

Chivers appeared silently out of nowhere and addressed his brother. 'My lord, the Reverend Reeves is at the gates, demanding to be let in. He is accusing Mr James of kidnapping his daughter and holding her hostage. How would you like me to proceed?'

Jamie surged to his feet. 'I will deal with him!' And deal with him he would. Once and for all. Without Cassie there to see, he was going to beat her father into a pulp, one which would need to be scraped off the driveway with a shovel by the time he was finished. His fists were clenched in preparation as he started towards the door.

'Wait!' Jack grabbed him forcibly by the arm. 'Whilst I completely appreciate your anger and whilst I would like nothing better than to see that man get his comeuppance, this is not your decision to make or mine. It's Cassie's.'

Yes, it was. Damn it. 'Marriage has made you soft, Brother. A few months ago and you would have been the first one out of the door.' Jamie's irritation at being thwarted disappeared when he saw Cassie's reaction to the situation. All colour drained from her face, eyes wide and clearly terrified. Without thinking he went to her and pulled her close. 'I won't let him harm you. You're safe here. I promise.'

'Jamie is right.' Jack came to stand loyally beside him. 'You are under our protection now and out of your father's jurisdiction. Do you want me to have him sent away or should I send for the constable? Or would you prefer Jamie to deal with him?' The brothers exchanged a look of understanding. Jack knew that it was not his place to step in and Jamie was grateful his brother acknowledged it.

'I would like to speak to him.' Her voice came out so small. She stepped stiffly out of his unwelcomed embrace and stood proudly. 'I want to tell him I am never coming back. I want him to see that he hasn't beaten me.'

They let him in. Cassie could tell Jamie wasn't happy with the decision, but he abided by it and stood next to her like a ferocious tiger ready to pounce as her father was led into the drawing room, flanked by the Earl on one side and a particularly burly footman on the other. Their presence reassured her, but did nothing to stop the nervousness and sense of vulnerability at seeing him again less than twenty-four hours after he had almost killed her. Despite that, her father showed not an ounce of remorse, although she had not really expected him to.

'These thugs of yours do not frighten me, Cassandra. We are leaving.'

'No.' In all her twenty-one years she had never said that tiny word to him. Even with the Warriners and their servants at her side, saying it still took every ounce of courage she possessed.

'I said we are leaving. I have had my fill of Retford and the patronising bishop. When we get home we shall pack.'

'And I said no. I am staying, Father.' The word Papa was too familiar and affectionate to use ever again. 'I granted you this audience because I wanted you to know I am never coming back to live with you again.'

'Under God's holy law, you must obey me.'

Cassie shook her head. 'I am of age. In the eyes of the law I can do as I please.'

'No law supersedes the word of our Lord! Honour thy father, Cassandra!'

She was done with being bullied. Done with all the punishments she did not deserve. Done with being a disappointment because of wayward character traits she could not suppress. 'Yesterday, by your own admission, you had no daughter. Only a harlot.' Her voice wavered on those terrible names because she suspected they were close to the truth. If only Jamie had not seen her completely naked and consumed with wanton lust. Though it made no difference to her decision concerning her father. 'You beat me.' Her fingers lightly touched the raised bruise on her cheek, yet her father's eyes did not appear horrified to see the evidence of his brutality. 'You tied me up. You put your hands around my neck and choked me until I passed out. I might have died. I will not live with the threat of such violence again.'

'You have duties to attend to.'

'Nor will I skivvy for you. I will find a job and earn money for my labours instead. That money you found, the money you accused me of prostituting myself for, it was my running-away fund. As soon as I had saved enough I was going to leave anyway. Your actions only served to expedite the process.'

His temper began to fray; she could see it in his eyes because she had never openly disobeyed him before. All her rebellions had been secret, but there were no secrets now. Her father had found everything and cruelly destroyed it. The only piece of her writing not torn to pieces was *The Great Apple Debacle*, and that was with a publisher and safe from his petty controls. And they *were* petty, she realised, because the paper he had ripped up so cruelly before her eyes was only that. Paper. The stories were still there in her head and they could easily be written down again.

'I am going to live my own life, exactly as I want to.'

"'Favour is deceitful, and beauty is vain: but a woman that feareth the Lord, she shall be praised!'"

His hand lurched out and grabbed her roughly by the arm, only to have it yanked away by Jamie with twice as much force. He glared down at her father, still holding the offending arm in a vice-like grip, and practically snarled as he spoke.

'How convenient, Reverend, that you should be sparing with that particular verse of Proverbs. I suppose the rest of the verse doesn't suit your particular needs. Do you remember it? Because I do. Word for word. *"Give her of the fruit of her hands; and let her own works praise her in the gates."* In other words— and do correct me if I am wrong—God demands you treat your women well, *Reverend*. Respect them. It says nothing about beating them, restraining them, imprisoning them like criminals, and it certainly does not tell you to try to strangle the life out of them!'

'You have turned my daughter against me and dragged her to this den of iniquity!'

'If you speak another vile word about Cassie, you will have me to answer to!'

Her father's lip curled scornfully. 'And who are you to usurp the word of her father?'

'I will be her husband and you can rot in hell, or a lunatic asylum where you belong! And make no bones about it, Reverend, I shall drag you there with my bare hands and make sure they throw away the key!'

Cassie stood frozen for several seconds, reeling.

Husband.

Where had that come from?

This morning he had left her naked because her wantonness was so abhorrent. She had seen the disgust and horror written plainly on his face. Almost the same sort of disappointment she received daily from her hateful father. A marriage on those terms did not bode well. All she would be doing was swapping one miserable existence for another, lesser one, doomed to disappoint another man with her wayward tendencies and break her own heart in the process. Because a bad marriage to Jamie, when he meant the world to her, would be a living hell.

'Over my dead body!' Her father managed to wriggle out of Jamie's hold to lunge at her again. Quick as a flash, Jamie caught him and twisted an arm painfully behind her father's back, effectively anchoring him in place.

'That can be arranged. Touch her again and I *will* kill you this time!'

'Oh, stop it!' Cassie felt bitter tears sting her eyes. This was all so awful. 'You need to leave, Father. I have made my decision and I am never coming back.' She turned, not to Jamie but to his brother. 'Can you show him out, please?'

Jack and the burly footman took an arm each and dragged her father from the room, all the while he spouted the scriptures and glared at her menacingly. Perhaps Jamie was right and he was a lunatic. Suddenly she felt chilled to the bone and more miserable than she had a scant few minutes ago. And so hopelessly lonely. She had believed Jamie was coming to understand her, like her even, but her exuberant personality had repulsed him, too, because she had let her guard down and allowed him a glimpse of the real her.

As if this morning had not happened, Jamie stepped towards her with his arms open, clearly intent on offering her more comfort, yet the thought of his hands on her again was too painful even though she desperately wanted to rush into them and absorb his strength. She backed up and held her palms up in warning. A warning he ignored. His fingers reached out and lightly brushed her cheek. 'Cassie…'

The tears fell then, noisily and filled with anger. 'Just leave me alone!'

'We need to talk.'

'No, we don't. I have nothing to say to you, Captain Warriner. I never want to talk to you again and I am certainly not marrying you!' Cassie picked up her borrowed skirts and fled from the room.

Chapter Seventeen

'Can I come in?'

The sound of her sobbing behind the door was breaking his heart.

'No! Go away!'

He heard something hard bounce off the wood, some missile she had found to hurl at his head no doubt. Ignoring her, he turned the handle. He had a hard head after all and he had procrastinated long enough, and in doing so had upset her further when she had so much to be distraught about already. Cassie had thrown herself on the bed, but raised herself quickly to her knees at his unwelcome intrusion. The murderous look she shot him could have curdled milk. 'I need to talk to you.'

'And I have already stated I have nothing to say to you!' She pouted sulkily and searched the vicinity for something else to throw. Finding nothing of any substance, she turned her back on him.

'Well, that is fine. I will talk to you and you can listen.' Stony silence. Jamie approached the bed gingerly and perched his bottom on the edge of the mattress, twisting slightly to address her back. 'Firstly, as has been loudly, most vociferously and completely unnecessarily pointed out to me by Letty, I should like to apologise for my horrendous proposal—if one could call it that. I did have every intention of asking you properly. I still have every intention of asking you properly. But I need to tell you some things first. Things I have been putting off because I couldn't find the right words to tell you.' Words Jamie was still struggling to find. 'The thing is…this morning I…'

'I definitely do not want to talk about this morning!' She practically jumped off the bed and stalked towards the window with her hands fisted against her sides. 'I would prefer to pretend *that* debacle never happened.'

'But I want to explain…'

'No explanations are necessary. I know perfectly well what I did wrong!'

Obviously he had made a spectacular hash of things if she thought she was to blame for any of this. 'You did nothing wrong.' He saw pain wash over her face and felt wretched. 'Why would you think you did anything wrong? I was the one who panicked.'

'You panicked? I didn't… I didn't disgust you?'

'Disgust me?' Where had that come from? 'Quite the opposite, Cassie. You were perfect.' Which actually gave him the perfect opening. 'And I am not. In so many dreadful ways. So I panicked because I did not know how to tell you and fled. I wish with all of my heart I hadn't if I made you doubt yourself in the process. You are the most beautiful thing I have ever seen and the simple, awful truth is I do not deserve you.'

This time when he reached out to touch her she did not recoil. She allowed him to take her hand and tug her to sit on the mattress beside him.

'I don't understand.'

Jamie took a deep breath. 'It's hard to explain. It might be easier if I showed you.'

The scars.

The guns.

He stood stiffly and tried to steel himself for her reaction to it all. 'Come. I need to take you to my bedchamber.'

She followed him warily without question, still allowing him to hold her hand. Jamie tried not to hope this was a good sign. Once she knew the truth she might not be so keen to hold it. No matter, she deserved the whole truth. 'You should probably sit down.'

She did, cautiously, her pretty face awash with questions while Jamie paced nervously to the window and then back again, wondering where the hell to start. 'When I escaped from that goal, I barely escaped with my life. The alarm had been raised and the whole garrison were searching for me.' He would tell her why that was later, if this part did not send her screaming down the landing. 'I was shot. Four times. The damage was substantial.' At a loss at how to explain the full extent of his injuries, He shrugged out of his jacket and began to undo his waistcoat.

Cassie sat watching him, alarmed. 'What are you doing?'

'I thought it might be prudent to show you what those musket balls did. It's more than just a limp, Cassie.'

Briskly he tugged his shirt over his head and tugged the waistband of his breeches down enough to see the raised pair of scars which sat like bookends on either side of his left hip. They were the least offensive marks and if she balked at them then there would be no point showing her the others. 'One bullet entered here and came out the other side.'

To her credit, she did not balk. Instead she bent her head to get a closer look and then surprised him by running the tip of her index finger over the mark at the front. 'That must have been agony.'

'Compared to the others, it was insignificant. It hurt like the devil at the time, but it was a reasonably clean shot and hit nothing important.'

'What did the others do?'

'They have left me deformed.' Jamie felt sick. 'Hideously deformed. This morning I was embarrassed. I didn't want to disappoint or disgust you and I blame myself for letting things between us go as far as they did...especially when you were probably expecting a whole man rather than what is left of me.' Her eyes widened and he fought the urge to flee again. Damn and blast, he had never been so humiliated or felt so useless.

Come on, Jamie. Be matter-of-fact about it. Show her. She deserves to know why you left her unsatisfied this morning. 'It's not pretty. Are you sure you want to see it?' Because if she did not, he would probably be relieved. And then truly miserable, because this was his only chance of any sort of future with Cassie. He wouldn't marry her without brutal honesty.

She nodded, but he could see her trepidation. He briskly undid the buttons on his falls and watched her eyes stare intently at the area of his hips as he began to inch the fabric down. 'There's nothing to be done about it and I can only apologise for inflicting this on you...' Revealing it inch by inch was pathetic and only served to prolong his agony and her horror. Better simply to do it quickly, let her see, then cover up the mess and promise never to sully her eyes with it again. He would suffer the dark to make love to her if she would have him. Which she probably wouldn't when she saw the state of him. Utterly degraded and mortified, he yanked the breeches down far enough to expose all of the vile damage and squeezed his eyes closed so he did not have to witness her initial reaction. As the silence dragged, he couldn't bring himself to open them.

After an eternity she huffed out a breath. 'But it is still there. Does it no longer work?'

'You know it works—you've seen it work—but it will always limp.'

'It limps?'

'When I walk, I limp. You know that. Did you think I had a wooden leg?' He had not thought his limp was that bad! Jamie risked cracking open one eye and found her staring not at his ruined left thigh, but at his manhood. It also brought him up short and had him hastily gathering up the sagging breeches and holding them in place. He had been so fixated on showing her the dreaded scars he had quite forgotten she might never have seen a man's privates before.

'And your...your...' She waved her hand in the direction of his jewels and blushed as red as a beetroot. '*That* part of you still works?'

'Perfectly well.' She still wasn't looking at his leg. Apparently her eyes were resolutely locked on his groin, something both strangely disconcerting and erotic at the same time when one considered the situation.

'Oh, thank goodness!' She started to giggle, her eyes never leaving that particular area between his legs, her lovely face as red as a face could be without the aid of paint. 'I assumed…when you said you weren't a *whole* man…well, I assumed that it had been shot off or damaged in some way as to render it…useless…but then I felt it this morning and it seemed to be functioning… as I am led to believe that part of a man's anatomy should function.'

Thank goodness?

Not at all what he had expected her first words to be when at best he had hoped for a cursory *it doesn't matter, just kindly keep it covered up*. A tiny part of him began to hope in earnest. A bigger part needed to hear her verdict on his deformity. 'The scars are repulsive, aren't they?'

Her eyes flicked to the covered damaged area, lingered, then slowly swept up his body to look incredulously into his. 'You were ashamed to show me them?'

'You're so lovely and so perfect and I am—'

'Brave and strong.' Her interruption brought him up short. 'Did you really think me so shallow that I would think less of you because of a few scars, Jamie? If I am completely honest, they humble me. To think that you have suffered all of the pain of those wounds and not only survived, but fully recovered leaves me in awe.' Her eyes travelled back down his body again, reminding him of the fact aside from bunched fabric in his hand he was stood practically stark naked in front of her. Her fingers reached up to trace the shape of the scar on the front of his hip. 'Does it still hurt?'

Jamie shook his head, transfixed on the peculiar sensation of being touched. There. And with affection. 'Parts of it are numb. Other parts over-sensitive.' The involuntary twinge as she found one of those places made her hesitate. 'Is my touching it uncomfortable?'

Uncomfortable. An understatement. Despite himself, Jamie laughed. 'My breeches were just around my knees, I am allowing you to scrutinise all of my imperfections and I inadvertently flashed you my...' He flapped his hand in the vicinity of his crotch and felt himself blush like a virgin. 'Why on earth would any of those things make me uncomfortable?'

'I suppose it is a little awkward, but...'

'But?'

'As you have already seen me naked, I think it is only fair that I get to see you in all of your glory.'

There were no words. Jamie opened his mouth twice to speak and twice he closed it while he digested what he thought he had just heard. 'Hardly glorious. My leg is a mess.' He must have misheard or misinterpreted her words out of desperation. He wanted her approval so very much, clearly his poor, besotted heart was attributing false meaning to the tiniest things. Yet she appeared totally sincere. Not even the slightest bit repulsed.

He watched in frozen wonder as the flat of her hand pressed against his abdomen, smoothed up his chest and then one finger traced the line of hair all the way down to his navel. 'To you perhaps it is a mess. My eyes find plenty of other bits of you to feast on which are much more interesting than a few insignificant scars.'

Cassie sucked in a breath of surprise and dropped her wandering hands firmly back into her lap. Gracious! Where had those words come from? She could hardly believe she had thought them, let alone said them out loud. But really, seeing him stood in all of his natural splendour in such intimately close proximity was making her giddy. Her palms itched to touch him again. All of him. Especially *that* part of him she had oh-so-briefly glimpsed and wished she were still able to see because it had not at all been what she had expecting and had held her momentarily transfixed.

Shocking thoughts which a proper young lady would never dream of thinking, but Cassie could not help because her passions were just too exuberant and always too close to the surface. With Jamie, it was impossible to control them—and with this morning's enlightening interlude still so fresh in her mind, knowing what those clever hands and mouth could do to her body— those passions had never been so close to the surface. She was practically vibrating from the force of them.

He caught her staring longingly at the arrow of dark hair on his abdomen which pointed down to *that* part— she supposed she was being rather blatant about it— and for a moment his dark brows drew together in a frown. Instantly, guilt and shame at her uncontrollable wantonness had her staring at her hands. She did not want to disgust him. 'I am so very sorry. I do try to control my passions—I really do—it's just that...' Her voice trailed off miserably and she buried her flaming face in her hands. She was hardly controlling her wanton tendencies if she was about to confess that the sight of him stood before her was making her think the most impure of thoughts.

Cassie felt the mattress depress beside her as he sat. Then she heard his breathing. Slightly erratic. More than a little heavy. Much like her own. 'Am I to understand the sight of me…naked…pleases you in some way?' His voice was gruff.

Hesitant.

Cassie risked glancing at him through her fingers and was surprised to see blatant longing in his deep blue eyes as if the idea of it was so preposterous, yet not unwelcome by any stretch. He was staring at her so intently. Waiting for her answer. It compelled her to be honest.

'Naked you are quite…splendid.'

He stood jerkily, still clutching the waistband of his breeches, and appeared bemused for a second. Relieved. Then in an instant he was all seriousness again. 'There is more, Cassie.'

'More scars?'

'Sort of—but not scars you can see… I am broken on the inside, too. Horribly broken and I cannot seem to fix it no matter what I do. The truth is, I have a morbid fear of the dark.' Not quite what she had expected his next words to be and unsure of how to react to them, Cassie merely blinked. 'I tell you this because if you marry me we can never sleep in the same room.' Not what she wanted to hear, but as he was speaking in such a rush now there was no time to interrupt. She had the feeling that whatever it was which was troubling him needed to come out; she suddenly understood he had held it all inside for so long, festering, because he could never say the words. Interrupting him in midflow now that he had finally found them was probably not the best idea. Especially when the poor man appeared completely mortified to be confessing it all to her in the first place.

'I am unsafe, Cassie. Dangerous. I have a tendency

to lash out at anyone who comes near me. I killed a man once. Snapped his neck. His name was Capitaine Du-Four and he was my gaoler in France. He used to come in the night and beat and torture his prisoners. That night I was exhausted—he had been interrogating me all day. He woke me from a deep sleep and I lost control. The savage inside me took over and I lost all reason. I was crazed, Cassie. It was as if I had the strength of ten men yet the sense of none. I wish I could say it was an isolated incident, one created by an extreme set of circumstances but it wasn't. I almost strangled my father for doing the same when I was barely fifteen. I wrapped his belt around his neck and watched him turn purple as he fought for life. When he fell to the floor I thought he was dead. I didn't feel any remorse, merely relief that I had killed him. I hadn't, as it turned out, but at the time I wanted him to be dead so very much. I tried to attack the surgeons who wanted to amputate my leg. They had to resort to tying me to the bed to stop me from lashing out. I even tried to kill my own brother when he woke me up to give me some laudanum. It took the other two of them to restrain me else he would be dead, too. So you see, you can never spend the night with me. I need you to understand that—really understand that and the dangerous implications before I dare take this further. I care too much about you…' His anguished voiced caught and he seemed to sag with exhaustion at the confession.

'But I have spent the night with you.'

It was almost too much information to take in and her brain was whirring, trying to make sense of what he was telling her and link it to what she already knew about him. Loved about him. 'I came to no harm.'

'A fluke. I could have killed you. This thing within me...' he clenched his fist and pressed it to his abdomen '...it feeds off the dark and kills all of my reason. When it possesses me it is as if I am outside of my body, watching myself. All that I feel is the urge to destroy. To kill. You have seen it for yourself. I wanted to kill your father when I discovered what he had done to you. I am a menace. I cannot control what I do.'

'Yes. You can. I watched you do it.' He had not been outside of himself when he had gone at her father. Jamie had been totally in control. And he had stopped because of her. Their eyes had locked and he had tossed her father to the floor. Stepped back. Centred himself. He had not been a crazed beast, merely her rescuer. Her knight in shining armour. A man who painted every detail of the delicate wings of a bee on a beautiful flower was not a man who would willingly harm anything—unless he had great cause to.

She remembered what he had said about his own father, of how the man had sought to beat the urge to paint out of him and pictured the little boy he had been, terrified and vulnerable at the hands of someone so much bigger, suffering for years and years at the hands of a sadist, and understood why he had eventually fought back so ferociously. If this Frenchman who haunted him had tortured Jamie repeatedly, then she hated the man with a vengeance just as much as she hated his dead father and certainly without needing to know any more. 'Your father and this DuFour were evil men who had come to harm you. Repeatedly. It is hardly surprising that you snapped eventually and fought back.' Cassie could find no sympathy for those vile men. 'Although extreme, they are wholly natural reactions. When your life is in danger you fight back. And you do the same for those you care about.' She had witnessed his loyalty to his family and now to her.

He cared about her.

How wonderful was that?

'I have spent my life cowering before my father in the hope it might make things better, yet it only made it worse. The more subservient I became, the more irrational and cruel his punishments. I fought my father when he tried to harm me and I will not feel bad for doing so. I am glad his face is covered with the scratches I gave him. His arms are covered in my teeth marks, too. If I had had a weapon to hand, I would have gratefully used it against him yesterday even if that action would have resulted in his death.' Cassie touched his arm gently. 'Tell me about the surgeons.'

He swallowed hard and tried to calm his breathing. Clearly that memory was also a painful one to recall. 'They wanted to cut off my leg when I first arrived. They said it couldn't be saved, but I wouldn't let them. When the infection set in they were adamant it needed to go, when I refused they restrained me. Tied me to the bed. It was too dark to perform the operation so they decided to leave it till morning. They left me strapped to the bed all night, but I managed to escape. Found a pistol. After that if any of them came near me I threatened to shoot them. They washed their hands of me. Said I was mad. Sent me home to die.'

'But you didn't die.'

'No. My brother Joe has been studying medical books since he was a boy. He made medicines and ointments to treat the infection. Even then it took months.'

'You were still ill then, when you attacked your brother, and drugged with laudanum.'

'I won't excuse it, Cassie. I cannot be trusted. I am not rational. I still sleep with a pistol because the darkness terrifies me.'

Aching with pity for him, Cassie went to him and wrapped her arms around him. No matter what he said, no matter what he had done, she knew he had a gentle soul and would never hurt her. 'Oh, my poor darling! After months of incarceration and torture, to then have to fight for your own life as well—it is hardly surprising you came home fragile and a little confused. Does your brother blame you for your outburst?' She had yet to meet Jacob Warriner, but if he was anything like the other three she suspected he was cut from the same cloth and would remain loyal to the end.

'No. He felt dreadful for creeping up on me and trying to drip the laudanum in while I slept. But Jake is my brother, Cassie!' His eyes were pleading now, desperate to convince her of his unworthiness. 'I attacked my own brother!'

'Almost a year ago, when on the cusp of death and still traumatised from your ordeal, and you are still flagellating yourself for it. Tell me, does Jake fear you now?'

This appeared to flummox him for a moment. 'He should—but, no, he doesn't. He's just the same as he always was around me and stiil does not knock before he enters my bedchamber when I have warned him a thousand times.'

'Perhaps because he trusts you and loves you.' Jamie clearly hated himself and did not think he was worthy of those things. 'Just as I trust you. And I love you, Jamie. With all of my heart.'

He stopped breathing and blinked. Swallowed hard, those fathomless bright blue eyes disbelieving. So she leaned close and kissed him, a soft brush of her lips over his, and took his hand. 'I don't think you are afraid of the dark, Jamie. I think you are afraid of yourself. Did you leave me this morning because you feared I wouldn't understand?'

She felt his head nod next to hers, felt his fingers lace with hers tightly. 'You love me?'

'Hopelessly. I have done pretty much since the moment you rescued me out of that stupid tree.'

'That's funny,' he said, not laughing at all, 'I think I fell in love with you at exactly the same time. Just after you flattened me. I remember opening my eyes and there was this beautiful creature staring down at me. Big brown eyes. Freckles. The most amazing hair filled with twigs and leaves. I never wanted a woman as much as I wanted you then. I painted you.'

The image of that lovely picture sprang into her head and Cassie realised that was exactly how he saw her. 'The orchard picture. And you want me?' He nodded again, perhaps a little uncertainly, and her heart soared. As he clung to her, Cassie choked out a laugh of relief. 'I thought you were disgusted by my wantonness.'

He held her out at arm's length and stared at her in shock. 'Are you mad? What would give you such a preposterous idea?'

'My father has always told me that desire and passion were a sign of wickedness. My mother left him for another man, you see. He was worried I had inherited her tendencies. Such things, he was adamant, were unwelcome in a marriage.'

To begin with he merely blinked at her, then he shook his head incredulously. 'As I said before, your father is a lunatic to have filled your head with such nonsense. I bet he had a number of convenient biblical quotes to prove his point. Sins of the flesh and all that. However, as I understand it, marriage was created to allow two people to enjoy one another without sin.'

'Enjoy? My father taught me that the only purpose of fornication is procreation.'

'But the marriage vows state *"with my body I thee honour"*—why would they say that unless they were acknowledging the physical manifestation of love between two people? If the act is solely for the procreation, then why did he design our bodies to find the experience pleasurable? In fact, the creator made a very specific part of the female body for no other purpose than to feel pleasure.'

'He did?' How shocking and wonderful was it to have a conversation like this with a man, although his claim baffled her. Every part she could think of had another, more important purpose. Giving birth. Feeding children. He saw her confusion and grinned. His hands let go of her arms and slid around her waist.

'It's very small. Very hard to find. Would you like to know where it is?'

The air became charged with an odd sort of tension. Of expectation. Cassie's own clothes suddenly felt tight and constricting. She became very aware of her breasts, her womb and all of the tingling flesh in between. 'Yes.' It came out in a whisper because he was pulling her to stand flush against him and she could feel his desire through her clothes. Felt it grow. Harden.

'I am afraid you are going to have to be quite naked again.'

'Will you be, too?'

She saw the trepidation, but he nodded. 'If you would like me to be.'

She licked her lips, she couldn't help it, and let her gaze drop to his magnificent chest.

'Yes, please.'

Was that really her voice? Urgent, breathy, laced with need, but she was hypnotised by the intense way he was gazing at her and the way all logic appeared to vanish when he was so near. When he bent his head and kissed her, she could taste his passion and happily gave herself over to it and to him. This man she loved and who loved her in return, despite all of her many faults and peculiarities.

He stood and walked to the door. Turned the key in the lock. Cassie's heart began to beat in panic, but when he came back towards her he pressed the key into her hand and she loved him for that thoughtful gesture which only he would understand. Cassie smiled and lifted the pillow, placed the key next to his pistol and carefully replaced the bedding to hide them. They both had their irrational fears and foibles. Perhaps together they would find the courage to overcome them. And perhaps they wouldn't. It didn't matter.

Jamie wrapped his arms around her, gently edged her back towards his bed and eased her to sit down on to it with a kiss. Then stood back. She watched the muscles in his arms bunch as he bent to tug off his boots. Only when they were gone did he allow the breeches to drop.

Except this time, her eyes got to feast on the sight of him aroused, a far more impressive state than before and that had been impressive enough. Wordlessly, he took her hand and pulled her back upright, staring deeply into her eyes as he began to undo the back of her dress. When it fell off her shoulders, he slowly peeled the muslin down her body, then did the same with her corset and petticoat. As each layer came off, Cassie's body came alive. Now, stood in only her chemise, he trailed his fingers over the aching tips of her breasts lovingly before he cast that garment to the growing puddle around her feet.

Both completely laid bare in every sense of the word, he opened his arms and she stepped into them, feeling for the first time the blissful sensation of his warm skin completely against hers. He kissed her again, deeply, and within seconds she was moaning into his mouth, her arms wrapped as tightly about his neck as she could to increase the contact of her breasts against his chest. Her belly against his hardness.

He picked her up like she was something precious and lay her reverently on his bed. 'I have to kiss your freckles first. All of them.' His mouth wandered over her body, licking and nipping every tiny blemish until she was writhing beneath him.

Unashamedly wanton, because he was not at all disgusted by it, she moaned her appreciation and those moans seemed to fire his passion further. Yet he still tortured her body mercilessly, kissing each of her breasts before sucking the puckered nipples into his mouth and making her cry out from the exquisite agony. By the time he came to lay alongside her, Cassie was desperate. 'You still haven't shown me the part of my body designed solely for pleasure.' Wherever it was she needed his hands and mouth on it. Immediately.

His fingers trailed lazily up her thigh, causing her hips to buck. 'I think you have an idea where it is, don't you?' And he was obviously enjoying her discomfort, a state wholly of his making. His hands were rubbing lazy circles on her abdomen. So close to where she wanted them and yet too far away. Her most secret area was screaming for his touch, but she was not brave enough to tell him. She hoped it was there so he would put her out of her misery.

'Please, Jamie…show me!'

His fingers toyed with the soft curls at the apex of her thighs and Cassie unashamedly opened her legs to allow him to explore her. This was no sin if they were husband and wife, and in her heart they were already married. Jamie was propped up on one elbow, watching her face intently and clearly enjoying the sensual spell he held her under. 'Let me see…' One finger probed her sensitive flesh gently and then—

'Oh, my!' He caressed something wonderful and Cassie's hips came off the mattress. With the tiniest amount of pressure and the smallest of movements he managed to create sheer ecstasy. With every stroke he watched her. With every stroke she lost herself.

It was bliss.

Heaven.

Yet it kept building and building and she kept wanting more and more until the need became almost painful. Her muscles tensed, her breathing became laboured and Jamie kissed her lips softly and nuzzled her neck.

'Don't fight it, Freckles. Relax. Let it happen.'

And it did. Something gave way inside her, hidden muscles pulsed and lights exploded behind her eyes. For an eternity all Cassie was capable of doing was feeling until she collapsed boneless on to the mattress, stunned. Too stunned to care that he was grinning at her so smugly, clearly feeling extremely pleased with himself for being the cause of her current state.

Yet as strange and wonderful as that state was, it still wasn't enough. Her hand reached out to touch him, closed around his hardened flesh. 'I want you, Jamie. Every bit of you.'

Those intense blue eyes instantly became almost black and he seemed to grow larger in her hand. 'If we do this, we have to marry. Will you marry me, Cassie? Even though I'm broken?'

'Yes. In a heartbeat.' There was no point arguing with him. He believed he was broken and unworthy and she would make it her life's work to prove to him that he wasn't. He was perfect. 'Although I think we might have to find another vicar to do the deed for us.'

He was laughing as he rolled on top of her, his lips nuzzling her neck, ears and then her mouth, and settled his body in the cradle of her thighs. 'I suspect the Bishop of Nottingham might be sympathetic. Will you marry me as soon as possible? Because I cannot wait.'

Cassie couldn't answer. He was doing wicked things to her with his lips and his tongue and her wonderfully wanton body was desperate for his. Everything about him was glorious, so she shamelessly ran her hands over the hard planes of his back, those broad shoulders she had always desired, his bottom, his face. Emotion clogged her throat when he began to inch inside her.

Jamie was so gentle, moving with such aching slowness so as not to hurt her, despite the fact she lustily
welcomed the intrusion. The discomfort was insignificant and fleeting. Then he filled her, his lovely blue
eyes locked intently with hers, and she saw the love
shining out of them and knew she was home. When
he moved inside her, further pondering was impossible. Nothing else mattered or existed aside from the
place where their bodies joined. She did not fight the
passion as it built this time. There was no point. She
gave herself to it completely, let it consume her, glo-
ried in it until they both cried out together, clinging
to each other for dear life. Exactly as they had been
created to do.

If his brother or Letty had any inkling of what he
and Cassie had spent the entire afternoon and most of
the night doing, thankfully they said nothing. Even
though Cassie's cheeks was reddened from the rasp
of his morning whiskers and her lips were plumper
and pinker than usual from his kisses. Nor did they
make mention of the soppy way he and Cassie kept
smiling at each other over the breakfast table. In fact,
it was a positively civilised meal. Far too civilised,
filled with a great many pointed and knowing looks,
and that amused him. Jamie knew the pair of them had
to be burning with curiosity and Letty at least would
have a million questions. Purposefully, he held back
from telling them that he and Cassie were engaged
for no other reason than that he knew it would irritate
them. Letty was gripping her teacup with such force,
he feared for the porcelain.

Chivers appeared out of nowhere and addressed his brother. 'A messenger has arrived with a letter for a Mrs Cassandra James.' Letty grabbed it and tore it open before anyone else had a chance. To vex everyone no doubt because her thirst for gossip was so far unquenched, she read it silently to herself, then smiled before folding it again. Both Jamie and her husband knew how the game was played and ignored her. Poor Cassie was beside herself.

'Is it from the publisher? Does he like the book? Does he hate the book? What does he say?'

Jamie hoped she would always babble when she was nervous, he enjoyed it immensely. It was one of the many things he loved about her.

'Please, Letty! What does it say?'

Letty sipped her tea, then blotted her mouth daintily with a napkin before finally caving and taking pity on her. 'It says he absolutely loves *Orange Blossom and the Great Apple Debacle*, as I always knew he would, and that he is keen to purchase any new stories by this wonderfully talented new author. He's going to publish it, Cassie. Do you have a new story?'

'We have been working on a story about a dragon.'

'Called Brimstone,' added Jamie as it had just occurred to him, 'He kidnaps the silly but intrepid Miss Freckles and locks her in a tower.'

Cassie was smiling. 'And Captain Galahad, Orange Blossom and Stanley come to rescue her.'

'Does it end with another wedding?' his meddling sister-in-law asked pointedly, 'With a guard of honour complete with an arch of crossed carrots?'

'Of course not.' Cassie's hand came to rest affectionately on the back of his. 'It will end perfectly. The silly but intrepid Miss Freckles and the brave and long-suffering Captain Galahad will ride off into the sunset together. Until the next adventure.'

Letty sighed and patted her protruding stomach. 'The perfect happily ever after. Cassandra James will soon be a household name.'

It occurred to Jamie then that things had changed. 'What your father thinks no longer matters. You are free from his rules. You do not have to hide behind a pen name now, Cassie. Perhaps it is time for Cassandra Reeves to step out of the shadows and shine.'

'The book was a joint effort and I rather like Cassandra James. As Letty pointed out, it is a marriage of sorts.' She blushed at her unsubtle hint for him to tell his family the good news because he had toyed with them for long enough.

Jack appeared perplexed. 'I fail to see why both of your names shouldn't be on the cover. Miss Cassandra Reeves and Captain James Warriner has a ring to it.'

'I'm no longer a captain.' It was time he was honest with everyone, including himself. 'My soldiering days are over, thank goodness, and I am resigning my commission. Even if a miracle occurs and this blasted leg heals, I am an artist now. An illustrator. And I like Cassandra James, too. The names merge perfectly to-gether…almost as if they were meant to be.' Which of course they were. For always. 'I was wondering, if you two have nothing better to do, then perhaps you would like to accompany us to Nottingham?'

This invitation earned a scowl from his brother. 'Nottingham! No, thank you. I loathe the place and I am certainly not dragging Letty all that way when she is so heavy with child!'

'That's a shame,' Jamie said, sipping his own tea nonchalantly. 'You will miss our wedding and I was going to ask you to be the best man.'

Epilogue

'Jamie!'

The voice was loud and he was being shaken. Quite violently.

'Jamie!'

'What the blazes?' His eyes flew open and it was dark. Very dark. He was in a strange bed. In a strange room. His chest constricted with panic.

Then he realised there was some moonlight. A lamp was burning low nearby. He was in the inn. In Nottingham. Simultaneously, he realised there was a very lovely, very dishevelled-looking naked woman knelt on the mattress beside him.

Cassie.

Her new silk stockings were hanging limply on the bedpost where he had tossed them after peeling them reverently from her legs last night. Heaven only knew where the saucy pink garters he had also bought her had gone, although he suspected they were somewhere in the tangled mess of his and her clothing scattering the floor. The moonlight glinted off her wedding ring and the lamplight picked out the copper fire in her hair.

As she continued to shake him with some force, her lovely breasts bounced and drew his eyes straight to them before he remembered she was distressed. 'Cassie?' This was not time for lust. He sat bolt upright, wrapped his arms around her, wishing he could recall where the devil he had put his pistols. 'What's wrong?'

'Nothing.' She was grinning and nudged him playfully.

'Then why the devil did you wake me up like that!' He was instantly furious. Didn't she realise the danger she had just put herself in? Hadn't he explained to her what he was capable of at night? Repeatedly. 'And what the hell are you still doing in my bedchamber?' He had taken two rooms at the Red Lion specifically to keep her safe. Two rooms at either end of the corridor just in case.

One for him and one for her.

'You promised me faithfully you were leaving to go to your own bedchamber.' At the time, he recalled hazily, his eyes had been drooping and his voice was thick with fatigue after they had made spectacular love for hours. Cassie had left him exhausted. 'Damn it, woman, I could have killed you!'

'But you didn't. Just as I suspected. You are far too fond of me to hurt so much as a hair on my irritating, odd little head. Admit it. The thought never even crossed your mind.'

She had a point. He had experienced a flash of brief panic before he had been distracted by the sound of her voice. Seduced by the sight of her nakedness. His wife.

Just thinking the word made him smile before he remembered he was livid.

'Next time you might not be so lucky. What would you have done if I had tried to strangle you?'

'I would have grabbed your pistol which is conveniently located under my pillow and clocked you over the head with it.'

Now she was giggling and Jamie wanted to remain angry, really he did, except the giggling made her fabulous breasts jiggle more and he couldn't seem to hold on to the anger for long enough to make it sound convincing.

'You woke me up just to prove a point?'

'Not entirely. Doing something simply to prove a point would be churlish and childish, wouldn't it? I did have another reason, seeing that you've asked.'

'Then spit it out, woman.' A difficult sentence to say with venom when her fingers were tracing the outside of his lips and she was so close he could smell her perfume.

'I want you again, Jamie. Do you mind?'

'Mind?' His lusty wife wanted him. Again. How splendid was that? 'For pity's sake, woman, have a care. You must be gentle with me—I am an invalid, you know.' Although he never felt like one with her, especially when she was already looking at his chest as if it was smothered in the finest roast beef and she was starving.

'You did promise to honour me with your body.'

'I did. And you promised to sleep in your own room.'

She sat back on her heels and pouted prettily. 'So you do mind?'

His arm shot out, grabbing her, and she tumbled giggling on to his chest. The blasted woman would be the death of him. 'For future reference, you never need to ask me that question again, Wife.'

Because she was the woman he had always dreamed of. That elusive soulmate who enjoyed nature's beauty as much as he did and who would want to sit with him while he happily painted, every day for the rest of his life. The woman his sensitive artist's heart beat for. His future. His bright and brilliant and purposeful future.

'You have made me the happiest man on earth, Miss Freckles, and if you want me, rest assured, I will *never* mind.'

And he never did.

* * * * *

MILLS & BOON

THE HEART OF ROMANCE

A ROMANCE FOR EVERY READER

MODERN

Prepare to be swept off your feet by sophisticated, sexy and seductive heroes, in some of the world's most glamourous and romantic locations, where power and passion collide.

HISTORICAL

Escape with historical heroes from time gone by. Whether your passion is for wicked Regency Rakes, muscled Vikings or rugged Highlanders, awake the romance of the past.

MEDICAL

Set your pulse racing with dedicated, delectable doctors in the high-pressure world of medicine, where emotions run high and passion, comfort and love are the best medicine.

True Love

Celebrate true love with tender stories of heartfelt romance, from the rush of falling in love to the joy a new baby can bring, and a focus on the emotional heart of a relationship.

Desire

Indulge in secrets and scandal, intense drama and plenty of sizzling hot action with powerful and passionate heroes who have it all: wealth, status, good looks…everything but the right woman.

HEROES

Experience all the excitement of a gripping thriller, with an intense romance at its heart. Resourceful, true-to-life women and strong, fearless men face danger and desire - a killer combination!

To see which titles are coming soon, please visit

millsandboon.co.uk/nextmonth

LET'S TALK
Romance

For exclusive extracts, competitions
and special offers, find us online:

- facebook.com/millsandboon
- @MillsandBoon
- @MillsandBoonUK

Get in touch on 01413 063232

JOIN US ON SOCIAL MEDIA!

Stay up to date with our latest releases, author news and gossip, special offers and discounts, and all the behind-the-scenes action from Mills & Boon...

 @millsandboon

 @millsandboonuk

 facebook.com/millsandboon

 @millsandboonuk

It might just be true love...